This b

The
a f

# Angel Dust

## SARAH MUSSI

HOT
KEY
BOOKS

First published in Great Britain in 2012 by Hot Key Books
Northburgh House, 10 Northburgh Street, London EC1V 0AT

A CIP catalogue record for this book is available from the British Library.

ISBN: 978-1-4714-0002-5

1

Typeset by Palimpsest Book Production Limited, Falkirk, Stirlingshire
This book is set in 10.5pt Berling LT Std

Printed and bound by Clays Ltd, St Ives Plc

**FSC**

Hot Key Books supports the Forest Stewardship Council (FSC),
the leading international forest certification organisation, and is committed
to printing only on Greenpeace-approved FSC-certified paper.

www.hotkeybooks.com

*For my two Seraphim, Sakky and Minty,*
*and my own little angel, Alyssa Serenity Tanya Mussi*

*The mind is its own place, and in itself*
*Can make a Heav'n of Hell, a Hell of heav'n.*
Paradise Lost ~ John Milton

# The Testimony of Zara Finer

*Return to the ground, since from it you were taken;*
*for Dust you are and to Dust you will return.*
*Genesis 3:19*

*You picked your time perfectly. It was a glorious summer's day.*
*The sky was blue and it was forever afternoon. I was almost*
*happy. A new trust had been placed in me. I was to keep*
*watch from the Twelfth Gate for St Peter. It is not easy to keep*
*watch from the Twelfth Gate. It is not easy for the Seraphim*
*to be allowed so far from the throne of God. It is not easy for*
*the Twelfth Gate opens on to the road to Hell.*

*Yes, you picked your time perfectly. I was alone. And for*
*some reason you were singled out in the last ray of the setting*
*sun. I was laughing at the way you sagged your jeans and*
*walked yourself down the street, as if the whole town belonged*
*to you, every brick, every kerb. I was enjoying the way you*
*ducked your head as you spoke. I was quivering at the deep-*
*ness of your voice. I was glorying in the breadth of your*
*shoulders and marvelling at how bold a man can be.*

*I think I was already half in love with you even then.*

*And you made your move. One minute I was so sure of*

myself, then you lifted up your head, as if you could see me, and you winked.

One look into your dark eyes was all it took.

I leaned out of the Twelfth Gate. There was music booming out of someone's car. I wanted to touch you. The car slowed down. A pretty girl wound down a window. Her boyfriend, a proper gangsta, shouted to you from the driver's seat.

You said, 'Oi bruv, tonight's the night. Man's eighteen at midnight!' You held up a bottle of champagne.

The gangsta said, 'Catch you there.'

He revved his car. He surged forward. You jumped into the street in front of him, waving your arms, being silly. I reached out my hand. Then stopped. I know the Rules. God's rules. I'm not allowed to interfere with your fate. The car swerved. You opened your mouth in mock surprise, like you were scared of nothing.

But the car was going to hit you!

I couldn't help myself. You were joking around. Playing with your life. But for your sake I broke all the rules in Heaven.

I touched you.

And you were safe.

Your friend, the gangsta, slammed on his brakes. The car screeched to a standstill. The pretty girl screamed, 'Idiot!'

'I'm Marcus,' you said. 'The original badman! I have angels watching over me!'

And you laughed and laughed and everyone knew you didn't care if you went to Hell and back.

Except there is no way back.

So I just looked wonderingly on. Wondering why I'd risked

*everything for you. Wondering what would happen next. Wondering at you.*

*And you were something to wonder at, with your coal-black eyes and your clothes and your gold and your girls. And an unexpected sadness caught my throat, because from the dust shimmering around you, I suddenly knew exactly why St Peter had asked me to watch from the Twelfth Gate. Why I was watching over you.*

*You were the one.*

*My temptation.*

*The one whose soul I had to Collect. And you were young, and you were beautiful, and you were flowing with energy. And my body trembled. I didn't want to watch from the Twelfth Gate any more. I didn't want to see you die.*

*You were only seventeen. It was your birthday. And I remembered then – another rule. Not a day more. Not a day less. It must be today. I had already trespassed once for your sake. I dared not again.*

*So there you were and here I was, stepping out of the Twelfth Gate to Collect you. And with a breaking heart I also understood something else. I was never going to save your soul. You were never going to pass the Twelfth Gate. You were doomed to step down the wide and pleasant broad-way, that so many take.*

*You were not bound for Heaven.*

*For your sake, I hoped death would be quick. You'd fall. I'd catch you. You'd see me. You'd understand. If there was time, I'd tell you to repent. If there was time, you would. Did I hope death would be quick? No, time should stand still. I should hold you for a thousand years, while you repented everything.*

*I did not think time would stand still for you. That is, after all, why they'd sent me, Serafina, the fieriest of the Seraphim, to embrace you. A brief caress of flame, for those bound for the fires of Hell.*

*What a waste.*

*The bell tolled.*

*The time had come.*

*I passed the threshold of the Twelfth Gate. I leapt across the broad and pleasant highway. I stepped down into the city.*

*For you.*

# The Book of Serafina

# Serafina 1

*Let me remember.*
*I have time without end. I will go on forever. I will*
*retell your story until the rocks melt.*
*I will fill eternity with thoughts of you.*
*I will make you immortal.*
From *The Song of the Seraphim* ~ 3:7

My God, but aren't cities fantastic? Chip shops and noisy traffic. I was nervous, of course. Anyone would be. We'd heard such tales: streets paved with bad intentions, how even a saint could lose his way in the Eden of those concrete gardens. Terrifying. So of course, I kept my eyes firmly glued to the pavement. I was not going to be tempted. I would be worthy. I would do everything right. I thought of St Peter and the trust he'd placed in me. I would not fail him again.

I bit my lip and kept my wings folded tight. I kept my thoughts focused on my mission. I hadn't got it very right so far, had I? I should never have touched Marcus. What'd possessed me? But if I got the rest right? If I delivered his death on time, asked him to repent, if I Collected his soul?

If I led him personally to Hell and left him on the shores of Styx? If I paid Charon, the ferryman, myself?

Such a huge unforgivable mistake.

That was it. No more mistakes. No more temptations. No more excuses. I would be the greatest Angel of Death ever. I would be darkness personified. My mission would become legend. I'd deliver Marcus the best Final Moments in the whole history of Final Moments. He would die at the right place, at the right time, in the right way. I'd add extras: ethereal music, golden glimpses of Elysian Fields, the keening of a thousand weeping souls and tears, bright, falling like shooting stars. Brilliant. I was going to get it so right and make it so romantic, even Azrael would be jealous!

Then surely God would understand?

Anyone can make a mistake.

Plus I'd tell St Peter all about the car thing when I handed in my mission. I'd come clean. After all, there was no actual way of telling if that car *would* have killed Marcus. Was there?

And it wasn't listed in the Manifest. I was in the clear.

It was going to be all right.

Wasn't it?


With the speed of angels I got there in good time. And my God, what a place! How it oozed with sin. There were late-night bargain booze bars, twenty-four-hour one-stop shops, kebab cafés and greasy pizza parlours. Oh, to be human! And there were the basements too. Such mischief. Illegal gambling joints, all-night blues parties, crack dens and dingy little rooms rentable by the hour. Imagine. I squashed my nose against the glass of a burger diner and breathed fire on the windows. I pressed my ear against the brickwork of a tenement block and listened to the groaning inside.

Thank Heaven I was early. No more mistakes for me. I dithered a bit until I found the nightclub where Marcus's party was scheduled. It was called The Mass and housed in the crypt of an old church. Then I checked the place out.

I wafted through the empty rooms with their black leather sofas and upholstered walls. It all reeked a bit, but I didn't mind. I like the smell of humans. I got out the Manifest and double-checked all the deaths scheduled for that evening. Yes, Marcus Montague was on it. There was my name next to his, and all the details. I peered at it very carefully. The Manifest gets updated all the time – at least the when, and where, and how. The day never changes. I super double-checked that the car wasn't supposed to have killed him. There was nothing to suggest it. I breathed a huge sigh of relief, and crossed myself in gratitude, and reminded myself that next time I'd triple-check. I'd put myself on super alert. Even if death was to be delivered at my discretion, no slightest detail would *ever* change without me being on it like a bonnet.

Quickly I found the spot where he'd die and decided where I'd stand. I tried out a strain or two of angelic harps and freshened the place up with a sweet southerly breeze straight from Heaven. That relaxed me a bit. If there were any demons to deal with, they'd find me more than ready. I drew a few fiery breaths and imagined cleaving them with a thunderbolt. On the way out I twirled my wings in the huge mirror by the door. I was very beautiful. My angelic glance alone could have enthralled all men. How perilous my smile! I twirled and spun and filled the club with stardust, made sunbeams dance on its polished floors. Oh, I was beautiful. I was even more lovely then.

I had the rest of the evening to kill. So I thought I'd wander down every back street I could. I'd eavesdrop on conversations and explore. I was quite invisible, of course. Nobody was going to see me. I'd make a thorough night out of it. Why not? We have so little time on Earth, we Seraphim. (No time, in fact, under usual conditions.) Anyway, snooping around back streets wasn't against any rules, was it? Come to think of it, now I was down on Earth, I could snoop anywhere I wanted. The Seraphim can travel in the beat of a wing, to the furthest corners of the sphere. I started wondering if I wouldn't prefer to go somewhere else. Paris? Rome? The summit of Mount Everest? Monte Carlo? What names!

But, you know, there's something about the perfume of the streets in Earthly cities that's completely beguiling. And I'd never been anywhere quite like this downtown place before. I was fascinated. I stood still and drunk in the night air. I wanted to make it all last forever. God, how I loved it. I wanted to stare into shop windows and listen to the roar of traffic until all the seas ran dry.

Traffic.

What *was* it like to ride in a car? I peeked into a late-night minicab office, just trying to imagine. Inside men sprawled on seats, smoking cigarettes. Real genuine nicotine.

They looked so bored. Imagine being bored! There was a girl with greasy hair plastered down one side of her cheek sitting behind the most incredible steel grille. She was reading a magazine. I wanted to have a look at it. It might have enticing images. How I would have treasured a magazine with enticing images.

But I couldn't wait until she put it down. And of course she couldn't see me, so I couldn't ask her. But I did look over her shoulder. When I did that she went all shivery and flicked her hair in my eye.

'Flipping freezing in here, innit?' she said to no one in particular.

I laughed. I loved her voice. It was all deliciously crispy and hoarse. And she wasn't even trying to be funny! One of the men grunted.

'Just had this weird déjà vu thing, like someone's standing on my grave,' the girl said.

I grinned and tickled her neck.

But of course, I was fooling myself. The real reason I wanted to hang around there was Marcus. Fooling yourself can be very convenient. And it's also not against God's rules, either. I decided to fool myself a bit longer and visit his home.

Marcus lived in a high rise called Curlston Heights. I adore high rises. On my last Collection mission I was sent to Manhattan, for a cleaner who died mopping the floor in a penthouse. I'd soared straight up the side of the building, straight through the downdraught, and peeked in at windows as I flashed by. I love lifts too, all that concrete and metal, that smell of humans! I love the way a lift clangs around you. It makes my skin flutter. I went up and down in that lift in New York five times!

Gosh, I make it sound like I was such an old hand at Collections. Not! The truth was I'd only been doing it for three days. I'd only ever done five deaths in fact. (The cleaner in the penthouse, a nasty old man and three sleepers.) Actually I was a complete novice.

You see, for most of my angelic existence I'd been praying for the Redemption of Humankind in the Cloisters of the Holy Heavenly Host. And if it hadn't been for the Declaration of War, I guess I still would be. It's really an awful reason to be allowed out, isn't it? Satanic war. Imagine. I really *shouldn't* have been so thrilled about it.

Anyway, the thing was, when Satan declared his 'New Offensive' against Heaven, God took it very seriously. Immediately we went into Code Yellow. I don't really know why everyone got so panicky – it wasn't like Satan was going to win, was it? But they did. And you know, you can't argue with God.

So you see that's why I was down on Earth in the first place. Because Code Yellow means that no lesser celestial creature or low-ranking angel is allowed out of Heaven. When we're on Code Yellow, God is always very fussy about whom he lets pass the Pearly Gates: only the brightest and the best. Those above temptation – just in case.

Still, it's an ill wind that blows nobody any good – I suppose. And Death Collections still have to be done. I mean people don't stop dying just because Satan challenges God, do they?

I soared up the side of Curlston Heights at an amazing speed, faster than Apollo 11. Imagine doing that at the Cloisters! What a flibbertigibbet they'd dub me! I landed on a tiny window ledge outside number 56, the home of Mrs Faustina Montague, her two daughters, Jasmine and Rayanne, and her eldest child, Marcus Montague.

We can do that, you know; just be somewhere and know everything – by touching it. I could tell you all the names of everyone who'd ever lived in that flat, plus the names of every builder, carpenter and plumber who'd ever worked on it. But only the facts: names, dates, figures, never the thoughts or feelings – plus it takes time and it's boring.

I was only interested in Marcus.

I pressed my nose up against the glass and peered through. Inside was a small front room bursting with furniture. A huge three-piece suite was crammed in beside a shelving unit of fake wood and brassy handles. The sofa and chairs were angled around a deep pile rug, which lay on a cheap laminate floor, in front of the widest wide-screen TV, ever.

On the sofa sat a woman. She was sniffing and talking on the telephone. Marcus's mother.

'I just don't know what to do any more,' she said.

There was a pause as if someone was telling her exactly what to do.

I slipped into the living room and stood beside her. I listened to the conversation.

'He's never here . . .'

'*It's his friends*,' said the other.

'He's gone for days, without . . .' Mrs Montague's voice broke.

*'He's using drugs.'*

'No . . .'

*'I hope you're not giving him money?'*

'No, it's Marcus who's bringing in money . . .' said his mother, rallying.

*'You'll have to tell him to go,'* said the person.

Marcus's mother sighed. 'But where to?' she said. 'And where is he getting the money?'

*'Give him a choice. Stick To My Rules Or Find. Your. Way!'*

Marcus's mother sighed again.

*'What he needs is a shock. A Big Nasty Shock!'*

'But it's his birthday . . .'

*'Fat lot to celebrate. He wants to be De Man, doesn't he? Then he better act like one!'*

The caller was getting irritated. I prowled around the living room looking at pictures: Marcus as a baby, Marcus with his arms round his mum, Marcus with his sisters, Marcus in a football team, Marcus posing like the Original Badman, Marcus in dark glasses. Marcus looking manly. My throat caught. There's something unbearably sad about being on Collection Duty. However beautiful you make the death, however gentle, however welcome.

I went into his bedroom.

What a delicious mess! Clothes thrown everywhere, ash trays full of butt ends, CD covers scattered on the floor, expensive trainers showcased on their shoeboxes, an Xbox still playing over and over the opening sequence to *Call of Duty*. And everywhere there were pictures of girls, tacked up alongside sheets of paper covered with lyrics in a small spidery scrawl.

> TO MY HOT GIRL
> *those fiery eyes*
> *Hot girl! hot girl!*
> *Soul on fire*
> *take out my heart*
> *i gotta do right*
> *i gotta talk true this time*
> *oh oh oh*
> *i'm fallin for you*
> *and that is so true*
> *i gotta do right*
> *I gotta talk true*
> *before i lose you*
> *oh no no*

I looked at a T-shirt flung carelessly on the floor. What was it, to be human? To feel the breeze against your face and know that nothing lasts? If Marcus could have lasted, would he have changed? I could smell change and goodness somewhere in his scent. Standing there, in his room, his life spread out before me, in clothes and music and passion, I saw the speed at which he'd lived. No time for regrets. No thoughts of the hereafter.

I didn't return to the living room. Right then his mother was grieving for the loss of that little boy in the photo with his arms around her. There was nothing I could do to comfort her. Not true. I could have touched her, I suppose.

15

I could have given her oblivion. Would she have wanted that?

I started to fret about the Collection again. The palms of my hands began to sweat. I could feel my feathers tingling. I had to get this absolutely right. Marcus had a definite time pencilled in against his name. There must be no mistake. I must get back to the nightclub. Maybe demons were already sniffing him out. Demons are foul creatures. They feast on unclaimed souls. They soil every death they touch. I went over my checklist:

- Catch him as he falls.
- Give him the chance to repent.
- Get there before the demons.
- Deliver him his Final Moment.
- Pinch out his life.
- Collect his soul.

Even if he was bound for Hell, he shouldn't fall into the hands of demons. What the heck was I doing wasting time snooping about?

I must get to the club immediately.

Ready to kill Marcus.

# Serafina 2

I think I was putting it off. I really *hadn't* been on Soul Collecting Duty very long (actually it was only two and a half days) and I still felt nervous. The sleepers had been OK. They were my very first ones. They were quite easy. I just arrived and sat at the end of their beds, and waited for them to drift into my arms. All very nice and quiet and respectable. Demons don't give a damn about them. And the ones I'd done had all been little old ladies, too. They'd all led nice little lives and put out food for the birds. They were headed straight for the First Gate. They had nothing to repent. St Peter fast tracked them through at once. God was very pleased with them.

Of course there'd been that one soul to be guided downwards. He'd been vicious and hateful. I was even happy when I'd pointed out the river he needed to cross. I didn't care if the demons got him.

Marcus was going to be *so* different. Not only was he young and full of life, but he'd seen me. That was so odd. Nobody had ever told me about being seen. I went back over it in my mind. I'd been watching him from the Twelfth Gate. He'd lifted up his head and winked. I was certain of it. Perhaps it meant something? No mortal has ever seen the Seraphim. Not like that. So that made him? I don't know what it made him.

And suddenly I realised that it was *very* weird. What did it mean? It must be some kind of omen, *or a sign?* I'd heard of signs – rainbows, burning bushes. There's *always* a sign when things are meant to happen – when something is predestined . . . when two people are meant to be together . . .

How strange. But now I'd thought of it suddenly I couldn't get the idea out of my head. It *must* be an omen. Somehow my destiny was entwined with his.

In the beat of a wing I got down to the club. And it was a good job I did. Immediately I could tell it was going to be much, much worse than I'd expected. For a start there was music. Loud music. I love loud music, but it's so distracting. And then there was alcohol too, lots of it: gin, whisky, cognac, champagne and alcopops. Imagine being able to drink alcopops! If I were human, and set on living at great speed, I might try one. But drink and music were going to confuse things. I didn't want confusion. I wanted to bring Marcus the best death he'd ever have.

And then there were the girls. Big girls, slim girls, girls in tight dresses, girls in high heels, girls with huge breasts and girls who were so drop-dead gorgeous I instantly hoped one of them would. Seeing all those girls clouded my judgement. And there were guys too: hunky guys, chunky guys, funky guys, guys in tight jeans, guys fresh out of sports cars, guys in gold chains, gorgeous guys and guys with amazingly sexy smiles. How in Heaven's name was I going to be able to stay focused on split-second timing?

And of course there was Marcus.

I smelt him as soon as I got there.

Marcus Montague. Birthday boy. Just turning eighteen and looking like he was already in Heaven.

I stood in the doorway quite overcome. Not just because of the music and the drink. I think I was grieving for the first time. Grieving for all the things that might have been, and never were. Someone turned the music up. I became disorientated. For a brief second. I tried imagining what it would be like to be human. Not an Angel of Death. Not immortal. I started to sway to the music. I imagined I had a body. A real body. Flesh and bone. A body that someone, some day could hold.

I watched Marcus. I watched him drag the prettiest girl into his arms. I watched as she moulded herself against his chest. Something inside pierced me. A strange pain tightened around my heart. I saw the muscles in his arms straining against his shirt. I saw the way he used the music to send the girl crazy. For some reason my throat went dry. I tried to swallow. I tried to catch my breath against a sudden longing. I saw Marcus smile, a lovely crooked smile showing off his pearly teeth.

But he was not smiling at me.

The chimes of midnight struck. I bit my lip. At any minute his death would arrive. I tried to prepare myself. I looked around. I was right. Demons were already gathering.

Someone put on a record for him. Marcus dragged the

girl into the centre of the dance floor. Everyone stepped back. Someone whistled. Marcus crushed the girl to him.

*Go, go, go, go, go, go . . .*

His eyes were wild with excitement.

*Go Marcus, it's your birthday . . .*

He shivered in delight.

The girl in his arms nearly fainted.

The pain inside stabbed again. I was confused. Why did watching him hurt so much? She was just a pretty little girl. She was nothing compared to me. I was a winged celestial creature more beautiful than a thousand stars. I laughed at myself. But as Marcus tightened his arms around her, I suddenly felt bewildered. In less than ten minutes he was going to be in my arms.

Not laughing, but dying.

I stood there. And for some inexplicable reason I felt angry. He was so full of life. Everyone loved him. Everyone wanted him. He was bigger, larger, more alive than anyone I'd ever seen. What was it to be alive? Like that?

Marcus raised the champagne bottle, shook it. It exploded like gunfire. A stream of champagne shot so high it splattered off the ceiling, drenching the girls crowding forward. But my mood was spoilt. I wasn't even remotely thrilled any more. In fact I didn't see the point in any of it. What was it all? This being born and celebrating birthdays, this living and dying, this going up to Heaven or down to Hell? If this was God's amazing creation – why had he created death? I know all the excuses: Eve, the apple, Free Will – but when all's said and done God created death.

It was the first time I've ever thought like that. And it spoiled everything. Earth was supposed to be fun and beautiful. Human life a sacred thing. Suddenly I wanted out. I was a bit shocked at myself.

As I waited I thought of Heaven, of the endless soft zephyrs that blew across its wide fields, of the delight of the Seraphim, our sheltered cloisters, our laughter. And I was confused. We Collected souls too, didn't we? That was our job, wasn't it? We killed people.

A car screeched to a halt outside the club door. I think even human cars could've heard it. It brought me back to earth. I focused my attention. And I saw everything. So this was how it was going to happen.

The guys in it were dressed in black. They had hoods on, sleeves rolled up, black gloves. The biggest one sprang out of the front passenger door. He was amazingly light for one so huge. In a single motion he drew two Mac 10s. He held them at hip height and kicked open the front door to the club. With angel's ears I heard the splinter of wood, the squeal of metal.

The main guy, massive, dark, hook-nosed, with thick jetty brows, paused, laid a finger over his lips, then ran down the stairs on tiptoe. Like a thief he crept through the arches and stood next to the large mirror by the exit. Marcus didn't see him. He was too busy toasting himself in bubbles. But the girl did. She screamed.

Marcus lifted his beautiful face up and looked at his killer.

'Yo bruv?' he said very softly.

The girl screamed again. She yelled at the huge guy with

the guns. 'Stop it, Crow,' she yelled. 'It's his goddamn birthday. Can't I go to any goddamn birthday I want?'

'Any except his,' said the Crow, raising the guns.

I prepared myself. This was it. I opened my mouth and said the words. *'I am Alpha and Omega, the beginning and the end. Turn and look upon your death.'* And Marcus did. He turned. *He looked straight at me and smiled.*

I didn't know what to do. *He could still see me.* How could that be? *It had to be a sign.*

In two strides the guy, the Crow, crossed the dance floor and reached the girl. She tried to resist. He yanked at her, pulled at her until she was in his line of fire. The Crow levelled his guns. With a shudder I realised he was going to kill them both.

The demons crowded forward.

'No!' yelled Marcus. He swung the girl behind him, shielded her with his body, faced the Crow.

*'Stop!'* screamed the girl.

Dazed, I moved in. Yes, this was how it would happen. Marcus would be shot, protecting the girl. She wasn't scheduled to die. I knew. I had the Manifest in my raiment. His blood would coat my wings. I would hold him as each throb of his heart beat and bled and ebbed.

*But he'd seen me, and somehow we were destined to be together.*

I wasn't ready. I was caught off guard. I didn't step forward far enough. I'd only ever done sleepers. I'd never seen a violent death, nor been to any with one so young. I froze. I was confused.

*He'd seen me.*

22

I got the timing all wrong. I stepped forward too late. So when the guns went off *I wasn't there.*

Everything went very quiet, except the music. It wound on, stuck on a phrase.

*Go . . . go . . . go . . . go . . . go . . .*

*But I wasn't there.*

And then all Hell broke loose.

# Serafina 3

Demons skulked forward. Shadows descended. Oily phantoms slithered down from the ceilings. I tried to move. My legs wouldn't work. I tried to jump to the spot where I should have been. Spectres groped their way across the floor. Nothing happened. My heart hammered. *I wasn't going to make it.* The demons, my God, how they smelt.

*And I wasn't there.*

*There was another burst of fire.*

Frantically I beat my wings. I commanded the air to let me pass. Nothing gave. I was frozen. Bewildered I thrashed my wings in panic.

*Nothing. Nothing. Nothing.*

Something was holding me against my will. The music cut. A crescendo of screaming tore through the club. Blood, thick and slippery, coated the floor. And Marcus falling. I couldn't reach him. *I couldn't reach him.*

'Oh God help me,' I screamed.

As if in answer, a figure detached itself from the crowd. A stranger, tall, graceful. He slid smoothly forward and seemed to push the demons aside. There was a slight smell of drains. The shadows fell back at his touch. He caught Marcus, held him steady by the shoulder. Marcus staggered and pitched into the centre of the dance floor. The stranger looked at me. *He looked directly at me.* And for the second time that evening I realised I'd been seen.

'Quick,' he said, 'I can't hold him.'

At that the demons seemed to flood everywhere. Shadows with greedy tendrils lurched out, clutched at the shining figure in white, at Marcus falling. But the stranger stood firm, holding them off, holding Marcus up, holding time back.

And just as suddenly as I'd been frozen, I unfroze. I didn't question that. I should have. I should have thought: What power could halt a Seraph in her divine duty? But I didn't. I was too relieved. I wanted to bring Marcus his perfect death. I wanted to get it completely right. Golden glimpses of Elysian Fields.

'There,' the stranger said. 'Catch him.' And he let go.

Slowly, gracefully, Marcus pitched forward. Thank Heaven I was there. Arms open, wings outspread, I caught him. I held him. I smoothed back his damp brow. I pressed his head to my bosom.

Hallelujah in the highest. And a huge sigh of relief.

Instantly I switched into action. I unfurled all my wings and beat the air. Without warning I sent hot fireballs raining down on the demons. We Seraphim have nasty tempers when roused, you know. The shadows fell back, the spectres squealed, but they cleared off before I tossed thunderbolts at them too. Demons aren't stupid, are they? With a toss of my thick locks I perfumed the air. Then I tended to Marcus.

I held him close. I felt the heat of his blood and the

hammering of his heart. Yes, he was still alive. I wasn't too late. Thank God. Outside a church bell was tolling midnight. *Not a day more. Not a day less.* I must be quick. I lifted up my face and with a blaze of my eyes I froze time. We, the Seraphim, can do that, if we really need to. (It's considered rather flashy, though, and we can't do it for very long.)

For an instant all sound ceased. In the silence that followed, I brought Marcus the Grace of Heaven. It would make him comfortable. His Passing Over would be pain free. I was just deciding whether to go for the heart-shaped tears or the shooting stars when Marcus, cushioned against me, opened his eyes and looked into mine.

His eyes were so full of trust they took me by surprise. My heart lurched. *He thought I was there to save his life.*

'So, angels *are* watching over me, after all,' he whispered, smiling up at me.

I held him so close then; I forgot who I was. 'Only one,' I whispered back, as if I really were his saviour.

'All I need for now,' he said and closed his eyes contentedly.

And I was so touched by his faith in me, I didn't know what to do. Except to wish I wasn't an Angel of Death.

Miserably I summoned a freckling of angel dust to shimmer in the air around us. 'Please repent your wrongdoings, repent your selfish life and the hurt you've caused others,' I said, my throat catching.

There was no reply.

All he needed to say was, 'Sorry.' I could have worked something out. Got him off Purgatorium, got him through the Twelfth Gate. I'd have done my best. Stayed with him while he did his penances; we could have gone straight up to Heaven together. Climbed the Staircase hand in hand. With a bit of luck nobody would have even known about the car thing, so when I came clean it'd actually have gone in our favour. I imagined St Peter saying: what a marvellous Seraph you are. Saving the soul of a hardened gangster like Marcus Montague. And Marcus, how brave to put your sins behind you. I'll be sure to let the Senior Team know that a lost lamb has returned to the flock and what a scrupulous, trustworthy angel they have.

I sighed. A spasm went through Marcus. I watched the pulse of his blood, feeling its warmth as it pumped out against me. I waited for him to open his eyes and speak. But for some reason I couldn't seem to bring myself to pinch out his life. Instead I just waited for him to repent. Willed him to repent – as if I could change his destiny.

*Just two little words.* That's all it would have taken.

*Oh Marcus, why couldn't you have spoken?*

Such is the will of God that we, the Angels of Death, may only ask once. One last chance before the clasp of fire and brimstone. And repentance must follow freely, because this is the hour and the minute and the second and after that Time. Runs. Out.

And Time did run out. I had to let it start up again. The bell tolled. The Crow and his crew left. The music coughed back louder than ever:

. . . *Yea though I walk* . . .

Someone screamed, 'Cut the sounds, man.'

Someone yelled, 'Call an ambulance!'

Another screamed, 'Joey Bigga's down! He's hurt.'

27

*. . . through the shadow of . . .*

I should have taken his silence as 'no'. But I was still a little bit unsure about exactly how long you *do* wait. Maybe it was longer than I thought? But when Marcus finally did open his eyes, he didn't whisper 'sorry'. He raised his gaze to mine and said, 'Did Candy make it?'

'She's safe,' I said and I was moved for a second time. Not only was he trusting, he was kind too. How generous that his first thought was for her. So I still waited, still hoped, still held death back.

But no word of repentance came. Instead his eyes danced. 'I like your feathers,' he said.

*Liked my feathers?*

'And the halo.'

*And the halo?*

I blinked. What did he mean? Nothing in my training at the Cloisters had prepared me for this.

His eyes rolled from me to the demons (who were already crowding back in loathsome number). I knew if I didn't claim his soul soon, they would, and like a shot too.

'Take heed,' I said, trying to bend the rules, trying to give him a hint, a last last chance.

His eyes widened. He flicked them heavenwards as if to defy all last chancing. I was bewildered. Nobody ever defies demons. A bullet had passed clean through his heart. Didn't he know the danger he was in? Maybe that was why he hadn't repented. He didn't understand.

*If only you'd understood, Marcus. You'd have repented. I know you would.*

So, you see, I couldn't act.

*I couldn't take you.*

The last stroke of midnight fell. In a panic I cast an aura of ethereal light around us. This was the moment when I should be making his death beautiful beyond compare, when lyres should be playing, when Paradise itself should envy him his Final Moment.

'Don't let me die,' he whispered.

But I *should* be letting him die. I should be easing his soul out of his body and taking it by the hand. I should be guiding it to the broad highway that stretches past the Twelfth Gate.

But I wasn't.

I was gazing down into the darkest, wickedest eyes imaginable. I was holding the firmest, tautest body I'd ever touched. Holding it as if I had no intention of letting it go. Anywhere.

What madness was this?

I crouched there, stunned at what I was doing (or rather not doing), when the stranger who'd caught Marcus (that glorious helpful being) knelt down close and laid his hand on mine.

# Serafina 4

It was a strange sensation. We angels don't have corporeal bodies. We don't feel the cold or heat in the way an Earthly being does; rather we feel through things – to the core of things. We feel in images. In essences. But the feel of that stranger's hand on mine was different. It was like the touch of an Archangel. It was tingly and warm and it sent delightful spirals of heat into my chest. The only thing that marred it was that slight whiff of drains again.

'Let me help,' he said.

I looked at him. 'Help?' I said, puzzled. For who can help an Angel of Death?

'There is a way,' he said.

'A way?' I repeated.

He laughed. 'Yes,' he said, raising his eyebrows, 'a way out even for you.'

I smiled up at the stranger. I pressed Marcus nearer. I cradled his head, covered his blood with my feathers.

The stranger smiled back at me as if I were being very slow. He cocked his head to one side in an enchanting way. 'You like him. Don't you?' he said.

I looked at Marcus. I looked at the stranger. Yes, I liked him. But 'like' was such a tame, human sort of word. It came nowhere near the feeling I had. I was mesmerised by the life force in him. I could never be alive, not in the way Marcus was. This was the nearest I would ever get. And I was appalled at the thought of pinching it out. *But most of all he trusted me.* And despite all his wickedness, I'd looked into his eyes and seen he was good and kind.

'And he hasn't repented, either, has he?' said the stranger. The lights from the disco ball sparkled off his teeth. They were very white teeth, very even, very clean.

'No,' I whispered.

'So you know what you must do.'

'Yes,' I nodded. I knew what I must do.

'But there is a way – *not* to do it,' said the stranger, a smile playing around the corners of his white teeth. 'A way to give him more time.'

More time? Yes! That's what he needed. *More time.* Oh, if only I could make time stand still forever. I would bend every beat of Heaven's great heart to help him. How could he not repent with such powers to guide him?

'More time,' repeated Marcus – as if he could hear my thoughts.

'What way?' I said, looking at the stranger.

'It's really *very* simple,' said the stranger.

I studied him, this stranger who could make everything very simple. He was beautifully dressed in a white suit, with a yellow rosebud tucked into his lapel. On anyone else that might have looked phoney, but on him it was exactly right. And he was good-looking too, clean-cut and smooth-skinned, with golden hair scooped back into

31

one of those adorable ponytails. I liked him immediately – did I tell you that already? No? Well, I liked him very much.

So there I was. Marcus lying in my arms, time behaving very strangely – in fact so strangely that all around us the club waited. In freeze-frame the revellers stood, caught between dancing and screaming, between living and dying. I couldn't make it out. Everything was not as it should be. Even the church bell seemed to be stuck. Perhaps this stranger really could help.

'You can ask for an Extension,' he said, and smiled another white-toothed smile.

Ask for an Extension?

What did he mean?

Frantically I looked up at him, clutched Marcus tighter, tried to think straight. The room swayed. Time shifted. Music blared out again.

Two of the girls screamed and screamed.

The crowd drew tight around me, around Marcus. They pressed in on us. Yet nobody touched him. While he lay in my arms none could do that.

'Don't move him!' a girl screamed. 'Don't move him!'

A knot of dancers crowded a little further off. Someone else was down. I peered through them. Marcus's friend, Joey Bigga, was sitting, heaving, spewing blood. He was hit, but he couldn't be dying – there was no other angel near to Collect him. It was all very confusing.

'An Extension,' repeated the stranger in a charming drawl. 'Think about it. All you have to do is ask,' he teased.

'Ask who?' I said. Wasn't I the Angel of Death? Wasn't

it my job to pinch out the light in Marcus's eyes? Wasn't I the one I had to ask?

'Oh, anyone,' he said airily. 'Ask the Grim Reaper if he's around! Hey, ask me, I'll stand in for him! Go *on*,' he added, 'give it a whirl, live dangerously. You can only ask, can't you?'

Marcus's eyes fluttered, looked up into mine, so trustingly. 'Then please, please, give us – I mean – give Marcus some more time,' I said, bowing my shining head over Marcus's dark one.

Marcus stirred a little and tried to raise himself. 'Shush,' I whispered, 'I'm trying to save you. Please,' I said to this golden-eyed, golden-haired stranger who had already helped me more than I deserved.

'OK, then,' he said and did a little twirl, as if I'd asked him to do a dance routine.

From far away the wail of an ambulance siren split the night air. I could hear it even over the music.

'How long d'ya want?' asked the stranger playfully.

'Anything: a minute, an hour, a day, a week, a lifetime,' I said. Anything. If only there was more time.

'Yes,' whispered Marcus, 'more time.'

'Done, dusted and delivered,' said the stranger. 'You can have three weeks! How's that?'

I stared at him in amazement. Was that all it took?

He nodded as if he could read my mind. 'Pretty straightforward, isn't it?' he said.

I think my jaw went slack. Lord, was I such an innocent! No wonder the other Seraphim got on OK on Earth. Even death, it appeared, was negotiable!

'Oh, thank you,' I whispered. I bent my head over Marcus and instead of pinching out his life with icy fingers I breathed fire kisses over his head. They landed in little tiny sparks. His eyes opened wide. He smiled. He tried to sit up. He was going to live.

*Marcus was going to live!*

I turned to the stranger, wanting to ask him how all this worked – to explain I'd never done Extensions before, that I hadn't been on Collection Duty long. I should have thought of Extensions straight away – I should have asked, shouldn't I?

'You just have to sign on the dotted line,' smiled the stranger. 'It tells you that you have taken out an Extension on Marcus Montague's life, the reason for the Extension: to enable him to fully repent and save his soul from Hell. And disco, *voilà*! *C'est tout!*'

'Oh,' I said, amazed that it was all so simple.

'And that, as his Angel of Death, you underwrite his life with various undertakings, blah, blah, blah. Boring stuff.'

'Oh,' I said, wondering vaguely what such undertakings might be.

'You'll have to sign soon, though, if you really do intend to save him.' He nodded in the direction of the demons. They were already throwing shadows out again, thick creepy shadows that coated the walls, slid to the skirting and slithered on to the floor.

'Yes,' I said. I took the pen he proffered and signed in the air with fiery letters.

'Good, good,' he said. 'Easy-peasy, really, isn't it?'

'Thank you, so much,' I breathed.

'Any time,' smiled the stranger. He swept my fiery letters into his grasp and said, 'Verbal commitment accepted. Will deliver paperwork in a tick.'

The crowd around me fell back. The ambulance reached the street door. The sirens wailed louder than ever. Someone hollered, 'They're here.' The paramedics rushed in, shouting: 'Stand aside! Give us space!'

I held Marcus so gently. Soon I'd deliver him to their care.

'You saved me?' he whispered, gazing up into my eyes.

I looked down at him and nodded. 'There's a condition,' I said.

He looked at me. 'Don't go,' he whispered, 'not yet.'

The paramedics made ready, unfurled the stretcher. I loosened my hold. He didn't want me to let go.

'You must repent,' I said. 'That's the condition.'

He hesitated, tried to clear his throat. 'I'm sorry.' His voice was deep. 'I'll try, don't know if I can.'

My heart stopped. *Don't know if I can.* What did he mean?

'I'll help you,' I said, 'I'll be there for you. We'll do it together.'

'If you're going to repent,' he said slowly, the blood rattling in his throat, 'your heart has to be in it.'

He was right, of course.

'Can't lie – about something like that.' He shut his dark eyes, and let his bloodied hand fall to his side.

'You'll change,' I said. 'You'll see it differently when you're better.' I stroked his brow. I was so proud of him. That was why he hadn't repented. He wasn't sure his heart was in it. Even on pain of everlasting damnation he'd refused to lie.

'I'll watch over you,' I said. 'On my Holy Oath I promise.' I don't know why I said that. On whose authority I could even pledge it. But I did. I swore in God's name to watch over him.

He smiled sadly. The paramedics moved closer. The screaming girls calmed down. I let him go. He was going to live.

I turned at once to the golden stranger to thank him. There he stood, leaning up against the great mirror, his hair tousled in a film-starry way. His cool, clean, white suit as crisp as ever.

'Happy?' he said, smiling, showing all his white teeth.

I nodded. That hint of drains was back. I was so happy. I'd saved Marcus. I shook out my feathers. I smiled. 'I'm very happy,' I said.

'Good,' he said. 'So that's that. Now there's only the matter of the small print.'

# Serafina 5

'Small print?' I said, puzzled.

'Sorr-ee,' joked the stranger, his bright eyes laughing. 'But we gotta do the small print.'

Perhaps I frowned, because he quickly added, 'Hey, it's not as bad as you think.'

'Oh, no . . .' I started to protest. I didn't want this kind, helpful being to imagine I'd quibble over a deal that had saved Marcus for me. 'It's just that I don't quite understand.'

'Ah!' he said. 'Small print on the contract.'

'The contract?' I said. I seemed to be repeating myself in a worryingly moronic way.

'Hey,' said the stranger. 'You're upset, stressed out – all that blood.'

'Yes,' I said faintly. It was true – my wings were coated, my hands too.

'Best get washed up before we go over it,' smiled the stranger. 'I'll get it all down on paper for you.' He nodded at the girls' restroom. 'And quit worrying. He's safe.'

I looked over at Marcus. The ambulance crew were bending over him, his dark curls almost hidden behind them. Marcus, the birthday boy who'd shone so bright. I could still smell his blood on my hands. Even from here,

I could smell the spilt champagne, the scent of perfume.

Even as I watched a paramedic cheered. 'Got a heartbeat!' He turned to his colleague. 'Stanley, get the BP cuff on him, get a reading. Quick – don't know how we're holding him. Bullet passed clean through the left ventricle.'

They fumbled with a blood pressure monitor, searched for a pulse. Then the other paramedic cheered too. '80 over 45, but rising,' he said. 'Pulse only 45, arrhythmic?'

They'd got a heartbeat. They were overjoyed. I smiled and made the sign of Our Father in their direction.

'Steadying, picking up . . .' said Stanley. 'Oxygen? Get the oxygen.'

'Freaking miracle.'

Suddenly the whole team swooped down on him: taking his pulse, checking his airways, attaching wires, staunching the bleeding, checking the bullet holes, putting an oxygen mask over his face.

'I'll buy you a drink at the bar after you're done washing up,' the stranger reminded. He was still nodding towards the restroom.

Angels don't need restrooms, actually, and I was too absorbed with Marcus. I stepped nearer to the busy medics, my hand ready to instantly freeze time – in case they should let him fall when they eased him on to the stretcher. Not for a second was I going to take my eye off him, not until I was absolutely sure he was OK.

'That's a drink, as in alcohol,' repeated the stranger.

Had I heard that right? I blinked. *Buy me a drink!* Buy an angel a drink? Gosh, almost as if I were human!

But angels don't drink.

Or do they?

Maybe on Earth they *do*.

The screaming girls had stopped wailing. Some of the guests were trying to get out. They were shoving and pushing like mad. The rest were clustered around Joey Bigga, shouting the place down. Except for one lonely being who was sat watching everything from a corner – strange how motionless he was amidst all the chaos.

'When you're ready,' prompted my saviour.

Now that Marcus lay on the stretcher breathing and calm, now that he had three medics checking him out and lifting him up on to the wheelbase of a gurney, I hurried to the washrooms. I slaked myself with water. I didn't really need to. I could have twirled in a sunbeam and cleansed myself straight away, if there had been a sunbeam – if it'd been daylight. I could have soared through moonlight and been purged of every stain if I cared to step outside. But I liked the idea of being a regular girl at a regular nightclub. What fun! I'd pretend to be human.

I sent a breeze of angel breath through the entire restroom. That would sweeten it. Next I pumped the soap dispenser about a hundred times. I worked up a wonderful lather. Then I turned on all the hand dryers at full blast. I pirouetted around and around in front of the mirrors until the restroom shone in fire and brilliance, soap suds and bubbles, and was one great rush of hot dry air.

That should do it. That should keep the gentlebeing in white happy.

Suddenly I paused in my dance. Wasn't it rather strange that there *was* a gentlebeing in white? And that he'd been able to see me? *What kind of a being was he?* Must be some kind of angel. I was sure I'd seen a glimpse of wing, folded very neatly beneath that white tuxedo. I ran through all the angelic possibilities: Announcer, Avenger, Destroyer, Guardian, Healer, Herald Mercy, Miracle-worker; none of them seemed to fit.

Oh no! I suddenly gulped: *Maybe he was an Inspector.* I'd heard some Collection Duties do get inspected. After all we *were* on Code Yellow, and there *was* a war going on in Heaven. Oh Lord! Just my luck, to get inspected on my very first week!

I stopped twirling. I'd better shape up quickly, get rid of all these bubbles, start behaving in a very professional celestial way.

*But oh my Lord, Marcus was alive! And had looked into my eyes! And hadn't wanted to let me go! And I hadn't failed him either!* I can't tell you the thrill it gave me. Everything was going to be OK.

I danced out of the washroom and over to the bar. There was Mr Lovely Golden Hair waiting for me, his suit immaculately white, his shoes spotlessly clean. The disco lights spun like sunshine off his blonde hair, bounced yellow from his bright eyes.

'Hey,' he said, 'you look great.'

I smiled nicely, thanked him for the compliment and told myself to be composed. Angels of Death should look dignified. I was being inspected. I must impress.

'What a night,' he said. 'You've been to a disco; you've fallen in love; you've saved your boyfriend's life and you still look dazzling! Let's drink to it!'

Laid out on the bar were two frosted glasses and an ice bucket with a bottle already chilling inside. But instead of reaching for a glass I turned to him, confused. I must tell him Marcus wasn't my boyfriend. Surely he knew love between a mortal and an angel was expressly forbidden. Perhaps he was testing me.

So I did. I told him that I'd only been doing my duty, that Marcus deserved another chance and angels love everyone (as he knew), that Earthly love was something very different: a savage thing, so I'd been told. A thing that drove men to murder and women to despair. That I couldn't possibly be in love, and that I'd been warned about it in the Cloisters.

He wasn't listening, though. He was pointing at the bottle in the bucket. 'Champagne,' he said, '*pink* champagne!' He winked at me. 'I'm Harry, by the way.'

'I'm Sera,' I said. 'Well, Serafina, but –'

'But you'd like an Earthly name too, eh?'

'Yes,' I said, surprised. I hadn't been going to say that, but: 'Yes, I would.'

'So you get to be called Sara then.' As if that was perfectly logical.

'Harry,' I said, touching his arm briefly.

'Sara?' he said, eyes widening in earnestness as he pointed again towards the champagne.

'Harry, I don't think –'

'Love you!' said Harry. 'I just love girls who don't think!'

I'd meant the alcohol. I didn't mean I was brainless.

Harry swivelled round on his bar stool and leaned up closer, widened his eyes and said, 'Hey, Klara, let's have a toast to true love, eh?'

'Sara,' I said.

'Oops,' he said.

He picked up the bottle of champagne, tapped the bottom of it a couple of times in a very professional way and loosened the wire. He took the white napkin that was draped over the bucket and, wrapping it in one smooth movement around the bottle, twisting at the same time, popped the cork – with a sound horribly reminiscent of gunfire. He picked up the first of the champagne flutes and poured the pink frothy bubbling liquid into it. How the liquid glowed and swirled, as if stardust was caught in its tiny tides.

Harry winked. 'Don't be shy,' he said, 'I won't tell. And he's one of us.' He gestured at a barman who was busy closing up.

'One of us?' I peered at the barman. He completely ignored me.

'Works for me,' smiled Harry. 'Very discreet. Now drink up.'

How strange it all was. An angel working behind a bar? Then I caught my breath. Perhaps he was working undercover! Part of the inspection team. Lord. I turned to look at Harry, eyes wide. He handed me my flute.

'But,' I hesitated, 'I've never drunk alcohol before.'

'It's quite easy,' he said, 'you lift the glass to your lips, tip it and swallow.'

'That wasn't what I meant.'

'No?' he said, all playful. 'Well, I think the evening you fall in love might be a good time to start, don't you, Lara?'

'But, Harry,' I started again. He seemed so sure I'd fallen

in love. *Had I? Surely not?* I shuddered. That would be a terrible thing.

'Larry,' he corrected.

*But what about the sign? What if Marcus was the one?*

'Sorry,' I said. 'I thought you said Harry.'

'You're as bad as me,' he laughed.

He *had* said Harry. I was sure of it.

'No "buts" allowed tonight,' Larry said with a mischievous look, holding up his glass. I felt confused. I felt embarrassed. Had I really misheard his name? It would be rude now to refuse a simple drink. And if he was an Inspector, it must be OK.

Mustn't it?

I thought of Heaven and all the rules. I was sure (although I'd never had the opportunity to check – believe me, in the Cloisters even mentioning manna-dew raises eyebrows) that alcohol on any kind of occasion was prohibited. I felt pretty certain of it, but as Larry filled his glass and peered at me: first through the bubbling nectar, with such teasing looks, such charming smiles; and then peeking his head around the edge of the glass as if he was hiding from the Big Bad Rule Book of Heaven, I burst out laughing.

If there were such rules as No Alcohol in Heaven, or No Alcohol on Heavenly Assignments, they were very silly rules! There, that's what I thought! And they'd probably been made up by old St Peter, who was the stickliest stick-in-the-mud ever, and had no authority to put them there in the first place.

I raised my glass.

'To our success,' toasted Larry.

'Absolutely,' I said.

'To your young man's next eighteen years,' he added. 'And to our little bargain.'

'Yes! Yes!' I said.

'Go on, then,' said Larry. 'Be a devil.'

I looked at him over the rim of my glass. We ought not to joke about the Devil.

He raised an eyebrow. 'OK, Barbara,' he said. 'Be an angel, then! Whatever!'

He drank long and deep, only stopping to say, 'Ah, the nectar of the gods.' Whereupon he refilled his glass again. Right up to the very top.

I felt a bit giddy. I felt a bit naughty. Larry was a very strange Inspector – so young and modern. But he was right – I should live a little (and I *had* saved a life *and* potentially a soul – *all in one go*). I sipped at the edge of my glass.

Oh my!

My first ever taste of champagne! It bubbled! It burned in fizzy strength against my lips. I could feel it. I could taste the ice-cold, tart flavour of grape and vinegar, of fruit and of something . . . something so intoxicating and thirst-making. It was wonderful.

'Good, huh?' said Larry.

'Umm,' I agreed.

Larry reached over, grabbed the bottle, picked up my glass and filled it up again.

'I know a much more exciting way of drinking it,' he whispered, his eyes alive with amusement. He leaned forward and whispered in my ear. 'A champagne kiss.'

I looked at him. I think I was shocked, despite the heady rush of wine.

'Naughty but very nice,' he winked.

'What's a champagne kiss?' I whispered, half guessing.

He waggled a finger in front of my face. 'Not for angels, Tamara,' he said. 'Only for bad girls!'

He made bad girls sound so exciting.

'Come on,' he said, 'hang out with me and everything's fun.' He finished off the champagne. 'But we can't be naughty all evening, and however many more bottles are chilling for us, we've business to attend to.'

He pulled a small case out of his pocket, flicked it open and withdrew a pair of thick horn-rimmed spectacles from inside. Sliding them on to his nose, he peered over them with an expression of the utmost mock gravity.

'Yes,' he said, 'to business and to small print.'

I looked up, confused.

'Of the contract, my dear.'

'OK,' I said.

'Thing is,' he said, smiling, half apologetically, 'Marcus's name actually *was on* the Manifest of those due to go off to the roaster tonight.'

'I know,' I said. Was he still jesting, or was he serious now? I replaced my glass carefully on the counter, the bubbles inside it bursting.

'So the thing is,' he repeated, 'we've got to sort of keep the Rate of Exchange balanced.'

The Rate of Exchange?

'How do we do that?' I asked.

'Simple as a pimple,' he said.

I looked at him, waiting.

'Send someone else in his place.'

# Serafina 6

*Send somebody in his place?* A sinking feeling plummeted straight through me. I looked at Larry, alarmed.

He grinned sheepishly. 'It's not as bad as it sounds,' he said, laying a reassuring hand on my arm. He shook his golden locks in a hit-me-I-am-so-guilty way. '*Really*, it's not.' He pulled a grimace.

*Send somebody in his place?*

'I know! I should have told you before you signed and stuff, but you and Marcus looked so perfect together, and I'm such a sucker for true love.' Larry looked at me with big blue eyes.

I couldn't seem to take in what he was saying.

'And he looks like the kind of young man who so *desperately needs* a Guardian Angel,' offered Larry, looking at me over the rim of his glasses and opening his eyes even wider.

Cold fingers plucked at my chest.

'And I could tell it would just break your heart to send him to the pits.' Larry twisted his champagne glass anxiously in his hand.

*What was he talking about?*

Behind him the police unrolled blue and white tape, cordoned off the dance floor, spoke into walkie-talkies. From outside a siren wailed.

'I just didn't want you to have to make that choice, not at that time, not in that way.'

*But to kill another to save Marcus?*

'Please, Tiara, don't look at me like that.'

I blinked. Of course I shouldn't look at him like that. He'd only been trying to help. It wasn't his fault.

'I got it wrong, didn't I?' he said.

He'd seen how I looked at Marcus. He'd wanted the world for us. And I could tell from the way he smiled so hopefully up at me, so remorsefully through his golden eyelashes, that he was a complete romantic. He'd just been trying to help. It was churlish of me to be so abashed. *But to send someone else in Marcus's place?* Yes, he'd got it wrong. Very. Very wrong. I couldn't. I wouldn't.

'But you've already signed,' Larry reminded me nervously.

And I *had* already signed. I'd thoughtlessly, carelessly, criminally committed myself to a contract without taking time to understand it. I'd messed up for real. And this time it was major. And now I was going to have to illegally Collect someone to put it right. It was as good as murder. I felt my cheeks rush hot, then cold. How could I have done that?

'You were flustered,' reminded Larry. 'I even had to catch Marcus for you.'

Yes, I was flustered and besotted and stupid and trying to pretend I was human, I was longing to be a teenage girl and imagining I was one, when I wasn't and never could be. I was vain and proud and envious. And I should've known better! I should. I was a Seraph (albeit only a teenage Seraph in Heaven's years – but that was no excuse); I was beloved of Heaven, a being that sat on the right hand of God. I should've known much MUCH better. I hung my head.

'I'll have to go and confess to St Peter straight away,' I whispered.

'Hey, hang on,' smiled Larry, 'it *really* isn't *that* bad, I hope. Honestly, it's not as bad as you think.'

*Not as bad as I think?* I couldn't think of anything worse!

Guiltily I jumped up, turned to go, to accept my fate, confess all and be banished to Soul Recycling Duty in Purgatorium forever. I'd failed in my responsibility. I didn't deserve anything better. It was that simple.

'Please,' said Larry, 'just hear me out.'

He put his hand again on mine; the bar lights swirled, the champagne sent a few tiny bubbles up my flute. I watched them peak and pop. The giant disco ball started to turn. Light sparkled off it, sparkled off the bucket, sparkled off the bottle, off the ice cubes and the glasses, but I wasn't sparkling any more.

'Please?' begged Larry again.

'Why?' I said reluctantly, knowing I should get up immediately and go and confess.

'Thing is,' he said, 'it's not such a big deal, you see . . . but I'm not sure I can say this . . .' He mumbled, seeing my blanched, worried look.

'Just say it,' I sighed.

'Well,' Larry took a huge breath, 'I know this may sound a bit heartless, but Marcus wasn't the only one who got shot this evening.' I looked up at him, trying to fathom what he meant.

'You see, his best pal, Joey Bigga, got shot too and . . .'

*What was he suggesting?* That I send Joey Bigga in his place? I couldn't believe it! This was too much. Condemn Marcus's *best friend* to the fiery pits? How awful. How heartless. How two-faced.

It was outrageous.

'*Please* hang on,' pleaded Larry.

I looked at him in complete shock. A new terror was forming. Why was he pleading with me to listen? If he was an Inspector, he'd order me to. I was confused. *Maybe he wasn't an Inspector at all.* No Inspector would ever even recommend swapping souls like that, would they?

'Who *are* you?' I said.

'Imagine . . . you really must let me explain. Let me do a little reconstruction – repeat the scenario. Please?'

'You're not an Inspector at all, *are you?*'

'Pleeeease.'

But before I could demand to know exactly who he was, Larry launched into a full explanation.

'Joey and Marcus are shot, both are bleeding to death; both are sinful creatures, both partners in crime, equal in guilt.' Larry nodded at me, keen to get me to concur.

'I suppose,' I agreed.

'The paramedics arrive. Joey happens to be closer to the exit. They attend to him first. Then they call up a reserve team for the other victim. *Voilà!* Disco! Joey lives. Marcus dies. Is that fair?'

'But that's was what was scheduled to happen,' I said dully.

'Chance, luck, fate, ill fortune! If Joey had crossed the

room a few minutes before the Crow and his crew entered, Marcus would have been closer to the exit, and *he* would have got the emergency first-aid treatment before Joey.'

'But,' I said, sighing, folding my wings in around my sides. 'Joey didn't.'

'I know,' said Larry, 'believe me. *I know*, and I feel *so bad* about it. And by the way I'm an Independent Celestial Advisor. I broker all sorts of Heavenly deals.'

'I see,' I said. I didn't see anything – except that there were further huge embarrassing gaps in the Cloisters' Angelic Curriculum.

'I really feel very bad about the Rate of Exchange,' he said. 'But it's beyond my control. Now if you could have placed your deal earlier, I could have spared you the un-pleasantries.'

'So you're a Business Angel,' I said.

'Sorry,' he said, 'but someone's got to broker loans, manage repayments, work out interest levels. Someone's got to be ready to sue for compensation in the Halls of the Dead.'

I sighed. Of course. I should have realised Extensions were far too simple to be true.

'Look, next time call me first. With a bit of time there could have been more choice. Here's my card: Claim Souls Direct.'

More choice? Did he mean he could have selected some other poor unfortunate being to send to Hell?

'None of it's personal,' said Larry dejectedly, 'but business is so cut-throat these days. Other celestial dealers would have demanded much tougher terms. It's no wonder I don't make any profit.' He put his head in his arms.

He sounded so upset. I put out a hand and laid it on his shoulder. 'Don't worry, this isn't your fault. I shall take the blame,' I asserted very magnanimously.

Larry looked at me through grateful eyes. 'I saw you and Marcus together. I saw a glimpse of a glorious future for you both. I love happy endings.' He sighed and looked sadly into his glass. 'I never had a chance at a happy ending.'

There was something in his voice, something broken and immeasurably moving that cut straight to my heart. He wasn't just giving me any old sales patter. He really meant it.

'I'm sorry,' he whispered. 'All I did was cause a bit of chaos; get the kids to cluster a bit more around Joey, so there was a clear path to Marcus when the meds came in. You really shouldn't blame yourself. It was the paramedics who decided which one to save.'

I felt too ashamed to follow his logic. How could I blame it on the paramedics? Here I was drinking champagne, in a nightclub, after having *not* Collected the soul that I was charged to Collect, after having signed an Extension Contract, *without* having read the small print. And now I was being talked into sending the best friend of the boy I'd pledged on my Holy Oath to watch over – to Hell. How could I blame all that on the paramedics?

I despised myself.

I was the worst, sloppiest, most despicable kind of angel ever.

Suddenly Larry looked like he'd swallowed a hedgehog.

'Christmas!' he said. 'It's a bit late to get upset now,' and he gestured behind me.

I turned. I saw Joey stretched out. The paramedics were giving up. One of them started to lift the thermal blanket up, to cover Joey's face. Another was unpacking a body bag.

*Joey was already dead!*

What the Hell was I going to do now?

# Serafina 7

Joey was dead. How could that be? Hastily I scanned the room to see if another Angel of Death had arrived. Nobody.

It was quite extraordinary. Joey had died all by himself.

'Why don't you go and give him a nice send-off, Kiara? That'll make you feel better. It really *wasn't* your fault,' urged Larry.

I should go straight to the Pearly Gates. I should tell St Peter immediately. I knew I should. But if I left Joey's soul unattended to, the demons would get it. I could see they were back already, greedily stretching out their diabolical tentacles towards him.

I could hardly believe he hadn't been provided with an angel. How could I abandon him? Leave his soul for those foul spectres to suck up? He was Marcus's best friend, for God's sake! I wouldn't leave a dog for those shades to feast on. I had to decide. Joey was Passing Over *right now*. I could see his soul hovering, peeking out from his body, scared, shocked, alone.

'Probably be a good idea to help him out,' repeated Larry, nodding at the wisp of grey bobbing up from the stricken corpse.

*What else could I have done? How could I have forsaken him?*

'If you leave him to the beasties, you'll be in even worse trouble,' whispered Larry.

I thought about it. He was right. To switch Joey with Marcus, for somehow I knew that's exactly what had happened, then condemn him to Hell without a chance to repent *and* leave him unattended to, *and* allow Lucifer's hordes to get him first. It was unforgivable, like being drunk behind a wheel and hitting someone and driving off at top speed and not reporting it. The Superiors at the Cloisters had certainly told me about *that* kind of wickedness. The sin of neglect. The sin of cowardice. The sin of being self-serving. No, I must help him. I had to do my best to put right the wrongs I'd created.

So I got up off my bar stool and hurried to Joey's side. The paramedics had already given up. Police were everywhere: taping off the dance floor, inspecting the corpse, chalking round the body. Obviously they couldn't see Larry or me.

Without a second thought I took up a fighting stand. Those demons as sure as Hell were going to get it. They crept forward, vile things. First I sent a volley of thunderbolts at them. Then I shook my tresses and summoned the great airy storms of Elysium to sweep them away. They turned tail and fled.

Then I caught the grey wisp in my arms. Joey Bigga's soul. I would help him for Marcus's sake.

'Hey Joey,' I called softly.

It turned and, seeing me, began to tremble like a naked child.

I unfurled one wing and sheltered it. I allowed it to

recollect itself, to know that it was going to be protected. It grew stronger and more defined under my touch. At last it managed to shake itself free of its body (always those last few wisps) and assume the full size that had been Joey. It clothed itself in the memory of its garments, and started to look again like Joey Bigga. Yes, Joey in his leather jacket, his designer sunglasses, his jeans and high-tops.

'I'll look after you,' I said, filled with pity – for as I spoke Joey hunted about him. On his face was disbelief, astonishment that all the good times had ended, surprise that the reckoning hour had come.

I took in his measure. Yes, Joey's soul was not overly large. He'd done a few good deeds in his life, but nothing remarkable – just little acts of friendship mostly inspired by self-interest. My heart eased a bit. There wasn't one spotless wisp of pure white on his soul. Perhaps Larry was right. I hadn't made such a huge blunder. Joey was damned anyway, and the world was well rid of him.

Nevertheless it was only right that I make amends. 'Would you like to repent?' I asked very gently.

'Repent what?' said the soul of Joey, checking himself out, patting his arms and chest. Souls like to do that. They find the Passing Over hard; the transition between corporeal reality and the nether world alarms them.

'Just repent,' I said. 'Atone for wrongs done, apologise for pain caused?'

'Repent?' He raised an eyebrow and peered at me. 'Repent all the good times? All the thrills, the spills, the guns, the game?' He shook his head. 'All those wild nights? Those hot babes! Why?' He looked around as if he expected to see a procession of wild nights filled with hot babes yet to come.

I clucked my tongue at him. How shameless he was.

'So I can save your soul,' I said. Although now he was already dead I doubted if I could. Technically you're supposed to repent whilst you're still alive. I'd never tried it the other way round. And actually you're not supposed to enter into any debate about it either.

'Nah,' he said shakily. 'I mean, OK.' He seemed unsure. 'I wanna go where the bad guys are.'

'Just as well,' hissed Larry from the bar. 'Breaking the contract could be messy.'

'Well,' I said, not quite knowing how to handle this, 'you have to be sure. Are you really sorry?'

Joey eyed me suspiciously as if I were trying to trick him.

'No comment,' he said.

I shot a desperate look at Larry. He jerked his head as if to say, Well, the chips are up for him, then.

'Joey?' I tried again. 'This is your last chance.'

'No comment,' he repeated as if he were being cross-examined by the police.

'Then you must come with me,' I said. He was going to go to Hell anyway – no need to continue the charade. 'I'll show you the way.'

With a heavy heart I took his hand. He'd been so nearly there. If the circumstances had been different – perhaps with some extras – a choir of cherubim?

'You mean I've got to leave all this fun at the club, right now? I never even got going,' he moaned.

I smiled. I didn't like to tell him there would be no

'getting going' where he was bound. Instead I said, 'Well, looks like the fun here is done for tonight. We shouldn't leave it too long. There's a kind of schedule involved. There might be a queue by the time we get to the river.'

'A queue?' he said, raising his eyebrows. 'Hell sure is a banging hot place, eh? All da crews lining up to get in?'

I nodded. Absolutely. It was a very banging hot place indeed.

Joey looked around and seemed to remember something. 'Where am I?' he said.

'Still at The Mass, the nightclub,' I said.

'No,' he said. 'Where am I? I mean *me.*' He tried to slap at his arms. 'Me. You know – Joey Bigga.'

'I think,' I said slowly, 'the paramedics took you away.'

'Then I must get me back,' said Joey. 'I can't die. You've got to save me. *I don't want to die . . .*' His eyes took on a haunted look.

'I'm sorry,' I said. 'You're already dead.' Then, more reassuringly: 'The worst is over.'

'No!' All his bravado was gone. He grabbed at me. 'I'm sorry, OK? You've got to help me. I can't die. I can't go to Hell!'

I looked down at him. Poor Joey.

Larry gave me an encouraging thumbs-up. He mouthed, *'That's my girl.'*

I tried to feel encouraged. 'Come,' I said, taking Joey under my wing. 'I'll keep you company. There aren't many hotter babes than me. We'll cruise on down the Highway and chat. You can have your pick of music – a few strains of the harp, perhaps? I'm good at the harp.'

Joey gave me an odd look, so I let some Welsh harp music drift across the street and swirl up into the club.

'That. Is. Total. Crap,' said Joey.

I didn't try again. Instead I led him off the dance floor, out of the club, past Larry (who smiled at me again, said, 'Good girl, Chiara, catch you later by the river'), and up the narrow stairs. We passed the bouncers' bay, the cloakroom, the upstairs café and stepped out into the still night of the city.

# Serafina 8

Between you and me, Joey wasn't the easiest person to play Guiding Angel to. He clung desperately to his human form, and he couldn't seem to quit weaving around and galloping forward.

'Hey, Joey,' I said, 'you'll get the hang of being dead quicker if you try walking first, and accept that your "body" now belongs to a different realm.'

As I said that, Joey launched forward and bumped into another soul and knocked it for six. He did it again. I found myself saying, 'Sorry,' and, 'He's so new to this,' to the other Seraphim escorting their charges down to the river. (In our own realm, sadly, we can't travel in the beat of a wing.)

'Taking it badly, is he?' asked a Seraph, someone I knew vaguely by sight (the Cloisters? Last year? Trumpet practice?).

I nodded, but what if Joey's erratic progress was less to do with him taking it badly, and much more to do with him taking it at all?

I smiled at the other Seraph and shrugged my shoulders. But I didn't feel as upbeat as I looked. The thought of St Peter's disappointment, his slow ponderous questioning, his melancholic disapproval sent shivers into even my most fiery bits. I'd have to confess, of course – but I *was* beginning to wonder if . . . you know . . . if everything went OK, with Joey, whether I couldn't put it off a bit? At least until Marcus had repented, and I could show some positive outcome?

My fellow Seraph smiled back. I liked her immediately.

I didn't much like the Highway, though. It was broad, of course, and they'd newly resurfaced it with lovely dark slate. On either side fields stretched away, filled with ripe corn, red poppies, myriads of wild flowers. But the Highway – gorgeous as it was, always sloping downhill, winding beside streams, curving out on to wide plains – was not a nice place. Its breezes were not the gentle winds of Heaven; they were stifling blasts of dry, hot ventilation. And they smelt.

'Hey,' I said, catching Joey, as he stumbled into a weary trudge. 'You've almost got the hang of it now. Brilliant!'

He gave me a scathing look. 'Don't need to patronise me,' he said. 'I'm the One and Only Joey B.'

How delightful he was! Calling himself Joey B. like that. Especially when he was just a puny little (dead) human. I wondered if the demons in the pits would like his charming arrogance.

'Tell me about yourself, Joey,' I said, trying to humour him.

'Why?' he said. 'You in league with the Feds?'

'The Feds?' I said. Did he mean cannibals? I shuddered. Maybe they were something like zombies.

'I'm happy to tell you I'm not in league with the Feds,' I said, smiling. 'Or anything else related to the undead.'

Joey gave me a funny look.

Of course, I was just longing to talk about Marcus, but I couldn't seem to find a way in. Every time I tried, Joey said something random that threw me off. I wasn't going to be defeated, though. At last I just burst out with it. 'Are you Marcus's best friend?'

Joey gave me another seriously weird look. '*Best friend?*' he said. 'Like college girls?'

'Absolutely!' I chirped. He'd understood me exactly. Just like college girls. I beamed up at him. 'Yes, like do you share secrets and things?'

'Joey B. share secrets?' he squeaked.

'Yes,' I said. 'I'm not asking you to be indiscreet or anything, but did Marcus ever confide in you – as his best friend, sort of thing?'

Joey started laughing. I couldn't really see why. I'd love to have a best friend. (Having close friendships was rather frowned upon at the Cloisters.) If I'd had a best friend I'd tell her everything: when I was sad, when I was worried, if I had a spot on my nose (I mean if I was human. Angels don't get spots, obviously).

'Yes, secrets,' I continued. 'Like do you know his favourite pizza topping, the book he's enjoying reading and um –' here I tried to keep my voice steady – 'what kind of girls he likes?'

'The *book* he's reading?' said Joey, looking at me as if I'd put my halo on upside down.

'And if he has a girlfriend,' I said.

At that Joey's face creased up. '*A* girlfriend?' He quite snorted with laughter. 'No, Marcus doesn't have a "girlfriend", he has *girlfriends*. He has so many *girlfriends*, he could start up an All Girls School, just on his own.'

'Oh!' I said, a sudden pang spearing me.

'Girls go crazy for that guy. He has to positively fight them off,' Joey said. 'Even then they come back, screaming for more.'

Beside us the road dipped briefly into the shadow of a huge cliff. The Highway narrowed a little to curve through a mountain pass.

'Oh,' I said again, thinking: Well, if he's going to repent, the whole area of 'girlfriends' might be a good place to start.

'Zillions of girls,' continued Joey, completely oblivious to the way my face was falling. 'They actually *pay* him to see them. Can you beat that?'

Once through the pass, the landscape opened up. Before us lay barren plains.

'And he treats them like shit. And they still come back for more!'

My fire dimmed and my splendour faded right out.

But all I said was: 'Oh.' As if the subject was boring and I'd had enough of it.

And then I nearly drove myself mad. Because I hadn't had anything like enough of it. I wanted to quiz Joey. I wanted to shake him, force him to take it all back. I wanted *details*. Huge details. Intricate details. Blow-by-blow details. Sordid details. Secret details. Any-details-at-all details – of every girl Marcus had ever dated.

And I wanted Joey to explain what it was that drove all those girls crazy, so that they paid to get near Marcus. What kept them coming back when he treated them so badly? What was his secret?

But I didn't need to. I knew. It was driving *me* crazy.

Had driven me crazy.

Would drive me crazy.

In fact I was already crazy.

So crazy I'd signed contracts, made promises, and here I was taking his best friend to Hell!

I knew just what Marcus Montague had.

And he clearly had huge amounts of it.

# Serafina 9

Together Joey and I hurried down from the mountain pass. As we drew near to the river, the air hung more heavily. Over the fields you could see it rising and shimmering, and from time to time you could catch a whiff of it too, a salty, sulphurous smell that made you twitch uncomfortably.

I started to feel ill.

When we reached the river we saw the queue. It was predictable, really: Saturday night, only port for a number of big cities – you can imagine the rest. We were going to have to wait for the ferry for ages.

Not that I minded. I was glad, even. Souls get impatient, the same way people do. So when the ferry came along, everybody was going to be in a rush to get across. That would make it much easier to get out of being cross-questioned. After all, I didn't want Charon bothering me about the life and death of Joey Bigga, did I?

But, God, was it hot! The river slid by – all smelly and greasy. Puffs of sulphurous smoke were constant and suffocating. The sky was streaked blood-red. The vegetation had all withered. The sound of clanging and wailing and (weirdly) of opera music drifted from the far bank. All the souls had lost their glitter. Each one looked as shabby as the next. It was quite horrible.

For the next few hours we shifted slowly forward in the line, the Angels of Death and the dead. There's no obligation on Seraphim to wait when there's a queue. But what with the Extension, I felt nervous about leaving Joey to answer for himself. Plus I had to collect the paperwork from Larry.

Soon my hair hung like a heavy curtain, and my raiment stuck to me. But I resigned myself. (Patience is a virtue and it's always good to practise it.) And as we waited I thought of Marcus. The way he'd seemed so determined to stay true to himself, even as he lay dying. So honest. I admired him for it. I'm an angel. I can't die, but standing there gazing out across that river towards the dull glow of the pits, I feared death. I think I'd have repented anything to avoid Hell.

I was relieved when I saw Larry. There he was, all clean and crisp in his white outfit. (He'd changed and had on white jeans and the cutest white tee under a white jacket.) His golden hair gleamed and his blue eyes twinkled.

All this time though, I have to tell you, Joey had *not* been waiting very patiently. He'd got quite excited ogling girls. And there were some pretty awesome females queuing up at that river to ogle at.

'Hey, Joey,' I said, 'you can go over to every girl on the jetty in a minute, after I've signed you in.'

'Whatever,' Joey said, not taking the slightest notice. He headed straight for a honey blonde with amazing buttocks.

I threw my wings up in despair. Larry didn't seem to mind, though. He crossed over to me, briefcase in hand, looking not a jot the worse for all the heavy air.

'Hello, my favourite cherub,' he said. (Just for the record, I'm a Seraph, six wings, tall and nothing like a cherub; plus, in the hierarchy of celestial beings – well, much higher.) He flashed me a perfect smile from a perfect set of pearly teeth. 'Are we ready to close our deal?'

I looked around me. All those poor souls bound for Hell. How blessed I was to have saved Marcus from this. I thought of Heaven, its glistening valleys, its sweet pastures; how lucky we angels were. It didn't seem fair. Somebody should do something about it all. The banks of Styx were surely where God's work should begin?

I nodded at Larry. Of course I was ready to close the deal. I tried to tug Joey my way without success.

'Hey, Angel-face,' said Larry, 'don't stress. You've had a rotten night. There's no hurry.'

'It's just Joey,' I said. 'I don't know, maybe it's because he's been brought here too early, but he's not getting used to it at all.'

'Don't worry, there are counsellors on the other side. They'll take him through step by step. He's making friends already.' Larry nodded towards Joey, who had slid completely from my grasp, and already had one muscly arm around the girl with the ginormous bum.

I smiled. I threw my wings up. Let him enjoy himself, then! The pursuit of Earthly pleasures wouldn't be his for long.

'So,' said Larry, 'just need your autograph here.' Larry held up the contract he'd shown me in the club. The writing was terribly small. I had to squint to see it. But even as I squinted it seemed to grow weirdly smaller. Must be the light, I thought. I didn't want to be rude and demand to see it, as if I was going to nitpick. I'd already committed myself anyway. This was just some kind of delivery note, wasn't it?

I have to tell you at this point something quite bizarre happened. I was glancing over at Joey by the queue and I swear – on my Holy Oath – I saw that shadowy figure from the corner seat of the nightclub again.

'I'm really sorry,' said Larry, 'but tonight's Extension was such a rush job, I've only got this one copy. Can I get yours to you later?'

I peered across at the figure just to be sure, but he'd slipped behind a knot of football fans in stripy scarves. I remembered there'd been an incident scheduled after a match. It'd been on the Manifest. (Quite a few fans had died, and one was only a kid. Thank goodness I hadn't been on Brawl Duty.) The shadowy figure was quite gone.

'Can I?' asked Larry again.

'Oh, sorry,' I said. 'Of course.'

'Brilliant,' he said.

I took the pen he offered and signed by the cross. It read:

Successful Delivery to Styx
Soul:         One
Description: Grey, stained, not suitable for reuse
Name:      Joseph Biggs
Deal #      19086600897
Broker:     Harry Laurence Schratz
Guarantor: Serafina Seraph
Signed:    *Serafina Seraph* & *Harry Laurence Schratz*

This delivery note relates to the contract of 20th October sealed at The Mass Night Club between and betwixt the above parties whereby an Extension was taken out on the life of Marcus Montague *provided a suitable exchange could be made on the same night. This contract expires on Halloween. If Marcus Montague has not repented by that date, his soul is forfeit with the rest of his Earthly life at that hour without prejudice. Collection time 12.00 Midnight, 31st October.*

Mr Harry Schratz. So I had heard right. That was strange. But I shrugged. Maybe he preferred his middle name. 'There!' I signed with a flourish and added a tiny drawing of butterfly wings. In the distance I thought I heard thunder rumble.

'Fabbo, fabbo,' said Larry. 'All's done!' and as he spoke two tall dark shapes moved in on Joey.

I glanced over to see what they'd do. But as I turned my head, I noticed out of the corner of my eye the word 'Marcus' in the small print at the bottom of the sheet. Larry was busy whisking it away, ready to file it in his briefcase, but I read it all the same. This is what it said:

> *. . . This contract expires on Halloween. If Marcus Montague has not already repented by that date, his soul is forfeit with the rest of his Earthly life at that hour without prejudice. Collection time 12.00 Midnight, 31st October.*

'Oh!' I said.

'Anything wrong?' asked Larry.

'Oh no,' I said. It would have been churlish, after everything Larry had done, to moan about the date on the Extension. But he had said three weeks, hadn't he?

Or had I misheard?

I smiled, but some of my gorgeous radiance drained from my face.

'. . . This contract expires on Halloween.'

And Halloween was only ten days away.

# Serafina 10

Only ten days.

In ten days, Marcus would still be recovering from his wounds. He'd be nowhere near repenting.

*Ten days.*

He hadn't even said he wanted to.

But even if he did want to, he was still going to need to turn his life around. How was he going to achieve that in under a fortnight? I opened my mouth to protest, but shut it again just as quickly. No un-kinder sin than ingratitude. Marcus had been given a second chance. For that alone I should be truly thankful. Amen. I was just going to have to make it work.

Straight away I started to plan. Repentance in word and deed. He'd have to go the whole way if I was going to get him into Heaven. Not just a quick 'I'm sorry' before Passing Over. That would only get him into Purgatorium. Even if I could swing it and get him through the Twelfth Pearly, we really should try for an early audience with St Peter. Not easy. But was it possible?

I thought about it.

Firstly I needed to get him to a priest or a pastor, a qualified representative of God on Earth at least: he could confess, receive absolution, be assigned penance: *Dominus noster Jesus Christus te absolvat: Amen.* That would be a great start. I'd explain it all to him; that bit should be reasonably easy.

Secondly he was going to have to forswear wrongdoing. That was going to be a bit more tricky: no more girls, no more crime (definitely no more girls), no more alcohol, no more meeting up with his gang and *absolutely* no more girls. All straightforward, but for some reason it made me terribly nervous.

The next bit was a lot more difficult: he needed to make recompense. I flipped my mind back to the exam paper I'd done on 'Penitence, Recompense & the Eye of the Needle: Advanced Paper, Higher Tier'.

*Access to Heaven through Penitent Recompense can be demonstrated in three ways. Please discuss:*
1. Sacrificial and noble action
2. Selflessness
3. Taking vows of chastity, poverty, obedience.

Yes, he could show he'd changed, either by doing something noble, like saving a life by giving up his own; or by doing a lot of selfless acts over a longer period. Sadly, there wasn't any time for the latter, and hopefully, no opportunity for the former: it was going to have to be chastity, poverty and obedience; starting by giving away all his worldly goods and ill-gotten gains (plus of course absolutely and completely abstaining from girls).

But then came the part that made me the most nervous

of all: what if – even if I got him to agree repentance was a good idea – what if he still didn't really *want* to do it? I mean, *really* do it.

That was the catch: Free Will.

If not for Free Will, I could have commanded him to. I could have flashed my eyes, blasted him with a few thunderbolts, sent hailstones to rain around him, until he *did* do it. That would have done the trick. It would've been a lot easier too.

But God had decreed repentance must be done freely and willingly. And the contract had decreed it must be done before midnight on the last day of October.

It was a lot.

One Hell of a lot.

'Hey, Shanara,' trilled Larry. 'You look far away. Sweet thing, what is it? Don't let this place get you down.'

I looked up at him and smiled, but not with the same warmth as before. He'd definitely said, 'three weeks.' And it really wasn't OK.

'I just wish I had a little longer,' I said.

'You mean, you'll be needing an Extension on the Extension?' he joked.

I think it was a joke.

'It'll cost ya,' he winked.

I didn't laugh. I glanced across at Joey. Another life prematurely snatched? Another person sent here to suffer for Marcus? My feathers curled at the thought.

Poor Joey. There were two dark shapes on either side of him now, dragging him away from the girls. One of the shapes whipped round and I saw its demonic face, red eyes,

71

gaping mouth. As he was led away, Joey glanced over his shoulder at me. His face stricken. His eyes pleading. All his toughness gone.

Even as I watched, a blood-curdling scream broke from the far shores of Styx. There was a rush of smoke, and the stench of singed hair and burning flesh belched out across the river. Someone tried to make a run for it. Another soul who only a moment earlier had been waiting patiently joined in.

The scream came again, nightmarish in its pitch. And before you could say 'Our Father' the whole centre portion of the queue went berserk and started running. Demons sprang from nowhere. They pounced on the souls trying to escape, sank claws and teeth into thin spirity bodies. They dragged them back, kicking, wailing, struggling.

I trembled. If I should fail? Could I leave Marcus here in less than two weeks? I remembered with a shudder all the stories I'd heard, told by candlelight, late at night, whispered under the arches of the quadrangles in the Cloisters. Stories of the things that demons did to souls in Hell: of how far a soul could be made to suffer; of the Devil, dark and squat, his horns, curved and sharp, chuckling over cauldrons of blood, of souls roasting in vats . . .

I looked again at Joey. His eyes still pleading, still begging. Could I face that look from Marcus?

An idea struck me: I could ask Larry. Maybe he could recommend someone to mentor Marcus? After all he had said he was an Independent Celestial Advisor, and could broker all sorts of Heavenly deals. Surely saving a soul was the most important sort of Heavenly deal there was?

I turned to Larry. I outlined my idea: someone constantly at Marcus's side to keep him on the straight and narrow, talk sensibly to him about his choices, persuade him to consider repentance, maybe even show him visions of Styx (not of the girls in the queue obviously, but glimpses of the pits in Hell where the damned were roasted, echoes of the screaming), to hammer home the point?

'Hmm,' said Larry. 'Not impossible.'

It wasn't a very confident Yes, I Can Do It, but his eyes did light up at the suggestion. I held my breath. I needed all the help I could get.

'I think I might be able to conjure up something,' Larry said.

I heaved a great sigh of relief. 'I'll pay, of course,' I said.

Another scream rent the air, another puff of stinking smoke spewed out across Styx.

'Oh yes, you'll pay all right,' said Larry, tweaking my cheek.

# Serafina 11

I was so glad to leave the shores of Styx. I wanted to get as far away from it as possible: the fetid river, the wilting foliage, the awful knowledge of torture going on just over the water: the burning, the stretching, the slicing, the tearing of sinew, the breaking of bones. For even though the souls of the dead had left their corporeal bodies behind, they still had their ethereal bodies that could be made to suffer. My spirits drooped. The heat oppressed me. I felt miserable about Joey. I tried to banish the image of Marcus dragged here, abandoned to those demons. But as I winged my way back towards the mountains, towards Devil's Pass, a different terror overcame me.

A vision of *me* led here in human shape, a trembling girl, dark-eyed, pale-faced, horror-struck. A vision of ghouls laying hold on *my* spirit, leading *me* away to the river. I trembled. My wings faltered. I beat the air and plummeted ten metres. I landed, shaking, on a rocky promontory.

But try as I might I couldn't shake the image off. Yet how could it be? Was I human – to be divided from my soul by death? How could an angel *ever* be cast into the fires of Hell? Angels don't die.

But the thought didn't console me. Instead I clung

shivering to the ledge. The vision was so clear. As in a nightmare, I saw my own eyes looking up at me, as two dark shapes pinned my arms and led me away.

And then a sad thought struck me: yes, angels can never be thrown into the fires of Hell. We don't fear death. We don't have to. Yet mortals such as Marcus must face that terror, must lie awake at night imagining it, must know beyond doubt that their lives will end and everything they love will be snatched away from them.

And this was God's creation?

Should I thank Heaven I wasn't mortal, then? But if I did, how could I ever hope to do God's work? How could I hope to save the souls of the damned when my immortality set me apart? Was I cursed to be an angel? Doomed never to understand the meaning of life?

For a split second I hated being immortal. On what authority did I judge those humans lining up by the ferry? If I were human who knows what choices I might have to make. I might be worse than the lowliest one of them.

I shuddered and curled my wings around me. What thoughts. Was I not blessed to be exempt from such a fate?

Did I say angels could never be thrown into the fires of Hell?

But wasn't that exactly what God had done to Lucifer?

For an instant I felt a terrible sympathy with the Devil. *To be thrown by the hand you love into that.* No wonder he wanted to inflict the same on mankind. No wonder he waged eternal war on Heaven.

But why by the stars above was I thinking all this? It must be the effect of these vile blasts from Hell.

I should get to Marcus quickly and wholly impress upon him the terrifying fate in store if he didn't do exactly as I said. And I must hurry.

Straight away I took to the air.

I was so preoccupied that I hardly noticed two shapes fall into flight beside me. When I looked up one of them dropped back out of view. The other was the Seraph I'd met on the road going down. I remembered her now. She was called Raquel.

She smiled at me and said, 'How was your day? Mine was crazy. I was on Road Call. There were so many souls to take to every kind of destination, I nearly got mixed up.'

I bit my lip, swallowed my worries and said, 'Well, next time, don't forget you can ask for an Extension, if you're really in a muddle.'

'Extensions?' Raquel said. 'What're they?' (Yes, I did remember her now. Genesis House. Cell 44. It hadn't been trumpet practice at all – it'd been the Thunderbolt Championships.)

I drew a deep breath and waved my feather tips vaguely. I decided to keep Marcus out of the conversation. I told her how a friend I'd known – aeons ago-ish – had met an angel, a Celestial Broker, on a business trip, and learned about Extensions.

'Bit like having a credit card, I suppose,' said Raquel. 'You know, buy now, pay later?'

'I suppose so,' I said. (I imagined having a credit card. I'd like a gold one with a super-shiny little chip on it. And I'd have my very own PIN number too.)

'What did you say your friend's name was?'

Had I mentioned a name? Well, I was going to have to now, wasn't I? 'Harry,' I said.

'Never heard of Extensions,' she said. 'Are you sure?'

'Yes,' I continued. 'I'd never heard of them before either, but Harry said apparently loads of angels do them, so I guess it's normal. Do you think if you ever did one, you ought to report it to St Peter?'

Raquel looked at me and rolled her eyes. 'Report it to St Peter!' she snorted. 'Like, only if you're mental, unless you *adore* long lectures on obscure trivia that happened millennia ago, in Israel probably. You *know* what he's like. Anyway, you off duty now?'

We'd left the wilted plains behind and were winging back up towards the poppy fields.

'Yes,' I said.

'Want to come over to mine later? I'm hosting an amazing choir you know, a proper ensemble and everything. Do say yes!'

'Oh yes,' I said without thinking. Why had I said that? I was going to see Marcus. It might take ages for me to get back to Heaven. I didn't have time for garden parties.

'Great,' said Raquel. 'It'll get you out of those dreary Cloisters. I'll introduce you to everyone and you can bounce the idea of Extensions around and see what they think.' She paused. 'I've never heard of any Harry, actually.' She laughed like it was totally funny for her not to know someone.

'He's in business,' I said.

'I know all the Senior Team, all the Archangels, everyone

in the City, really . . .' She was obviously puzzled she couldn't place him.

'He's got his own company,' I said, suddenly. 'I remember now. Claim Souls Direct.'

'Oh,' she said. 'That kind of business.'

# Serafina 12

I left Raquel by the Twelfth Gate, promising to see her later, and hurried to Christ the King's Hospital. In a heartbeat, I flicked my wings and was inside Marcus's room. It was a lovely private room. I was so glad. I wanted the best of everything for him.

There he lay as beautiful as ever. His dark hair tousled on the starched pillow. His long eyelashes brushing his cheek. There were his sweet full lips. My heart stopped. I caught my breath. There was his hand curled into a loose fist, slung outstretched in his sleep, as if even in his dreams he were waging war on the universe.

In the chair opposite sat his mother, her face crumpled, eyes bleary, knuckles pressed into a clenched ball in her lap. She couldn't see me, and I didn't change that. Anyway, she wasn't looking at anything. She could barely see beyond her own misery.

I went over to her. I touched her on the hand and sent her the balm of oblivion, not permanently, of course, just so she could get some sleep.

Then I stood beside Marcus trying to decide how I should wake him. How I longed to smooth back his tangled hair, to run my finger down the sculpted lines of his cheek, to take his hand.

I tried to work out exactly what to say. How to broach the subject of Joey, for a start. Imagining how it could all go terribly wrong.

ME:        Hi, just stopped by to see how you were doing.

MARCUS:   Not too bad. Where's my crew?

ME:        Ah, yes, they're probably in church.

MARCUS:   In church?

ME:        Arranging the funeral.

MARCUS:   Why? I'm still alive.

ME:        Yes, but I killed Joey off to keep you that way.

How was I going to tell him that? Not only was his friend dead, but it was all my fault and the reason he was still alive. I cringed. I really needed to think this through.

But should I wake him at all? He really didn't look very well. All around his bed, machines beeped. Above him a bag of blood dripped slowly through a tube into his arm. He wasn't going to be well enough to be told anything for ages.

Could I perform a miracle, then? I'd done Miracle Working as an Option at the Cloisters and got A* on the term paper. I could heal Marcus, I knew I could. It would be a textbook case. Nothing difficult or supernatural, not like turning water into wine, just hastening up healing time in normal tissue. But dare I?

I held my breath. If I was caught doing miracles, I'd probably have my wings stripped, be cast out of Heaven and sent to do five hundred years' Community Service in Purgatorium.

I didn't dare. Not a full miracle anyway, but I could do a Healing Hands Blessing. It would certainly speed up his recovery a bit.

I extended my hands over his heart and lightly touched his wounds. I let the power flow through me and whispered a full consecration. Immediately his breathing eased.

Then I just sat there perched on the end of his bed, nervously twiddling with a loose wing feather. He wasn't going to like the repentance thing. I knew it. I was going to have to be very careful. Timing was everything.

And right now was definitely not the right time.

I left the hospital. I'd got no idea what to do next. It was already late afternoon, and I'd been away from Heaven for nearly twenty-four hours. Twenty-four hours. Now there were only nine days left till Halloween.

With a troubled heart, I set out for the long journey up to Heaven, for the Pearly Gates and home.

But the minute I'd climbed the Staircase and got through the last Pearly, I knew something was wrong. Very wrong.

Firstly a strange new scent wafted on the evening air. It was faint at first and hard to place, but as soon as I passed through the Jasper Arch and on to the Golden Promenade, I knew what it was: the odour of diesel engines, of boot polish and cold metal. The smell of God's Army.

Then I heard the sirens. They were coming from the

three northern Gates. I stopped and listened. I sharpened my gaze. Something seared across the sky. Thunderbolts. God's Army are never allowed to use thunderbolts, unless we're under direct attack from Hell. Sirens and thunderbolts. Saints above, we must already be on Code Amber.

Quickly I looked around for a newspaper. Usually they're everywhere. But today no cherub flitted by with copies tucked under an arm. I threw a coin into a fountain by the huge pieta in the Virgin Mary Square, and I made a wish. But no paper plopped into my hand.

Where was everyone? The best I could get was a half-torn copy of the *Daily Trumpet*, a terrible publication produced by the Saved. The headlines read: GOD'S ARMY FIGHT BACK and WE'LL THRASH LUCY WITH CODE AMBER and SATAN'S CHALLENGE SPECIAL ISSUE – FULL STORY STRAIGHT FROM HELL.

I sighed. Half the stuff printed in the *Trumpet* was rubbish. If only I could get a copy of the *Celestial Herald*. Hastily I hurried through side streets to the Cloisters. Somebody was bound to have one there.

Over the cobbles I sped, until I reached the main arch to the entrance. Then I barged through the huge doors, slamming them behind me. The place seemed completely empty. I couldn't even hear any singing.

'Hello? Anyone there?'

The ambulatory was deserted. My friend Celandine's cell was locked. I hammered on her door just in case she was resting. Nothing. From far away I heard a murmuring. Had everyone gone to Devotions? Already?

I raced down the corridors and round the quadrangle to my cell. I let myself in, and bolted the door behind me. When I was safely inside I went all shivery. *We were on Code Amber. God's Army was bombing the Abyss.* I shook my head. I didn't understand.

Why couldn't God just meet up with the Devil? Weren't they once friends? Maybe if they both said sorry then the Devil could stop being so angry. I couldn't see how a terror campaign was going to help anything. Plus God's Army scare me, more than Satan. I probably shouldn't say that – after all I've never met Satan, so I don't know what he's capable of.

Inside my cell I tried to calm down. I put on music. I put on fairy lights. I lit some incense. But it was no good, I was so jumpy. Why had we escalated to Code Amber so quickly? Were we about to be overrun with demons? I put on the Announcer, and tuned it into the Prair Waves.

*'Please, Holy Father, help me . . .'*

I tuned in to another channel.

*'God's Army have been interrogating suspects . . .'*

If only Marcus were here. That would calm me. I could take care of him. He'd be safe. I imagined his cheek pressed against my pillow, my arms comforting him . . .

*'. . . denounce those found attending séances, trying to contact the living.'*

Why is it when you want to get the news up you can never find the blessed right frequency?

*'. . . will be instantly vaporised . . .'*

Or if I could be on Earth with him.

Was I crazy? I was a Seraph. He was a man.

'. . . *new offensive from Hell . . . the Challenge issued by the Devil . . . the Senior Team having declared war . . .*'

For some reason my throat went dry. A sudden ache made me catch my breath.

'. . . *serious breach . . . state of emergency . . . no quarter left unexamined . . .*'

Was that a noise outside?

I rushed to see. I pressed my nose to the leaded pane. In the darkness beyond I caught a glimpse of something: a shape flying, material swirling, then it was gone.

Every feather on every wing curled up and shrank. Had someone found out about Marcus? A chill blasted through me. What if Extensions were against the Rules when we were at war! *What if someone had denounced me to God's Army?*

*What would they do to Marcus?*

Trembling, I drew every blind. I put out the lights and sat down in the dark. Someone might still be watching. I got so scared. I didn't want to be alone. I tried to think. Who could I turn to? Where were the other Seraphim? I strained to listen. Finally I heard a distant whisper of prayer. Of course, those not on Heavenly Duties would be keeping Vigil. Even my two closest friends, Celandine and Haniella, would be praying and fasting until the threat from Satan was past.

And then I remembered the invitation. Glory be! Thank God for Raquel.


I hurried through the overshadowed streets. I kept my hearing on full volume, my vigilance on super alert, my wings unfurled ready for flight. In my hand I conjured thunderbolts to hurl even if the tiniest shadow appeared.

I made my way down bejewelled lanes to the outskirts of the town where Raquel lived. She'd had moved into the campus villas on the west side of the City by the sixth foundation stone of ruby. (You can do that once you've graduated from the Cloisters. Although you still have to do the duties, of course.)

All around me the sky flickered, sirens wailed, the air quivered. And I couldn't swear to it, but behind me I kept getting the feeling that something was following. Just a tweak of movement, a swirling of air in the twilight, and the tiny hairs all down my neck prickling.

I can't tell you the relief it was to arrive at Raquel's place and slip inside her gates. I heaved a huge sigh and waited until all my feathers stopped quivering. I leaned up against an old yew tree near the fence, my heart still racing. Even the strains of the choir tuning up took a while to calm me. At last I collected myself. I shook out my wings. I tossed my head and let my tresses burn with fiery radiance. I composed myself, ready to go in.

Inside Raquel's garden there were angels everywhere, saints too, and lots of souls. Little cherubs carried round trays loaded with delicacies: ambrosia, scent of sandalwood, fragrant nectar. I wasn't tempted. I needed to know what was going on. I rushed past everything, looking for Raquel.

She met me on the steps to the lower garden. She unfurled every wing around me, held me close, as if we were quite old friends. 'Serafina!' she cried. 'How wonderful! You came. With all this palavering going on too. Here, have

85

some honeydew.' She put a flute of clearest amber dew in my hand and kissed me on both cheeks. I was very grateful that she hadn't mentioned anything about the ascent from Hell, or how dimmed I must look.

'What's going on?' I gasped. 'Why are we on Code Amber?'

'Meet Clothilde,' she said and waved vaguely at a middle-aged saintly-looking creature.

'Pleased to meet you,' said Clothilde. 'I think there's been a breach.'

'A breach?' I said, eyes widening.

'I'm going to introduce you to all my friends.' Raquel grabbed me by the arm and hauled me off towards a cluster of angels.

I seized hold of Clothilde and said, 'What kind of a breach? Has Satan got into Heaven?'

Clothilde trotted unwillingly along beside me. Raquel ducked and dived through the guests. 'No, I think it's more of a security breach,' she said.

'Here's Georgia and this is Daniel; here's Maria and David,' Raquel chanted in a charming singsong voice.

'I *must* know, Clothilde,' I said as Raquel swept me on again.

'It's Saint Clothilde, actually,' said Clothilde. She was falling behind, stopping to sniff at perfume thimbles.

'*Saint* Clothilde, then,' I yelled. I was almost losing her in the throng.

'They say . . .' Clothilde shouted out, but her voice was lost in the hubbub. And that was that.

I surrendered. I allowed Raquel to give me the Full

Induction. I followed her around and smiled a lot. I'd find Saint Clothilde later and get the whole story. At least Satan hadn't stormed Heaven.

Across the party I saw the silhouette of a lone angel standing by the garden's edge. Behind him the sky was sinking in fiery red. The angel stood dark against the golden sky. He had one wing folded behind him and his profile was turned away from the party. He stood quite motionless. Strangely quiet.

Unlike Raquel.

'Meet Dahlia, you'll know her, of course, and Saint Sebastian, oh gosh! Yes, Seb, it *is* All Saints' Day in a week or so . . .' Raquel chatted on.

All Saints' Day. All Hallows' Eve. I trembled.

After today, only eight full days left.

The sun sank a fraction, touched the still angel by the garden's edge, caught his profile. He turned his head. I held my breath. He was mind-shatteringly beautiful.

'Who's that?' I asked, pulling on Raquel's arm. Raquel followed my eye.

'Oh, that's Kamuel,' she said. 'He's a darling, knows everything about everything and then some more.' She steered me away in another direction and whispered conspiratorially, 'Too intense; not really chatty. We'll greet him later.'

At that moment he lifted up his face. His gaze shot across the garden. His eyes met mine. Clear grey stormy eyes with deep centres. His formerly still outline suddenly quivered a little, as if a shiver had gone through him, as if he had suddenly seen in me something that he'd been waiting for.

I shuddered too. I couldn't take my eyes off him. He had such sad eyes, such lonely depths to them.

'Come *on*, Serafina,' hissed Raquel. 'You can meet Kamuel later. He won't disappear, you know – he's not a will-o'-the-wisp.'

But I couldn't get him out of my mind. Why did he look so sad? Maybe he knew why God and the Devil couldn't make up.

As it turned out there was no later. There was only the choir recital.

Resignedly I found myself a bower. Brushing rose petals to one side I curled up, prepared to be frustrated. How could I settle down and listen to cherubim?

Suddenly my reverie was interrupted by a cool, clear voice.

'Would you mind if I joined you?'

I looked up to see the elegant form of Kamuel standing over me.

# Serafina 13

'Raquel didn't introduce us,' he said.

'She wanted to,' I said. 'She was very busy.'

'It wasn't a reproach,' smiled Kamuel. 'I saw you and I waited.'

'And now you've saved her one more job,' I laughed.

He sat down beside me, smiled. Suddenly I felt embarrassed. I could see by the shining light above his head he was an Archangel. *An Archangel!* I'd never even *met* an Archangel before – I mean, sat with one at a garden party and tried to pour them a drink, like I was trying to now, reaching for a flute, fumbling my lines, slopping the nectar on to the grass and my wing.

'Glory be,' I said, 'you're an Archangel.'

'Yes,' he said very kindly, 'rather a troubled Archangel tonight.'

I gulped. He did look troubled. Lonely, even. And I understood what lonely was like. With every chord of music I'd been thinking of my empty cell, been longing to be back on Earth, be nearer to Marcus.

My mind flitted back to the 'breach'. Could I ask Kamuel what was going on? But Archangels are so formal. You can't just chat to them as if they're normal beings.

Kamuel graciously took a (sticky) flute of nectar and looked at me. 'You're troubled too, I think. Does something weigh upon your spirit?'

Did it show so easily on my face? I smiled nervously. Did he know about Marcus? What if that's why he'd come to talk to me?

'No,' I said, making a supreme effort not to let my voice tremble. 'It's nothing.'

'I'd like to help,' said Kamuel.

There were so many things I needed help with.

'You remind me of someone,' he went on.

'I do?' I said.

'Yes,' he said, 'Someone I loved very dearly and lost.'

'Oh,' I said, unable to say anything else. How had he lost them? It must have been something pretty dreadful. Angels don't exactly die. (I hoped to High Heaven his friend hadn't been vaporised.)

'I'm so sorry.'

He inclined his head, just a fraction.

'Oh,' I said again, not wanting to pry, not wanting to ignore (but I could hardly say: did they get vaporised, could I?)

'They fell,' he said, 'to Earth. Fell in more ways than one.' He sat motionless. 'And paid the price.'

We didn't get any further, which was probably just as well, because there was a loud knocking at the gate. The smell of diesel burning, of boot polish and cold metal was back. The choir stopped right in the middle of an aria. Raquel ran to the gates, looking very worried.

'Nobody moves,' barked a gruff voice. It was so loud you'd have thought it was Judgement Day come early.

Two uniformed beings flung open the gates, ran forward, then stood to attention in full view of the crowd. The Being with the voice marched through. He was huge, and in his hand he held a long whip.

'Archangel Jehudiel,' whispered Kamuel, 'the Mighty and Strong Opposer of Lucifer, the General of God's Army.'

Trumpets blared, a booming clap of thunder sounded, the stars seemed to dim, some of the non-celestial beings started screaming. I shrank into the shadows of the bower. Kamuel put his arm forward and shielded me with a wing.

'What do you want?' said Raquel, her voice shrill and scared.

'Stand aside,' barked Jehudiel.

A tank, huge and dark, rolled through the gates. On its front a giant flame-thrower turned ominously from side to side.

Kamuel pushed me behind him so that I could hardly see out. 'It's a platoon of God's Army,' he whispered. 'It's the breach. The Devil has made a move on one of the Angelic Host.'

'The Devil?' I breathed, terrified. Any sympathy I'd had immediately evaporated. I imagined a dark, squat figure with horns. His eyes gleamed red and behind him danced an army of vile demons.

'Call your guests forward,' barked the voice.

'Why? What are you looking for?' squeaked Raquel.

'That was a very clear instruction. Don't make me repeat it,' snapped Jehudiel. He stood there like a preacher who'd stepped straight out of history: knee-length frock-coat, high boots, white collar, tall black hat, prominent insignia, the sacred heart and flaming crown stitched on everything – and massive wings. He cracked the whip twice as if he was not at all happy about being questioned, and there was a level of threat in his voice that I'd never heard this side of the Pearly Gates.

'Of course,' said a subdued Raquel. 'Please, everyone – please come into the drawing room. May we go to the drawing room?'

But no sooner had a few of the guests stepped forward than Jehudiel bellowed, 'That's him! STOP HIM!'

A squad of God's Army marched forward. They were dressed in greatcoats belted at the waist, caps with the same insignias, armbands, breeches, boots, just like the Schutzstaffel. As I watched they broke into a charge. On the double, in paired ranks, they pounded forward with heavy tread, their boots crushing the turf of the garden. There was something so graceless about them; I shrank still further behind Kamuel's wing.

The flame-thrower on the top of the tank turned slowly until it was pointing straight at a tired, mild-faced angel who had been trudging obediently towards the open French windows.

The man froze.

'ARREST HIM UNDER SUBSECTION 32!' barked Archangel Jehudiel.

'We need to get you out of here,' said Kamuel suddenly. He grabbed my hand, pulled me towards the tangled under-growth at the edge of the garden.

'But –' I said.

'There's no time for that,' hissed Kamuel as if he could read my mind. 'We need to go *now*.'

He led me through the shrubbery. Behind us the grating of iron on iron, scattered screams and the heavy clash of chains echoed into the evening. Within seconds we were out on to the street behind.

When we were at least a block away, Kamuel stopped. He pushed me into a shadowy alcove in the perimeter wall. He stepped in close beside me. His nearness, his terrifying beauty robbed me of speech.

*Oh Marcus, how nearly I spoke out to him, begged him to help us. Why didn't I?*

Kamuel stood there, poised. At last I managed. 'What's wrong?'

'Danger,' he said, his voice low and urgent.

'Danger?' I repeated.

'They came to Stop and Check everyone at the party.'

'Why?' I said.

'They had an arrest warrant for Vincent. But they won't pass up an opportunity to hound others.'

'An arrest warrant for who?'

'If it hadn't been for the breach, God's Army would never have known.'

'What breach?' I asked again. 'What did Vincent do?'

'Vincent ends lives that aren't on the Manifest,' said Kamuel.

'*He Collects people illegally?*' I gasped.

'He took one today when he was on Domestic Violence and Family Duty Collections. He didn't know we'd gone up to Code Amber and it would be checked up on.'

I felt as if I'd been thrown into the fiery pits. All the little hairs down my spine stood on end. *Vincent killed someone while on Collection Duty?* I shuddered. I remembered the stricken look on Joey's face, his pleading eyes.

'It was a mercy killing. The lady was old and in great pain. She had an incurable disease. He does it out of pity,' said Kamuel. 'It's his work. He's an Angel of Mercy.'

Of course. I'd heard of the Angels of Mercy, lawless beings who obeyed only their own conscience.

'God knows these things happen. He turns a blind eye.'
*God turns a blind eye?*

'Then why the flame-thrower, and the tank, and bursting into a choir service?' I said.

'That's not God. That's the Army. That's Jehudiel. He's a fanatic. He sees everything in black and white. And he carries the Whip of Justice. He thinks that gives him the right.'

'And does it?'

'He is the Great Avenger. At the whip's touch all things return to dust. It was given to him by the Ancient of Days, when the firmament was in chaos. He alone can wield it, and he takes his work very seriously. Too seriously, sometimes,' sighed Kamuel. 'He is empowered to defend Heaven, and now, because there's been a major breach, he's taken that as full permission to check everything and go after anyone.'

'Oh,' I said.

'Poor Vincent,' said Kamuel.

'But what was the breach?' I whispered.

'Someone signed a pact with the Devil,' said Kamuel

very softly. 'It was probably something minor, but that's how the Devil works. In small ways, cunningly, deceitfully, moving cautiously until he has Heaven under siege – and angels falling like summer rain.'

I stared at him.

'With this signing coming so soon after the Challenge, we've gone straight up to Code Amber.'

'What was the Challenge?' I whispered.

Kamuel straightened himself up. He looked me directly in the eye. His face so lovely, so sad. 'Lucifer threw this gauntlet before the Senior Team:

*'I will pick your brightest and your best, your loveliest and most innocent, from under your hand, and I will so corrupt and drive your chosen one that they will rather Fall and die and live in Hell with Me, than stay in Heaven with You.'*

I let air whistle out between my teeth. 'Saints preserve us,' I whispered.

*'And you cannot stop me.'*

'But they can, can't they?' I said.

'It's very serious,' said Kamuel, 'and very possible. If he succeeds and God cannot stop him, there will be chaos in Heaven. Already you can see how God's Army have responded.' Kamuel sighed again. 'And now this pact.'

'How did they know about the pact?' I breathed.

'The Devil has his ways,' laughed Kamuel. 'He whispers into many ears. He gave enough details for the Senior Team here to know he tells the truth, but not enough to pin anything on anyone. That's all part of Satan's diabolical plan too. Cause panic, have us all suspecting one another, looking over our shoulders, turn Heaven against itself. Turn

Heaven into Hell. That's why they're Stopping and Checking.'

How awful.

I thought of the contract I'd signed. A terror started to grow in me. What if they got to know about that? What if Larry was not only untrustworthy about names and dates, but indiscreet as well? Or worse – a shivering took hold of me – *perhaps he didn't work for God at all.* At least not exclusively. He'd said – for what it was worth – he was an *Independent* Celestial Advisor.

*Perhaps he worked for the Devil too?*

I went icy cold from head to toe.

*Perhaps the Extension I'd signed was the pact Kamuel was talking about.*

But there's nothing evil in a contract to extend a life so that a soul can be saved – is there?

I took heart. Saving souls was God's work.

But I must be careful. When I next saw Larry I must ask him. And I mustn't sign anything else. Perhaps I'd better tell St Peter after all. Better to make a clean breast of it, if it were all my fault – but then . . .

Like a cold hand around my heart came the thought of Marcus.

*What would become of him?*

No, I must stay quiet, stay on my guard and not trust Larry again.

'God gets very worried about Satan,' continued Kamuel. 'They were old friends once.' A faraway look came into his eyes. 'Yes, God knows his adversary well. He doesn't under-estimate him. Lucifer was his greatest Archangel.'

I wanted to ask then, why, if they'd been such good friends, couldn't they just make up? But I didn't dare. Instead I said, 'What about the angel that made the pact?' My voice was shaky, my chin trembling. 'What will happen to her?'

Why had I said 'her'? I mustn't give myself away.

'Nothing,' said Kamuel.

'Nothing?' I repeated.

'Nothing at all.'

I couldn't believe it. 'How come?'

'Because I will make sure of it. If I have to go to Hell to do so,' said Kamuel in a sudden hard, bitter tone.

And I knew he meant every word of it.

# Serafina 14

We got the announcement the following morning:

## NO MORE DUTIES INVOLVING HIGH-RISK ACTIVITY WILL BE ASSIGNED TO UNDERGRADUATES AT THE CLOISTERS.

'What does it mean?' I asked the Superior on Duty.

'It means you're off Collection Duty and on Ministering to New Arrivals,' she said. 'Lucky you, no more trips down to Earth – you can safely stay far away from Hell and all the problems that go with it.'

Lucky me? My heart shrank. *No more trips down to Earth?*

'But I have to get down to Earth,' I said quite simply.

The Superior looked at me and raised an eyebrow.

'I have to save souls,' I said. 'I want to do God's work.'

'It's an order, and it's come from On High.'

I opened my mouth to protest further, and shut it again. *Obedience is the third holy vow.* I went slowly back to my cell before I betrayed myself.

Inside, I sat down. I didn't move. I couldn't take it in.

*No more trips down to Earth.*

*Marcus would die and go to Hell.*

*I'd fail.*

*Joey would have died in vain.*

I sat in front of my mirror and watched all my fiery beauty fizzle out in little sparks until I looked like a firework party from last year. What was I to do? *No more trips down to Earth and only eight days left.* I put on a cloak.

I needed to get out before a Superior called me to go and start ministering.

I was trudging down towards the West Gate, lost in thought, when I met Raquel. She was in a hurry. Half-heartedly I greeted her.

'Thanks so much for the party. I'm sorry I left early.'

'Oh, thank *Heavens* I've seen you!' cried Raquel. 'You've *got* to help me. I'm on duty again. Look at this – *and* I'm late.'

'Oh,' I said.

'Here,' she said, thrusting the Manifest at me. 'They've doubled my workload. I've been put on Motorway Duty *and* Hospital Collections in my district. There's no way I can guide seven souls to Hell *and* Purgatorium *and* back here today. Not with my morning shift at the Announcer. Look at that! Not one of them can be fast tracked. The aerial tolls alone will be horrendous. You *saw* the queues by Styx yesterday! If I'd got up earlier, but the party, that *dreadful* being with that *dreadful* voice, and now all the checkpoints to get through with this beastly breach business. I'm tired already.'

I looked at her she was like a gift from God. A desperate plan formed in my mind. Greedily, I ran my eyes over the list of hospitals. *A way down to Earth!* Yes, there it was: Christ the King, three deaths to Collect. Oh YES! I punched the air. Hallelujah.

'I'll help,' I said, 'I'll do that hospital,' before she could argue and say: wouldn't you rather be on the motorways – where at least there's some fresh air? I ripped the schedule in two and pocketed my hospital portion. 'There,' I said, 'your duties are halved, nearly. But don't let St Peter know. I'm officially underage to go on Collection since the breach, *apparently.*' I rolled my eyes. 'It's a new announcement – security overkill. Don't be worried. I'm not.' I bared my teeth in a kind of grin. 'So I'll need your spare pass.'

'OK,' said Raquel. She looked surprised. I guess she wasn't used to seeing Seraphim quite so keen to get out and kill people.

'If you don't mind,' I said, 'I'll bunch them and take them to their Collection points in a group. It'll be quicker that way, unless you think they've all got to have an individual send-off?'

'Well,' she said, a bit at a loss for words. 'It depends . . .'

I pulled out the schedule. 'Oh dear,' I said, 'there's a girl who's overdosed, there's an old guy who's very ill, and a baby, poor thing.'

'Look, honey, you do what you like. Just be there at the right time and Collect them, and get them to wherever as soon as you can. I'll probably catch you later at the river or back here – or if we get any repenters, then I'll see you at Black Point.' (Black Point is a particularly tricky aerial toll on the way to Purgatorium where demons give angels a really rotten time.) 'Looks like I've got a whole family to

Collect off the hard shoulder.' She unrolled her section of the Manifest and peered at it.

I squeezed her arm. No wonder she'd rather have done the hospital. 'Oh, poor you,' I said sympathetically.

'Poor *them*,' she said. 'They don't even know it yet. They're probably still having their cornflakes.'

She looked at me, and I looked at her. It was hard to take.

I know the whole thing about Original Sin and the Dominion of Death. Believe me, I majored in it for a decade of semesters. How God was totally miserable (still is a bit miserable sometimes) about the whole Garden of Eden thing backfiring so badly. But I'm still not sure unleashing death on the world as a punishment was a good idea. Plus think of the cost in angel hours alone.

'Don't worry, I'll manage,' said Raquel. 'I'll make their deaths pain free and if it's truly terrible, I'll try your tip about Extensions.'

I shuddered. 'Oh don't,' I cried. I shuffled my wings. For some reason a feather had come loose.

'You're right,' she said. 'I don't think any of them would really like to be the only survivor.'

I thought of a lifetime apart from the ones you love. I thought of Marcus lying with his cheek on the white pillow. I thought of his mother sitting there with her hollow eyes and her sagging shoulders.

'No,' I said, 'keep them together.'

'But the dad isn't coming here. Even if he repents he'll have to do time in Torium,' said Raquel. 'So they'll probably be split up anyway. He was drunk. I mean, will be drunk. He's probably hitting the bottle right now.'

'And we can't do a thing?' I asked wistfully.

She shook her head. ''Fraid not. That's Free Will for you.' She rolled her eyes. 'You know: You Better Choose To Be Good Or You'll Be Sorry.'

Suddenly I wasn't so sure I liked Free Will. If it were Marcus about to be crash-victimmed, I'd knock the bottle out of *anyone's* hand. And I wouldn't be up for any Free Will rubbish either.

I blinked at myself. *What a forbidden thought!* I blinked again; can you have a forbidden thought if you have Free Will?

The rest of that morning was a whirl. I rushed back to my cell. I didn't know where to start: had to fix my nails, do my hair, choose a new raiment, fluff out my feathers, practise a few 'fire and glory' moves, and get down to the city checkpoints, get *through* the city checkpoints and make it to the start of the Staircase.

I was just going to have to hurry. Now what should I wear? All my raiments looked so – well, frankly, angelish. I wanted to be more funky, more trendy, more girly, more human, more like someone Marcus would go for.

I remembered the girls at the nightclub. Yes, I'd wear leggings and a tight top and a tiny skirt. Of course I didn't have any, so I decided to raid the new arrivals' wardrobe.

But it seemed like the new arrivals didn't arrive in nightclub outfits. There were a lot of night*dresses*, pyjamas, a few denim jeans and loads of hospital scrubs. In the end I chose a sweet white cotton bodice with spaghetti straps (quite accommodating for the wings) and a long floaty floral skirt.

Even though I say it myself. I did look nice. Very human, but still angelly. I wanted to impress Marcus with my celestial status yet still look very approachable – you know.

*Oh, how I wanted to see Marcus.* It made me burn up like fire. At the very thought my mind was a whirl. And he'd be so much better today, a full twenty-four hours after the Healing Hands Blessing. I'd be able to talk to him. I got the flutters in my stomach and went all dizzy and breathless.

If I hurried, if I got down through the twelve Gates quickly and into the hospital, I could Collect the girl; find her somewhere to rest – so she could gently accustom herself to the Transition – give the old man a little longer on his life support machine, let the baby and her mother have a last sad farewell and squeeze half an hour free to meet Marcus.

I'd stay with him long enough to tell him everything; to impress upon him the very urgent need to repent. To repent in word and deed. I'd try to give him a few hints on how he could put that into action (Please God, let Raquel stay on double shifts). What could I suggest? Something while he was recovering? A donation to charity? If he could build up a bit of a portfolio of good deeds over the next week, at least we'd be in with a chance. If all else failed, it'd be grounds to appeal on. Get his soul weighed in the Halls of the Dead.

Why is it that when you're in a hurry everything goes wrong? I'd borrowed a hairbrush from the new arrivals' wardrobe and was busy trying to use it. I was only having a little practice at being human. (We angels don't need them.) But it was one of those circular types, and it'd got itself all tangled up in my hair.

Ouch.

Never mind. I tossed my tresses back. I was still more beautiful than a thousand stars.

This was it.

No more mistakes for me.

Today was a fresh start.

Today everything would be OK.

Today I'd save Marcus.

# Serafina 15

No wonder Raquel was stressed. Getting across town was horrendous. For a start nobody was allowed to fly. I suppose the thinking behind that was that if Saints and the Saved had to walk, then angels should too. (Of course, apart from Archangel Jehudiel, God's Army was all made up of the Saved. So they could hardly set up checkpoints in the sky, could they?) Anyway suddenly there were a zillion tanks everywhere with their flame-throwers pointing ominously upwards, just to make sure no angel broke the rules, I guess. We had to trudge on foot. God, was it slow.

And scary.

I joined in with a line of workers heading back to the Suburbs-of-the-Saved after their shifts in the City. It was actually kind of good I was in human attire. I put my cloak over my wings and mingled in better. As we walked I wondered about Vincent. What had happened to him? There was nothing on the front page of either the *Trumpet* or the *Herald*. That was weird. Was there a news blackout too? Overnight it seemed the war had moved from the far north by the Abyss to the centre of the Kingdom – and we were more under attack from God's Army than Satan. But I didn't say so, obviously.

I met Raquel as planned by the South Gate. She gave me the pass and told the guards I was just seeing her off. As we went through my throat completely dried up, but I put on my most angelic smile and thank the Holy Star of Bethlehem I passed unchallenged.

After she'd gone I raced. Every minute counted. The more time I had, the longer I could spend it with Marcus. But my God, did it take *for-ev-er* to get down the Staircase. I tried floating, waltzing, Cossack dancing (you never know), sprinting, jumping two at a time, I even tried sliding down the banisters. It still took forever. By the time I stepped out through the Twelfth Gate I felt a million years older. I didn't know if my halo was straight and my feathers looked really soft and floaty or whether I looked like a dead parrot.

But I was through.

In the beat of a wing I was beside Marcus. I *know* I should have gone to check out the venue for the girl's Collection first. I should have made sure about the demons, decided on my exact position, chosen music, all that stuff, but I didn't. I just didn't. OK? I wanted to see Marcus, so I just didn't.

And there he was. His mother had gone home. There were cards by his bed (I noticed one was from Candy) and flowers (which I hoped weren't from her too). And he was still asleep. (She needn't have put quite so many kisses on it.) But oh, how beautiful he looked! His gorgeous mouth curled into the tiniest smile. His long eyelashes resting so perfectly on his dark cheek.

I crept up close. I could feel the heat of his skin and

smell the tang of his scent. I reached out and held my hand under his nose. Imagine. Here I was standing in the room right beside him. Just the two of us. Just for a moment, no God's Army, no stupid rules separating us. Just Marcus and me. I felt his breath warm and tickly on my fingers.

*Oh Marcus! Why couldn't it have lasted?*

I breathed. He stirred as if he could hear me. I held my breath. Best to let him sleep on, while I got the girl. (OK, I *was* feeling guilty about her.) I needed to go and sort her out like a quarter of an hour ago. But I wanted to be there when he woke up, to find me standing beside him.

I waved my hand over his brow, 'Sweet dreams, my prince,' I murmured and sent him visions of fantastical waterfalls, of ethereal clouds being chased across deep blue skies by the winds of paradise. I blew him an angel's soft kiss.

He sighed in his sleep.

I left.

I'd get back to him as fast as possible.


The girl was lying in a room all on her own. She was very ordinary in a thin way, and she was in a coma. Her face was twisted up, as if she'd tried at the very last to vomit up her decision and expel the pills she'd taken, as if life itself was distasteful to her and death not much more appealing. I stood there a little shocked. What tragedy was this?

The Superiors at the Cloisters would say: suicide is sinful. It's one of the most wicked trespasses, such a soul should go straight to Hell. But as I looked down at the girl, I couldn't find it in my heart to blame her. And why was it so wicked? Was one's self not one's own, to live in or escape from? And what about Free Will? Were some acts less free than others?

I felt so sorry for her. What was it to be human and to hate mortality? What was it to inhabit one flesh for eighteen years only to hate the life it brought you, to cast it off in despair? I wondered what despair was like. And again I felt that sudden confusion about being immortal. The unfairness of it. How estranged I felt. How could I ever be alive (even in the same way as this tired, forlorn creature) if I could never die? How would I ever understand despair? How could I understand *any* emotion if I were not truly alive? And suddenly I saw death in a new light: not as the end of life but as its whetstone, how it must sharpen each second of living.

I gazed into the girl's face, as if I could read all the answers to the puzzle of life written there, as if I could understand what drove a person to such depths. But I couldn't really understand. You see, I longed for a chance to have a live body. Just for one hour.

I felt so sorry for her. Her thin pale hand, her pinched red lips. This girl had not known love – for it's love that redeems and keeps the spirit going, isn't it? How sad she looked. How I wished she could have been loved just once in her short sad life.

Quickly I closed the doors to her little side room. Nobody had come to sit by her. She'd had a mother, I remembered from the summary on the Manifest. A mother who must now suffer the horrors of her only child committing suicide. That was very wicked. But a mother who wasn't bothered enough to come and visit her, even though she lay dying? Yes, she was dying after all – wasn't that why I was here?

Demons were already peeking in at the window. They'd made an oily web that was seeping in through the casement joints. I flashed my eyes at them. Pure amethyst. That sorted them out. I really *should* have come straight here. What was happening to me? I was normally so reliable. I'd always been there for every duty, never broken any rules, done my best to be perfect. But since I'd met Marcus, I'd become so wayward.

I reminded myself today was a fresh start. I would do everything right. So I chose a haunting lullaby, to help the girl's Passing Over. She looked like she needed something gentle. I wondered if anyone had sat beside her when she was a child, held her hand, soothed her brow, played for her, sung to her. I'd sing to her. I'd sing her to sleep. I started straight away.

*'Rest your head my own sweet child;*

'Won't you wake up, dear one, and repent?' I whispered.

But she did not stir. Only a slow tiredness fell over her thin face as if she would sooner die than wake.

> *'Close your eyes and sleep,*
> *Rest your heart my own sweet child,*
> *And I your soul will keep.'*

I stroked her cheek. I sent her dreams of skies unlimited, of golden sands by turquoise seas. I took her hand and pressed it to my lips. I felt her spirit stir, felt it rise to my touch, drift towards me. I crooned on until it rose from her inert form and sought around itself, and seeing me gave one piteous cry and came into my arms.

'Good girl,' I murmured. 'There, there, was that so terrible?'

And her life ebbed away.

I watched the monitor zoom into one flat line. I heard the alarm sound in the charge nurses' office.

The girl whimpered, clung to me. Her form stirred now as if it were loath to be parted from its animated spirit. So after all she would have hung on to life, despised as she saw it? I marvelled. Felt jealous. Oh to know that unknowable thing. Mortality.

Her soul seemed to rise off the bed, then sink reluctantly down. I was used to this: the attachment that the body has for its soul, so I let the memory of it follow us as I guided her out of the little room.

Nurses came racing down the corridor. I held her close as they passed. I held the shade that used to be her body close too. It wasn't her real corporeal body, just a memory, a sad imprint of flesh and bone. I let them seek the comfort of each other, her soul and her shadow self, and then I took her by the hand. I said, 'You will have to stay with me, my dear one.'

'I'm Robyn,' she said. She looked like a robin, her small, bird-fragile form, her thin nose, her light brown hair.

'Come then, Robyn,' I said gently. 'Stay with me. I'll be

your guide today and deliver you to your final home by nightfall.' She tucked her thin bird-like hand in mine, and we walked quietly back together to Marcus's room.

Robyn was very quiet. She was disorientated, of course. But I think she'd probably always been a quiet soul. I felt a twinge of guilt, even though I'd really given her a very gentle Passing Over. I should have taken her straight to Hell, of course, and come back on cue to Collect the old chap and the baby. I could probably have even slipped back early to spend an extra five minutes with Marcus too. But I wanted more. Five minutes was no longer good enough. Neither was five hours, nor five days, nor five millennia.

How huge and hungry was my greed for him. How terrible my desire. How deadly my sin. If I had known then what it would lead me to, would I have done things differently?

Marcus was still asleep, still in his private room, in the private wing of the hospital. I crossed through the space by the side of his heart monitors and opened the French windows on to the sunniest, sweetest patio. Light glanced in through the room, spearing Marcus on his bed. From the edge of the patio, gardens swept away like Elysian Fields. The verges of them were graced by cedars and pines. Quickly I scanned their reaches. Then I bent my gaze back to the patio. I sighted a bench. I took Robyn by the hand and led her through the open glass doors.

'Here,' I said, indicating the bench. On its back was a brass plaque on which was written: *I lift up mine eyes unto the hills from whence cometh my help*, and a dedication to Mrs Spenser, late of this parish.

'Lie down,' I told Robyn. 'I'll cover you. The sunshine will warm your spirit; you can breathe the fresh scent of roses from here.' I created a bed of gossamer and silk and conjured a choir of doves to coo to her.

She lay down without a word and closed her eyes. I covered her with the gossamer. I didn't need to, but her phantom body was still unused to its new self and was shivering; strange really, as if it could actually feel the chilly breeze that swept down from the pines.

Then I returned to wake Marcus.

# Serafina 16

Once inside his room I checked myself in the mirror. I straightened my top and swished the floaty skirt. How did teenage girls stand? I tried a hand on my hip. I tried lifting up my chin with my eyes downcast. I tried a twirl. I knew how to do a twirl, but it wasn't very humany.

What else? Make-up! I didn't have any, but nevertheless I managed to effect a dark smudging around my eyes.

What sort of things did girls say? They commented on each other's shoes. They said 'Oh My God' in lovely perky tones. I tried it out beneath my breath. They said 'awesome' and 'totally' and 'so' and 'like' and 'yuk' and 'ta-da'. Well, I thought they did. I'd have a go.

I straightened my shoulders. You can do this, Serafina, I told myself.

All a-tremble I turned to Marcus. My heart beating wildly, my throat like I'd swallowed the entire Sinai desert. I pursed my lips, tried a smile, let shimmering glory glow around me. 'Yuk', that was so angelly. Got rid of the shimmering glory. *It was so scary*. I glanced at the clock. If I carried on dithering there'd be no time left.

This was it.

'Awake, dear one,' I breathed. I stood over him. I blew two fiery kisses, one for each closed eyelid. He stirred. He turned. He opened his eyes. He stretched his arms.

'Ouch,' he said.

I smiled my most radiant smile to date. It was hotter than a thousand suns; starlight danced in my eyes, roses bloomed on my lips.

He coughed. He coughed and coughed. He carried on coughing. At last he muttered, 'Oh Hell.'

It seemed a strange greeting. I stopped, bewildered. I'd never tried to have a relationship with a human being before.

His arms were still outstretched. Unable to restrain myself I closed my eyes, and leaned forward. I felt his heart beating; felt his bodily reality *so near*, felt *my* heart pounding, *my* pulse racing. And as he closed his arms around me (well, closed his arms. Not exactly around me, because I'm not of the same ether), I imagined the fierce touch of his skin. I imagined the way he'd tighten and tighten his embrace, his muscles crushing me to him.

I opened my eyes and looked up into his.

His face was grey and strained.

'Marcus?' I whispered.

He closed his eyes.

I waited. When he opened his eyes again and reached for a tumbler of water, I waved a tiny fingery wave in front of his face. 'Marcus?'

He ignored me.

I frowned, puzzled. I tried again: the kisses, the smile; I skipped the imagined hello hug and the Heavenly crushing and made the finger wave much more haughty, an angelic summoning.

He missed my smile.

He didn't notice the angelic command.

He was oblivious to everything.

My heart stopped. I grew cold all over. Something had changed.

Marcus couldn't see me.

I took a step back. Confused. I didn't get it. The night before last, he'd seen me. He'd winked at me, for Heaven's sake. It'd been a sign. I knew it had. It was one of the reasons I'd broken all the Rules for him.

Our destinies were entwined.

They had to be.

I flumped down on the chair. Now what was I going to do? Why couldn't he see me any more? There must be a reason.

I tried to remember everything I'd ever learned at Early Years Angel Academy in the junior section of the Cloisters, but honestly that was aeons ago, and I couldn't remember much. I'd probably been too busy passing notes or worrying about getting on the swim team (not easy for us fiery angels). Though now I came to think of it, I did sort of vaguely remember something about angels appearing in their true glory to humans at near-death moments.

I made my mind go back, until I actually remembered the textbook. It'd been written by one of the visiting apostles who'd made the study of angels his afterlife's work. I recalled the actual page: 70.

75. Angels appear in their true glory to humans at near-death moments.

76. Angels appear in their true glory during the actual instant of Passing Over.

77. Angels appear in their true glory at their own demise.

78. Angels appear in their true glory at their own volition through a process called *apparitioning*.

That was it! *That's why he'd seen me.* It hadn't been an omen or anything extra-ordinary or destined. Just the same old near-death stuff. My shoulders slumped. I felt very small and very miserable and very stupid.

You see, I had to talk to him, and short of taking him to the point of death again, there was obviously only one other way to do it. I sighed. My shoulders sank even lower. My feathers drooped. I was going to have to break *more* rules. I was going to have to apparition.

Apparitioning, except on Heavenly business and on express commission from the Senior Team, is forbidden. Plus it's risky. It means stepping into semi-human form with all its frailties. You're really vulnerable when you do that. What if a bus hit you? Imagine the problems that'd cause for the Senior Team.

But as I contemplated it, I saw its advantages too. A real body, well, very *nearly* real. One realm closer. What *would* it feel like? A hand I could hold Marcus's with, sort of – even if it felt a bit funny. And the fact that I'd had always secretly wanted to do it.

But there was no getting round it being forbidden. I'd

have to take all the responsibility for doing it myself. But I had Free Will, didn't I? And my intentions were pure. And actually I didn't care what the Senior Team thought. Marcus had seen me. It *had* been an omen. We *were* destined to be together. And I was going to save his soul even if I had to break the Rules to do it.

So I did it.

I apparitioned, right there and then, right in front of Marcus. Like I said, I'd never actually done it before, so that's why it was a bit sudden and clumsy. Probably next time I might want to do it more slowly, with fade in and out effects, rather than atomic-bomb style. But I wanted to hang on to the amazing smile with the stardust in my eyes impression – and it was kind of tricky.

I guess I was pretty 'awesome'. (Although I was a bit disappointed with the texture of the body. It didn't feel quite right. It still didn't have that 'totally human feel' I'd expected.)

But I did it, and I was proud of myself. I looked eagerly at Marcus to see his reaction.

Oops.

His face had blanched. He'd gone completely grey beneath his skin. He closed his eyes and clutched his chest. Perhaps I'd overdone the sparkling aspect. A nearby monitor started bleeping very worryingly. I crossed the room and looked at it – tried to turn it off – couldn't work it out – so I raised my hand and said a quick Our Father over it. That shut it up.

The bleeping stopped. I looked again at Marcus. He squeezed his eyes. The look on his face was peculiar, almost as if he were in pain. (You know, I really should have practised a bit first.) He closed his mouth and twisted his lips. His breath grew shallow (I think he was blaspheming). He spread his arms forward and got hold of the steel supports on either side of the bed.

'Hello?' I said.

'Hel-lo,' he gasped back.

'Did I overdo it?' I asked, a bit worried.

He shook his head. I think he didn't want to upset me. He tried to smile. He looked at the bottle of pills beside his bed. He looked up at the drip going into his arm. He looked at the machine that had stopped bleeping. He looked at me.

'*Are you for real?*' he croaked.

I laughed. He looked so cute. 'Of course,' I said.

He blinked. 'Like really?'

'Would you like me to prove it?' I asked.

He just stared at me, eyes round as saucers.

'I can do a twirl,' I said. 'Just watch this.'

'A twirl?' he whispered.

'Exactly,' I said. And then I twirled. It was the best twirl I'd ever done. I was faster than the mightiest maelstrom ever. All the machines in the room started beeping and I swear even the walls rattled.

I looked at Marcus to see what he thought. He looked like he was about to choke, maybe cough again. Then suddenly he kind of snorted. Finally he *laughed*. Well, coughed and laughed. He wiped his eyes on his hospital gown, dabbed blood off his lips and sighed like he'd understood something. (There was nothing actually that funny.) 'What do you do for an encore?' he said.

He'd laughed. I'd just apparitioned in all my glory, in defiance of Heaven, to save him. I'd done my best-ever twirl and he'd laughed. A blaze of hot indignation swept over me. I think I quite forgot myself.

He wanted me to prove myself? OK, he could have the full works. With a flash of my eyes thunder rolled in the distance. A sheet of ice crusted over the window. Flames leapt from the palms of my hands. I unfurled my wings (all six). I beat the air and made ready to sound trumpets.

Marcus struggled into a sitting position.

At once I saw the pain he was in. His flawless lips were driven quite pallid with the effort. His brow knitted up and tiny beads of sweat broke out along it. An understanding seemed to register in his eyes. '*You really ARE real?*' he stammered.

He looked about ready to pass out.

'*It's really you? You're back?*'

Instantly I stopped all the theatrics. I crossed to his bedside and laid a hand on his.

'I thought it was the morphine,' he said.

I let the Balm of Paradise flow through my fingers, and the Stars of Heaven shine in my smile. His brow relaxed, his breathing became less laboured. I relaxed too – for touching him sent the oddest sensation into me, as if I'd been the one in pain – and by touching him my aching had been healed.

'Have you come to take me?' he said, a curious vulnerability in his voice.

I stood there, dazed, beside him. So strange, this touching. And yet I wasn't truly corporeal at all.

I shook my head gently.

'OK,' he said. He clutched at his chest in a fresh spasm of pain. 'Sorry, I didn't rate the twirling. I thought I was seeing things.'

'Oh,' I said.

'It *was* a bit showy, though,' he whispered. 'You didn't need to try that hard – you've already got the advantage.' He closed his eyes and laid his head back on the pillow.

I kept my hand on his, marvelling at the feeling it gave me.

'So?' He feebly tried to smile up at me.

'I've come to save your soul,' I said, getting straight to the point. (I was quite proud of myself for that.)

'You've come to save my soul?' he repeated.

Right, this was it. 'Yes,' I said. 'Your soul's in danger.'

Marcus struggled up a bit and raised his hand in a stop sign. 'Please,' he whispered. 'Man knows you saved me – and I owe you – and man's really grateful. But Angel – it's just not that easy.'

Well, I wasn't giving up. I drew in a deep breath. 'I know what you said.' I smiled in what I hoped was an encouraging way. 'And I think it took great courage to say it – and the reasons you gave were honourable.' I must make every word count, however pompous I sounded.

'And it was your very honesty and integrity, how you said, *your heart had to be in it;* how you averred you *couldn't lie – not about something like that –* that persuaded me to keep on trying.' I kept my voice steady. 'But I believe once you fully understand the peril you're in, you'll think differently and change your mind.'

There was a silence.

Finally Marcus spoke. 'The trouble is,' he said, 'if you repent you have to make a change, don't you?'

'Definitely,' I said. 'It means you can make a fresh start and live in a new way without sin.'

'That's the problem.'

'You don't wish to change your sinful ways?' I said, alarmed. 'Even though you may lose your soul to the fires of Hell?'

'Even if I wanted to, I can't,' said Marcus sadly. There was a very final note in his voice.

I was astonished. How was that? Surely that was the whole point of Free Will. He could choose to change – *especially* if he wanted to.

'You don't understand,' he said. 'Other people depend on me. If I don't bring in the Ps the mortgage won't get paid, Jasmine won't go to college, my nan won't get her care-home costs met . . .' He tried to give me a What-the-Hell smile. 'And that's just the simple end of it.'

I opened my mouth to speak. I closed it again.

'Once you're in,' he said, 'I mean in a gang, you can't just leave.' He coughed.

This was a new complication. Nobody ever told me about being *trapped* in a life of crime . . .

'It's all about the money, Angel,' he said.

Instantly I knew I was out of my depth. Money is not something we deal with in Heaven. I'd have to think about this. No wonder it was called the Root of all Evil.

Marcus must have seen my face fall for he tried to smile again and said, 'But if you want me to give it a go, don't let man put you off. I could try.'

I would not be put off. I'd go for an entirely different tack – an angle I felt much more confident in. 'Surely you desire salvation?' I started. Didn't everyone?

Marcus rallied a little, as if he liked a good discussion. 'Forget salvation,' he said. 'Life's for living, not creeping around afraid of your own shadow, or thinking about what comes after.'

I looked at him startled – stunned even. Forget salvation?

'But aren't you afraid of death?' I asked. This was possibly my strongest argument.

'No,' he said. 'What's the point? Why waste time on it?' He tried a smile. 'Life's too short.'

'But isn't that the point?' I said. If life was too short, then death was to be feared.

'Fear's dumb – who wants to live a boring life?'

I could hardly believe my ears. Was he teasing me? 'Then what of demons?' I cried. I'd have him there.

Marcus laughed at that – or tried to. His laugh became another coughing fit. 'Demons?' He opened his eyes, a little bit of colour returned to his cheek. 'You really haven't got a clue, have you?'

I thought of their oily presence, their foul smell. I was on home territory. I did have a clue. I knew a lot about demons.

'You know something?' Marcus reached for a tissue and wiped more blood off his lips. 'I think when they learn what I can do, demons might actually be afraid of me.'

My eyebrows shot up.

There was noise outside. A trolley was turning into the corridor.

*Not afraid of death? Not afraid of demons?* How was I going to convince him of anything?

'You're sure you *really are* here?' queried Marcus suddenly. 'Not some kind of hallucination?'

This was going to be a lot harder than I thought. Much harder.

The trolley rattled nearer. Someone might come in at any moment.

'You might just be morphine,' Marcus mused.

But before I could reassure him that I really was real and no hallucination, the trolley rattled to a halt.

A voice cried out, 'Mr Montague?'

I laid my finger over my lips and signalled at him to stay quiet.

'Mr Montague,' insisted the voice, 'are you awake?'

'Exactly,' whispered Marcus.

He pointed at me, his dark eyes wide.

'Am I?'

# Serafina 17

We needed to go somewhere much more private. If someone else were to see me in full apparition form, and fall on their knees and send a prayer up to Heaven, they'd probably get straight on to the Prair Waves – I could just imagine it: Angel Seen on Earth. I'd be discovered straight away.

'Come,' I said urgently, touching his hand, pulling at him. 'Come and walk. Let's stroll in the garden. I've got so much to tell you and time is already fleeing away.'

He looked up. He put his head charmingly on one side. 'I really love the way you talk,' he said.

I looked at him. What was wrong with the way I talked? I'd just used a completely standard expression from the *Angel's Guide to Common Phrases on Earth* as recommended by the Archbishop of Canterbury in 1506 or something. I tried again (updated version 2012). 'Let's make a move, an' roll an' chat, because I'm on the clock.' There, was that clear enough?

He shook his head. 'I'd love to but –'

Good. I cut him short and pulled at him. *Oh, please God, don't let anyone come in.*

'But hey, Angel, haven't you forgotten something? This man's a bit tied up right now?' He gestured at the drips and monitors and medical paraphernalia holding him captive to the bed.

He was right. I *had* overlooked that. *What was I going to do now?* How I wished I could freeze time, but in apparition mode you can hardly do anything. My angelic powers were practically zero, and I'd used up far too much energy already on the twirl.

Quickly I removed everything from him. I pulled out all the tubes and whipped the little sticky pads off his chest. He grimaced in pain. He clenched his jaw and flinched.

Oops, I'd forgotten that might hurt. 'Sorry,' I whispered. *The trolley was rattling right at the door.* Never mind. He needed to get better, and we didn't have time for the human approach to recovery. I breathed the Light of the Lord over him and gave him another Healing Hands booster. That pretty much drained me. 'You'll be strong enough for now,' I smiled. *We needed to get going.*

'Yo, now *that* feels good.' He stretched. He opened his eyes wide and rubbed the back of his hand where the drip had been. 'Whatever you've given me, it's the best.'

The glow those words gave me! *The best!*

'Thanks,' I breathed, tugging at him.

He smiled. 'You're a real lifesaver, aren't you?' He looked so much better. 'Though being near you could be fatal.' He raised one eyebrow.

'Fatal?'

'My heart.'

'Your heart?'

'You make it beat faster.'

Oh, his heart! He'd been shot. Of course, I mustn't get

125

too near him. I must be much more careful. I must not alarm him.

'I'm sorry,' I said. *The door handle began turning.*

'That was a compliment.'

I shook my head. He confused me. Was it *not* dangerous to elevate his heartbeat then? I didn't understand. So all I said was: 'Come now,' and kicked an armchair against the door.

'And you've got a killer smile.'

Oh dear, I hadn't realised humans were so fragile. I must try very hard not to overdo the smiling. 'Are you ready?'

He slid his feet to the floor.

'Mr Montague?' The voice from outside was not giving up.

Someone tried to shove open the door. The chair shifted a bit, scratched over the floor.

'Have you got visitors, love?'

Marcus looked up. I signalled again at him to be quiet.

'Should I come back later?'

Marcus frowned at me. 'Yeah,' he said.

I exhaled in sparkles of flame.

I hoped that meant a *lot* later.

Marcus swayed a little as he stood up. I steadied him. He leaned on me. I felt his powerful body through his hospital scrubs. It tingled in my grip, quite unlike any sensation I'd ever had. He must have felt it too, for he said, 'Weird, it feels like man's leaning on a hurricane.'

Together we walked out on to the patio, past Robyn who was curled up and quite sunken back into her coma, past the rose bushes, down a short private path and on to the grass. The pressure of his weight on mine seemed to rush to my head and make me giddy.

126

'Come,' I urged. I was going to try again. There had to be a way. If I told him everything? Maybe that would help.

'You're the boss,' he said, his crooked smile dancing over straight teeth.

There was so much to tell – of Joey and Larry, the Extension, the contract – and me. What should I tell him first? That I was the Angel of Death who'd come to take his soul, that I couldn't, that one look at him had undone me? Should I really tell him absolutely *everything*, how I'd broken all the rules? How I thought we might be destined to be together?

We passed out across the grass and down towards the spreading cedars. We left Robyn behind, a faint outline under a webby gauze. The sun was already high and the quiet of another lazy hospital afternoon had begun. I love Earthly afternoons. I love hospitals, that smell of antiseptic, that perfume of bleached floor, that aroma of clean starched kindliness. Marcus smelt so powerfully of it all. I wanted to press my nose against him and inhale him like a flower.

We reached the first huge spreading tree. One of its long limbs had grown so close to the ground it formed a horizontal seat. To this branch I steered Marcus. He lowered himself gingerly on to it. I sat too. I took a deep breath and resisted the urge to start scratching. (Being in apparition mode is really itchy.)

We sat awhile, quietly. He seemed a little out of breath. If only we could have sat there all year – caught in between the past and the future – we could have created a paradise for ourselves. I glanced across at Robyn and sighed. I had to tell him. The time had come.

I bit my lip. How to start?

'So,' he said, looking at me, raising one eyebrow again. 'If it's my body you're after I'm afraid it's already in Heaven.'

I stared at him. *What did he mean?* Had another Angel of Death come in the night and taken him? I touched his arm – no, he wasn't a physical shadow like poor Robyn.

'Very holy,' he said.

I still stared.

'Bullet holes? Holy?' he offered.

I shook my head.

'Holy? In Heaven?'

'Oh,' I said. I got it! This was a joke! He was having a joke with me!

'Sorry,' he said, 'I guess in the presence of an angel, I should be more reverent.'

'Yes,' I said. Reverence was definitely good.

'But life's a bit of a bad joke, isn't it?'

I jerked back. That was a strange thing to say. Life a bad joke?

'You don't get it, do you?'

I looked at him, very puzzled.

'A joke. Get it?'

He was playing with me. Joking again?

'No, I don't get it,' I said.

'That's the point,' he said, 'Nobody gets it. Life's for living, like I said. How could it be for anything else?' Suddenly his face grew serious. 'Look,' he said, 'can you tell me something? You're an angel, you're bound to know.'

I nodded.

128

'Nobody will tell me anything – and I want the news about Joey. Is he OK?'

I must have blanched, because Marcus leaned forward and peered at me. 'You do remember Joey, don't you? He was at the club with me. He got shot too.'

My heart hammered. What should I say?

*'He is OK, isn't he?'*

He was far too ill. If he should become faint, I had no power left to help him. My voice cracked. 'I can't speak of Joey,' I whispered. 'I'm here to talk of your destiny.'

Marcus looked disappointed, lapsed into silence, grew pale. A slight beading of sweat broke out again on his brow.

'He's been taken very good care of,' I said carefully, trying my best to comfort. I fidgeted with my wings. (Misleading another is a serious trespass.) Marcus's face regained some colour. There was an awkward silence. I didn't know what else to say.

'OK,' Marcus said at last. 'So let's talk then, get on with the agenda.' He raised his hand (well, tried to) and winced. 'Is man about to die? Is the world about to end?' I heard his breath, each intake a struggle, each exhalation unsteady. I'd done the right thing not to tell him, hadn't I?

'Not yet,' I reassured. 'It's as I've said. I've come down from Heaven to save your immortal soul.' I liked the way I said *'come down from Heaven'* – it gave the whole conversation a certain gravitas. Perhaps that would convince him.

'A being from another world, eh?' He bent his head quizzically on one side. 'Yes! You have a look of something other-worldly about you – might be the wings – could be the halo . . .'

I looked at him wonderingly. This strange, fascinating boy. I wasn't sure if it was me, or him, or humans, but I had the feeling I was standing on the edge of a chasm. Every word Marcus uttered was confusing. Was he in jest? Was he not? Should I be stern? Should I chastise? Should I laugh? Could I tell him the truth? How could he be so frail? Yet seem so strong? How could he be so sinful? Yet look so divine? Why did my heart flutter like this? What was I to do?

I shook my head.

'Do you remember anything about the night before last?' I asked. I had to start somewhere, didn't I? I had to try and find a way to reach him, before I told him everything.

'Of course,' he said. 'It was my eighteenth birthday. I was in the club. Let me guess . . . those dimples – you're a cherub?'

'Please continue,' I said, prompting him as gently as I could.

'There were a lot of guests. I was dancing; the Crow showed up.'

'Who exactly is he?' I asked.

'He's *the* hardest meanest dude this side of the city, discounting me,' he said. He flashed me a wicked smile. (I just love gold teeth.)

'Why did he want to kill you?' I asked.

'Ah,' said Marcus. 'Now *that*, you don't want to know. Some things we do to survive on Earth might upset you, Angel.' He stared moodily into the distance as if before his eyes scrolled scenes he'd rather forget. 'Gang stuff,' he said, a bead of sweat trickling down the side of his jaw.

'Please try me.' I really was quite interested. I imagined blood and body parts and guns and motorbikes and fast cars, dark nights, loud music and gold, heaps of gold.

'Well,' he said, 'these neighbourhoods are mine. I run these streets. I treat my boys well. Nobody's family goes without things on my patch. There's a reason why I get a nice private little room and all. I help out, see. Folks are grateful.'

Overhead the tree creaked, swayed slightly. A ray of sunshine lit up the lawns. A light breeze scuffed the autumn leaves. I wondered what exactly 'helping out' meant.

'And that makes some people jealous.'

'The Crow was jealous of you?'

'He's jealous of the loyalty I get, the streets I control, jealous of the love people show me – and he specially didn't like it when his girlfriend showed me the love too!' Marcus leaned forward, tried to laugh, but folded his arms and broke into a coughing fit.

'Candy?' I asked.

'Yeah,' coughed Marcus. 'She's really something.'

I looked at him confused. *He liked Candy?* A hole opened up in my chest. I felt my insides drain out. But all I said was 'Oh' in an unhappy little way.

'And she knows it.'

'Marcus,' I said, suddenly stern. 'It's right and good and proper that you confess all your mortal sins to me, but you must try to turn your back on them, however far you are from repentance, however much you feel you cannot fully renounce your life of crime. Small steps count. We cannot speak of sin, or the . . . um . . . the affections of a young

131

lady, without in the same breath praying for forgiveness and . . .'

Oh dear, it just wasn't coming out right. I sounded as boring and longwinded as St Peter. And he *had* pushed Candy behind him. He wasn't all bad. I'd seen kindness in his eyes, smelt goodness in his scent.

Maybe he really liked her . . . I suddenly felt quite flat and deflated.

Marcus looked at me. 'OK, Angel,' he said, 'I won't speak about them. But you asked me why the Crow came after me. That's why. I control these hoods – I closed down his business – that's what I do – and his girlfriend won't leave me alone. Any of those would do – and I'm not sorry about none of it.' He clenched his fists until they turned quite pale. A muscle flexed in his jaw. His brow clouded over.

A sharp wind blew across the lawns. It bit into my skin. He was right, I had asked. I did want the truth. I ought to be happy he'd told me. But I can tell you there's nothing pleasant about contemplating sin. The thought made me feel quite ill. And if he liked this Candy so much that he was ready to take bullets for her, and if he really wasn't anxious to change, then what was I doing here?

The thought made all the fire inside me die. A horrid cold congealed in my throat, a sudden pain stabbed at my chest. I shivered. 'Just the wind,' I choked, almost as if I felt it too.

*Just the wind?*

What was I thinking of? Marcus might catch a chill. Human beings are so fragile. One cold breeze and they all get the plague. I looked at him. His lip still bloodless, his brow all tense.

I needed to take care of him. 'Come,' I said. I took his arm and steered him towards an arbour covered in climbing roses. Inside was a sheltered seat. Over everything spread the branches of a fruit tree.

I tried not to hurry him, but he shouldn't stay out in the wind. When we were seated I took his hand. 'Marcus,' I said gently. 'You are troubled; you must trust me; please tell me what it is that eats away at you, what drives you to this life of crime? I'm not at all sure it can just be about the money.' I was in deadly earnest.

A frown darkened Marcus's face. I lifted my finger to the crease lines between his eyes. I smoothed them away.

'I know I sound serious, but we have so little time to put everything right and much has gone so wrong. This is why I'm here. I think if we can get to the bottom of your sorrow, to the thing that causes you such pain, we can start to mend it. And solutions may follow – then repentance will be much easier.'

'You are quite lovely,' he said, suddenly. 'And you really do care, don't you?'

Was this another joke? Was he trying to divert my attention away from everything that needed saying?

'Is Heaven full of serious angels, like you?' he asked.

'Of course,' I said.

'You almost make me want to go there.' He considered this for a minute. Then whispered (conspiratorially), 'Do any of you get up to anything . . . you know – naughty – behind the big G's back?'

He *was* joking again.

I laughed and the sun broke from behind a cloud. Then I laid one finger across his lips. 'You mustn't think like that,' I whispered. 'Heaven is wonderful. There's nothing impure in anything we do.'

'So,' he said, 'that adds up to paradise, eh?'

Was he still joking?

I couldn't tell. He was such a perplexing creature. So I just answered his question as best I could: 'Well, it's not like Earth. Not that I don't like Earth, but here you have such sad things to deal with.' I thought of all the pain etched on faces. I thought of the dark nights, and the desperateness of everyone at that disco, all trying to have fun, as if fun was something that the minute you grabbed it just evaporated in your hand. I thought of the sad lined faces in the queues at Styx. I thought of the thin girl over there, huddled beneath the gossamer trying to accept her death. I thought of death. To know that everything ends there, to fear there's no afterlife, to count your days and see each dawn break and finish, each evening close down on another day of your life, and to know they're finite.

'You are so beautiful when you're sad,' he said and reached out to me. I smiled. His hand hovered, touched me, ran a thumb down my cheek.

A confused look came over his beautiful face. 'Your skin feels strange,' he said, 'I can't seem to *really* touch you.'

'No,' I said. 'That is how it is. We Seraphim are of a different realm. You cannot touch me, not in an Earthly way.'

'Not touch you,' he said, as if this were quite a new

idea. 'But I *must* touch you,' he said simply. 'I have to touch you.' He raised his arm and reached out as if he intended to break through all the regions that lay between us. His face twisted and I could see it hurt him. He was struggling with himself. And when his arms found nothing, he let out such a cry of pain that it issued forth in a half-strangled sound. '*There must be a way,*' he cried. '*I have to touch you.*'

I looked at him. I saw his eyes ablaze with something so fierce it almost frightened me.

'Teach me how to touch you!' he demanded.

'I don't even know how,' I whispered. 'I have appeared before you. You can feel me, here is my hand. But I don't think any mortal can touch the Seraphim. Not in the way you desire.'

'Maybe this is really it,' he murmured as if he had asked himself a question. 'I can't hold her. I can't touch her. She talks to me of goodness and of righteousness, of saving my soul and healing my pain and I want to touch her.' He seemed to find this funny and smiled a strange savage smile.

He made as if to take my hand and once again shook his head, puzzled.

How disappointed he looked. How I would have given anything to have had a real human hand, just for a few minutes, just to feel his touch on my skin. What would it have been like?

Far away a buzzer rang.

'That means they're closing the ward,' he said. 'It's the end of visiting.'

I smiled. The arbitrary opening and closing of hospital wards meant nothing to me.

135

'And I'll have to go and be there for the pill round,' he added. 'They've got some pretty massive painkillers. Give you one hell of a kick.' He tilted his head. 'Who knows, if I don't get my next fix you might disappear.'

I jumped. What was I thinking of? *I had to get to the surgical ward and Collect the old man! I had to get down to intensive care and kill the baby!*

In a swirl of flame, hair floating wide, wings risen, I jumped up. I'd wasted all this time. I hadn't told him about the deal, or how Larry had helped, or Joey, or what should have happened. What was *going* to happen! I hadn't informed him about my repentance plan: the charity dona-tion, the appeal to the Halls of the Dead.

I started to feel terribly angry with myself. I could feel thunderbolts building up inside me. How remiss, how unfor-givable, how incompetent.

'Hey, Angel, calm down. You can come another time,' he said. 'I'd like that. You can appear in a flash of light and wow me all over again.'

We had to get back to the ward. Right now.

Marcus struggled to raise an arm. He unhooked a lanyard from his neck, gathered something in his hand and pressed it at me.

I looked at him, uncertain, and helped him to his feet.

'It's a key,' he said, 'to my place. I haven't got anything else to give you.'

'But you don't have to give me anything,' I said.

'I do,' he said. 'You saved me. I owe you. That's how it is in my world. It's the street code. Now you can call on me any time you like.'

I shook out the lanyard. Looped through it was a key.

'I've never given that to anyone before,' he said. 'It's just a way of saying my yard is yours, and if you want me to change, I'll give it a go. And that's a promise. I know you don't need a key. You can walk through walls.'

I was so stunned I didn't know what to say.

'I'll look out for you, then,' he said. 'We can argue a bit more – you know, about life and truth and reality.'

Argue? Had we been arguing?

'About sex and drugs and rock and roll.'

Sex and drugs?

'Just kidding,' he laughed. 'Only drugs.'

Oh, he was joking. He didn't want to see me again.

'Please come,' he said. 'I'd really like it.'

# Serafina 18

I was late.

So I did everything in a rush.

I got Marcus back to his room, helped him on to his bed, but I couldn't fix all those tubes back. I couldn't wait till a nurse came to do it either. It might take forever. But if I left him?

There was nothing for it; what was five hundred years in Torium anyway? So as soon as I got out of apparition mode and back to my full powers, I performed the advanced Pick Up Your Bed And Walk Miracle (adapted, obviously). I healed him completely – right there and then. And I was right, I made a perfect A* job of it. I know, don't say it. I don't even want to think how many rules I broke.

The miracle knocked him out, though. With a strange little cry he collapsed on the bed, completely flattened. (OK, maybe it would only have got a B+.) I made him as comfortable as I could and left him lying there insentient.

Then I got moving. And I would've been OK, if I could've flown from one bedside death to the next and hurried the souls along, but Robyn slowed me down. She was so attached to her human form she insisted on walking.

I got quite cross with her. I told her to let it go. I ordered her to hold on to me and allow me to guide her. I even threatened her, told her I'd leave her if she didn't hurry up. I wasn't very nice. I'm so sorry for that. I really didn't give her a great send-off: making her wait and then bullying her to keep up.

Somehow we made it to the baby in intensive care. That was horrid. She was such a tiny little thing and was struggling so bravely to breathe, her minuscule chest inflated by machines, her incubator just a mass of tubes and plastic. It wasn't her fault she was born too early.

Her mother was hardly more than a girl herself. She looked tired and strained. She must have been sitting beside the child for days. She knew the little thing couldn't survive. She knew that each breath was a fight, each heartbeat took such courage. It was a mercy to release the infant from her painful brush with life. Maybe Marcus was right. Maybe after all life was a bad joke.

Anyway, she didn't slow me down. I simply cradled her in my arms and soothed her with a song until she fell into such sweet oblivion. It was sad she wasn't bound straight for Heaven. The mother should really have had her baptised. It would have been so much more sensible than wringing her hands. Human love. Such a complicated thing, so much emotion, so little sense.

I carried her gently for all that. Poor little soul. Life isn't fair, is it? I wondered how God explained her in His understanding of Free Will.

Free Will. So much seemed to revolve around that idea. I glanced down at the Manifest. The child's name was definitely on it. So that meant the Senior Team knew she was going to die. They knew she wasn't going to be baptised. They knew Robyn was going to die. They knew Robyn was going to kill herself. And so they knew both of them would not be bound for Heaven. So how could their actions ever have been free, if the Senior Team had known about their sin in advance? Didn't it mean God had determined their actions in advance? It confused me. Did God know about Marcus's future? Was there any hope? Any point in trying to save him at all? And how unfair on the baby. Was she to blame for Satan having tricked Eve? Why did she have to go to Hell?

So, weighed down by heavy thoughts, I finally made it to the geriatric ward. Straight away I saw the reason why we're supposed to deliver souls individually to their destinations. Bunching them up like this was very problematic. For a start the man was bedbound. He was too weak even to sit up. My arms were full, plus I'd got Robyn still comatose in tow – how the hell was I going to get them all to Hell?

I ended up having to give the baby to the girl, which wasn't ideal. Not that she could have dropped her or anything, neither of them actually having a body.

Anyway, she held the baby, or rather thought she did, because the baby wasn't too worried about bobbing about in her microscopic spirit form, and leaving the memory of her tiny little shape floating around too. While Robyn did that, I coaxed and carried the old man until he figured out that even though he was dead and wanted to stay with his body, it was much easier to leave it behind and glide.

We must have looked a very odd little band going down

the broad and pleasant highway. I got quite a few disapproving looks from other Seraphim. But I just smiled and nodded. I was getting only too used to doing everything wrong.

Still, it was a relief to turn off towards Mount Purgatory and escape. I'd made a decision. I was NOT going to take the baby to Hell. If she couldn't go to Heaven then I'd take her to Torium. Not only that, I figured while I was at it, I'd give Robyn and the old man a break as well. I'd take the whole bang lot of them there.

That was probably against every Rule in the Book. But sometimes, you know, you've just had enough of rules. Plus I could interpret a piteous cry as repentance if I wanted to, couldn't I? And I don't care what they say at the Cloisters, I don't think suicide should be a sin – and Hell is no place for babies. And as for the old man, well, he was so . . . (I don't like to say it – but 'forgetful' will do); he'd been far too confused to give a straight answer when I'd asked him to repent.

So, what the hell, I took them to Purgatorium. There you are, I did it. I handled all the aerial toll-houses on the way – the baby was too young to speak for herself, the old man too old, Robyn still thought she was in a deathly coma and I was in no mood to be trifled with.

I was in a very strange mood. Although I'd just spent the whole afternoon with Marcus, and I ought to be feeling deliriously happy, I wasn't. Instead I was feeling very flat. I didn't understand his jokes. I'd been too cowardly to own up about Joey, and I was no nearer sorting out what we were going to do about the contract. Half the time I wasn't even sure he'd believed I was really there. The rest of the time I got the distinct impression he didn't want to repent at all, and that he'd only give it a go because he felt indebted to me for saving his life. I was pretty sure that didn't count as repenting 'freely and willingly and with a whole heart'. Plus I'd somehow managed to break a zillion more rules without even trying. I told myself that if I carried on messing up, I'd *have* to go and tell St Peter everything. Without fail.

That gave me a shock. It would no longer be a matter of Ave Marias and Our Fathers. Even if I escaped Community Service in Purgatorium, he'd have me totally grounded. But that wasn't the worst of it. If St Peter reported me to Jehudiel, not only would my fate be sealed, but Marcus's too.

There'd be no more going down to Earth, he'd have Raquel's spare pass off me like a shot and Marcus's Extension would be cancelled.

A shudder went through me. Raquel's spare pass was the only thing left that allowed me to get in and out of Heaven. What with the new checkpoints and the curfews and the breach and the Army, I *had* to hang on to it.

# Serafina 19

I said as much to Raquel later, when the day's work was done and the jars of amber nectar filled. We were hanging out under some palms by a crazy beautiful beach, south of the City. Raquel was in a hammock and she'd got on an 'awesome' sarong filled with all the colours of the rainbow. And I was telling her I adored Collection Duty (and thank God for her spare pass).

'Why?' said a sad voice I remembered from the evening of the garden party.

I turned my head. There was Kamuel, the same tall, sombre, melancholy figure, still as breathtakingly beautiful, still as noble.

'Why,' I stammered, suddenly overcome by the sheer grace of him. 'Why, because Collection Duty is the only real work of God.'

Kamuel pulled himself up a chair and sat. 'Why do you say that?' he asked.

I thought of Robyn and the senseless waste of her life. I thought of the baby, so innocent, so damned by man's Original Sin. I thought of Original Sin and the Devil and his waging of war against us. I thought of the stench of Hell, the fiery pits. I thought of Joey and his pleading eyes.

I thought of Marcus and how he'd laughed in the face of God's bad joke.

I turned to look up to Kamuel. 'I've seen things,' I stammered. 'I've seen the darkness. I've seen it and I can't forget it or unlearn it. I . . .' My voice trailed off. Why the hell had I said that?

Kamuel studied me gravely.

'I think, I've seen it for a reason,' I continued. I didn't know why I was telling him this. I shouldn't be. I clamped my mouth shut.

'Here, honey, have some angel cake.' Raquel slid a dainty slice of pink and yellow and white gateau at Kamuel. (We angels practically *never* eat; we live on fresh air, ambrosia, honeydew and perfume.) 'Just a nibble, it won't hurt.' She smiled, all dimples, all charm.

The sickly-sweet smell of the cake mingled with the salt tang and the ocean breeze. I thought of the streets on Earth. Life wasn't all romantic beaches and cake there, was it?

Kamuel, noticing that my bounce had gone, that the fiery brilliance of my eyes was dimmed, placed a hand upon my shoulder. And Raquel, tiring of such gloomy faces, got up and said she was going for a dip. She picked up a towel and headed off down the beach.

'So thoughtful,' murmured Kamuel. But whether he was referring to Raquel or my gloom, I couldn't divine.

But I nodded anyway. I was thoughtful.

'And very beautiful,' he added. I looked after Raquel's departing figure. She was very beautiful.

I didn't reply. I'd started worrying about Marcus again.

*What was he going to do when he found out about Joey?* I quivered from my neck to my wing tips. There was something about Marcus that frightened me – something so volatile and reckless. He might do *anything*.

Kamuel lifted his hand from my shoulder. 'I need to ask you to help me with something,' he said.

I was so glad he'd spoken. I immediately said, 'Yes, of course.' (And to be asked by an Archangel for assistance is the highest honour.)

'It will not be an easy task,' he said.

'No?' I looked at him.

'It will demand loyalty and sacrifice.'

I nodded, suddenly worried that I might mess it up. 'I'm a bit scatty,' I said anxiously.

'You'll be fine,' he said, 'if you truly see your mission as to ease suffering and save souls.'

I nodded. I hoped so. I waited for him to tell me what to do.

'Then meet me later after you've left your friend.'

I nodded again.

'Meet me by the North Gate.'

*'The North Gate?'*

'Yes, where the Army is watching over the Abyss.'

I gulped. I blinked.

'I'll meet you there,' he said, 'by sundown.'

He stood. He bowed to me. He took my hand and kissed it in a strange old-fashioned way. Then he left.

I sat there, faintly shocked.

*The North Gate?*

That was madness! God's Army would be everywhere.

All my feathers curled up at the thought. For Christ's sake why had I ever opened my big mouth?

Raquel returned. She towelled down. '*Cripes*, thank *God*, Kamuel's gone!' she cried. 'He makes me feel so *serious*. Everything is so *solemn* and he's so *brooding*. Even you started getting glum.'

'I like him, though,' I said loyally.

'Of *course* you do, darling, everybody *adores* him.'

'But I do like him,' I said.

She threw her marble-white arms around me. 'What a serious little softy you are,' she cried. 'What was all that "I've seen the darkness" rubbish? When you've been down to Earth as many times as I have, you get pretty fed up with the darkness; it's all so boring and useless and nobody'll ever sort it out. But you're a legend! You completely saved me today.'

'It's nothing,' I said. 'I like all work, and I love Collection Duty.' I started to wax lyrical about the timing of a Passing Over and how wonderful it was to make it serene and how an extra slanting ray of sunlight or a rainbow shimmer worked miracles on a half-repentant soul. Raquel looked at me, wide-eyed.

'Wow,' she said, 'if you like it that much, you can help me out every day!'

'Yes,' I breathed. 'Yes, please.'

'There! Aren't you a treasure,' she said. 'I told Maybelle just as much, though she seemed to think God's Army were after you for something.'

'God's Army?' I said, instantly petrified.

*The contract?*

146

*Larry?*

Raquel laughed. 'Said she'd heard it on the Fig-Vine.'

'Heard what?'

'Oh, just that. God's Army are on to you, sweetie.'

# Serafina 20

When the sun was just sinking below the crest of the Sapphire Mountains I left my cell. The Seraphim were still holding their vigil, the Superiors attending devotions. The Cloisters were practically closed since the breach, so there were no new arrivals, no one to spy on me – thank God.

I didn't know what work Kamuel intended to give me, but God's Army were camped north of the North Gate, so knowing we would meet near there, I tied my hair back and chose a dark raiment with cloak and hood. Raquel's words still rang like a knell of doom in my ears: *God's Army are on to you.* I had been warned. With a pounding heart, I drew the cloth close around me. I must stay as invisible as possible.

I glided out of the building, more quietly than a cloud passes across the face of the moon. But no sooner had I reached the Cloister gates than a uniformed being suddenly materialised out of nowhere. My blood froze.

'Who goes there?' he hissed.

I didn't answer.

'Halt. Show yourself.'

I stayed in the shadows.

'Don't try to leave the Cloisters without one.'

'Without one what?' I whispered.

'Standard-issue Cloisters-Only Identity Bracelet,' he ordered, and thrust something at me.

I backed away, heart hammering.

'Your choice,' he said.

I stepped forward very cautiously.

'Hold out your arm.'

I held it out. He slipped the security band over my wrist and fastened it. 'Don't remove it if you know what's good for you,' he hissed. 'It's the new curfew rule. Just be grateful they haven't put your number on it yet.'

'My number?'

'Show it if you get challenged, or you'll be arrested.'

*Arrested?*

'You can go.'

I did.

I moved as only the Seraphim can – silently and with the speed of the west wind through the shadowy streets.

The Golden City is not very big. Only angels dwell in its confines. The souls of the dead live in the huge Suburbs-of-the-Saved, which stretch in every direction across the great Elysian Plains. They're lovely places. Sometimes I wander there, through the leafy green lanes of the un-living, but even dead humans have their own ways; it's not easy to mingle amongst them.

So it didn't take me long to reach the North Gate. I stayed close to the Jasper Wall all the way. Shadows dappled off its jewelled ramparts and threw enough variance of light to confuse any watching eyes. Not many would have been able to make me out gliding through the darkened streets. Even if they had, they would have been confused, for angels don't slink around in their own city.

At least I supposed they didn't. Up until then I'd never had any reason to suppose differently. But perhaps there were others like me – out on clandestine missions, weighed down by guilty secrets. Hurriedly I cast a glance behind me to make sure I wasn't being followed. What was that? A darker patch of darkness? A figure ducking into an alcove?

I pulled my cloak tighter and broke into a run. No flying, and now identity bracelets. Maybe it was all my fault God's Army were clamping down on everyone. Suppose Larry *was* working for the Devil? Would signing the contract for Marcus's life mean I'd made the 'pact' with him?

And if it did, was I sorry?

I thought of Marcus. I put my hand to my throat and held the key he'd given me. To know that Marcus was alive, to hope that I could save him from Hell – I couldn't be sorry for that.

*I wasn't sorry.*

*I'd do it again.*

And that scared me more than anything. I wasn't sorry, and part of me didn't care who the hell Larry worked for.

Even if it was the Devil.


At the North Gate I waited. I hid myself behind a buttress. From there I could see down a long valley. God's Army were still at work far off, bombing the edge of the Abyss.

Every now and then flares lit up the night sky. I wondered if demons were already crawling up its cliffs, already seeping in their oiliness out of its depths.

'How clever of you to come so quietly,' murmured a voice at my ear. I spun round to see the noble figure of Kamuel just at my right shoulder. 'But no more than I expected.'

I glowed at his praise. I had done right to be secretive, to cover my fiery beauty with such a dark cloak

'Yet still quite brilliant,' he said. 'No raiment, however dark, could hide that.'

My glow turned a little hot. I think I blushed. It was very sweet of him to say so. I knew he was sincere. And I was sure he didn't say such things often, maybe hardly ever. His voice had a kind of unpractised air about it. But despite all that it was sort of embarrassing. The earnestness of his tone made me shrink from him. How perverse I was! When Marcus laughed at me, I longed for him; when Kamuel praised me, I cringed.

'Thank you,' I whispered, 'but I don't think you summoned me here to admire my dark cloak.'

'No,' he said. 'Tonight we have a difficult and dangerous mission to accomplish; know that this night I intend to break all the Rules of Heaven. I do not ask you to join me in this – I hope that you will. But if not, then you may turn back now.'

My eyes flew wide. What, was I to break yet more rules? But Kamuel was an Archangel so all I said was: 'Tell me what I must do.'

His beautiful face softened and he smiled with such

radiant happiness, I was almost afraid. 'So lovely, so inno-cent,' he murmured.

But I said nothing except: 'I don't understand.'

'No,' he said. 'Now you have chosen your path, do not seek to understand, only to obey.'

Obedience is the third vow and a prized virtue. I couldn't refuse. No one can refuse an Archangel, anyway.

'Your will is my command,' I said.

'Good. You are not to tell of anything that happens this night,' instructed Kamuel. 'And for your loyalty, know that I shall not forget you when misfortune knocks at your door.'

My feathers tingled. Misfortune was certain to come, then? A cold shiver ran through me.

'It's right to be afraid,' said Kamuel. 'Did you not say – only earlier today – that you have seen the darkness?'

I nodded, swallowing.

'Remember, then,' said Kamuel. 'In your darkest hour, I will not desert you.'

'Thank you,' I whispered.

'Then know that there is one whose soul we must save tonight.'

I nodded again, suddenly wondering if we were to go down to Earth.

'You did say you believed that the saving of souls was God's true work, didn't you?'

'Yes.'

'Then meet the one whose soul will be forever in your debt,' he said.

He waved a wing. Out of the shadows came forth a dark figure. He was cloaked as I was and with faltering steps he slunk along the edge of the Jasper Wall until he reached us.

'Vincent,' Kamuel said. 'Come, take courage, this young Seraph will lead you to the edge.'

I peered through the shadows at the cloaked figure. It was the same tired angel I'd seen at Raquel's garden party. He looked even more tired than ever. His eyes were red. His arms hung limp. The lines of his face told of things that chilled my spirit.

What in Heaven's name had they done to him?

# Serafina 21

Vincent bowed slightly to me, but didn't speak.

Kamuel drew nearer. 'Together we will guide him to the Abyss,' he said. 'You must be ready to carry on alone should God's Army detect us.'

'Carry on alone?' I faltered.

'You can command thunderbolts, I hope?' smiled Kamuel.

'Yes,' I said.

'If for any unforeseen reason we are found out, on the beat of a wing I will repair to the topmost peak of the Sapphire Mountains and hurl thunderbolts into the sky. I will make a fine show. Dazzle and terrify. Let obscene wailings be heard from the depths of the void, create shadows that dance against the starry sky. Fearing a new offensive, God's Army must and will turn their steps towards me. When they are upon the foothills, I will disappear and meet you by the very rim of the Abyss, right at the point where Lucifer fell: the place they call Devil's Drop.'

'Yes,' I said, although the idea struck terror into me.

'Well said,' commended Kamuel. 'You will not regret this hour.'

'But how did you free Vincent? Where will he go?'

'Do not ask how I released Vincent, which angels helped

me, which broke into God's Army's camp and shattered
the chains that held him. That is how we work.'

'We?' I said.

'Ah,' smiled Kamuel, 'so you have not yet heard of the
work of the Mission?

I shook my head. In all the long hours spent in study or
devotion at the Cloisters, I had never heard of any group
called the Mission.

'It's just as well,' said Kamuel. 'No one should know
who we are.' He drew his cloak closer around him. 'If God's
Army should arrest you, you will not betray us. And I will
not forget you.'

I nodded. Already it was too late. Was I not here, cloaked
in darkness, already assisting an escaped criminal?'

'What about Vincent?' I said, looking at the thin angel
beside us.

'He will fall to Earth,' said Kamuel. 'He will fall from
the edge of the Abyss and he will escape.'

'But . . .' I said.

'And he will dwell among men, forever invisible, forever
unable to return to Heaven, but he will survive. He will
work doing the will of the true faith, until the day we
triumph. He will become one of the Outcasts,' said Kamuel.

'One of the Fallen?' I said.

'There are many.'

I blinked. Where had I been for the past few millennia?
Why didn't I know about this? About Outcasts, about
Falling, that unseen angels trod the pavements on Earth? I
opened my mouth to ask: can they apparition to humans?
Can they command rainbows? Do they touch mortals?

But Kamuel held a finger over his lips and I said nothing.

'They all worked for the Mission. They all knew the price they might have to pay,' said Kamuel. 'They live on Earth in secret. One careless flash of angelic power would give them away. Retribution would be swift and entire.'

I thought about that. Had I passed Outcasts in my duties on Earth? Had I not noticed they were there? Had that lonely figure in the club been one of them? I suddenly knew he *must* have been one of them. It had been *him* at Styx! The cities of Earth were probably thronged with the Fallen.

'Unless they cross over to the dark.'

'The dark?'

'Join Satan.'

I shivered. Join Satan?

My thoughts were interrupted. 'Are you ready?' Kamuel asked.

Kamuel took Vincent's arm. Vincent nodded.

'Come, brace yourself. Take courage, Vincent,' said Kamuel. 'Lucifer shall not have you, and God's Army will not find you.'

Vincent seemed to shrink under the fortification. His cheeks sank in, and his eyes stared back out of deep hollows.

'So, Vincent, can you do God's work on Earth in secrecy, in silence?'

Vincent nodded. His thin shoulders twitched a little.

'Can you renounce Heaven, and Fall?'

'God bless you, Kamuel,' whispered Vincent, 'for offering me the chance.'

'The work will be hard and thankless. You will go unnoticed, often cursed.'

Vincent looked like that had been the case for a very long time already.

'You will be called upon to deceive out of Kindness, to be cruel out of Love, to kill out of Mercy.'

'I'm ready.'

'Then go with the Mission's blessing.'

'What were God's Army going to do?' I squeaked.

Vincent smiled. 'God's Army would have taken me to the Day of Judgement Courts to be tried before the Senior Team. The penalty for unlawful killing is vaporisation.'

I shuddered. In my mind's eye I saw Vincent shattered into a million tiny fragments of dust, each angelic speck doomed to waft in the air for eternity.

'If I had only done it once,' continued Vincent, 'perhaps they might have just stripped me of my wings and banished me from Heaven . . .'

'Oh,' I whispered. I wanted to ask more – who, why, how many – and did Extensions count as unlawful Collections? And why had he chosen to become an Angel of Mercy? But I just couldn't.

Vincent smiled.

Kamuel silenced us with a wave of his wing. He beckoned us forward. 'Now,' he hissed.

The three of us hurried through the North Gate and down the narrow lane that led out to the wasteland beyond.

Silently, like shadows in the night, we passed the barren plains that stretch northwards towards the Sapphire Mountains. None heard us pass, none stopped us with shout nor alarm. On we flew, quiet as the grave, skimming the land and keeping low so that no careless moonbeam would betray us.

At last we came to the first postings of rock that signalled our closeness to the Abyss. No fields, nor woodlands, adorned this part of Heaven, only the bones of the mountains, austere, unwelcoming. I'd never in all my days been this far north.

'Devil's Drop is not far off,' whispered Kamuel.

We alighted upon stones as quietly as snow falls. I drew my raiment tight around me. I was so glad I'd chosen such a thick one. It was very cold. The wind wailed like a disembodied spirit out of the depths of the Abyss, blasting us with icy particles. I could hear it moaning even from where we were.

'Draw close,' said Kamuel.

The three of us huddled together in the shadows of the rocks. From amongst the folds of his robes Kamuel drew a rope.

'What's that for?' I asked, imagining somehow that Vincent was going to have to climb down it into the Abyss.

'To bind his wings. Come, Vincent,' said Kamuel. 'Let me tie them for you.'

Vincent shuffled forward.

'Why do you tie his wings?' I asked.

Kamuel smiled as he pulled the knot tight. 'If I do not, once he has jumped he will use them. There is no other way. None can withstand the Fall if they have wings to save themselves.'

Kamuel finished his work. Vincent tested the knots. I

shuddered to see his feathers broken in places, crushed, deformed. But Vincent didn't murmur.

We walked the rest of the distance on foot. In single file we tiptoed silently between the overhanging rocks, crept round the curved mass of the boulders, and made our way quietly to the lip of the Abyss.

There it was. I'd never seen it before. The rocks so perilously smooth. One wrong step and you'd slip, fall, plunge. Instinctively I unfurled my wings. The edge beckoned; seemed to tempt. I felt a sudden overwhelming urge to slide forward, to peer over its edge, to look into the void beneath . . .

Kamuel caught my shoulder. 'Have a care,' he said. I stepped back. The wind moaned up. Mists swirled out of the deeps below – sometimes thin and wispy in phantom shapes, sometimes thick and treacherous. My pulse raced. I balanced precariously on the rocks.

A sudden noise.

*What was that?*

A squeak of leather on stone.

I jumped, slipped, tipped towards the edge, unfurled my wings, beat the air. Kamuel held me steady.

It happened so fast. Before I knew what was going on – there they were.

'STEP AWAY FROM THE EDGE,' boomed a dreadful voice.

I whirled around. Wildly I stared into the mists. Not phantom shapes at all. There they stood, as if they had materialised straight out of the Apocalypse. A whole regiment of God's Army.

*God's Army!*

*How had they surrounded us so quietly? Why had I imagined their tramping would give them away?*

'Stand off,' commanded Kamuel, instantly summoning a swirling fog to hide us.

'BEWARE! We act with authority,' ordered the voice I remembered from Raquel's party. 'Show yourselves. Someone has signed a pact with the Devil. They must be found and punished. You cannot stand in our way. Do not protect the wicked. Until the threat is dealt with everyone is at risk.'

There he stood, whip in hand, towering over all the others. My heart beat. I made to step forward. Kamuel and Vincent should not be caught because of me.

'We know a Seraph is amongst you. We know you are assisting an escaped convict.'

Instantly Kamuel turned to me, grabbed my arm, exposed the Cloister's identity band. Without hesitation he ripped it off, hurled it into the Abyss and whispered in my ear, *'Do not argue. You have been tricked. Fly.'*

Confused, alarmed, I beat my wings. I rose straight up.

*'Jump!'* Kamuel screamed at Vincent.

But Vincent hesitated, undecided.

*'Jump, for God's sake!'*

Archangel Jehudiel raised his arm. The huge whip curled into the air. 'STEP AWAY FROM THE EDGE,' he ordered. 'FALLING IS FORBIDDEN ON PAIN OF VAPORISATION.'

Kamuel rose in the air, sent a fury of thunderbolts. The ranks of God's Army scattered. The fog thinned.

*Vincent just stood there.*

'*JUMP!*' screeched Kamuel.

I beat the air, soared ten thousand feet.

Kamuel followed, but Vincent remained motionless, like a rabbit caught in a finger of light.

And Archangel Jehudiel flicked the Whip of Justice up into the whirling air. 'STEP BACK FROM THE EDGE NOW OR I WILL WIELD THE WHIP,' he commanded.

*And still he didn't jump.*

And Jehudiel cracked the whip down.

And a length of white-hot fire – thinner than a flower stalk – snaked out.

And shattered Vincent into a million shining pieces.

# Serafina 22

After Vincent was vaporised everything came to a full stop. Of course. The paperwork was endless. The searches took forever. I didn't dare use the spare pass, and it was all chaos.

But if Marcus had called me I'd have heard. I'd have found a way to reach him. All he needed to do was whisper: *'Angel?'* We Seraphim can hear the rustle of a butterfly's wing as it beats the air a continent away. I'd even have braved using the fire escape if he'd called.

But he didn't.

I thought he might. Hoped he would. He'd said he'd like to see me again. I grew impatient waiting. I had to talk to him. But perhaps it was just as well he didn't.

Heaven was in uproar.

The *Daily Trumpet* had a field day:

EVIL ANGEL ATTEMPTS ESCAPE!
KNOWN KILLER DONE IN AT DEVIL'S DROP!
VILLAIN VAPORISED ON VERY VERGE OF VICTORY
DEVIL'S DISCIPLES AT WORK IN HEAVEN
JEHUDIEL CRACKS DOWN THE WHIP

It was all obviously part of Satan's campaign. And it was all major news. And oh, poor Vincent. Poor, poor Vincent. Vaporised by the swirling Abyss. His poor sunken cheeks. His tied wings. His empty eyes, those staring deep hollows. Would I ever forget? The terror. The horror. The moment of impact – how the whip had turned him white-hot, fused his wings, sent a web of fissures out into every vein, every artery, his face a mask of pain. How for one moment he'd appeared in his true glory – beautiful beyond compare – then the shattering of his limbs, how they'd melted down, cracking, twisting, breaking . . .

*Why hadn't he jumped?*

*Why had we just flown away? Couldn't we have saved him?*

*The terrible look of retribution on Jehudiel's face.*

I hid in the Cloisters. I joined the vigil. I went to devotions. I covered my guilt and my terror with white raiment and endless prayer. *Had they seen me?* Every time a door opened I started, every time it closed I heaved a sigh of relief. *Did they know who I was?* The identity bracelet. *Would I be recognised by the guard?* I'd been followed – hadn't I? I'd been tracked and tagged. It was the bracelet, wasn't it?

I tried never to be in my cell; I stayed away from my friends, lest in my eyes they read my terror and asked of it; when the Superior demanded details of all our movements, I didn't own up. *Thank God I hadn't been recognised.* When Jehudiel searched our cells I trembled in silence and hid Marcus's key. When the Seraphim were issued new Individualised Identity Curfew Bracelets, I accepted mine as if I'd never seen one before.

*They'd vaporised Vincent.*

*God's Army were on to me.*

And I didn't dare use Raquel's spare pass. Not until it had all died down. Not until I was absolutely sure it was safe.

And so three days elapsed before I could get back down to Earth. Three whole days. That left only five before Halloween, and it was torture.

But at length the day came when I could slip out. I removed the new identity bracelet, fearing it would betray me. I hid it inside the Announcers' Offices, where I pretended I was going to work all day. Then I tagged along with a choir of Seraphim who were going down to sing at the inauguration of a new bishop. I slipped through the checkpoint – waving my pass – hiding in their ranks.

Once on Earth, in the flick of a feather I got to the hospital. I hurried to his room. Made ready to apparition.

But Marcus had vanished.

I panicked. Had they moved him to another room? Was he in intensive care? Had something gone wrong? *Had my miracle not worked?*

He wasn't in another room. Not in intensive care. Immediately I was terrified. Was he dead? What had happened? I looked in the morgue. *Thank God he wasn't in the morgue.*

I tried touching the bed he'd lain on – but it wasn't his. I flicked from ward to ward, trying to find the right bed, but when I did, it told me nothing, except that he'd left it yesterday. *Where was he? How could I find him?*

I remembered hospitals keep notes. Instantly I scanned

through records, found his file. He'd received a phone call and discharged himself on 22nd October. Nobody had come to pick him up – that's what his notes said.

*Why had he done that? He was still so weak.*

Stay calm. There must be news of him. Use your powers. I tuned my ears into the music of the spheres to see if any chance refrain sang of him. But there was no mention of Marcus. Alarmed, I tried listening in to a thousand conversations, whispered across the spinning globe, but none revealed his whereabouts. In desperation I gazed with angelic vision through thicket, stone, cement, steel, to north, south, east, west – yet *still* I could not find him.

In the beat of a wing, I was at his mother's address at Curlston Heights. I soared to her flat, feeling the wind rushing in my wings, feeling the stars crashing towards me.

But he wasn't there.

He'd been there though. *He had been there!* I could smell the scent of antibiotics clinging to the sofa. I could tell from a packet of tablets thrown down by the TV.

His mother was in the kitchen cooking. She was chopping onions far too quickly. I tried to use that as a clue. She wasn't happy. I shivered. Was he in danger? I touched his mother (always risky to touch those not scheduled to have an angelic visit) to see what she knew. But she didn't know where he was.

Had the Crow shot him? Was he lying dead? I searched in my memory for the Manifest. No death today with his name on it. Should I be relieved? But would it appear on the Manifest? After all as far as Heaven knew, Marcus was already dead. My head suddenly started to throb.

*Had he gone to see Candy?*

He'd said she was 'something'. What madness if he had! There'd been a card from her at the hospital. I'd seen it. I searched my memory – had it contained an address? Was he with her? The card had been covered in kisses.

I whirled through the flat looking for Candy's address. I stormed through the kitchen. I blasted through the tiny congested hall and tore like a hurricane everywhere else.

His mother drew the windows tight, checked they were locked. I lasered through papers, letters, mail, magazines. Nothing. Nothing. Nothing.

I raised my head and threw back my chin, and called his name in a voice that would have woken the dead. But there was no reply, only his mother dialling up a friend, saying she felt spooked, saying she could hear the wind whistling down the Heights.

I left. I tore down to the street. I couldn't believe what I was doing. I swirled through gardens, through parking lots. There was ice in my eyes. There was something hurting my throat. *Where was he? Where had he gone?* I sank to the pavement. I pressed my ears to the concrete slabs. I listened through a million hurried steps, searching for his.

*And at last I found them!* Light, slow steps as if he was in pain. I drew in a long, deep breath. He'd been here. He'd been here recently. He wasn't well. I could feel it in his tread. Now I could follow him – as long as he was walking – as long as he didn't take a bus, or get in a car. Please God, let him not disappear again.

I must stay calm. His footsteps were very faint. I must focus. I'd read his intent. I'd conjure it out of the very earth.

I must listen to see if he took anything from his pocket, used a bus pass, or if he opened his cell to call a friend. I found his next step and I pressed my hand against it. I listened. In between the beats, in between the silences. I heard his intention.

He hadn't spoken on his cell. He hadn't thought of a bus or taxi. He hadn't slowed, nor stopped. He knew where he was going. A little relieved, I followed.

Step after step, I traced him. At the corner, at the end of the street, he took a left. I swung a left. Halfway along the street he crossed the road. I crossed it too.

He stopped. I stopped. He stood there for a full five minutes. Why? In front of me was a flower shop, its windows brimming with bouquets: roses, carnations, rich red peonies.

He'd stopped to buy flowers.

I stepped into the shop determined to fathom this new mystery. Flowers? Had he come to buy flowers for his mother? If not, who? I stopped. I couldn't help myself, I sank to my knees. *Please God, not Candy.*

If he'd bought flowers for Candy, if he loved her – what was I to do? I suppose I'd hoped somehow – in some way – he might have loved me, or grown to love me. If he'd loved me he might have changed, repented freely, willingly, with a whole heart, for my sake. With love on our side we could have done it – we could have faced his responsibilities together – found ways to help those who depended on him. I'd have stopped time. Read lottery numbers. Made cards fall. Fixed races. Thrown dice.

167

But if he loved her, it was hopeless. He might 'try' to repent because he 'owed me' but it would not be from his heart, nor of his own Free Will. I'd fail. He'd burn for eternity. And I'd have to tell St Peter.

I'd risked everything for him. I'd be handed over to God's Army, have to appear at the Day of Judgement Courts. I'd have no soul to show, no reason to explain my actions, only broken rules and bad judgement.

No Joey. No soul. No Marcus.

I'd be vaporised.

I couldn't bear it. Not because I feared God's Army. They could do their worst. I unfolded my wings in defiance. Damn You! *'Do your worst!'* I yelled. The flowers swayed, a leaf detached itself from its garland and tornadoed across the shop. And not because I dreaded failure. I'd rather fail a thousand times – in the eyes of everyone – than see Marcus brought to Hell.

I couldn't bear it. How he'd suffer.

I rose from the floor and swept the freesias and petunias aside. I would not let this happen. Even if he loved another, I could bear it. I'd still save him. Even if I could not bear it, I must bear it.

For I loved him.

It was the first time I'd admitted it to myself. And it felt like a blow struck hard against my chest. *I loved him.* This was the feeling that drove men to murder and women to despair. I must not despair. I repeated the words directed by God to be written in his Holy Book:

*'Love is patient, love is kind. It does not envy . . . it is not self-seeking, it is not easily angered . . . it keeps no record of*

*wrongs . . . It always protects, always trusts, always hopes, always perseveres.'*

My love for Marcus must be just as pure.

So I rose up from the mess of petals on the flower-shop floor and bowed my head under its new burden. I closed my eyes in acceptance of my new understanding of love and felt humbled. I loved Marcus. I loved him so much I wasn't going to let anything stop me – even if he loved another.

I left the shop and followed his steps. The ice in my eyes hurt. The beating of my heart was overshadowed only by the nervous fluttering of my wings.

It's better, I told myself, that he should have a human love. Easier. A love between an angel and a mortal could come to no good. If the girl was sweet and ready to die for him, had led a good life and wasn't bound for Hell, then he might repent for her sake. And I would try my best to help him.

And then, when I was sure he had repented, I'd deliver sweet death to both of them, at the same moment, in the same way. I could make their deaths glorious and beautiful – perhaps they could die together drowning in a great flood or like Romeo and Juliet for the love of one another.

Marcus didn't take the bus. Instead he walked along the riverbank. He didn't seem to be in a hurry, but he kept a steady pace nonetheless. He cut through back streets, dodged a huge shopping mall and passed through parkland. It was easier to follow him over grass. He ducked through tangled trees until he came to an opening, a green vista with the view of the city. He stopped there by a pool filled with water lilies and rested on an iron bench. I sat there too, aching at every thought of him. Where was he now? Why had he come here?

*Then I got it!*

He was going back to the club. This was a short cut. I was puzzled. Had he arranged to meet Candy there? Maybe in the upstairs café? In the flick of a feather I was at the door. The instant I was, I knew he was there too.

He was not in the café. He was downstairs in the club. Like an arrow I was inside, through wood and steel, through brick walls. With the speed of light I arrived at the foot of the staircase. Before me stood the great mirror. I twirled in its silvery depths, letting for an instant my fire and beauty invade every atom of the place. That cheered me up. Gave me courage. Then I folded my wings and looked around.

It was just the same as the night of the birthday party. The same black leather sofas, the same upholstered walls. It all still reeked. I caught my breath and remembered how I'd stood there waiting for Marcus's death, how I'd missed the moment, how Larry had saved me, how I'd saved Marcus, how I'd held him in my arms, how he'd looked into my eyes . . .

There is nothing as heartbreaking as memory. When you're all alone, when you've been passed over for another, when you remember that hour when you first met – memories so bittersweet . . .

There was the dance floor; there the tired disco ball, no longer shedding its glittering light; there the bar stools.

There was where Larry had sat, where Larry had talked me through everything. There was where I'd held him. I looked across at the spot.

And there was Marcus.

# Serafina 23

My heart stopped at the sight of him. I stepped back, involuntarily, as if my presence were toxic. I hid in the shadows. I waited.

He was standing still. I sent an eerie show of moonbeams across the walls. Outlining my silhouette. Did he see me? No. He couldn't see me. But like a thief I still stayed hidden.

He sighed. I imagined how eager he was, how anxious for her to come, how he needed to hold her. *Oh, to be held.* I tried to imagine it. Imagine his arms around me, feel his mouth on my neck, feel his lips against my skin.

He sighed again. I longed to jump from my hiding place, to apparition before him, rush to him, fling myself into his arms. Arms that couldn't hold me. Hands that couldn't touch me. But I didn't. It wasn't me he was thinking about. So we waited, the two of us.

It was only when he moved that I noticed exactly where he was standing. He suddenly bent down and lowered himself gingerly to the floor. Then he knelt – almost as if he was going to pray. I stared, hardly believing it. He closed his eyes. His shoulders shook. He seemed smitten by some blow. Was he going to ask forgiveness? Pray for her to come? I held my breath. His head dropped to his chest. His arms hung slack. In his hands the flowers quivered.

I bit my lip. He seemed to be intoning something.

*. . . Yea though I walk through the valley . . .*

A prayer, perhaps?

*. . . of the shadow . . .*

No, not intoning: singing. I strained to catch the words.

*. . . of death . . .*

There on the disco floor, Marcus laid a wreath, a simple circle of white lilies, of red roses.

Right on the spot where Joey died.


How could I have imagined he was meeting another? Oh, faithless Seraph: miserable, culpable, guilty, ignominious angel. He hadn't come here to meet anyone. He wasn't up to anything. How full of distrust, suspicion, doubt: I wasn't fit to be a celestial being. I closed my eyes. I asked for forgiveness. I asked for faith. Recklessly I sent my prayer straight up to Heaven.

But I didn't move from my hiding spot. I didn't apparition. I couldn't. It wasn't because I wanted to snoop or anything. It wasn't because I even wanted to be near him. No, I had no right to hide and spy on his private grief. But I didn't want to interrupt it, either.

And I had to talk to him.

*Oh, Marcus, from the moment I met you I was trapped.*

After a while Marcus stood up. I'd wait until he was composed, then I'd leave my alcove and appear before him, tell him the truth about Joey, why he died, how he died,

173

how he owed Joey everything: the morning, the breeze on his cheek, the afternoon to come, the days he had left. I'd brave his fury. If he blamed me I'd ask his forgiveness. That's all.

Marcus drew a red rose from the wreath and, crossing over the disco floor, held it aloft, and said: 'To my angel. This is for saving me.'

*To my angel!*

I watched, held my breath. He kissed the rose, right on the spot where I'd first held him.

*He kissed the rose!*

'I wish you were real,' he said.

He stood looking at the rose. Should I reveal myself *now?* I held my breath, wondering where to apparition. How beautiful it would be to appear right before him and accept the rose . . .

But just as I prepared to do so, it seemed a vision appeared right before *me*, exactly as it had at Devil's Pass. I saw myself as a young girl, thin and trembling, with angel wings coated in blood, lying there, bleeding to death, right on the spot where Marcus had fallen.

And whilst I stood there dazed, trying to understand, I heard Marcus sigh. He crossed to a leather couch on the far side of the room and sat down. And holding the rose quite steady, he tore out a petal.

He let the petal tumble to the floor. Then he tore another. Marcus ripped out a third. He let it fall as before. He ripped a fourth, and a fifth and again and again. He tore savagely at the rose until, by his feet, strewn all around him, was a battlefield of red fragments. There they lay like drops of blood staining the floor. The poor rose had only a few petals left, but Marcus was on fire, relentless.

I watched, horrified, mesmerised. I watched until there were no more than two petals on the carcass of the flower. Marcus tore out the last but one. He held it between his fingers as if it were accursed.

Then he let it go. As it floated down to rest with the others, he said something.

I'd been so busy watching, I missed it.

Quickly I listened. When the Seraphim listen they can hear a strand of coral rustle at the bottom of the ocean, they can hear the dew settle on Mars. I pressed my ear against the wall and searched for his words through boards, through tiles, through space and dust, until at last I found something, still hanging unsteadily in the air. It was only one word.

Liar.

Marcus had said, 'Liar.'

That was it.

Marcus looked at the last petal as it trembled there on the stalk. His fingers quivered. He went to pluck it. His lips squeezed up, as if he was going to say something else. Then he flung the stalk with its one remaining petal straight against the mirror. The petal smacked into its reflection, blossomed in mirrored petals, came to a standstill, twisted, twirled and fell.

I shrank back.

Marcus's face grew bleak. He laughed a sudden savage laugh. Then a dark fury seemed to settle over him. I could have apparitioned. I should have. *I'd come all this way to speak to him.* But suddenly I didn't dare. He looked half wild and mad.

And I was afraid.

How could I tell him, now, that I'd killed Joey?

So I turned.

I was a coward.

I left him alone with his lilies and his roses, his memories and his grief.

I left him alone with his fury.

And I fled.

# Serafina 24

I shouldn't have done that. I should've stayed and faced him. How cowardly. *And he thought I was a liar.* I'd blown my one chance to get to Earth. Wasted. And now I was back in Heaven, wearing my identity bracelet, back on curfew, a virtual prisoner and frantic to see him again.

*I wasn't a liar. I'd just not told him everything.*

And going down to Earth was Absolutely Out Of The Question without a proper job spec and probably an armed escort.

Immediately I went to find Raquel to see if I could do a Collection Duty for her, but she had the rest of the week off. I went to the Angel Roster to see if I could swap myself in for something: a prayer meeting, a revelation, even watching over the beds of sick children (which is really heart-rending, but has to be done). Nothing. With all the new rules, the checkpoints, the curfews and curtailments, hardly anyone was going to Earth at all.

There were a few choir duties. I marched straight into the Celestial Job Centre and applied for them – I didn't even feel ashamed about trying to deprive a trainee cherub of a chance to visit the Vatican – *anything* to get down to Earth; but they didn't take me. Perhaps they knew about the ban on undergraduates from the Cloisters, perhaps they'd been given orders not to let me out of Heaven by Jehudiel himself – I no longer cared. I had to get a glimpse of Marcus. I had to explain. I had to reassure myself he was all right. I wasn't a liar. I had to find him.

It was listening to the Prair Waves that afternoon that gave me the idea. I'd been trying to figure out when the next Angelic Host was due to go on tour, hoping it was soon and that I could slip down amongst its ranks. I tuned into a God's Army broadcast by mistake and someone on it was having a rant: '. . . *we must stamp out every trace of sin . . . Heaven has gone slack . . . what we need is another Great Purge . . . venial sin . . . the illegal communication with those on Earth . . . haunting . . . reincarnation . . . those using the Channel . . . clean up the Summerlands . . .'*

Those using the Channel.

The words struck home. *The Saved used the Channel to get down to Earth when they went haunting.* Why not me?

Without a second thought, I put on a cloak and headed for the Summerlands, beyond the Suburbs-of-the-Saved.


Down Shamballa Street in one of the less shabby suburbs of the Summerlands, I found the offices of Lily Rose's Psychic & Astral Travel Agency. Actually it wasn't an office at all. It was the back room of somebody's house, the somebody in question being Madam Lily Rose.

As soon as I saw her name above the door I knew I'd made the right decision. It was a sign. An omen. The same flowers that Marcus had chosen. I shuddered again at the memory of that torn rose.

Madam Lily Rose ushered me into her home and, peering quickly up and down the street to make sure we'd not been seen, slammed the door to behind us and locked it. Five bolts.

'Can't be too careful,' she whispered, 'with bloody thugs out there like Jehudiel.' She shook her head as if she expected far better from an Archangel. 'I had a premonition you were going to be followed. Quick, in there and wait. I'll spread a bit of mystic fog outside. Give me your identity bracelet.' She beckoned me to follow and showed me into a darkened back room. Then she disappeared behind a curtain.

In the centre of the room stood a table. It was covered by a dark red velvet cloth, and on it was a crystal ball. There was a low couch under the window, and the walls on every side were hung with maps. Framed above the fireplace was a huge certificate which read *Psychic & Astral Travel Agents' Guild award this certificate to Lillian Rosemary Higgins.*

Soon Lily Rose reappeared, rubbing her hands and looking satisfied. 'That'll bamboozle him,' she exclaimed triumphantly.

I looked at her, alarmed.

'It's all right. Sit down,' she said and slid out a chair. 'I saw you coming ages ago, and that great fat whip-bearer too. He doesn't know where you are now, though!' She chuckled in a high squeaky tone.

I sat down, suddenly faint.

'It's all sorted,' she said. 'I've got a couple of disembods to go for a walk with your bracelet until further notice.' She chuckled and chuckled. 'He'll have fun following them all afternoon.'

I hoped that was a good idea. I hoped Jehudiel didn't catch them and realise he'd been fooled.

'You can't catch disembods – that's the whole joke of it.' She chuckled as if she'd read my thoughts. She sat down, folded her arms over her ample bosom and looked at me. 'Now, angel, what can I do for you?' she croaked. 'Charms or curses?'

I stared back at her. 'Oh, not curses,' I said.

'Charms, then?' she queried.

'My name is Sera—' I started.

'Oh, no names.' She lit a candle. 'It's better that way.'

'I want to get down to Earth,' I said, 'as soon as possible. Now – if you can arrange it?'

She looked at me, shook her head. 'You're an angel,' she said, 'you don't need me to get down to Earth. You can take the Staircase, the back stairs, the fire escape, plus you've got wings if you really want to do it the hard way. It's only the Saved who use the Channel – for them there are no other routes.'

'I want to use the Channel too,' I said. 'I have my reasons.'

At this she nodded her head. Everybody has their reasons, don't they?

'It'll be expensive,' she said. 'More – now that God's Army have outlawed it.'

'I'll pay,' I said, 'whatever you ask.'

She thought for a moment. 'Cheese,' she said. 'I need cheese.'

I raised my eyebrows.

She laughed. 'Oh, there's a good market up here for cheese. Since that blasted bloody whip-wielding freak banned imports, my customers will pay anything – even for a slice of rat trap.' She shook her head. 'The souls of the Saved like their food, you know. I could do good business with a bit of cheese.'

'But –' I said.

'You just get it. Put it in this bag (she thrust a crumpled bag at me) and leave me and the Channel to do the rest. I'll get it through in an eatable state.'

I blinked. So I was to pay in contraband goods.

'Ever done it before?' she asked, as if she knew I hadn't.

I shook my head.

'Here're the rules then. You leave your body there.' She pointed to a couch nearby. 'You'll fade in and out a bit at first. Head for the colder patches, stand in draughts – it helps stabilise the haunting. If you get too intense your feelings will boil up and you'll overheat. Overheating must be avoided at all costs. You won't be able to communicate. Even angels won't see you. But you can blow the air around. Skilful ghosts can write messages in dust and on windows, direct Ouija boards, slam doors, howl down chimneys.'

I nodded. I had no intention of howling down chimneys, but the tip about staying as cold as possible was useful.

'Nobody will be able to hear you or see you.'

My heart sank. How was I going to explain anything to Marcus if I couldn't talk to him?

'I only do person-haunting,' she said. 'If you want to

181

haunt a building or go on holiday you've come to the wrong travel agency.'

'No,' I said, 'I want to haunt a person.'

'Right, you'll have to go where they go. If you try to stay behind or go elsewhere, you'll feel the Channel tugging you along and it'll be uncomfortable. Bit like diarrhoea,' she whispered. 'You'll have a window of about a quarter of an hour – if you're away from your hauntee longer, you'll ricochet right back to them like a boomerang.'

I blinked. Diarrhoea. How ghastly. Not that I'd ever had it. Angels don't get those kinds of problems.

'You can slip out and get the cheese within fifteen minutes, can't you? Any cold section of a supermarket will have it. The chill will help you stabilise as well.'

I nodded. I supposed I could.

'And you can affect atmosphere. If you want to bring about a change in the fortunes of others, just focus on an image.'

'OK,' I said. Instantly I thought about cheering Marcus up. If I could only make him feel better about Joey.

'Now, have you got an object that belonged to the person you want to haunt? You need that, otherwise I can't direct the Channel.'

My eyes flew wide. She needed something belonging to Marcus? I didn't have anything. Not even a picture.

*I wouldn't be able to go.*

'That'll do,' she said, pointing at my throat.

I looked at her, confused.

'The key.'

*Of course, his key! Thank God I had his key.* How had she known it was *his* key?

'I am a clairvoyant,' she said reproachfully.

I looped the lanyard off my neck and handed her Marcus's key.

'Very good,' she said warmly and, picking up the key, held it firmly between her two hands.

'Yes, yes, excellent,' she commented and directed me to the couch. 'I've got a few other things to do this afternoon, so you'll have to be back by four.'

I nodded and, wondering if she'd prefer Cheddar or Camembert, let her push me gently on to the couch.

Lily Rose sat down at the table and, still holding on to the key, she spun the crystal ball. 'Relax,' she said.

The crystal ball turned. The edges of the velvet tablecloth began to blow. The maps from the walls swirled towards me. Like pages of a book they flicked before my eyes. One map hovered, drew nearer. It was a map of city streets. As it whirled closer I caught sight of the name Curlston Heights. I caught my breath. I tilted forward. I was really doing this. The little square on the map widened. I felt myself leave the couch. *What if something went wrong? Or Jehudiel found out? Or Marcus didn't want to see me ever again?*

I tipped head first through the square, into a long dark tunnel.

Then suddenly, without warning, I seemed to be stuck. I froze, not knowing whether to try and struggle back, or shove myself further in.

Then – *whoosh.*

I pitched forward again. Air dashed against me. I was sucked downwards. There was a stretching, a tugging, a

183

guttering and sinking. A tornado bruised my face. I gulped.

I gasped.

Down I fell.

Down into the Channel.

# Serafina 25

I feel my feet hit ground. I sway and stand. All around me blurred shapes come into focus.

Immediately I know where I am: the CD covers are scattered on the floor, expensive trainers showcased on their shoeboxes, everywhere pictures of girls.

Marcus's bedroom.

'What about Film and Media?' says a voice I don't recognise.

I squint, slitting up my eyes and peering out into the small room through a dim greenish fog.

'Or Music Technology. You like music.' The voice is sweet and musical and female.

'Nah,' says a voice that sets my heart pounding. 'Don't see myself as a technician.'

The fog clears. In front of me – so near I could almost touch him – sits Marcus. He's bending over a keyboard. His eyes are fixed on a computer screen. Thank God he's well. Thank God he's calm. I pray he's forgiven me too.

'I'm sorry,' I say shakily, moving straight to his side. 'You mustn't ever think I'd lie to you –' But the two of them don't look up. I go nearer to the desk. 'Marcus?' I try a burst of sunlight. It doesn't work. He doesn't move. I remember. I'm completely invisible, without powers – just a voyeur.

'What about Sports and Leisure?' says the girl. 'Or personal trainer?' I step round her and look. She's petite, pretty, about sixteen. She has such a smile. She adores Marcus, I can tell. I recognise her from the photos. She's Jasmine, Marcus's younger sister.

'I'm not sure about that.' Marcus peers at the screen. 'Criminology, that looks cool . . .'

Jasmine frowns. 'Are you sure?' she says.

'Why not?' he says. 'Man knows a lot about it, and I told you, man's just looking, so don't get too excited. I promised someone I'd think about making a change.'

'But . . .' she says, '. . . it's really great you're looking at colleges, but –'

'You think I'm too old, too stupid?'

'Oh no, not that.' She strokes his head. 'You're the cleverest, nicest person ever. It's just that in lots of the jobs these courses qualify you for . . .' She hesitates, then says in a low voice, '. . . Marcus, you need a clean police record.'

Marcus throws up his hands. 'So you're saying there's no point in even thinking about fixing up?'

'Well,' said Jasmine thoughtfully, 'I just think you need to go for something where that won't matter.'

'Like?' says Marcus. He types something into the search engine. I try to look over his shoulder, get as close to him as possible. He's very angry about something. I can feel his energy, the way he punches the keys. I hope he's not still angry at me.

'Well,' he says. 'At least I can ask about it, can't I?' He

looks over his shoulder and mutters, 'If you're watching, Angel, know that even though you don't deal straight with me, man's dealing straight with you. I may be a gangsta, but I don't lie.' And he types in 56 Curlston Heights and then his postcode, clicks on *Request A College Prospectus*.

I want to cry out, protest, defend myself – *what else could I have done?* You were so ill. I was so weak.

But I don't, because he's telling the truth.

I was a liar.

I step forward and put my hand on his. I want to make him know I'm sorry.

'You know, Jazz, I think I'd look good with a backpack and glasses and a stripy scarf,' he says suddenly and flashes her a wicked smile.

The fog suddenly swirls back, right at me. I sway. Lose my balance. There is a terrible emptying-out feeling. A tugging at my intestines. I panic. *Find a cold spot!* I'm slipping away. I'm losing the Channel.

Instantly I step through the window, land on the street, press myself against iron railings. The cold metal refreshes. The nausea passes, the swaying steadies a little, but before I can step back into the room another fog rolls over me. I fall headlong into a thick dark cloud. The tug on my stomach is too much.

'You'll have to try a lot harder than that,' said Lily Rose and she pinched me. 'We got a perfectly good frequency and the Channel coverage was strong. You stood far too near the humans. I told you find a cold spot immediately you got down there and stay in it.'

I groaned and clutched my stomach. 'Please let me try again,' I begged.

Lily Rose snorted. 'If you want me to send you again, it'll cost more,' she said. 'I want wine *and* cheese – and I notice you haven't even got the cheese.' She pinched me again in a cross sort of way.

'Alcohol?' I breathed.

'Yes, 12.5%, and none of your grape juice. A nice Pinot Grigio suitable for a summer's evening in a wine bar. Get me that, six bottles, and I'll even give you an extra hour.'

'OK,' I said and, clasping my hands tight over my stomach, prepared myself again for the stretching feeling.

The room is changed, but the fog is just as thick. I hear a voice I don't recognise.

'If you can just relate incidents as they happened, and answer the questions clearly.'

'But officer,' says a voice I know: Jasmine's.

I peer through the mist. It swirls a little. I look around for a cold spot. There by the window.

The room clears. I can see immediately I'm in a police charge office. I recognise it from my course: *Crime & Punishment – Should Earthly Justice Systems Replace the Day of Judgement?*

In front of a wide desk sit Jasmine and Marcus. Behind it sits an officer. I seem to remember him. Yes, the scene at the nightclub.

'But,' carries on Jasmine, 'I'd like to speak on behalf of my brother – unless . . .' She nudges Marcus. 'Go on,' she says.

He shakes his head.

'Well then,' she says, 'I'll say it anyway. You see, officer, last week my brother was shot.' She lays an envelope on the desk. 'In there are the hospital details. We know you interviewed him at the hospital, but there were reasons why he told you he didn't see anything . . . But now Marcus wants to say that he –'

Marcus looked at her and frowns. She carries on. I make sure I'm standing right in the blast of the open window.

'He wants to be a witness, but we need to be sure that we get protection.'

'Well,' says Marcus, pushed into speech. 'It's not for me. My family . . .' He puts his hand on Jasmine. 'My sisters, my mother . . . they shouldn't be put in danger because of me.'

The officer looks up. He says, 'As it's a murder charge, we can arrange to have an officer outside your block.'

'That may not be enough,' says Marcus.

'If we have to rely on your testimony to bring about a successful conviction, we can think about putting you in a witness protection scheme.' He reaches for the phone.

'I can take care of myself,' says Marcus. 'You don't understand these guys; it's my family who need safeguarding.'

'You were shot too,' says the officer, changing the subject, reaching for the envelope, pulling out a hand-held tape recorder. 'Let's go into an interview room.'

They stand up and open the door. A rush of hot air from the corridor blasts in. Immediately the fog thickens, swirls up in front of me. I stagger sideways. Marcus, Jasmine and the officer hurry off into the corridor.

I hang my head out of the window and let the fresh air revive me. By the time I feel strong enough to move, I've lost them.

I try to catch up. By sticking to draughty corners and even gliding up a blocked-in chimney – in an effort to stay cold – I manage to work my way through three offices and two interview rooms.

I don't find Marcus in any of them.

I remember Lily Rose saying: *'If you stray too far from your hauntee, you'll be ricocheted straight back into their company, like a boomerang.'* I start thinking I could go for the wine and cheese and keep on going until the pulling starts and snaps me back to Marcus. I decide I'll do that.

On my way out through the front foyer, I see a figure leaning over the reception counter. Immaculate white suit. Gleaming white teeth.

It must be.

It *is*.

I'm pleased and a bit scared. My heart starts to race. I want to talk to him. I'm resolved to talk to him. I'm going to say: 'Larry, do you work for the Devil?' Well, maybe not exactly that. Maybe more like: 'Larry, you *do* work for God, don't you?' I bite the corner of my lip. It's not going to be so easy. I can't just walk right up to him and say that, can I?

I glide nearer. I'm worried he won't be able to see me. This is when writing in dust might be extremely useful.

I call out anyway. 'Larry?'

He turns. His face lights up. 'Hiya there!' he says. 'You lovely thing!'

I'm relieved and puzzled both at the same time, and still pretty nervous. Lily Rose said, 'Even angels won't see you.' I'm glad he can, though. I must know if my Extension was the cause of the breach. My heart thumps. I'm terrified he'll say, Yes.

Larry nods at me to wait. Then he turns to the policeman on duty. 'There's a young man here called Marcus Montague. I'm with him,' he explains. 'We came together to make a statement; he witnessed a murder. Yes, yes, I'm his sort of social worker – I got him to come. I can corroborate what he says. If you need me to – I can do that now.'

His suit is wrinkle-free. His golden hair flawless. I'm so impressed with his apparition mastery. I'm almost jealous. He does it *so* well you'd think he was actually human.

Suddenly a woman behind me steps completely through me. Clothes, boots, blood and bones. Everything. Straight through my chest and I've no time to get out of the way.

'Ugh,' she says, 'this station's chill-ee. I've gone all shivery It's like someone's stepped right over my grave.'

Believe me, I want to say, that's nothing to the way I feel.

But as I'm trying to get over the shock, she moves straight up to Larry and says: 'So what brings you here? More trouble at the club?'

I'm puzzled. I thought Larry had seen *me*. Maybe it was this woman he saw. It's very confusing. I'm a little disappointed. I'm pleased he's helping Marcus, like I asked him to. But I desperately want to know if I've signed a contract with the Devil or not.

Before I can try and talk to him again, I feel the pulling on my stomach. Marcus has left the building.

I have to go. Lily Rose was right. It's not a nice feeling. My intestines feel like they're dissolving.

I'm out in the street. I'm glad of it. Outside, away from the central heating, I feel much better. I'll have to speak to Larry some other time. Perhaps he wouldn't have heard me anyway. I wonder vaguely why he didn't come with Marcus; why Marcus hasn't greeted him, or arranged to meet him now, after making his statement.

Quickly I look up and down the street. Marcus and Jasmine are already walking away – he's leaning on her. I glide after them. Soon I've caught up. I fall into step along-side. I hear everything.

'That was amazing,' says Jasmine. 'You're so brave.' She ruffles his air. 'I thought you'd never do that. Joey'd be so happy. I know it. He wouldn't want his death to start a gang war.'

'Yeah,' Marcus says, 'but you don't know the Crow. If he finds out man's snaked him up, none of us is safe.'

'We know,' she says, instantly serious. 'We talked it over, Mum and Ray and me. You don't realise, Marcus, how much we want you to get out of this gang thing. We really, *really* want it.' Her voice drops, cracks a little. 'You don't know the hell we've been through with you getting shot.'

'It's not fair, though. And it's man's fault.'

'But we love you,' says Jasmine simply, 'so we're gonna stick together, and anyway, I'd like to see any gangsta try and get into Curlston Heights. Mum knows better than to buzz strangers through when she's alone.'

Marcus lifts his head. 'Oh, Jazz,' he says. 'It's not an

excuse, but I only ever started all this to try and help. You know when Mum . . . and the job.'

'We know.'

'And because man can't stand seeing the Crow doing all that shit.'

'Exactly,' says Jazz, 'so you did the right thing just now. You actually put the finger on the Crow, named him as Joey's killer – nobody's ever dared do that before. Look, I think that's so amazing, I'll buy you a drink – even if they won't allow me in the bar.'

'Nah,' he says, 'I don't fancy a drink right now. But if you're loaded, we could grab a couple of Cokes and a burger?'

They turn into a burger place. I stay outside. It'll be too hot in there. But oh, how happy I am. Marcus is changing. I look fondly after him, his dark hair, his broad shoulders then I hurry to a One Stop Shop. I collect a selection of cheeses and six bottles of wine. I put them in the bag Lily Rose gave me and am surprised how a fog quickly gathers around it and it's tugged off at speed.

I smile. Lily Rose has got it all worked out. I bet she's right about shifting things too. 'You can blow the air around,' she said. 'Skilful ghosts can write messages in dust, direct Ouija boards, slam doors, howl down chimneys.' Who knows, I might try howling down a chimney after all.

I start with trying to blow a paper napkin that someone's dropped. Nothing happens. 'Blow the air,' she said. I focus all my energy on moving the air rather than my chest. I find I can get the edges of the paper to twitch a bit.

It suddenly occurs to me that if I direct the air *under* the tissue, rather than at it, I'll have more success. So as I wait for Marcus and Jasmine, I practise. By the time they come out of the diner, I've shuffled the paper right down the street and back.

I try lifting the edge of Marcus's jacket. 'Bit windy out here,' he comments. He hugs the jacket close. I smile. I've cracked it.

Learning how to blow objects around isn't the only thing I've cracked. While I was practising on the tissue paper down the street, I hatched a wild plan. I saw a church and I checked it out: St Jude of the Lake. (Dear St Jude. I know him well – Patron Saint of Desperate Causes and Hopeless Cases.) I cross my fingers and pray my plan will work. I send up a plea. *St Jude, please help us, no one more desperate than I, no cause more doomed.* Then I catch myself. No prayers. No Prair Waves. If Jehudiel is after me, he mustn't know I'm here.

I fall into place alongside Marcus and start to perfect my idea.

*'You can affect atmosphere,'* I remember Lily Rose saying. *'If you want to bring about a change in the fortunes of others, just focus on an image.'* I need to get Marcus in the right mood. So I pour forth the most generous, peaceful thoughts I've ever had. I remember the glory of the sunrise in Heaven, with choirs of cherubim praising God on high as the sun breaks over the horizon in a fiery ball.

'I feel good, Jazz . . .' says Marcus suddenly. 'You know, I reckon it isn't so impossible to change. She was right, you know . . . she probably was.'

Jasmine smiles and looks quizzically up at him.

'Don't laugh,' says Marcus, 'but I think I've got a guardian angel.' He leans forward and whispers conspiratorially, 'I think she's right here, watching over us, right now.'

'Oh Marcus,' says Jasmine, 'I hope you have; you deserve one.'

'She saved my life, Jazz. She visited me in the hospital, she told me to change; you-know-what-I'm-talking-about.'

'Good for her,' Jasmine laughs. 'I suppose next you'll be telling me she's pretty too.'

'Woo,' says Marcus, 'she's more beautiful than –' he looks up, throws his arms in the air, 'than the morning stars.' He pauses.

Suddenly his face falls.

I pause too.

'But she's tricky,' he says. All happiness drains from his voice. 'She doesn't tell it like it is.'

I wince. The rising sun bobs down and drowns in water.

'I hate that,' he says moodily. 'In my world you shoot it straight. Man hates a liar worse than anything.'

'You're crazy,' says his sister affectionately.

*I don't tell it like it is.*

'Maybe,' says Marcus. 'But she saved man's life and man promised her he'd give it a go – gangsta's honour – so it's back to college one of these days, and who knows, maybe not so much hanging with the crew, either.'

He flashes her a thoughtful smile.

'And no more shootings. I'm definitely gonna do the family ting from now on.' He puts his arm through hers. 'What do you say, sis?' His crooked smile stretches over his straight teeth.

I swallow my hurt. One day I'll explain. Now for my plan. *He's ready to give it a go.* I race ahead.

I stand outside the church and blow. Lily Rose said ghosts can *'slam doors'*. I heave my chest and blow as hard as I can. If you can slam a door, it means you can open it too. Doesn't it?

At first nothing happens. I try again. The door is slightly ajar. It rattles a little. I remember the trick with the paper napkin. I blow hard at the crack under the door and I'm a lot more successful. The door rattles and shifts. The dark wood heaves, its blackened brass fixings shudder. It starts to swing on its frame. But there are heavy counter-lever chains on the inside that make the doors swing shut. Against the pull of these weighted chains I set my breath.

And I blow.

Marcus and Jasmine stroll nearer. Jasmine crosses to the railings, on the street, by the church, to put her Coke container in a rubbish bin. I blow at the door with all my breath, all my hope, my entire being.

The door creaks. Slowly it opens. I hold it so with a gale straight from my heart. Then with a sudden puff, I blow the paper Coke cup out of Jasmine's hand and send it bowling towards the church.

Marcus brings his head up, his beautiful eyes flick wide. 'It's a sign,' he whispers. 'I walk beside a church . . . the door opens . . . it's like she's showing me the way. Man, this is freaky.'

Jasmine stops and stares. She points at the cup rolling in through the old oak doors. She walks into the vestibule of the church, picks it up and gazes at the chain that strains open against gravity.

'Angel,' calls Marcus softly. 'Ang-*el?*'

'This is weird,' says Jasmine.

Marcus follows her, steps forward, stands on the threshold of the church, raises his head. 'Hey, Ang-el,' he calls, '. . . are you there . . . can you hear me? Is this what you want?'

With my last ounce of energy I conjure up an image of the Pearly Gates opening for him. Heaven waiting behind. Blue skies. Happy days.

Marcus steps forward. 'OK,' he whispers, 'this is totally unreal, but I've got a good feeling about it. And if you're listening, Angel – this is for Joey. Nobody in my crew needs to die because of me. Man's done with all that. You-get-me?'

'Silly,' says Jasmine. 'You're talking to yourself.'

'Maybe I am,' says Marcus, and puts his arm over her shoulder. 'Here, let me lean on you, sis, while we pay God a visit, eh?'

'Yes,' breathes Jasmine. She hurries back to help him. 'But Marcus, it's a church – you need to be a bit serious, you know.'

'This is way beyond serious,' he says, 'this is in the realm of the bizarre. Imagine. Me In A Church.'

The strain of keeping the door open is telling on me. A thin mist is beginning to hover around the edges of things. A fog swirls up.

At last Marcus steps right in. Only just in time. With a huge convulsion I stop blowing the wind and sink on to the pavement. The church door slams to behind them.

Lord be praised. Marcus is in a church.

And I've helped to bring him there.

# Serafina 26

Thank God churches are cool places. The effort of holding the door open is too much. The sucking feeling on my stomach returns. The fog swirls up to meet me. In a last effort to stay near Marcus, I hurry through stone walls. I press myself against the cold marble of the font. I splash Holy water over my face.

I can tell you one thing, Holy water is miraculously refreshing. Instantly my vision clears. The inside of the church is as sharp and crisp and in focus as a spring day in Heaven.

Quickly I glide down the nave. Marcus and Jasmine are standing before the chancel, looking up at the altar.

I want to let him know I'm here. That I'm happy. That I know he can repent. That I've seen that he's keeping his word.

I blow at the huge white candles on the altar. They gutter and waver. I whirl around the church. I blow on all the little candles that burn by statues, by shrines, by the door. The church quivers in flickering light. I blow on the flowers in their stately vases and petals swirl in the air. I race up the tower over the north transept and blow on the big bell. It rocks. I blow harder. A solemn peal resounds. I whirl back to Marcus.

Jasmine is looking at him, clutching his arm.

'It's her,' he whispers. 'She's here. She likes flashy stuff like that.' He squeezes her hand.

I smile. I laugh even. Already Marcus knows me so well. He'll forgive me everything when he knows the truth. I conjure up an image of Marcus nodding his head, understanding why I lied.

Jasmine walks over to a stand where the candles are still guttering and stares at them in wonder.

I can't resist it. I glide up the nave. I stand beside Marcus. I stand in front of the altar. I blow on all the petals again. They swirl above me. I imagine the air filled with confetti. I lift the white lacy veil that covers my face. I whisper, '*I do.*' I turn to Marcus. I lift up my chin.

He turns. He bends towards me. I raise my lips.

The sun pours in through the stained glass. It lights us up and pools at our feet.

Our lips touch.

I gasp.

The fog swirls up.

I race to the font. Am I insane? I splash my face like crazy. I nearly spoiled it. Whatever possessed me? He's here to repent.

Instantly I run down the front of a pew beside him, exhaling in one long breath. I flip open all the prayer books. As the pages flutter, Jasmine lets out a startled: 'Oh.'

Marcus, smiling with angel dust in his eyes, forgiveness in his heart, picks up the prayer book beside him and murmurs out in a whisper, 'Jazz, see where the pages have opened to.'

He starts reading. '*Forgive me my trespass, for I have sinned . . .*' He stops, looks up at the stained-glass window overshadowing the chancel. There in the glass is an angel. She is as beautiful as me. Golden light flashes through her. She raises an arm in blessing.

Marcus falters, stops reading, seems mesmerised by the glittering angel.

'It's for confession,' whispers Jasmine.

'It's so surreal,' he says.

From across the other side of the nave, a man emerges. From the expression on his face, so full of peace and goodness, I can tell he's a holy man. He walks evenly towards us and, smiling down at Marcus and Jasmine, he stops and greets them. Then he lifts up his head and beams straight at me, as if he can see me as clearly as the glass angel.

'So calm in here, isn't it?' he says. 'Such a refuge from the world outside.'

Marcus nods. 'It's a different world,' he says.

Jasmine moves closer, smiling.

'How do I repent?' says Marcus suddenly. 'Can you help me? I've never tried.'

'You can pray for forgiveness directly to God,' says the man, 'or if you prefer you can confess to a spiritual guide who will, in the name of Christ, forgive you and advise you how you might make amends.'

'I've been in a shooting . . . there's things I've done that might have caused that. My friend died. I didn't kill him – but I'm to blame.' Marcus hesitates. 'I don't know if . . .'

Instantly I jump to his shoulder and I lay a ghostly hand on his arm. I think of tired creatures laying down their heavy loads – of plunging themselves into the clear waters of the River Jordan and arising born again, free from sin.

'Yes,' says Marcus, 'I want to unburden myself. I want to – can I confess to you?'

'I am only a lowly servant of the Lord,' says the man. 'My name is Christopher. But I will hear your sorrows, and bless you, and can absolve you of your sins, if you so wish.'

'Go on,' urges Jasmine. 'You've been so sad and down since Joey died. It may help. It wasn't your fault – if you confess and do what this man says, you'll feel so much better.'

Marcus stands up and smiles at his sister. He turns towards the stained-glass window with the picture of the bright angel. He murmurs, 'You know I'm doing this for you, Angel.'

I smile and blow on the pages of the book in his hand until it opens on Luke 15:10.

*'And likewise I say unto you there is joy in the presence of the angels over one sinner that repenteth.'*

Marcus smiles. His mind seems made up. I dare to smile too.

*We are so nearly there.*

Christopher leads Marcus aside. They sit apart by a statue of Our Lord Jesus with a little screen protecting them from any stray eyes. I hear Marcus start: 'Listen, Christopher, I confess . . .'

I hold my breath. I imagine the light of the Lord streaming in through the stained glass. The angel is alive in colour, with burnished fiery wings, radiant as a thousand suns.

A mobile phone buzzes.

*Marcus's mobile phone.* I want to jump forward, knock it from his hand, scream in a voice that would make the mountains tremble: 'LEAVE IT!' But even though I jump, I cannot touch the phone. I blow. I breathe. I wish. But Marcus stops murmuring his confession. He looks at Christopher. He raises his head.

Christopher nods. 'Answer your phone,' he says. 'Be composed in your mind.'

Marcus raises the phone to his ear.

*Nothing can be important enough to stop for,* I want to scream at him. I do scream at him. He doesn't hear.

'Hello?'

Let it be a wrong number, a simple request. I tune in my hearing. I listen. 'Marcus?' Someone is sobbing at the end of the phone.

*'Marcus?'* They can't get their words out.

Marcus waits patiently. He whispers, 'Sorry,' to Christopher.

'When you're ready,' Christopher murmurs back.

*'They've shot Melly,'* sobs the voice. It catches. It whispers. It breaks.

'Sharissa?'

'They're here,' sobs the voice. *'They've got me and Lil Joe.'* Her voice is bleeding like a knife wound.

Jasmine jumps forward, hurries to Marcus's side. 'What is it?' she says.

Marcus holds the phone against his chest. 'It's Sharissa.'

'Sharissa?'

'Joey's girlfriend's little sister.'

Jasmine's eyes widen. 'What's wrong?'

'She says someone's shot Melly, Joey's girlfriend . . .'

Marcus returns the phone to his ear. 'Shariss,' he says, 'Calm down, take a deep breath. I'm gonna help you. I need to know everything.'

There's a spluttering and sobbing. *'The Crow's crew are here. They shot Melly.'* The voice rises to a scream. *'They've got Lil Joe and me. It was my fault. I opened the door –'*

The scream ends abruptly. A new voice on the phone shouts: *'Listen, wasteman, we've got the kids. We've popped the bitch. You withdraw your statement or I swear down we'll waste them too. We're not fucking about. You've got twenty minutes. Your sister's next.'*

Marcus looks up at Jasmine. She looks down at him.

His face changes, grows grey, hardens.

*'Please, Uncle Marcus,'* screams Sharissa's voice again. *'Please . . . '* Her voice is so shrill I think even Christopher can hear it.

Marcus takes one look at him. 'I'm sorry,' he says. 'I can't confess anything no more.' He turns back. 'Stay calm, Shariss,' he says. 'I'll withdraw my statement. Do what they say.'

'OK,' she sobs.

Marcus raises himself up out of the confessional box. I see a mask of control slip across his face. 'I'm sorry,' he says again. 'I wanted to make a clean breast of everything. I wanted to give myself a fresh start.'

'May God go with you, my son; return here when you're ready. The confessional is sacred. I will not reveal anything you tell me or break confidence with you.'

'Yeah,' mutters Marcus. 'Yeah, cool.'

'But do not perjure yourself before the police,' advises the priest. 'Speak your truth plainly and leave everything in the hands of God. He will take care of it.'

'*Yes.*' I want to add my voice to his, scream out. '*I have heard. I will help. I will move Heaven and Earth to help.*'

'Yeah, yeah, yeah,' sighs Marcus. 'You know. I once thought I saw an angel and she said something like that – she said my friend had *been taken very good care of.* The image of Marcus covered in angel dust, nodding his head, understanding everything, forgiving me my trespass explodes.

I cringe. I falter. I remember the torn rose. The fog swirls up.

'C'mon, sis.' Marcus grabs Jasmine's arm. 'This is what I knew would happen. Someone else shot. It's all my fault.' He hurries her down the aisle out of the nave into the vestibule. 'I might as well have pulled the trigger myself.' His voice breaks '*Oh God, Joey . . . I'm so sorry . . .*'

'Marcus,' sobs Jasmine. 'Sharissa'll be so scared . . . she's only eleven . . .'

'There's no way out. No fresh starts,' says Marcus bitterly. 'No guardian angels.'

I hold on to the font. Splash myself anew with Holy water.

'The police can't protect us. There's only one way to settle this. Man'll do as they say, but after . . .' He crashes out through the huge wooden swing doors into the bright autumn sunshine.

The church, pews, pillars and windows swirl around me. I must follow. The tugging at my stomach starts. Outside is so hot. What did Lily Rose say – that if you can't go somewhere, hang on until the last minute, and the pull will tug you to the next place. I hang on. Literally. I get hold of a stone gargoyle carved into the base of the font. Its leering face like a demon's own seems to smile triumphantly into mine. Its white marble teeth gleam.

I can withstand the tug no longer. I reach out. I blow out my raiment; a flyer from the church is trapped in its folds. I let go of the gargoyle and, like a rubber band released from its stretching, I zip through air, stone, glass and concrete and with a ping find myself back in the police station, back in the charge office.

The police do not look happy.

'Step in here,' says the charge officer with a voice that could crack cement.

Marcus is led on his own into an interview room. The officer steps in front of Jasmine in a none-too-friendly way. He motions her to go and remain in the waiting area. I glide through into the interview room. Thank God it's cool inside.

Marcus sits on a metal chair. His head between his hands.

'You are being charged under Section 5(2) of the Criminal Law Act 1967 with causing wasteful employment of police time by knowingly making a false report which shows that a criminal offence has been committed, creates apprehension for the safety of any persons or property, or indicates that you have information material to any police inquiry. The offence carries a maximum penalty of six months' imprisonment and/or a fine. I shall now read you your rights . . .'

Marcus nods; a vein in his temple throbs. His fists are balled tight. 'I'm sorry, officer,' he says. 'Please read me my rights, and I'd like to call a friend to see if they can bail me – if I can. There's things going on I need to see to.'

'Got somewhere more important to be?' mocks the police officer.

The scene whirls.

Something snaps at me. What's this? I'm cool. I'm not too near Marcus.

A dark tunnel opens up. I feel the all-too-familiar tugging again. What's wrong? I must know how this ends. I can't leave Marcus alone, shamed, trying to save Sharissa, regretting his decision to change, *in a prison cell*. I can't leave him still angry at me. I can't leave him just when . . . just when I . . . A sudden realisation begins to dawn.

*I just can't leave him.*

That's the problem. And I remember Lily's warnings: '*If you get too intense your feelings will boil up and you'll overheat.*'

I take a deep breath. *Oh Marcus*. I push away my feelings. I must.

The tugging lessens. The scene clears.

Time has shifted.

I am outside the police station. There is Marcus. Thank God he's free. Jasmine is crying. There are four young men with him. They all look the spitting image of Joey. I think they must be his brothers. One of them is venting.

'Man's not happy about this y'know, Big M. You think grassing on Crow dem gonna do the business? Man coulda told you he's too big to take down like that! Now look what you've done. Melly shot an' all and those two kids fucking freaked out. And the law's got a charge on you. There's only one way to settle that creep and when we've put Joey to rest, man dem gonna pop him like a birthday balloon. You get me?'

'Yeah, I get you,' says Marcus, 'an' I ain't gonna offer up no excuses. I was doing my own little thing there, trying to straighten up. But I hear what you're saying, Spider. Thanks for bailing me out. Man owes you big time for that.'

'We could get you legal aid. Claim you were threatened?' squeaks Jasmine.

'Please, Jazz,' silences Marcus.

'Cool,' says the other. 'We's a team; we're there for you, Big M, you know that – and we know you taking it personal about Crow dem. We know Joey was your main man, we know Crow popped you one – so we're safe.'

'Did you get to Melly's yard? In time?' asks Marcus.

'Yeah, we chased them off, but it ain't looking good for Melly. She bled out on the kitchen floor. They took her to hospital, but you know. We got her junior and Joey's kid with us now. We told the po, they can't answer no questions now. They don't know nothing. Nobody knows nothing and we keep it that way till we fix Crow ourselves.'

'Thanks,' said Marcus and hung his head.

'You're up for that, innit?'

'Man needs to think,' says Marcus slowly.

'You watch your back then,' says the other. 'Crow gonna feel he whupped you this time, so he might get cocky and try to take you an' yours out next.'

'Yeah,' says Marcus. 'I know.'

They walk off down the street.

I follow. The fog is seeping back

I manage to blow the church flyer on to Jasmine's hand. She catches it as it flutters past. She scans it, smiles briefly, hands it to Marcus, saying, 'Look what the wind blew at me – so strange.'

Jasmine hands him the flyer.

He looks at it, shrugs and screws it up. He tosses it in the gutter. 'Where are you now, Guardian Angel?' he mutters. 'Still out there rearranging the truth?'

The fog closes in; I feel myself falling. With a crash, I land spreadeagled on the couch in Lily Rose's parlour.

The Channel snaps out.

And I'm back.

# Serafina 27

I was confused. I needed space to try and think. He'd been so near. It wasn't his fault. It wasn't fair. He didn't have Free Will at all – did he?

*It was all a myth. God's great creation, mankind, weren't free at all.*

I had to ask someone. Was the very principle salvation was built on a lie? The thought made me faint. I needed to talk to Kamuel. I knew he went walking at daybreak.

So I got up early the next morning and lay in wait.

Kamuel was as tall and elegant as ever, as kind and good-tempered, as sad and thoughtful. He didn't mention our last meeting. We might have strolled for the entire day and never referred to Vincent or Falling, let alone Free Will.

So I stopped and asked him

'Kamuel,' I said, 'you're so wise and well versed in everything.' That's the appropriate way to address an Archangel (they are such sticklers for etiquette). 'I believe you may even have been there when God first created Earth.'

'Yes,' he said simply, 'I was.'

I noticed he was looking at me with large melancholic

eyes. We reached a brook. We entered under the shade of swaying willows.

'Why,' I asked, 'did God create the world?'

We sat down on a fallen trunk and watched the brook rushing past.

'He wanted to do something beautiful to console himself,' Kamuel said. 'It saddened him when Lucifer fell. They were like brothers. From morning till night they talked.'

'Argued?' I said.

'Yes, argued.'

'About what?' I asked.

'Free Will, mostly,' said Kamuel.

*I knew it.* This was the root of the problem. But all I said was: 'It puzzles me too.' And then I added, 'It seems to me that Free Will is just a nice idea that doesn't really work.' I waited.

He said nothing.

So I continued. 'What exactly is it, even?'

'Free Will means allowing another to do what they want, in the way they want, when they want. That's the short version, anyway.'

'But you can't really have Free Will if every decision you make affects someone else badly, can you?' I said. 'Isn't it just a choice of the lesser evil?'

Kamuel looked at me thoughtfully. 'You have hit upon the nub of the problem.'

'And,' I added, 'I don't think it's fair to judge someone if they haven't really got Free Will – if they just decide to choose the lesser evil and not what they really want to do.'

Kamuel didn't laugh. 'Be guarded in what you say,' he

whispered. 'Make sure God's Army do not hear you.' Hurriedly he looked over his shoulder. 'Their first premise is that everyone is responsible for their own actions – their own destiny, their own suffering.'

I opened my eyes wide. Kamuel pointed at my bracelet. I nodded. I understood.

'If everyone has Free Will, why did God make all the Rules?' I asked in a low voice.

Kamuel laughed in a deep, soft way. 'How exactly you have hit upon the other problem,' he whispered.

'Lucifer didn't like the Rules, did he?' I mouthed.

'Ah,' he returned thoughtfully, his sad eyes fixed on mine, as if he could see into my future. 'But there have to be Rules. What if an action you take hurts another? Should God set no limits?'

I thought about limits and rules, and how once rules are made there are consequences, and when the rules get broken and the consequences are unpleasant – Free Will, if it ever existed, ends and punishments begin.

I pulled a face.

'Look, let's backtrack,' he said. 'What about responsibility?'

I felt uncomfortable under his scrutiny, so I stood up and picked a pebble up to throw it into the stream.

'Of course everyone has to be responsible,' I said.

I threw the pebble into the water. It made a very satisfying splosh. But I saw how it created waves and the waves were beyond my control. What if one of them should flood a tiny creature and drown it? Would that be my fault?

And I thought of intention. How Marcus had intended to do the right thing. *Had* done the right thing by reporting the Crow. *Hadn't* broken any rules. But he hadn't foreseen the consequences, either. Was he to be held responsible for things that might or might not happen? Was Melly's death his fault?

And what was he supposed to do after he got Sharissa's call? Obey the rules, and risk her death too? Or break them and be damned?

Lucifer was right – there was definitely something wrong with rules.

'If we don't have rules,' said Kamuel, reading my mind, 'how can we be sure that where one person's Free Will ends, another's is not compromised?'

I sat down again. Well, exactly! Marcus was compromised by the Crow. But did that mean he should do nothing about it?

'The only way we can have Free Will is to have rules,' he said. 'If you want to break the rules, you can. But when the consequences descend, don't complain.'

'I see,' I said. But I wasn't happy. Kamuel seemed to be saying that Marcus should have done nothing to save Sharissa and Little Joe – should have left it in the hands of God – and should *do* nothing to stop the Crow – when it was obvious the police couldn't. That he should just take care of his own salvation and own skin and stick to the rules. That somehow the Crow would get his comeuppance – and to Hell with Sharissa and everyone else.

All my fire rose up at the idea.

*And I'm glad you didn't, Marcus. I'm so glad you obeyed a higher instinct. And I love you all the more for daring to disobey God's petty rules even in peril of your soul.*

Kamuel put out a hand as if he wanted to stem my thoughts.

*And God, shame on you, for you would have done nothing to help Sharissa. You would have sat back and let the Crow enjoy his 'Free Will', wouldn't you?*

'Choice *is* Free Will,' said Kamuel carefully.

There was something in his tone. As if he understood only too well what I was thinking. And I wondered, had he been there when those two great powers disagreed? And if so, which side had he erred on?

I sighed. 'So if there really is Free Will then there's no Divine Fate?' I said. No omens. No signs. No destinies. No soulmates. I frowned. 'Is the future not written in the unchanging Book of Days? Doesn't God know everything?'

Kamuel laughed. 'So now you want to discuss Fate and Omnipotence?' he said.

*But if He did know everything, how could He just let some of it happen?*

'Have a care, for it was into that abyss Lucifer strayed.'

Was thinking so dangerous?

'One day you will understand,' he said.

How very like an Archangel to be so mysterious.

'Understand Fate?' I said.

'Of course,' he laughed.

'If it's a safe subject,' I said bitterly.

'And Love.'

I was sure that wasn't safe.

'Nothing's safe,' he said.

'Nothing?'

'Not when it comes to tasting fruit from the Tree of Knowledge.'

# Serafina 28

The 26th October was past. There were barely four days left until Halloween. And I had to see Marcus.

Properly. Not as a ghost via the Channel. But so that I could talk to him, in full apparition.

I could have staked out Curlston Heights, hoping to meet him there, but it was risky. I might only get one shot at another trip, and I needed to be certain I'd find him.

There was only one place where I could be a hundred per cent sure I would.

Joey's funeral.

The only problem was I didn't know when and where it would be. So I set myself the task of finding out. I searched the Prair Waves. I listened in to all the obituaries, paid attention to Bible readings, confessions and church schedules. And my diligence was rewarded.

Strangely enough, it was on a funeral home channel that I didn't even know we could tune in to. I heard his funeral referred to three times by two different undertakers. Joseph Biggs, Saturday 29th October. 11.30 a.m. St Rita's Crematorium, full cavalcade, brothers as coffin bearers, wreaths and special requests, polished brass handles, embossed A5 six-page programme: prayers, hymns, tributes, service led by family friend Marcus Montague. Arrangements, Gurn & Soley; hearse and limousines, Murdly & Seagrief.

He'd be there. And so would I. By hook or by crook.

It was by crook. I left my curfew bracelet in my cell, sneaked out over the cloister wall and took the fire escape out of Heaven. I slid through the Pearly Gates in the shadows and hid beneath a borrowed cloak of woven mistiness.

I didn't have a job spec from the Senior Team and using the spare pass was totally risky. I was bound to be missed, but I just *couldn't* use the Channel again.

When St Peter saw me he scowled and wagged his finger and would have detained me. But since there'd been no further offensive on the part of Satan, things were a tiny bit calmer. So I smiled briefly, flashed Raquel's spare pass and said, 'Left a prayer unspoken at a bedside,' very quickly, and raced through before he could stroke his beard over it.

It was a hopeless lie. And I realised if I was going to keep breaking rules, I needed to get a lot better at lying. I pulled a sad smile at that, and thought of Marcus. He was right, you know. I really was a liar.

So step by step, shadow by shadow, lie by lie, I came down to the cemetery, and to the cremation of Joseph Biggs late of that parish.

There is nothing so bleak as an Earthly cemetery. The rows of graves, the dismal dull tarmac of the drive, the pathos – the sadness of forgotten lives, spent and gone, mouldering under slabs of stone.

Joey was being cremated. I didn't know how I felt about that. He should've been buried in a Christian graveyard with full blessings, not burned in a furnace as if everyone knew he was already roasting in Hell. But I said nothing. What could I have said anyway?

I got there early. I wanted to make sure I saw Marcus before it started. But as I stood in the chilly morning waiting for the hearse to arrive, for the mourners to gather, a heaviness settled upon me.

The cemetery was so drear, so gloomy. The crematorium was already creaking from an earlier burning, and except for one lonely figure standing by a grave far away, the place was quite deserted. I shuddered and looked at the plastic roses in their stone urns. The red had faded from their petals. They looked faintly drained, like tired slices of cooked meat, brown-yellow at the edges and lacklustre in the centre.

Plastic roses, a metaphor for immortality? Roses that never died, never shrivelled, were never alive, could never be full-blooded symbols of love. It made me shudder. I was immortal. I never shrivelled. I never aged, never changed. Was I also dead? Had I never been alive? Was I incapable of love?

As I mused, over my left shoulder I saw a figure approaching. It wasn't the lonely figure by the gravestone, but another dressed in a white suit; his golden hair glinted in the morning light. He had on a pair of white gloves and carried a snow-white briefcase tucked under his arm. I forgot about the meaning of plastic roses and turned to greet him.

'Larry,' I said. I went to fold him in a polite embrace. He smiled as I curled my wings around him and laid my cheek close to his.

'Hey, Cara,' he laughed. 'Fab you could make it! Isn't it fun meeting up like this?'

I nodded. Although I would hardly have called it 'fun'.

'We'll give young Joey a wicked send-off,' said Larry. 'You can do Choirs of Angels, and I'll do Solemn Dignity.' He laughed and pulled a mad, bad, crazy face, as if it was quite beyond him to ever be dignified.

'Larry, can I check something out with you?' I asked, my heartbeat suddenly accelerating.

'For you, darling, anything,' he said in that lazy way of his. 'Except of course my steel guitar.'

I looked at him, puzzled.

'Rod Stewart,' he said. 'So retro.'

I was no clearer. Anyway, no matter. Instead I launched straight in with my question.

'Larry, it's important I understand something. I've been very worried. You said you were an Independent Celestial Advisor – I just need to be sure exactly who you were working for when I signed the Extension contract. It was God – wasn't it?'

Larry threw back his head and laughed. 'Bless you, Abracadabra! Did you think I was working for the Horned Horror?'

I mentioned the fuss in Heaven and the breach and how it had really shaken me.

'My dear,' he said, 'I work for *myself*.'

'Oh,' I said, not entirely sure that answered my question.

'Oh golly gosh, you poor child,' he chuckled. 'Luckily for you, you don't have a *clue* about being self-employed – but if you did, you'd know that even self-employed beings are regulated.'

'Oh,' I said again. Of course they were bound to be regulated. God loved Rules.

'There – are you reassured?'

I was. At least I think I was. The idea of rules and regulations certainly calmed me. But I needed to find out a lot more about the regulations to be certain. Now, though, wasn't the right time and I didn't want to annoy him. So I put on a smile and said, 'Could I ask you something else?'

'Let me guess! It's about your little project, Reforming the Bad Boy, isn't it?'

I wasn't completely happy about the word 'little', but I carried on anyway.

'Larry, I was so confident when I took out the Extension that I'd be able to just explain everything to Marcus,' I said, 'and I hoped the love of an angel would be enough to –'

'Absolutely, Angel-cakes, I should think *so*,' said Larry. 'Anyone who isn't half in love with you must be totally retarded!' Larry looked at me, his pale blue eyes shining like a cat.

Deep inside them I saw something that jolted me. *Was Larry interested in me?* I stared at him. *Like that?* There was no mistaking the hunger in his eyes. If I'd have given the word he'd have devoured me on the spot.

'Oh,' I said, because I'd lost track of what I was going to say.

'You thought he'd fall for you,' smiled Larry, prompting me.

'No, but –'

'But what?' said Larry. 'I think you two would make a lovely pair.' His voice dropped as he said it. I saw the light in his eyes die a little, as if the idea of Marcus and me happy together hurt him.

'But Marcus is so trapped,' I said. 'He wants to change. I know he does. He tried to repent. But it didn't work out. In fact it went terribly wrong. Everything backfired. And now I'm scared he won't try again – in fact he might do *anything*. He's not in the least bit worried about death and damnation. He just seems to obey his own rules. I'm scared he may not take any notice of me, however much I talk to him.'

'Oh dear,' said Larry, but I noticed the fear had gone from his eyes.

'And I was wondering if you've had any success – mentoring him? I know you helped him out at the police station – thank you so much. Do I owe you anything for that?'

Larry smiled at me, a big broad confident smile. 'Getting him to turn Queen's evidence was only part of my strategy. And it's all on the basis of no win, no fee! How's that?' He said it like he'd just caught a cricket ball with one hand.

My heart settled a bit. It was very generous of him, but I wasn't so sure about his 'strategy'. Turning 'Queen's evidence' had actually made things worse. But all I said was, 'Thanks.'

To tell you the truth I'd have been a lot more easy in my mind if he been a bit less flippant and had charged me properly. No win, no fee might just mean, if you don't pay anything – you don't get anything.

'I'll be at his side constantly,' said Larry. 'I'll whisper in his ear all the time. Except when you two are together, of course!' He tapped the side of his nose knowingly.

I blushed.

'But it may not be enough,' he warned.

My heart sank. That was just what I thought.

'What else can I do?' I said, my voice breaking.

'You need to try to see more of him,' asserted Larry firmly. 'When the girl you love isn't with you All The Time your imagination goes crazy. You ask yourself: where is she, then? What's she doing? Shagging my best friend? Why isn't she here? Probably shagging all my friends. He'll be driving himself completely mental thinking about you.'

I gulped. I'd no idea humans thought like that! So base. So –

'Sorry to say it like it is,' smiled Larry, 'but would I tell a lie?'

Well, he had come straight to the point, however, um . . . indelicate.

I sighed. 'But I can't always be on Earth, you know that, and it's so difficult at the moment.' I thought of God's Army and shuddered. 'Even now I shouldn't really be here,' I said.

'Poor you,' said Larry sympathetically, 'but Marcus won't understand, will he? He'll think: well, you're an angel; you can do what the hell you want, so if you're not visiting him that means you don't really want to. It'll drive him nuts! Just imagining you off with the next guy.' Larry slid his arm around my waist.

'Oh no,' I cried.

Larry dropped his arm. 'But talking about the next guy,' he said silkily, 'I don't suppose he has a chance, has he?' Larry looked at me. There was no mistaking his question.

'Oh Larry,' I said. 'No chance.'

'Oh well, just trying,' said Larry, 'but I totally get you, and honestly, if you want to reassure Marcus, you've got to spend a lot longer with him. If he slips up and takes a wrong turn, it'll be Hell and Damnation for him, before you can spit out a blessing and flick up a wing feather.'

I trembled. The idea of Marcus burning in the fiery pits. I folded my wings in tight until they were all flight shafts standing stiff around me. My brilliance wavered; the stench of Styx wove itself nightmarishly close. I could feel its appalling breath on my skin.

'*Larry, help me,*' I pleaded. '*Please* help me. Is there any way angels can get down to Earth? I don't mean as an Outcast or a ghost   that wouldn't help   I'd have to stay invisible . . . and I've got to be there   solidly with him – all the time . . . '

'Only one,' muttered Larry, 'and you don't want to *even consider* it.'

'A way!' I cried.

Larry shook his head. 'You don't want to know,' he replied.

'But I do,' I said. 'I'm ready to do anything to save Marcus.'

'Anything?' said Larry.

'Yes, *anything*.'

'You're crazy!' he said.

'I think . . . I'm in love,' I said slowly. It was the first time I'd said it out loud. And it felt right. So right that I laughed in a sudden mad way and wondered why I'd never said it before. 'And love will do anything – it can conquer everything, can't it?'

'Not this,' he said.

'Please tell me,' I said.

'No. You don't want to know. You could never do it, anyway. Never should do it.'

'Please tell me,' I said quite coldly. 'I assure you if there *is* a way, I'm quite prepared to take it.'

He paused. 'You have to Fall,' he said flatly.

My God. He was right. I'd have to Fall.

'Yes, Fall,' he said, 'fall from Heaven completely, fall from God's grace. Cease to be an angel.'

To Fall.

The thought sent shivers into me. To renounce Heaven. To lose for ever the Elysian Fields, the gentle winds of Heaven. The smiles of my friends, the laughter of the blessed.

'Exactly,' said Larry. 'I told you it was a non-starter and you couldn't do it.'

But couldn't I? What was love, then, if I wasn't able to cast away everything for its sake? My love would be as empty and shallow as a plastic rose, mere show, lifeless, insubstantial, a flame in the wind. Marcus was right to doubt me. He'd seen through me at a glance. I remembered the single word he'd said at the club. 'Liar.' A deep shame swept over me at the thought that I wasn't ready to love him above and beyond everything.

I turned to Larry. 'What is love, then,' I asked him, 'if it can't commit itself even to save a soul?

Larry put an arm around my shoulder. 'Cast it out of your mind, Candelabra,' he said, 'I should never have told you. I regret doing it. It was silly and irresponsible of me. And I won't give you the kit.'

'Larry,' I said, 'don't blame yourself. I forced it out of you. I wanted to know. I truly did. What is a kit?'

'You've got yourself all tied up in knots wondering about the nature of love and doubting yourself.' Larry smiled kindly. He laid a hand on my left shoulder. 'And that's confusing you. Of course you love him – enough. Of course you do, but nobody in their right mind expects you to give up immortality for the love of a stupid human boy, and (let me remind you) a very sinful, ungrateful human to boot.'

I flinched at that.

But to give up immortality?

I dropped my head. Larry meant it kindly, I suppose, but his words stung. Was that all Marcus was? A stupid, sinful, ungrateful human? Something that didn't qualify for the love of an angel? And if that was so, what did God's love mean? Why did we bother saving humans at all?

Love, then, was a silly shallow emotion.

I couldn't bear it. I couldn't think like that. Marcus was worthy of loving, worthy of sacrificing everything for. Love could leap even the divide between Heaven and Hell. I would save Marcus. I would. I'd prove my love. Even if I had to Fall.

I stood there suddenly stronger, more resolute, more in charge. There was nothing that I couldn't do for Marcus.

As if Larry could read my mind he suddenly winked at me. 'You'd have to go all the way, you know – inhabit a human body, become fully mortal, no messing around, no hanging on to your eternity. You do understand what real Falling is? Although,' he added, 'of course there might be advantages to being mortal.'

I looked at him, confused. I would not consider any advantage! If I Fell it would be for the most pure and noble reasons.

Larry winked. 'Like touch,' he whispered. 'Real sensation! Oooo!' And he ran a finger across my feathers.

Touch. As soon as he said it the image of Marcus at his birthday party rose up to haunt me.

*Me, in the doorway, quite overcome. Grieving for all the things that might have been, and never were. The music turned up. Me disorientated. Me imagining what it would be like to be human. Not an Angel of Death. Not immortal. Me swaying to the music, imagining I had a body. A real body. Flesh and bone. A body that someone, some day, could hold . . .*

And Marcus with his smile, his lovely crooked smile, showing off his pearly teeth, dragging the prettiest girl into his arms. *Me watching as she moulded herself against his chest, seeing the muscles in his arms straining against his shirt, trembling as he used the music to send her crazy, imagining it could be me with Marcus . . .*

Oh yes, there could be advantages to having a human body!

I shivered in delight as I thought about them, *imagined*

*his hands hot on my skin, his broad strong hands cupping my*
*chin, lifting my mouth up to his. His pearly teeth biting gently*
*on my cheek, sucking my lower lip in, nibbling it with sharp,*
*sweet bites. The pressure of his mouth at last, his tongue forcing*
*my lips open, penetrating, exploring, filling my mouth with*
*sweet savage kisses . . .*

I blinked. *Where had those images come from?* I held my
breath; deep strange carnal longings shuddered through me.
Things I'd never imagined. *Could never have imagined.*
Things I never knew a human body could do to another
human body. *And they felt good!* I squeezed my eyes tight.
I tried to push the visions away. They left me panting and
yearning and feeling an exhilaration that thrilled me more
than a thousand sweet Heavenly breezes.

I looked up at Larry. He was smiling at me gently, looking
so kind, so concerned, but as I turned my head I thought
I caught a gleam of triumph in his eyes.

'Hey, Shara, I can see just where your mind's going,' he
said, winking, 'but Don't Go There. That's an order. Wait
and see how Marcus is today. There, that's sensible advice,
isn't it?' Larry pulled a stupid face, as if sensible advice was
nasty, pinch-your-nose-and-swallow-it medicine. 'Talk to
him first. He won't want you to risk so much for him. He
won't expect that of you. He knows he's only a human.'

I know Larry was trying to reassure me, but I wasn't
reassured. What, expect Marcus to feel he was *'only a
human'* in my eyes? That was hardly likely to reassure him,
was it? Plus, he wasn't. He was everything. He was a God
(among men, obviously). He should be treated like a God.
He should expect everything from me. And I should deliver

225

it. No, Larry was wrong. I wasn't going to tell Marcus I was prepared to Fall to Earth for him, and then ask him if he was important enough for me to do it. What, tease him? Make him refuse? Make him admit his worthlessness?

Never.

I would do it.

# Serafina 29

I'd never actually been to a funeral before, so I'm probably no judge, but I thought it was phenomenal. The hearse led a cavalcade of cars up the long drive to the crematorium. Joey's family had spared nothing. (The size of the hearse alone totally amazed me.) White lilies woven into flamboyant wreaths rode like figureheads on the prow of each limousine. They read: OUR JOEY BIGGA THAN EVA and LUV U MUM and RIP JOEY.

His family followed in a second equally huge car. It sailed up the long drive to the crematorium as if blown in by a typhoon. There was his mother all dressed in black and his father with a top hat on that looked vaguely out of keeping with the white flower tucked in his lapel.

There were Joey's brothers, the whole crew of them. I recognised them immediately from outside the police station. Today they looked different. There was something almost indecently sexy about the way they walked. Their dark pinstriped suits sat on their square shoulders and narrow hips like they were fashion models.

All four of them wore dark glasses and trilbies with white crown bands, and had hands so feverish they looked like they longed to feel the throttle of a motorbike beneath their touch, or were itching to draw a weapon. Pow.

And then came Marcus.

My pulse leapt. He stepped from the next limousine as if he were an archangel himself. Gone was the downcast air of yesterday. Now there was something bold and reckless in his step. I compared him with the other mourners. What was the grace of the brothers, the smartness of the father compared to him?

He spoke to Joey's mother. I wondered how she could receive with such composure his glance, which seemed to slice through me. I expected her colour to drain; but I was pleased when it didn't. He isn't the same as them, I thought: he isn't of their realm. There is something celestial about him. I can see it. He's like me. Though the firmament should separate us, I recognise him. He's mine. I'm his.

The third car arrived and coasted to a standstill. Marcus crossed the drive and held the front door open for his mother. After she had stepped down and hurried to greet and hold Joey's mother, Marcus opened the back door for his sisters.

And my God, how beautiful they were. Rayanne, the older, was slim and tall with legs that reached her armpits. And the cut of her skirt, just above the knee (with such heart-lurching promise of things higher up) got all of Joey's four brothers fixated on her – from the moment she lowered her lacy veil to the way she set her high-heeled shoe (four inches!) so daintily upon the path.

Instantly the eldest of Joey's brothers pushed his siblings back, jumped towards her, offered her his arm, his smile, his heart (and other body parts too, I guess, if she gave him the chance).

Marcus's younger sister got down from the limousine. Sweet, kind Jasmine. She ran to Joey's mother, hugged her, helped her, guided her along walkways, up steps to the crematorium, pressed her arm, offered her tissues. She smiled shyly at Joey's father and greeted the older relatives so respectfully. As soon as Joey's mother was in the right place, she raced round the side of the parking lot and checked on the undertakers. I honed my hearing.

Had they remembered the wreaths from the house? Had they got enough programmes? Did they want her to get the brothers ready to bear the coffin in? Had the photographer arrived? No? They couldn't start till he had. I listened in on all. Marvelling. How she whirled around, all sympathy, practicality, compassion.

When her mother needed a hanky – she was there; when her sister couldn't find the restroom – she was there; when Marcus needed a crutch – she stood up straight and let him lean affectionately upon her.

And all the while I stood with Larry, far off, in amongst the graves, watching.

Larry pressed my arm and whispered, 'Courage, Demerara, you're so brave.'

I gave him a smile, but it didn't reach my eyes.

'I've got a few deals to close today,' he said, 'but I swear I'll watch over your boy. I just had to drop by to see you were getting along OK. But, just in case you wanna live

229

dangerously,' he said, raising his eyebrows like Groucho Marx, 'and be mad, bad and completely cuckoo!' He blew me a kiss. 'Here.' He drew something out of his briefcase. 'Gotcha,' he said. And he hung a small silver whistle on a chain around my neck.

'What's it for?' I asked

'Whistling,' he said.

Then before I could say, 'But what's it *really* for?' he dived into his briefcase again. This time he pulled out a small package and pressed it into my hand.

I took it. 'Thanks,' I whispered.

'Don't worry,' he said, 'it's a freebee, a twofer.'

'A twofer?' I asked.

'Two for one!' he giggled. 'You find a crossroads – then you blow the whistle or go mad, wondering what would have happened if you had!'

I didn't have a clue what he meant. My face must have shown it.

'Nothing to it,' he said. 'RTBM.[1] And if you make it to Earth and feel like partying,' he started humming, '*I'll be in da club with a glass full of* . . .' Then he winked and left.

I stood there, nonplussed.

What had Larry meant? RTBM?

I looked at the package he'd given me. It felt like there was a box inside the plastic bag. I drew it out. It *was* a box. On it was written:

---

[1] Read The Blessed Manual

# Serafina 30

The rest of the gangsters arrived: Marcus's crew. Oh, those gold chains, those diamond-studded ears, those low-slung belts, tight jeans, edgy haircuts, dark looks, glittering eyes, rough-shaved chins. They hung back after greeting the families and formed a well-dressed, dangerous wall around the gathering.

When they were in position Joey's younger brother moved over to Marcus.

I tucked the D.I.Y. kit into the sash of my dress, wondering how exactly it worked and why Larry happened to be carrying one. Was Falling from Heaven so common? Did he do daily deals with kit boxes? And giving me the whistle too? There was something worrying about it. Larry – charming as he appeared – didn't seem like the kind of being who gave things away for nothing. I remembered something about whistles too – or was it bells? Yes, it was bells. Bell, book and candle. Excommunication.

Still feeling uneasy, I turned my attention back to Marcus.

'Just give us the nod, bro.' Joey's brother was saying. (The youngest one looked like an oversized Al Capone.) 'If the Crow shows up to mess with Joey's send-off, we're ready. All the boys are tooled up, you-biz?'

Marcus looked at him and nodded slightly. Then he put

his head to one side. 'Hey, Spider,' he said. 'Man wants to thank you again for bailing me yesterday.'

Spider gave him the brotherhood salute, knuckle to knuckle, fist to chest.

'You know man was shot,' continued Marcus. 'Well, man had to do some computing. When you brush with death, it calls for brain activity, you-get-me?' He laughed like brain activity was something none of them rated.

Spider nodded. 'Yeah, man,' he said.

'Man wanted to step right out of the gang thing, true,' said Marcus.

I wanted to shout out. *But don't give up. I couldn't help you yesterday. But I'm here now.*

Spider looked at Marcus. 'You was nuts,' he said, not unkindly.

'But I learned one thing, bro,' said Marcus. 'The po can't protect you. Innocent people get hurt. Joey, and now Melly, and what am I gonna tell Lil Joe when he's big? Your mum and dad died and the guy who killed them is still sipping Bacardi?' He laughed. 'I don't think so. But I don't need no back-up for this one, that's what I mean to say. Nobody else gets hurt. It's me an' da Crow, now. You-get-me?'

My jaw dropped. My heart sank.

Somebody shouted, 'Yo, my man, M! How ya doing?'

Marcus nodded at Spider. 'Keep it close,' he said, 'but I'm going for him. Trust me.' Then he turned aside and walked back towards the crematorium reception area.

Spider slipped away, and sidled up to his older brother. I listened.

'Marcus wants to take out da Crow solo,' Spider said.

233

*Take out the Crow?*

The brother nodded. 'Yo, da Big G's taken it bad. Joey was his main man, you-know – and now this Melly thing.'

'But he's talking cutting us out,' said Spider.

'Allow it,' said the brother. 'He was waving hello to God too, d'you-know-what-I'm-saying. He's as mad as Hell; but he'll call for us, bro; he knows we're fam.'

'Seen,' said Spider, looking very doubtful.

'He won't cut us out,' reassured the older brother. 'He knows man dem need to spill blood.'

*An emptiness opened up inside me. Not that.*

'Marcus needs to chill,' said Spider. 'He's not well; he needs to find his-self a likkle wifey and let man dem settle this beef.'

The brother laughed. 'The day Marcus gets a wifey is the day I get a job.' He bust himself up laughing.

'What are you two sniggering over?' said the lovely Rayanne. She strolled over and leaned up against Spider.

'Marcus getting hitched,' laughed the brother.

'Not. Going. To. Happen,' said Rayanne, all sassy. (You know, on reflection, she wasn't as good-looking as I first thought.)

'Told you,' said the brother.

'Probably aching for a bit of you-know though, and scared he'll pop an artery!' suggested Spider.

I turned to look for Marcus. Where was he? There, standing alone by the edge of the party.

Time to act.

I positioned myself. I made sure I was absolutely right in front of him, although some distance away amongst the graves. I quickly checked my clothes. I'd put on a very sober, tight-fitting long black dress. It was off the shoulders and flared from the waist into a full romantic skirt. I wore long black lacy fingerless gloves to match. I tossed my head, my hair spread out in unparalleled beauty.

One the count of three I apparitioned. Just for the briefest of seconds. I did it perfectly. A sudden burst of sunshine through the grey October morning; to the uninitiated just a stray shaft of sunlight, to Marcus a greeting.

The guests, shivering in their thin designer gear, looked up, pointed, remarked that perhaps the sun would break through, perhaps Joey was amongst us. But not Marcus. He didn't bat an eyelid.

He must have seen me. Surely I'd done it properly?

I tried again. I let a chorus of songbirds trill.

Nothing. Except Marcus shrugging and giving me the cold shoulder.

So he had seen me.

And as if to rub in the point he turned his back and started walking off in the opposite direction. He took up a place at the furthest side of the cemetery, as far away as possible. He leaned over and steadied himself on some railings.

Jasmine, seeing he was in pain, rushed to be with him. *Surely he must look at me?*

But nothing – not a nod, not a shrug, not a glance.

I was shivering with a new feeling I couldn't understand. I folded my wings in tightly around me. *Those stern eyes, that cold resolute frown. The sight of him turning away from me.*

I couldn't bear it. Without meaning to, I cast a rainbow right across the Heavens. I wanted to make him smile. I made the breeze drop. I wanted to see his face light up as he saw me. I made the grey clouds scud away. I made a sunbeam single him out like a stage spotlight. He must forgive me.

He didn't even twitch an eyebrow.

Not a goddamn eyebrow.

I think I lost my temper. I'd been under a lot of stress. It was either that or burst into tears. And angels don't cry. They don't need to. Not when they can command. Marcus was deliberately ignoring me. Did he think he could give me the silent treatment? After everything I'd been through just to be with him? A fury started to burn inside me. I wasn't having it.

I got rid of the sunbeam and the rainbow, brought back the grey clouds and grasped his shoulders with a tornado. I *made* him turn.

Almost as if he too were fighting himself, he turned. He looked up.

In a flash I switched to his side of the cemetery, took up a new pose, apparitioned, like a blaze of lightning – right beside the statue of a stone angel. Just for a second. There I was, visible, in a pillar of light.

And our eyes met.

Jasmine grabbed his arm, as if she was concerned about him. 'We all need to go in now,' she whispered.

But I held him with the hand of the hurricane. *He would see me. He would talk to me. I would not be ignored.*

'They'll start the service soon,' she urged.

I drove the wind hard at his back and forced him to step towards me.

'You're still not well,' she added.

'Sort the others out,' he sighed wearily. 'Man's received a summons. There's someone I need to talk to.'

# Serafina 31

I sent a sudden gust of wind. Jasmine's hat sailed off. She looked confused. She didn't know whether to chase it or stay with Marcus.

'Is it her?' she whispered. 'Is she here?'

I lifted the hat off the ground and bowled it away.

Marcus smiled at her, gently released his arm from hers.

'Don't worry, I'll be in soon,' he said.

He gestured towards me. His shrug seemed to say, *You don't need to drive the wind at my back. I'll come, if it's that important to you.*

Jasmine looked even more puzzled. She peered around. I stood there trembling by the tombstones, quivering with the force of the cyclone.

'Well, hurry,' she said and went to chase the hat.

She chose well. For delightful as she was, she couldn't stand in my way. Heaven nor Hell nor anything that lies between can stop the divine might of an angel when she's doing God's work. And I was. I knew I was. How dare he be angry at me. I'd save his soul by force if that's what it took. I held the wind steady. I would tell him to repent. And then I would see with the help of thunderbolts what *he* chose to do.

Marcus moved forward. When he reached near, I apparitioned seamlessly. He held out his hand, palm facing out in a please-stop-this-nonsense gesture.

'Ho! Angel,' he said. 'Are you *that* desperate?'

'I am,' I said.

He sighed in a most hurtful way. But I paid no attention to it. I put aside all pain, all thought of self. 'Marcus,' I said in a voice like the End of Days. *'You may choose to pretend I don't exist. You may believe that there is no God. But I say unto you, repent. I exhort it in the name of the Lord.'*

'Tried it already. Long story. Didn't work out. Not doing it again,' he said.

I gulped a bit, knowing full well just how hard he *had* tried and just how seriously it *hadn't* worked out. I nearly stopped right there. But I forced myself to think of Styx, to remember Joey's eyes and the terrifying screams that echoed out of Hell.

*'You don't understand,'* I thundered. *'You have to repent. I command it!'*

'Actually you've got a nerve,' he said back, 'showing up here, ordering me about.'

With a massive effort I conjured the clouds to roll down, to contort themselves into Joey's pleading face. Behind the terror in his eyes I let the sun glow red-hot like the fires of Hell.

There, let him see it for himself.

He raised his head, took one look at it, went grey, then seemed to settle into a cold fury.

'Hello,' he said icily, 'that's not very nice.'

*'Let it be a warning to you!'*

'And this is a funeral, in case you haven't noticed. Not just another opportunity for you to show off.'

Show off!

'Appearing in sunbursts, all that boring birdsong, animating stone angels – now *Joey's face* – that's sick. This is his funeral, for fuck's sake! What're you thinking of?'

I looked at him, stunned.

'So disrespectful. You should know better. For God's sake, you're an angel!'

'But your soul?' I said. 'I've heard what you plan to do. Do you think that will bring Joey back? You must not take another human life. I command you not to. It's wrong. It's wicked. You will pay for it with your immortal soul.'

'Oh pul-lease,' he said, rolling his eyes. 'Marcus do this, Marcus do that. Get real. You don't control me.'

'But do you not tremble at the thought of Hell Fire and Brimstone?' I was astonished.

'You're so predictable, Angel. So one-dimensional. And frankly, I don't give a shit if you're real or not. You're bang out of order,' he muttered.

'One-dimensional?' I gasped.

'OK, half a dimension.' He made a gesture with his hand that upset me.

I couldn't stop myself. The feelings all boiled over. Before I knew it I'd raised a storm cloud, a dark cumulonimbus. It rolled over Marcus's face and hovered ominously above his head. 'Have a care how you address God's messenger,' I threatened.

He looked up. 'Go on,' he said, 'do your worst.' And he

set his jaw tight and met my eye. 'Nobody tells me what to do.'

I couldn't help it. *Something inside snapped.* I felt my full powers return. I let the thunder crash, the rain pelt. *I couldn't stand the contempt in his eyes.* I made the trees shake. *Together we'd been going to work everything out.*

'Amen,' he said. 'Very supportive.'

He was mocking me. This time I meant it. I sent lightning lancing down upon the ancient yew tree by the cemetery wall. For a good two minutes the tree writhed in flame, danced in fire, split, crashed, fell. There. He better damn well get the message. Then I raised a gale that howled through the tombstones and moaned at the graves like a disembodied spirit.

All the mourners hurried into the crematorium.

Marcus shook his head. 'And you reckon I need to worry about the Devil?' he said.

I made the earth shake. *'If you don't repent,'* I screamed, *'I'll crack open the very tombs of the dead and make their ashes swirl before you.'*

*He must see. He must understand. He must realise.*

'With Guardian Angels like you, who needs demons?' he answered.

I stopped. Dead. The wind dropped. The rain ceased. The clouds broke.

'Hello, Angel? Now can you guess why I don't want to talk to you?' He looked at me steadily. He seemed to be debating with himself. At last he spoke. 'Apart from your gentle, comforting presence – you did something that really hurt me.'

*I did something that really hurt him.*

'Why didn't you tell me?' He stopped. He seemed to be unable to carry on. *'Why didn't you?'* he whispered, his voice suddenly cracking. *'I thought you cared . . .'* He hesitated. *'I asked you about Joey – you made me believe he was OK.'* He looked at me. *'Do you know what that feels like – to believe and then . . .'*

Men like Marcus don't cry. Their eyes just become set like obsidian. Their grief destroys everything around them. *'You made me believe you . . . when you should have told me.'*

My jaw dropped.

*'And all the time he was dead. And you knew.'*

I dared not look at him.

*'And even after that, I still tried to do what you wanted. Not just because I owed you – but because I wanted to believe . . . because I gave my word and I don't lie.'*

He waited for me to say something. But I couldn't. *I just couldn't.* He shook his head in disbelief. 'You don't give a toss about me, do you?'

I had to speak. I opened my mouth. I tried to defend myself. 'You were too unwell . . .' I started to explain.

His face grew dark. 'You don't care about Joey, either.' He narrowed up his eyes. 'Oh, just push off back to Heaven and leave me to show some respect.'

'But your soul?' I whispered.

'Christ!' he yelled. Then he stopped. He looked up at the sky. He shook his head. 'What is the fucking point! You girls are all the same. You've got only one thing on your minds.'

I blinked. I did care about Joey. And I felt guilty. And

ashamed. And I didn't want to talk about it. *I should have told him.* I was a coward. I wanted to think some good could come out of it. *I should be telling him now* . . . about Joey's death . . . but if I could save him . . . I could make it OK . . .

'Girls!' he snorted. 'And I thought you were different.'

I was different. And I did care about him. I loved him so much. More than God or Heaven or anything I'd ever known. I'd have frozen suns, melted rocks. I'd have even gone into the heart of Hell if he'd asked me to.

Marcus shook his head. 'Always telling a guy to fucking fix up. You're just the same as all the rest.'

But as for us 'girls' being all the same . . . I raised a column of fire before his eyes. I stepped into its burning heart. We. Were. Not. All. The. Same.

That made him smile. 'Except you're very Old Testament.'

My jaw dropped. Old Testament? Me?

'Two little words,' he said.

I looked at him amazed. Earthquake, fire, flood wouldn't shake him. 'Old Testament?' I whispered.

'No, those aren't the words you need to learn.'

'What are they?' I said, bewildered.

'My. Life.'

I snapped my mouth shut.

'I don't want to be saved any more. Get it? Savvy? Capisce?'

'But,' I said.

'I tried it and it's a joke. So I don't want salvation. I don't want Heaven. And I don't want you telling me what to do.'

'Then what do you want?' I said in a confused half-strangled squeak.

'I wanted Joey to be alive,' said Marcus, his voice suddenly dangerously soft. 'I wanted Melly to be alive. But they're not, and so now I don't care about anything except getting even.'

'*No!*' I cried. *'You mustn't give up. I'll stay by you. I'll be there!'*

'Like you were there when I needed you?' said Marcus. 'When Melly was bleeding out, and I was trying to do what you told me?' His voice was breaking but he stood firm, looking me straight in the eyes. 'Nah,' he said. 'Repentance, what crap. What about justice, Angel? *What about that?* What is salvation, Heaven, everything – *without justice?*' He flung the words at me with such force that I stepped back.

'But,' I said again. 'You don't understand.'

'No. *You* don't understand,' he said. 'Joey was my friend.' Marcus spoke slowly, sadly. 'I don't know how it works up in Heaven, but down here your mate is your mate.'

He looked at me to make sure I understood. 'He puts up with you when everyone else walks away. He's there when you're down, when you ain't got a dollar to your name. He shares his crummy cheap burger with you – when neither of you've got nothing he makes a joke to cheer you up. He opens his crib to you, when you're out in the cold, alone, drunk and in trouble. He don't have to be smart, or kind, or clever, or good. Joey wasn't any of that shit. He was a joke. A crazy bastard. But he was *my* friend. Understand? He was my friend. My friend.'

I tried to understand.

'So Angel, I know you're good. Maybe you care, but if you really care, you'll start showing it, and respecting my decisions. Heaven and Hell don't matter if you can't protect the ones you love – and when your best friend gets murdered, and his killer is still out there, you've got just one mission in life and until you finish it, you're only half a man.'

For a split second I saw. *I saw what he meant.* But this was madness. He didn't understand.

'Joey would've died for me,' said Marcus.

'Wait,' I said.

'And I'm ready to die for him.'

'Please, Marcus.'

'Wait for what?' he said. 'I've waited long enough, waited until I was well enough to walk out of the hospital, waited for the police to sort it, waited while the Crow murdered Joey's girlfriend – waited right up until now – until we've given him his send off. But do you think Joey'll rest in peace? His soul will *never* rest in peace until his murder is avenged.'

'But there's something you don't know,' I said. My voice breaking.

'I know everything I need to,' he returned. 'The Crow's got it coming. He better sit up and enjoy his last few days, because this man's going to kill him or die trying.'

'Won't you at least *listen* to me?' I pleaded. '*You must listen.* It's not as clear-cut as you think –'

But Marcus stepped away from me. 'I've got a funeral to go to.' He turned his back. 'And I'd appreciate your support.' He shrugged.

*He stepped away from me.*

*He turned his back.*

I don't know what happened. A feeling possessed me. *I had to make him listen. I had to tell him. I had to take the blame. I had to stop him. I leaned out.*

*I touched him.*

*The purity of my desire broke all the fetters of Heaven.*

*I really touched him.*

I BROKE THROUGH FROM HEAVEN AND TOUCHED HIM.

*He felt it.*

*He jerked back. He looked into my eyes.*

*Time shifted. Froze. Was frozen. Will freeze. Becomes one. Together. Merges. The moment goes on for ever.*

*'I'll support you,' I whisper, 'I love you . . .'*

*He sighs as if he's been waiting for those words. I open my arms. He steps towards me. We embrace.*

*'Let me kiss you,' he says. 'I've needed you so badly.' Stardust is in his eyes. Angel dust is in his heart.*

*He leans to kiss me.*

*I press my lips against his. I feel him through the boundaries that lie between us.*

*He reaches forward. He holds on to the marble of a tombstone. I see how his knuckles are pale against the grave. He's straining to reach me. His eyes. I meet them. We are locked together.*

*His tongue slips into my mouth.*

*We are one.*

*It's like sunlight. We are each other. We've known all our lives. We fuse. We want to be one. We are one. We must stay one.*

*The moment ends.*

*And we stand there trying to understand.*

*I say, 'I'll do whatever it takes.'*

*The Dust of Angels settles around us. All around us in the sunshine. And time – its shortness, its length – means nothing.*

*We grasp the sunshine.*

*We have kissed in the shadows of the cemetery.*


And everything I wanted to say, everything I wanted to tell him was driven out of my mind, except that as we parted I whispered, 'Be careful, Marcus, our days are short; don't return unto the path of evil, forswear all wickedness.'

But he lifted up his hands as if he wanted to shush me. And such a look of longing and of sadness dawned in his eyes that I became quiet.

'We're doing it my way,' he whispered.

I nodded. He was right. He'd asked for my support. I would give it – even if he chose to go to Hell. I would go with him.

'If I could always be with you,' he whispered. 'If it was always like this, all the time, I could be OK. I could stay strong. If I could always feel like this and you were always there.'

'You are with me,' I said. 'And I'll be with you.' And in that simple promise I sealed my fate. For if he wasn't to die and come to Heaven, the only other way to be with him was to cross the great divide myself.

And I didn't regret it, for I could give up all eternity, all my future in Heaven, for just one day on Earth with him.

\*   \*   \*

Don't judge me. Please don't judge, all you Heavenly beings that weigh the souls of humans on your scales in the Halls of the Dead, those of you who hold their destiny in your hands; those of you who blow the trumpets for the great Judgement Day – don't be too sure you have it right.

For if you have never felt the tug of passion – the wrench of desire as it floods your chest, the ebb of blood in your belly – you can't know what inhuman power it takes to stay true to anything. For Earthly love has an authority that can't be denied, won't be denied. So don't judge too quickly.

Yes, I should have told him. Yes, I should have bared my truth until he understood. He could hear me, could see me. Yes, there was no reason not to.

But I was afraid.

Afraid to tell him that his life was won through Joey's death. Afraid to face his pain. Afraid he would turn away from me. I could not bear that. I could not.

And so I started a new intent, a plan to save him, a way to be with him forever.

I trembled at the thought of it.

I trembled at my boldness.

This was no joke. I really would do it.

I really would Fall from Heaven.

# Serafina 32

Marcus left me shaking amongst the headstones, left my fire and brilliance shimmering uncontrollably in the grey morning. I clutched at a gravestone to steady myself: oh, the feel of that stony surface – so cold to the touch, rough-hard like the pressure from dark lips. I tried to regain some measure of restraint. I pulled my fire inwards. I straightened up my wings; but they shivered and shivered.

And though Marcus was gone, I still sought him. I looked through cement and stones. I gazed into the crematorium. He was supporting his mother, giving her his arm. They were settling on chairs. I must go – already St Peter would be wondering. Oh, Marcus. His broad shoulders. His smooth muscular chest. I must get back to Heaven.

One last look.

Joey's older brother moved away from his family, crossed to Marcus. I saw Rayanne smile; I saw Jasmine take her mother's arm. Joey's brother drew Marcus aside.

'Man knows you took the bullet. Man knows to show you nuff respect for that.'

Marcus nodded.

'But Man's bro is lying there deaded in the coffin, you-know-what-I'm-saying?'

Marcus nodded again and held up two fingers in the everlasting victory sign – a way of showing respect.

'Safe, bruv,' said Joey's brother. 'So man dem *need* to see the Crow's blood running too, you-get-me, don't ya?'

Marcus nodded.

'So that every time your bullet hole bites you, you gonna check Joey and you gonna know his peeps showed you da love and respect. So we've taken a decision. We're keeping it real. We're in with the beef. We're gonna do the business. For our Joey – you're still de man, it ain't like that. Give us two days to tool up, get clean heaters and a disposable ride. Then when you're ready – you say the word.'

Marcus smiled. 'Yo,' he said.


Heaven is not Heaven if you're not happy, and I wasn't. I was miserable. I was in despair. I was panicking. It was 29th October. *The 29th*. Halloween was only two days away.

So as soon as I got back I chose a dark raiment, checked I had the D.I.Y. kit, threw away my identity bracelet, left a note which simply said:

> *Dear God, I'm so sorry.*
> *Please try to forgive me. S.*


Then I closed up my cell, and raced out, across the Golden City. I charged through the all-pervading smell of boot polish and cold metal, up towards the North Gate.

Outside the North Gate was awful. God's Army had wrecked the place. The fields were scarred. Great wounds of earth lay furrowed where tanks had left their tracks; swathes of corn had been ploughed dark; soil turned and left in heaped clods, flowers lay crushed, hedgerows trampled, saplings broken.

I didn't care. I raced straight for the Abyss. I even took to the air and flew. Who cared any more about stupid rules. Let God's Army catch me if they could. I was going where none of them could follow. I was so upset I didn't even notice another angel flying behind me – not until I reached the far wastelands.

Kamuel.

'Don't try to stop me,' I shouted.

'Be careful,' he said. I glanced across at him. His lovely face, so breathtakingly beautiful, was set hard like flint. 'What you think you do for love may only be a trap, a different kind of temptation sent by the Devil to catch the unwary.'

'Love in any form is Heaven sent,' I yelled back. He wasn't going to dissuade me.

'Self-love is not,' called Kamuel sternly. 'Seeking to ease your own pain is not love,' he warned. 'It is self-serving. Have a care, Serafina, that you do not mistake the two.'

'How?' I replied. 'To do something noble and self-sacrificing to save another can never be the Devil's work!'

He flew closer, reached out very tenderly and touched my wing feathers. 'Oh Serafina,' he cried, his face quite melted in tenderness. 'Don't be hasty. You are the dearest, the most beautiful of God's Seraphim. Don't forget He loves you and has sheltered you in His sacred Cloisters, prepared you to do His work. It would grieve Him to lose you.' The sadness in his voice made me want to weep.

Kamuel was so lovely, so kind, so wise, but I did not think it would grieve God to lose me. He had everything. He didn't need me. But I kept my own counsel. I didn't want to argue.

'And I would grieve too,' said Kamuel, 'if anything evil should befall you.'

'Why is it so evil to Fall from Heaven?' I said, suddenly defiant.

A shadow passed overhead. The sun blinked out like the shutting of a great eye. Kamuel sighed.

'*Tell me,*' I persisted.

'Look,' he said, pointing at the landscape ahead. 'See the mountains hard and bright?'

'I see them,' I sighed. I wished sometimes Archangels would give you a straight answer.

He plucked a feather from his wing and released it into the air. Immediately the wind took it, whipped it around and bore it away.

'Temporal things do not endure,' he said, 'and neither does Earthly love. Be not like the feather, Serafina. Seek to be hard and bright like the mountains.'

And he pressed my hand and in that gentle pressure I understood. Kamuel cared. He wanted to save me from myself. He knew.

'I have something for you,' he said. He held out a small gold crucifix on a golden chain. 'Wear it for me,' he said, 'so that God's Grace will be with you wherever you go.'

I could not refuse a blessing so gently given. I took the

crucifix and fastened the chain around my neck. It felt so light against my throat, like the caress from the tip of a feather.

'But I can't be yours,' I said, looking into his eyes, determined to tell him the truth. An Archangel as great as he should not be deceived.

'Why, what courage you have, my Serafina,' he said.

'I just can't,' I said.

'Yes,' sighed Kamuel. 'I would keep you if I could: together we could chase rainbows and create such beauty in the universe that even the Devil should bless us.'

'I can't,' I repeated, beating my wings faster. 'I love another.'

Kamuel looked at me and smiled. 'Then I pray that whoever he is deserves you, will cherish you, will adore you for all eternity and humble himself before you, as I will – as I do.'

'You are too good,' I murmured, thinking of Marcus, his wild moods, his bitter resolve, the press of his lips, the strain of his body against me, the heady smell of life lived in the fast lane that clung to him. How he didn't care if he went to Hell and back.

The cloud passed from the face of the sun.

'Don't try to change my mind,' I said.

'I won't,' he said sadly. 'But you must consider this: none have returned. Falling from Heaven is the one thing God forbids. The one thing he does not forgive.'

'But others have,' I said. 'Vincent would have Fallen.'

'But in the end he chose not to.'

'But your friend Fell,' I pointed out.

'Ah, yes,' mused Kamuel, 'but not by choice. And remember, anywhere that is not Heaven is Hell.'

So Hell was carnal knowledge: skin on skin, pulse beating, blood thickening.

'Brimstone and fire,' said Kamuel.

And kisses wild and sweet, I thought.

'And death and disease and sorrow,' said Kamuel.

'But this immortality isn't life,' I said.

'No,' he agreed. 'It's not life.'

In the distance the faint thrum of thunderbolts rolled towards us. I saw the sky flicker with lightning. 'Please,' said Kamuel, compressing his fine lips, 'come with me, before you make any decision.' He seized my hand. He shook out his feathers. 'There is something I have to tell you.'

# Serafina 33

Up he soared into the air. Obediently I followed. The sky throbbed around us; the clouds parted, soft like swansdown. At every beat of Kamuel's great wings a quiver of sunshine leapt from his feathers until all the countryside below was speckled in honey light.

'Behold,' he said. He pointed to the Golden City, now tiny beneath us. 'See how beautiful Paradise is.' He raised one arm and pointed at the skies above. From his fingertips beams of light shot forth until a fan of sheer radiance ran right across the Heavens.

I looked at him, awestruck: so mighty, so full of splendour.

He stopped soaring and hovered beside me. 'All this is yours, Serafina,' he said. 'The wide fields, the flowers, the city, all yours.'

It *was* beautiful. If I were to fall, I would lose it. And gain what? At best a few forbidden nights with a wild human boy? A grimy soul saved from the pit it should've been tossed into long since?

Kamuel turned towards the Sapphire Mountains. 'Follow me,' he commanded. Soon the peaks rose about us and quite shut us in.

'Let us stop here,' he said, as we reached the first outpost, a regiment of rocks that guarded the way to the summit. There were no fields there, only the raw fabric of the mountain, bleak, savage. When the rush of air and cloud cleared, I heard the work of God's Army clanging much nearer.

'Listen,' said Kamuel. 'They are preparing for the Great Purge. They will start their March soon,' he said. 'No one will escape their scrutiny, no stone will go unturned, no deed unexamined.'

'Will they discover everything?' I asked.

'Only if you show them your thoughts. God's Army purge the mind as well as the soul.'

'Oh,' I said.

'But perhaps you will not be here when they come?' He looked at me with his steady eye.

I made no answer. I knew my mind. He knew it too.

'Follow me,' he said abruptly.

Kamuel took my hand and led me to the summit. I hadn't been expecting that. I hadn't quite realised where we were – but suddenly, yawning at my feet, was the Abyss.

Sheer rocks of fall.

Vertigo.

Dizzy.

Plunging into mist and chaos.

Head swimming, I clung to him, my mind falling, plummeting down into those depths below.

'Lord save me,' I whispered.

A column of white swept up at us. Kamuel unlaced my fingers from his arm. He took a rope from the folds of his robe. He twisted it into a noose. He handed me the rope;

looked at me with a cold clear eye. 'Jump,' he said, 'if it's what you want.'

I read his message only too plainly: you think you want to Fall. I know your mind. You wish to become mortal. Go ahead, Fall, sin, reap the joys of temporal existence, reap the kisses and the touch of flesh. Reap the whirlwind. Throw away immortality. Live. Die. Perish!

I couldn't speak. I just stared dumbly up at him.

He waved a wing. A rainbow sprang up over the Abyss, a giant portal.

'Serafina, perhaps you see into my mind as I see into yours,' he said. 'I will not stay for the Great Purge. I intend to leave Heaven, soon – perhaps for ever.'

'Why?' I said, confused. 'Where will you go?'

'I will go far,' he said, 'to that wasteland where the dead await salvation, even as far as Mount Purgatory itself. I will set up our Mission there and work tirelessly to save souls. I will do God's Will in Purgatorium.'

The air around us trembled. I was sure I could hear the distinct tramp of feet. Hard boots on hard stone.

'You said you wanted to save souls?'

The pounding of feet grew steadily nearer.

'Come there with me, Serafina?'

God's Army were on the move.

'Why jump into that Abyss?'

The trumpets sounded and the drum beat began. Maybe they were coming for me.

'What do you say?' demanded Kamuel. His face was as hard as the granite drop before us. 'You want to leave Heaven. I need a fellow worker. We can both escape from the madness of this Purge – and I need you there.'

*Go to Purgatorium with Kamuel? Work amongst the unsaved souls?*

'Surely this is more important work than anything on Earth?' demanded Kamuel.

'I suppose it is,' I whispered, but inside I was yelling, NO! NO! NEVER! NEVER!

Kamuel unfurled his dread wings. 'Surrender yourself to God's Will, relinquish Earth, rise to a higher purpose.'

'God's Army are coming,' I cried. 'If we wait here a moment longer, we'll be discovered.'

Kamuel smote his breast with a clenched fist. 'The work, Serafina, is all that matters.'

*'I can't!'* I cried. And I bent my head, for to refuse an order from an Archangel is a terrible thing.

Over the crest of the Sapphire Mountains lightning flashed.

Kamuel looked as fixed as the rock around us.

I looked from him to the Abyss. A spectre seemed to rise before me, the image of Marcus standing at the River Styx. He'd turned his head and called out to me. My feathers shivered, all the little wisps of down on my under-wings stood on end. The flesh on my bones chilled. My mind was made up. Marcus could not do it alone. I had promised him I'd be there. I would go to Hell with him if he wanted. Who else would?

'I can't come with you,' I said to Kamuel. 'I can't.'

The trumpets sounded nearer, the tramp of feet, the smell of boot polish. I heard over the rush of air the sound of Jehudiel. 'SURRENDER YOURSELF. We know who you are. You have betrayed Heaven.'

'*You do not want to save souls at all, do you?*' said Kamuel, suddenly understanding.

I shook my head, for I too understood. Gone were my pretences, gone my self-deceit, and in that instant I knew my own heart. Marcus wanted me. I wanted him.

*I longed for his touch, his skin on my skin.*

I wanted to feel his love, surrender to his force. I wanted union with him so that we could truly be one.

Nothing else mattered.

I loved Marcus.


I drew myself proudly up, I spread my fiery wings. I kept my fires ablaze. I was no longer ashamed. I thought of Marcus. I burned for him. I burned and burned and filled the sky with scorching heat.

I kept my eyes smouldering; I swept Kamuel's arm off me, I stepped right to the edge of Paradise where the Cliffs of Fall began. I looked over the rim of the great Abyss. That twisting drop, seething in smoky plumes, falling away into wispy nothingness. The wind moaned up. The boiling clouds churned in the very depths of the void.

I stepped out on to the furthest pinnacle.

I slipped the noose around my wings.

I stood with the bottomless chasm at my feet.

I pulled the rope tight.

'*Please,*' cried Kamuel.

'Marcus!' I shouted.

And I threw myself down.

*Marcus.*

My choice.

# Serafina 34

Air dashed against me, bruised my face, tore at my raiment. Gasping, guttering, sinking, I gulped and found only the void. Vainly I strained with my wings to fly. Vainly I crushed my feathers: but the rope held tight. Down, down into the ever-darkening Abyss, twisting, turning, straining.

On and on, I fell.

Sometimes upright.

Sometimes spun in strange vertigo.

Down. Ever Down.

*'Oh help me, Lord,'* I cried. But barely had the words left my lips when tornadoes of air ripped them apart and scattered them behind me. There was none to hear. My head swam. Clouds blasted against me. I closed up my eyes. *'Oh God forgive me,'* I whispered. And with a cry of despair I remembered something terrible: they said Satan fell for nine days. *Nine days? Surely not? I should have checked. I would never get there. The 31st was the day after tomorrow.*

A hurricane howled. I pulled at my wings. The noose held firm. I remembered my purpose. I remembered the kit and Larry's words: *'You find a crossroads, you blow the whistle.'*

I was at a crossroads. Above me lay Heaven – below me surely Hell.

Between Heaven and Hell, between Good and Evil, between angel and mortal, what greater crossroads?

So I twisted in my fall. I threw aside my raiment until it tangled with my limbs. I drew from around my neck the whistle.

And I blew it.


Far way through the firmament I heard them. Cruel voices singing. No, not really singing – chanting maybe, intoning, howling. I rode the air. I set my fires to burn brightly. But even as I did so, a gale howled up out of the Abyss.

*'We are the hounds from Hell*
*We come when you ring the bell.'*

'Whistle,' said one very loud flat voice. 'Not bell. Whistle.'

'Doesn't rhyme,' said another voice.

The song continued:

*'We are the hounds from Hell,*
*We come because you Fell.'*

And through the mists I saw something. At first it looked like a huge fireball bowling straight at me, but as it drew closer I saw that it was a giant wheel the colour of beryl, tinted by impurities; green, blue, yellow, red, and white – and all along its circumference flames raged. It was being rolled through the air – half pushed, half dragged by two gigantic dogs.

As they drew closer I saw my mistake. Neither were dogs. The larger was definitely a wolf. The smaller was a being with a jackal's head. From the oily blackness slipping all around them I knew at once they were both demons.

'You called, madam?' said the first demon. 'Allow us to introduce ourselves. This is Marchosias, and I'm Anupu, King of the Abyss.'

'You're not King of the Abyss,' said Marchosias.

Anupu opened his jaws, lunged at Marchosias and cracked his teeth together with a ghastly snapping sound. All around us the elements writhed.

'Missed,' remarked Marchosias. 'Get her to the eye of the storm.'

The two hounds suddenly pounced at me. Desperately trying to escape their deadly teeth, I spun sideways.

The wind dropped.

They dragged the wheel closer. They flipped it on to its side. Marchosias slavered and sent up an eerie howl. 'Come on,' he said. 'Hurry up and get on it – we're not doing overtime.'

'*Get on the wheel?*' I gasped.

'*We are the hounds from Hell*

*We're here to perform the spell,*' chanted Anupu.

'Ritual,' said Marchosias. 'Not spell.'

'Doesn't rhyme,' said Anupu.

Then without warning the two animals jumped on me. Legs, arms, head, shoulders. Their teeth clicked too, imprisoning me. I screamed. They stretched me out. I kicked at them, fought as best I could. I tried to escape.

'Hey you,' snarled Marchosias. He slashed me with a razor paw. 'D'you want to become human or not?'

'Yes,' I whispered, terrified.

'Then let us get on with the job,' he growled.

Without further notice they tied me down, spreadeagled me on the burning wheel: north, south, east, west, until my body made a five-pointed star. I opened my throat and screamed. Then with one mighty heave they spun the wheel.

The vacuum twisted. The flames leapt. A vast spiral of air – and I was spinning at the centre of a thin whirlwind.

'OK,' barked Marchosias, 'this is your cue, Anupu. Give it your best.'

Before I knew what was happening Anupu jumped on to my chest and in fierce biting motions snapped his teeth together over me, crooning:

*'I am a hound from Hell*
*And this is the bit I do well*
*I'm making the sign of the cross . . .'*

He snapped again in a ghastly parody of the Kabbalistic cross. His spittle dripped down on me and the stench of sulphur overcame me.

*'You summoned me up from my lair*
*Spirit, water, fire, earth and air . . .'*

'Give it some proper poetry,' yowled Marchosias.

I tightened my lips, praying I wouldn't faint.

'Whatever – it'll have to do –' snarled Anupu. 'Get the kit; I've got the whistle.' He ripped it from around my neck.

Marchosias jerked the D.I.Y. kit out of my grasp. He swept the contents into his grip. The instruction sheet flailed beneath his paw, flapped in his muzzle.

I struggled, but all the bands held good.

In that gloomy light, in that rush of vile air, he read: *'Guidelines for casting extreme Black Magic. Once you have performed the Supreme Invoking Ritual of the Pentagram* ("I'm not doing it again," growled Anupu) *it's time to Summon the Devil.'*

263

# Serafina 35

'Check everything's there,' yelped Anupu. 'One black candle, a packet of dust, a handful of bones, a blade, a bottle of water, a rock of salt.'

'Yep,' said Marchosias.

'Right, you can do this bit,' said Anupu. He threw the whistle at him. 'Blow the whistle at Raphael. Pour the water over Gabriel. Extinguish the candle for Michael. Throw the salt at Ariel.'

With what seemed like one smooth, practised motion Marchosias did it all. In some kind of twisted irony I thought how easily – thus – is the power of the Senior Team dismissed by the gyrations of a devil dog.

'Place the bones in her right hand. Sprinkle the corpse dust over them. Slice her palm. Let the blood water it. Chant the conjuration: *Power of Death, Power of Life, Let the Devil Live and Rise Again.*'

Marchosias jumped to my side, slit the palm of my left hand open, crushed the bones in, sprinkled the dust on, squeezed my hand into a fist until the blood trickled through. And then he chanted the summoning spell, the words of power:

*'Bagabi laca bachabe*
*Lamc cahi achababe*
*Karrelyos*
*Lamac lamec Bachalyas*
*Cabahagy sabalyos*
*Baryolas*
*Lagoz atha cabyolas*
*Samahac et famyolas*
*Harrahya.'*

'Right, we're done,' said Marchosias.

And just like that they turned and trotted off, leaving me still tied to the wheel.

*'Come back,'* I yelled. But they didn't even twitch their tails.

I let out a deep groan. They crooned as they disappeared into the void:

*'We are the hounds from Hell*
*And this is our dog-ger-el.'*

'Rhyme,' said Marchosias.

'Doesn't,' said Anupu.

And they were gone.

A howling sounded out of the Abyss. I waited, heart beating. The chasm swirled with choking sulphur. *My wrists. My ankles.* A fog of brimstone ascended. Oily shadows slithered and seeped into the air around me. *Help me*, I screamed.

But no help in the form of either devil dogs or demons came.

Instead ice formed on the wind. From far away came the sound of screaming. Invisible hands plucked at my raiment. The vortex shattered. The sulphur contracted into a dense column. It swirled as if a thousand snakes had been enchanted to writhe in it. Thicker and thicker, bubbling and howling.

Then silence.

Pale as a corpse, a face materialised. White like death, it turned towards me. Two eyes stared out of its shadowy depths.

Beads of sweat broke out on my brow. My teeth rattled. A shivering took hold of me. This was it.

I'd summoned Satan.

'What do you want?' echoed a booming voice. I'm not sure now if anyone really spoke or the words just sounded in my head.

My throat dried up. I quaked at the thing I was about to do. I remembered Marcus, his eyes, his crooked smile, my promise, remembered that Halloween was only two days away.

So I took courage. 'I want to become human,' I said, teeth chattering, 'and I wish to live on Earth. And please take me to Curlston Heights by 30th October,' I squeaked, for I remembered that the Devil is tricky and unless you are very clear about what and when and where, he will twist your wish until it becomes your curse.

The column of sulphur seethed.

This was it. I was really doing it.

And so I should be.

Marcus had tried to change for me. And he deserved no

less. And if only he'd succeeded everything might have been different. If only the Crow hadn't found out about his statement. Suddenly that seemed odd. How exactly *had* the Crow found out?

Only Jasmine and the police officer knew.

And Larry.

Yes, Larry knew. I'd heard him: *'There's a young man here called Marcus Montague . . . I can corroborate what he says.'*

A cold terror suddenly tightened around my heart. *What if Larry had told the Crow? What if Larry had betrayed Marcus?* But surely that was impossible. Larry was on our side.

A new horror struck me.

*What if he wasn't?*

*'Wait!'* I cried.

The yellow column gave a revolting shudder. There was a terrible silence, as if never in his entire existence had the Devil been asked to wait.

'Do you not wish to become human?' hissed the voice.

But I did. I did wish to become human.

And what was the use of wondering if Larry had betrayed me now?

It was all too late.

'Yes,' I whispered, 'I'm sorry.'

'So you will pay the price?' said the voice.

'Yes.'

'You will sign the contract?'

'Yes.'

'Your soul will be forfeit.'

'Yes.'

'There is no going back.'

'Yes.' There was no going back.

'If you fail. If he does not repent. You will be mine, however long you live.'

'Yes.'

'Then drink this.'

A hand, thin, yellow, emerged from the sulphurous column; in it, a phial.

The liquid inside seemed to have a life of its own.

'Drink!'

I opened my mouth. In one movement the hand uncorked it, dangled it above my lips and then violently tipped it down my throat. Oh, bitter potion. How it seared my tongue. How I felt it burn all the way down through my chest.

For a moment, nothing.

Then I jerked in a spasm of pain. Icy tendrils writhed inside. 'This is it!' I cried.

'It absolutely is,' said a voice.

I twisted in the air, suddenly shocked. I knew that voice.

There was, I thought, a chuckle from behind the gyrating fog.

'Who is it?' I screamed.

This time I was sure there was laughter. The column of smoke definitely billowed out. And I almost recognised that laugh.

*I did recognise it.*

Not Larry.

Or Harry?

And suddenly, like a lock clicking open in my brain, all the pieces of the puzzle slid together and formed a picture.

Larry who was not Larry at all, but Harry.

Larry who didn't work for the Devil. But worked for *himself*. The Extension that Raquel had never heard of. Joey dying all by himself. The date that wasn't three weeks. The breach that had raised God's Army. God's Army after me, collecting my stuff, following me. The police station where he hadn't met Marcus. The D.I.Y. kit he just happened to be carrying.

What if Larry didn't work for the Devil?

What if Larry *was* the Devil?

The laugh. I recognised the laugh.

*I knew it. I'd always known it.*

Old Harry.

Old Nick.

*Claim Souls Direct.*

*I was the one who'd signed the contract.*

Arch Fiend.

*God in Heaven preserve me.*

Prince of Darkness.

Fallen angel.

*Lucifer.*

*Satan.*

*The Devil.*

'*Voilà!* Disco! There you go,' said Larry, his voice echoing through the column of sulphur. 'It was fun while it lasted, though, wasn't it?

# Serafina 36

*Oh God.*

*Forgive me.*

*How I had fallen.*

*Larry was the Devil.*

I screamed out at him through the writhing sulphur. *'Why me?'*

'Just because,' he laughed. 'You'll find out.'

'Larry?' I whispered, as if I could somehow appeal to him.

'My name's not Larry,' he said. 'And don't you think my two dogs are completely delightful? Did you like the poetry? I knew you'd appreciate a bit of ceremony.'

'But I thought –' I said.

'No you didn't,' said Larry. 'But never mind, I told you right at the start I just love girls who don't think.'

I opened my mouth to protest, to plead, to reproach, and found there was nothing left to say.

'Now fly!' he commanded.

In one brutal movement something broke the wires that held me. The wheel shattered into a thousand fragments of stone and fire. The rope tying my pinions snapped. Instinctively I unfolded my wings, beat the air.

Instant pain.

I slashed at the emptiness. The pain drove everything out of my mind. I tried to stop myself plummeting downwards. *For God's sake stop the pain . . .*

The ice inside me spread.

'Fly!' came the voice again.

I stretched out my wings. A force blasted them. I felt feathers ripping – being snatched out. Tears sprang to my eyes. Flight feathers broke. I let out a terrible cry.

*'Fly!'*

I was so cold.

The hurricane plucked out every fibre of down at my wing base. *I screamed and screamed.* Frantically I beat the air. At every stroke feather after feather shed away.

'Fly!'

Hysterically I turned, I looked over my shoulder. Behind me my wings were just a fan of bone, *all my feathers gone*, only the skeletal frame remaining.

*Larry was the Devil.*

I was freezing over.

And then I fell. I couldn't stop myself. I plummeted straight down. Inside me a voice confirmed:

Yes, down you must go. Down you will go. Down, down. Down, down. Sheering down.

I gave a little cry. My body twisted in space. Everything exploded around me. I burst through the horizon, right over the rim of the world, into the skies below.

I rushed towards Earth.

I arched my back – the bony span of my wings ripped free. I screamed. The air tore my voice from me. My back hurt, a dizzying agony of blood darkened my eyes. I was squeezed on both sides. Air pressure.

Falling.

Gasping.

Blind.

Frozen.

Lungs bursting.

I have to breathe.

Can't breathe.

No air.

Darkness.

The Devil.

D

o

w

n

# The Book of Zara

# Zara 1

*Because you have done this, you are cursed*
*above all cattle, and above every beast of the field;*
*upon your belly shall you go, and Dust shall you*
*eat all the days of your life:*
Genesis 3:14

Bright light. White light. The sun like I've never seen it, burning my eyes. There must be something wrong. I blink. I shut my eyes. Sun doesn't hurt. It doesn't burn. I try to open my eyes. My lids feel weirdly heavy, like they're really too heavy. I touch them; skin, real flesh. What?

They're real.

They're flesh.

I cover my eyes with one hand. I touch my face, my neck. I feel the small hard crucifix at my throat. My crucifix. Kamuel's blessing. Larry didn't hurt me. I'm OK. I try to stand. It hurts. I never imagined anything could hurt like this! I explore the ground. It's hard and dark like solid stone, like it's come up from inside a volcano. I rub my hand over it. My hand's bleeding. Ow, how it hurts, like fire stinging. I watch as red spots erupt across my palm. I raise one palm to my mouth. I lick it. It tastes of salt and

275

iron. I run the taste of blood around my mouth, amazed at its sharpness, its power. How it hurts.

I have blood.

I bleed.

It's a new sensation. I try to raise my face again. The sun burns. I blink. I shade my face. I'm on my belly. I roll to my back. I sit up. How strange. I wobble. The green of some field tilts away: now towards me: now from me. A field? A green lawn? Larry betrayed me. Not a lawn, the green grass of a park. I'm in a play area in a park. Slitting my eyes up against the sun, I peer out. There's a girl. A teenage girl. She's sitting on a swing. She bends her head low and peers back at me. She tilts her head to one side. She tilts her head to the other side. She's looking at me.

'You fall?' she says.

I look at her. I look at the swing. I shade my eyes again and look up into the blue yonder. I nod. I run my tongue around my mouth and try to form words. 'Oh,' I say, 'fall.' I just spoke. How strange. That was my voice.

And suddenly it astonishes me. I did. I Fell from Heaven. I survived the Devil. I betrayed God. I'm here, sitting on the spongy, black tarmac of a play area in a park. Larry is the Devil. I fell. What time is it? *What day is it?*

I try to get to my feet; my legs don't work. I stumble up. Like I'm rising from the grave. I look at the girl. 'Can you see me?' I say.

She wrinkles up her snubby little nose. She points at me. 'You hurt yourself,' she says.

I look at my palms again. They're grazed. They're bleeding. I touch the blood and smear it around. I'm not sure how they feel. They're prickling like they've been pierced by sharp needles. It's actually not very nice. It burns.

'Yeah,' I say.

'You run away from school?' she says. I look at her. I don't understand. School?

'They gonna catch ya,' she says, 'if you run away from school.'

I smile. She's seen something in me. Obviously. I'm a runaway. But I haven't run away from school. Heaven isn't a school. It's kind of a nice idea, though: Heaven, the school for good little angels run by the headmaster, God. Serafina the truant, who made a pact with the Devil.

'Yeah,' I manage to say, 'I ran away.'

'Me too,' she says, rocking awkwardly on the swing.

I wobble to my feet. I try to use my wings to balance me. No wings. I'm cold. What day is it? *What's the date?* So strange I can remember my wings. I turn to check. I'm sure they must be there. No wings. I'm very cold. *Please don't let it be after the 31st.* I realise I've only got on a twist of cloth.

'You look funny in that,' points out the girl. She tilts her head to the side again. 'Well funny.' She tilts her head the other way. She's thinking.

I clutch my raiment around me. It's all twisted up and bunched around my waist. I want to ask her what the date is. But I'm not sure yet my voice will work properly.

'Want to wear my gym kit?' she adds. 'You've got to wear something.'

I do want. I'd love to have a gym kit (what *is* a gym kit?). She tosses me a bag. I catch it. Oh, I can catch a gym kit.

'Quick,' she says, 'you gotta cover up.'

I notice that above me the sky is bright; a bird is singing. So it's morning. I pray it's the morning of 30th October. I pray hard because I know Larry is treacherous. The bird's notes are repeated, as if it's alarmed at me holding a gym kit. How extraordinary. I open the drawstrings. Inside is a black T-shirt and a short black gym skirt, and a pair of black stretch leggings.

'You can wear the leggings,' says the girl. 'They ain't too dirty.'

I smile at the girl. What a lovely girl. She gives me her very special own gym kit. I'm quite delighted.

I sit on the black spongy felt tarmac and pull on the leggings. They're very thick black leggings. They are quite delightful leggings. And they fit me well. Tight. I'm very skinny. I notice the soft curves of my angelic shape are all gone. I really Fell. I'm not an angel any more. So the Devil played fair about that. I'm hopeful.

'Look, leggings on.' I make do with squeaking it out. The girl tilts her head to one side again. I balance on my feet and try a twirl. I can't twirl. I can't command the elements. I stagger and trip.

'Put on the rest too,' she says.

I pull the T-shirt over my head and stick my skinny arms through the sleeves. It's long-sleeved and the wrists of it drape down nearly over my hands.

I smile at the girl. 'What is the date?' I say. It was too long a mouthful, I didn't know when to breathe. The words feel thick. They roll around on my gums – but bless this girl, she understands.

She looks at me kind of weird, and she says, 'It's the 30th.'

I laugh. My laugh doesn't tinkle any more. It's rather flat and loud. I like it. I think I like it. I'm not sure. It doesn't matter. *I'm not too late. Larry didn't cheat me.*

'And the skirt,' says the girl.

I fasten the short skirt around my waist.

'You still look silly,' says the girl, 'but at least they won't arrest you now.'

I laugh again and so does she. *Thank God, I'm not too late.*

'Do you know Marcus?' I say.

'Marcus?' she says. 'Marcus who?'

Maybe she doesn't know Marcus.

'Is this Earth?' I say, suddenly panicking at a new thought. Am I in the right place? This is the joke he'd play on me, isn't it? *I'm in the wrong place.* I try to calm down. It didn't take nine days. Everything else has worked. It's 30th October. I must be in the right place. Where else could it be?

'That is,' she says, pointing at the green grassy area behind me.

'Oh,' I say.

'You talk funny,' she says.

I stop. Do I talk funny? Suddenly I'm worried. I thought I was speaking more clearly. Will everybody be able to tell I'm not human? I pick up the cloth and tie it around my waist. I must learn how to talk human. I must practise. When I speak to Marcus I mustn't sound funny.

'You look all Gothy,' she says. 'Do you worship the Devil?' *The Devil. I belong to the Devil.*

But before I can answer she jumps off the swing. 'All

you need is shedloads of piercings and you'd be one,' she says. 'Hey, hang on a minute, you need some make-up too.' She reaches into her handbag, pulls out some tubes. She walks straight towards me. 'Relax, Goth girl,' she says. 'I'm going to make you beautiful.'

She pulls me after her and pushes me down on to a park seat. She pinches my face between her hands. 'That's it,' she says, 'chin up, head back. Hey, I love your hair dye. What colour is it? Stay still, I'm going to give you huge eyes with tear drops.'

'Oh, OK,' I say. How lucky I am, to fall right in front of this girl. She's preparing me to be human. She's making me beautiful for Marcus.

'Do all human girls carry around make-up?' I ask. Perhaps I need some too?

'Like, yeah,' she says, as if that's the dumbest question anyone ever asked.

'And are they all Goth?' I ask.

'You're a retard,' she says. Her voice is deliciously grumpy. Then she tilts my chin right up and draws lines around my eyes. I can feel the point of the pencil. It's not a pleasant feeling.

'I'm Serafina, actually,' I say.

'Zara who?' she says.

'Serafina.'

'Zara Finer?'

'Yes,' I say.

'Pleased to meet you, Zara Finer. I'm Kookie.'

'Oh,' I say and smile.

'Don't smile,' snaps Kookie, 'you'll mess it up.'

'Kookie.'

'Kookie by name and Kookie by nature,' she says as if she's said it a hundred times. 'The curse of every classroom, the despair of every teacher.' Like it's a little rhyme she's learned by heart.

'Hi Kookie By Name,' I say.

'There,' she says, unpinning me. 'Wanna take a look?'

I nod.

Kookie pulls a phone out of her handbag. She holds it up. It's a little mirror. I peer in. There reflected back at me is a small heart-shaped face, very pale with huge dark eyes. It doesn't look like me. I didn't know I would look so different. It's not just the loss of the wings and fire. *I'm totally not me.*

Suddenly I panic. Will Marcus still know me? If he looks into my eyes he'll know me, won't he? I can't get used to this new face. It's very odd. It's kind of thin and the lips have been drawn on in bright red lipstick. Across the forehead is a thick fringe. And all around the small face is a curtain of straight black hair.

I never had black hair.

I look at it. It's not me. I was beautiful.

I touch my hair and run my hand around my mouth. The lipstick smudges.

'Stop it, silly,' says Kookie and smacks my hand away from my face.

*I used to have flaming hair; the setting sun used to hide in my curls; the morning star streaked liquid fire through my tresses. When I tossed my head, every shade of autumnal blaze burned and flashed, like gold and amber . . .*

It's thick and black and very, very straight.

'You'd look good in bunches,' says Kookie. 'Like goofy spaniel ears.' She ties great loops of my hair up until it cascades down around my face.

'You got a lot of hair,' she says. 'I could cut it.' She searches through her bag. I sit on the bench, knees all scrunched up. My legs are very thin and very long.

'Can't find them.' Kookie shrugs. 'And I gotta go,' she says. 'You can keep the gym kit. I hate sports.'

She snaps her handbag shut. She shakes herself down in a very pretty kind of way and gives me a little finger wave. 'Bye-ee,' she says.

'Kookie,' I say. 'Don't go. Is this Earth?' I really do need to know.

'It's Earth, of course, worse luck,' says Kookie. 'Woohoo, Earth to Zara, come in, you're orbiting planet Earth.'

I smile, I laugh even. I Am On Earth!

'Got. To. Go,' says Kookie. 'If they find me here they're going to take me straight back to Planet School.'

'D'you know where Curlston Heights is?' I say. 'Fifty-six, Curlston Heights.'

'No,' says Kookie.

I catch my breath. How will I find Marcus? My heart starts to pound.

'Don't smudge your eyes,' says Kookie. 'Just walk into any newsagent and look in an A–Z. I'd get it up on my mobile, but I ain't got no credit.'

'Your mobile,' I say. 'How did you get it? Can I get a mobile?'

'You're kookier than me,' says Kookie. She tilts her head

to the other side. 'Look, if you fancy bunking school again, I'm usually here until the kids all go in, especially on Wednesdays. So we could hook up, but today I got a plan, so ta-ra.'

'OK,' I say.

And I sit there looking at Kookie, and I don't care where I am, except that I'm on Earth! And I'm smiling and smiling. I did it. I Fell. I'm a girl. I check my breasts. I *am* a girl. They're not very big. I check my hands. They're really human hands. I reach out and I feel the seat of the bench: they are real human hands and they are feeling the bench.

'Kookie,' I say, 'before you go, will you hug me?'

Kookie puts her head on one side.

'You're weird,' she says.

'Will you?' I ask. I look at her. I want to know if Marcus can hold me, if I will be able to feel his hands on my waist. If I will be able to be strained against him. I remembered how Marcus dragged the prettiest girl into his arms, how she moulded herself against his chest. How the muscles in his arms were taut against his shirt . . .

Kookie shrugs and says, 'Whatever, Zara, you're a perv, but I like you.'

'I only love Marcus,' I say.

Kookie puts her arms around me and squeezes. My God, but it's good. It's all squidgy and soft and firm and warm and immediately I fall in love with hugging, so I fling my arms around her and hug her back.

'Hey,' she says.

I put my head on one side like her, and I say, 'Hey,' back.

'And don't forget to put on the plimsolls,' she says.

# Zara 2

Kookie is gone. I sit on the park bench and look at the sky. I see clouds. I think of how Raquel will miss me, how Kamuel will be sad. I was sorry to hurt Kamuel, but I couldn't go to Purgatorium with him. 'I'm sorry, Kamuel,' I whisper. *You tried to stop me leaving, but without Marcus there's no need to be immortal.*

Then I stand up. I need to find him. I don't know which park I'm in. I don't know where I am. But I've two days left. I'm so happy about that. I've never really wondered how humans get around. I try to blink my eyes – just to test. I whisper, 'Curlston Heights,' but I don't move. So I just follow the way Kookie went. I put on the plimsolls. I feel the pavement. I look in wonder at the world. God's shining creation. I hug myself. I've no wings, no fire; I'm cold; I've been betrayed; I've abandoned Heaven; I've sold myself to Satan and I'm totally on my own, but I don't care. I'm human. Marcus can have me now. Together we can be and live and die. Together go to Heaven or Hell. My heart swells up.

I walk out of the park gates. I smile at a mum with a buggy and two toddlers. She gives me a weird look back, as if I was about to pinch candy off the little boys. I smile

284

again anyway. I'm so happy – even if I'm cold and haven't got a clue where I am. I'm in love. I'm in love with thick black leggings, gym skirts, black T-shirts, plimsolls, pavements, weird looks, make-up and spaniel ears. I love Kookie for welcoming me so kindly to Earth. I think she's so free and happy making her own choices. I love the trees and the cars and the wild city tumbling all around me.

And I love the perfume of the streets. It really *is* beguiling. I've never been anywhere like here before. Not in this way. Never. I walk down by the park. I run my fingers along the railings. My fingers are going bump, bump, bump. I'm going to try skipping. I'm going to try hopping. It makes my breath go all fluttery. I stand still and drink in the morning air. I want to make it all last forever.

Hello Earth. How I love you. I want to stare into shop windows and listen to the roar of traffic until all the seas run dry.

Traffic!

Cars!

Suddenly I know what I'm going to do. I'm going to take a minicab! I've always longed to ride in a minicab. Today I'm going to do it!

Here is a minicab office. I peek in. It's just like the first minicab office I ever saw. On the wall above the counter is a clock. It says 09:15 – 30th October. There are drivers sprawled on seats. They're smoking cigarettes. Real genuine nicotine. I look around. It's like déjà vu.

*Then suddenly I realise it is the first minicab office!*

*I am in the right place!*

*It worked. Everything worked. Larry played fair. There may still be a chance. I'm in the right place, on the right day! I can hardly believe it.*

The drivers still look bored. They are bored! There's the girl with the greasy hair plastered down her cheek. She's sitting behind the incredible steel grille. I'm so happy. *This is my minicab office!* This is just like it should be. Just like it was on the day I met Marcus. She's reading a magazine again. I say, 'Can I see your magazine?'

She points at a pile on a small square coffee table. I pick one up. They don't have enticing images. I'm just a tiny bit disappointed.

'D'you just wanna look at magazines or are you taking a car?' says the girl. Her voice is deliciously crispy.

'I'm taking a car,' I say.

I'm taking a car!


I follow a long-faced man out into the street. He yanks open the door of the minicab. He gets in. I stand there a bit unsure. I'm unsure how to actually open the door.

I don't get it quite right. I pull on it. It doesn't open. The cab driver leans out through his window and yells, 'Hey kid, press the goddamn handle.'

'Oh,' I say, and I try pressing the handle.

The door opens, and I get in. There's a newspaper on the seat. I push it aside. I slide along the smooth material and feel it squidge beneath me.

'So where to, kid?' yells the cab driver (I love the way he calls me *kid* – like I'm a real teenager). There is a strange weary note in his voice. Perhaps he works too hard, maybe he's tired.

286

'Are you tired?'

'Just tell me where to?' he says.

'Oh,' I say, 'Curlston Heights. Fifty-six.'

'The street, lady,' he says, 'gimme the street.'

'I don't know the street,' I say, 'is that a problem?'

He shakes his head like he really is very, very tired. 'Whatever,' he says. He types 'Curlston Heights' into a strange boxy thing on the dashboard, and sighs again as a map comes up.

'That's southside,' he says. 'It'll be more.'

'Oh yes,' I say, a bit puzzled by the 'more' comment. More what? More miles, more time?

He starts the car up. It coughs into life. A voice from the boxy thing says: 'You are approaching a roundabout. Take the second exit.' It's a funny voice. I look around to see who's speaking. I clutch at the seat as we slide forward. My stomach feels very strange. The cabby looks in the mirror and catching sight of my face says, 'If you're going to be sick, kid, you can get out right now.'

'Oh no,' I say, 'I won't be sick.' How can I be sick, when I'm going to see Marcus?

'Because this ain't my car and I don't want no trouble.'

'Of course,' I say. I smile at him.

And we're away. Streets flash past. Police sirens wail. The funny box voice says things like, 'Turn left at the next junction.' Traffic lights flick from amber to red. The roar of the engine. The tug of the morning air. We slice round corners, spin down side streets and I feel a mad, wild, crazy feeling: freedom and a rush of hope.

Past us speed bargain stores – 'Turn, first on your right,'

one-stop shops, kebab cafés, pizza parlours – 'Keep in the inside lane.' News-stands, bakeries and buns and oh, the smell of roasting chicken!

I pick up the newspaper. And see it's called the *Herald* – just like in Heaven! I smile. I double-check the date. 30th October. One day left. My spirits suddenly plunge as I fully realise. *Only one day.* I read the headlines: POLICE WARN OF HALLOWEEN DISRUPTIONS: *Traffic will be re-routed away from key residential areas tomorrow evening* . . .

*Halloween.*

*One day left.*

We draw up outside Curlston Heights. I recognise it immediately from that evening, from that other life when I soared up its walls, when I perched on its windowsills and peered in through its windows. I remember adoring lifts.

I'm going to use the lift now. I shiver in excitement. As soon as the cab draws to a standstill, I jump out ready to bound over to the grey painted front doors.

'Not so quick, young lady,' shouts the cabby. 'What about my fare?'

'Fare?' I say, turning and looking at him in astonishment. What does he mean, 'my fare'?

'My ride, my loot, my lolly, my spondulicks.'

His spondulicks?

I laugh. I've never heard such a word – *spon-du-lix*! Amazing.

But the cabby's not laughing. 'Hand it over. I ain't got time to play. I don't do this job for my health. I want my money. All of it, and don't try to fob me off with any *come back later*. I need hard cash. The full amount. I got bills to pay.'

Money?

My heart falls. He expects money for the ride in his car? Even Charon the ferryman doesn't expect *full* payment, just a token coin, a crossing of his hand with silver. But I see at once this cab man does expect it. Not a blessing – not even cheese. I remember now from the textbooks in the Cloisters. I remember Marcus in the hospital garden. How foolish of me. Money, the root of all evil.

'Money?' I say. I haven't got any money.

'Yeah, money.' He spells it out.

'M. O. N. E. Y.'

# Zara 3

I can see he means it. He's in earnest. My eyes widen. I look at him. He looks angry.

'I don't have any money,' I stammer.

'You don't say,' he guffaws (not at all in a jolly way). Clearly he doesn't believe me.

'I'm sorry,' I say, 'I didn't realise I had to pay. I don't have anything, but I promise as soon as I find my friend, as soon as I can, I'll pay you back.'

'You get one every day, don't you,' he snarls. 'A grimy little hooker without a penny to her name.'

'I'm not a hooker,' I say, shocked. What is a hooker? It sounds horrible.

'Tart, floozie, whatever the hell you are. Look at you plastered all over in make-up and obviously no older than sixteen.'

'I'm much older than sixteen,' I start to say.

'Yeah, yeah,' he says. He eyes the gym kit and the pumps and my (rather tattered) raiment in disgust. His eyes travel to my neck. 'Hand over that crucifix, then.'

My hand flies to my throat. I clutch my crucifix. *Not my crucifix.* It's the only blessing I brought from Heaven. '*Wear it for me,*' Kamuel said, '*so that God's Grace will be with you wherever you go.'* I need God's protection. Not my crucifix. I can't give it away.

'Hand it over,' he says roughly, 'and count yourself lucky I don't take you straight to the police.'

The police?

He gets out of the car. He's big. He smells of cigarettes. He grabs my arm. 'Don't even think of running,' he says. He pulls my hand away from the chain. His hand is hurting my arm. He closes his fist on the crucifix. He turns a wrinkled-up lip and scowls at me. 'Hand it over.'

I can't. It's mine. He yanks the chain. Stinging pain. The chain snaps. He takes my crucifix.

'Flipping whores,' he mutters, and then he gets back in the minicab, jams the gearstick into place, revs up the engine far more than he needs to. He screeches away.

I watch him go. He's taken my crucifix. My eyes start pricking. My arm is hurting. My neck is hurting. I would have paid him. I sniff. I don't like this feeling. It's like everything is lost. I think of Kookie. She was so kind. Why wasn't he?

A pang starts somewhere deep in my chest. A sudden longing for Heaven. No way home now. No more Elysian Fields.

I walk slowly up to the side of Curlston Heights, to the main front door of the tower block. At least he didn't take Marcus's key. It's still on its lanyard. I loop it off over my head. Curlston Heights is so huge and strange. The doors look like the fabled adamantine gates that bar the road to Hell. They tower above me, grim, shut fast.

*But oh! Marcus will be there waiting for me.* These are

just the last doors. I've come all the way from Heaven. I am not afraid of these doors. I've jumped into the Abyss, been tied to the wheel, been tricked, stripped of my wings . . . bargained with the Devil. What is my crucifix compared to all that? No doors can stop me now. My heart starts to flutter. *Marcus will be there!*

I push on the doors. They are barred fast against me. I can't see where to flex the handle. There is no keyhole for the key. I stand like a small child perplexed in front of the fastened doors, unable to pass.

How do they open? I drive myself against them. In frustration I rush at them. But I'm no longer made of Heavenly stuff. I can no longer pass through rock and stone, wood and water. Instead I'm hurled back from the door. It has a force and power of its own. My shoulder hurts. The bones inside squeal with the flinging and the battering.

'Oh, please help me God,' I whisper. But no help comes, only the bitter wind, the downdraught from the huge walls. I shiver. The gym clothes aren't very warm. I try to tighten the raiment around me, but it makes no difference. My skin is bumpy with cold. My teeth start to rattle. I have to get in. Today is 30th October. *There are less than two days left.*

But I don't fling myself against the doors again; instead I observe them closely. There's a number pad, a series of little steel grilles – there's a sign which reads CCTV IS IN OPERATION ON THESE PREMISES. I wonder what CCTV is. I look around to see if it's a person, someone I can ask. But CCTV is not a person. It must be some other thing that humans do. I don't know what to do. *The History of Life on Earth* we studied at the Cloisters did not inform me about CCTV.

I bend down to see if I can smell Marcus's scent, as I did before. Find his tread on the pavements, but I can't smell anything. This human nose I have can only catch the faintest whiff of dog and dirt and cement. I wait. I decide to sit and wait on the sidewalk until he comes. He must come soon. This is his home. Maybe if his mother comes, she'll know where he is. Maybe if someone else comes, they'll let me into the building. I know his door number. I'll find him in his room, in that joyful wild room of his where everything is such a delicious mess. But my heart shudders inside me, as I remember the conversation I heard the very first day I met Mrs Montague.

*'I just don't know what to do any more,'* she said.

*'He's never here . . .'*

*'It's his friends,'*

*'He's gone for days . . .'*

What if he's gone for days? What if his mother has thrown him out? How will I find him? A horrid sinking feeling begins. I haven't thought this through. I haven't prepared for anything. I'm alone on Earth, without a coin to hold, without a home, without a friend, without a coat, without anything other than these gym clothes to keep me warm.

I look anxiously around. A few people pass me on the street. I run to them, hold out my hand. I say, 'Please can you help me . . .'

But before I can explain about Marcus, about how I must find him, they brush me off. One woman gives me a cruel push and yells, 'Baggage! Shame on you!' I drop back. I slip. I land on the cold concrete.

Such anger. I don't understand. I bite my lip. I pick myself up. I wait. One man passes twice. I'm sure he's looking at me, in a sad, lonely kind of way, but I don't try to run to him. Another person comes. She's going up to the door. She's carrying a green bag slung across her shoulders. She picks a flyer of paper out of the bag and starts trying to push it through a crack between the two front doors. She looks kind. Timidly I walk up to her.

'Please excuse me,' I say, 'I'm trying to get into this building; can you let me in?'

She looks at me and tries to hide a sudden expression of pity and disgust. 'Why d'you want to get in?' she says warily.

'There's a boy –' I start.

'Listen,' she says. 'If you need love, turn to God.' She dips into her bag again and pulls out a flyer. She goes to shove it into my hand.

'No,' I say, 'it's not like that. I love him.' I say it simply; it's the truth. I love Marcus. 'I need to get in to see him.'

'Accept Jesus into your heart,' she says.

I don't know what to say about Jesus, about God. My mind is quite blank.

'I just love Marcus,' I say.

The lady shakes her head. 'Poor thing,' she says, 'that's what love does to you. Rips you from on high and pulls you down.'

Suddenly I understand. I only have my love for Marcus left. Everything else is gone. Yes, she has made me understand. And instantly I panic. If I should fail? If I should lose Marcus? What would be left?

'And suddenly you're vulnerable and lost and anything can hurt you and it usually does.'

I look at her. She is a prophet. She is warning me.

'Listen.' She scribbles something on to the back of the flyer. 'That's the address of the refuge. If he's beating you, locking you out,' she is looking at my bleeding hands, my smudged face, 'if he's abusing you, you can go there. They'll take him to court if he comes within a mile of the place. They're Christians.'

'Oh,' I say, looking at her, perplexed.

She thrusts a little folded pamphlet at me. 'Book of Job,' she says. 'Read it and see if you can't find your way to our church.'

I remember Job. He came to the Cloisters once and gave a series of lectures on Loss of Faith. I nod. 'I do love God too,' I say.

She stops and frowns at me. 'I'll remember you in my prayers,' she says.

I watch her go. I clutch the flyer to me. I try to understand what she means, but I can't. Human love is sacred. I tell myself, 'It's sacred.' It is. On Earth as it is in Heaven Once you've found your true love, once you've waited all your existence for your one and only, once you've been united with them, that's all there is, isn't it?

# Zara 4

The morning turns into afternoon. The wind whips more fiercely down the side of Curlston Heights. I wait and I wait. My hands are numb. I'm shivering. I wait a long time. At last I see people intent on entering the building. I'm shy now to approach them. Shy in case they turn me away with harsh looks, with shoves. Instead I watch. I start to notice something very curious. As each person approaches the main door they tap something on to the number pad. I try to creep closer to see what exactly they're doing. But a man there sees me coming and covers his hand so I can't know the trick he uses to get into the building. I try to call to him. I say, 'Please, I would like to enter this building with you,' but he gives me a funny look and bolts through the door when it opens, like a small frightened thing. He yanks the door back after him. I'm once again locked outside.

It's only when an old woman comes to the door that I suddenly understand. She balances her shopping basket on the paving slabs and punches in 103 on the number pad. I wait hoping to see the door open, if 103 will open the door. As soon as she's gone, before I can alarm anyone else, I'll tap in 103 too. Once I'm inside the building I know I'll find my way to Marcus.

But the door does not open. Instead a funny tinny voice rattles out from the little steel grilles arranged beside the number pad.

'Hello?'

'Hello, dear,' says the woman. 'It's me, Margie.'

'OK,' says the tinny voice. There's a strange buzzing – very faint – like a fly trapped in a cup.

The old lady, Margie, hastily pushes on the adamantine doors and lo! they crunch open! There's a click and the sound of an electronic lock opening (or closing). Then Margie pushes through.

I'm left outside.

But now I've an idea. I think my idea is good. I think Margie tapped in the flat number of her tinny-voiced friend. I think I'm beginning to understand how I might get into the building.

When nobody is looking I pull my cloth over my head. I sidle up to the keypad. I know Marcus's number by heart I should, it's engraved on it: 56, Curlston Heights. I tap in 56. I stare at the door waiting for it to pop its lock, so that I can push it open, just like Margie did. But it doesn't pop. It doesn't do anything. I even give it a tiny shove, but it stays well and truly locked. Instead I hear the tinny voice. It's ringing out of the steel grille. 'Hello,' it rings.

I almost recognise the voice. It seems to belong to another life. 'Hello,' it says again. I cross back to the little steel grille.

'Hello,' I say.

'Who's that?' says the voice. It's a woman's voice.

'It's me,' I say.

'Go away,' she says. I hear a click.

'Hello,' I say again, but the tinny fuzzy sound has gone. I stare at the steel panel – maybe I should have put my lips right up against it. I don't know what to do. I stare at the steel grille, hoping the tinny voice will speak again, but it's not going to. As I try to make sense of what just happened, I push away thoughts of Heaven. There are no locks there. Every door will open for you, if you want it to. There are no tinny voices there, nobody will tell you to go away.

Just as I'm starting to take pity on myself, I remember whose voice it was. Mrs Montague! I peer at the steel grille with more interest. Mrs Montague is using the grille like a mobile phone. How has she done that? How I wish I still had my angelic powers. I touch the wall again to see. I know it's hopeless. It's just bare brick, cold cement. I can't tell who built it, who lived in it, who designed it, what creatures wandered over its soil before it was raised from the dirt.

I sigh and my eyes start watering in a sudden horrid way. I brush my hand across them, and make-up comes away on my fingers. My heart sinks further. Kookie took so much time over me. I don't want to spoil it. I want to look right for Marcus.

I take a deep breath and press 56 again.

'Hello,' says the tinny voice, angry now.

'Hello, is that Mrs Montague?' I say.

'You again?' she barks.

'Yes, it's me. Please don't go,' I say. 'Please, is Marcus there? Can I speak to him?'

'He's not here,' says Mrs Montague, as if that settles the matter.

'Oh,' I say, completely stunned. 'Can I come in and wait?'

'No,' she says. 'Who the hell are you?'

'I'm not from Hell,' I hastily reassure her.

She snorts. I'm not sure what to say next. I can see why she'd be upset, if she thought I was a demon sent to get Marcus.

'I've come a long way to see Marcus,' I say. 'He knows me. He's been expecting me.'

'My dear,' says Mrs Montague, her voice suddenly kinder, but all sort of stiff and pompous, 'it may surprise you to learn that Marcus knows a lot of young women and that you are not the first to come hanging around the flat.'

'I know,' I tell her. Of course I know. I saw him with so many beautiful girls. I do know.

'But that was before me,' I say.

She laughs. It's not a mean laugh, just a laugh like she's sad and happy and knows more than I do.

'Well, not to upset you, dear,' says Mrs Montague, 'but you don't look his type.'

I quickly look over my shoulder. Can she see me?

'What do you mean,' I say, 'his type?'

She coughs as if she's made a mistake.

'Look,' she says, 'I'm sure you're a nice girl, but shouldn't you be somewhere? School? College? Here's a piece of advice; Marcus is my son, but he's not really the kind of boy you're looking for. I'm sure you're a nice girl, now go on home and forget about him. Don't get yourself mixed up in trouble. I'm his mother, and I'm saying this!'

'But,' I say.

'I'm tired: tired of standing here talking to you. No, you can't come up, and, no, I'm not going to get involved, and no, no, no, I'm tired of it all, far too tired. And if you don't go away I'll call the police.'

'Oh,' I say again, but the tinny machine has clicked off. I wait a while. I'm afraid. She may call the police. I remember Jasmine saying how 'Mum knows not to buzz strangers through when she's alone'. How Sharissa didn't. How everyone is afraid. But I must get in. I screw up courage again and press 56.

But this time she doesn't answer. I dare not press it again. She must be really worried about people pressing her doorbell. She must be really worried about me.

So I sit down on a bollard and wait. If Marcus *is* up there he'll have to come out, won't he? But why would his mother lie? Suddenly doubt seizes me – what if he's with somebody else?

I push that thought away from me. That is an evil thought, beneath me, and born of the Devil. I won't believe it. I won't be tricked by him again.

When I find Marcus everything will be OK. He'll sweep me up into his arms. He'll strain me against his chest. I'll feel him, his hard muscles, his arms like steel. I'll mould myself against his body, like the girl in the nightclub did. If human love is like that taste I had at the cemetery . . . oh, I hope it is. He'll be there pressed right up against me. I'll breathe when he breathes. I'll look up into his dark eyes. I'll tell him everything.

The afternoon turns chill, evening approaches. I'm so cold. This bollard beneath me is frostier than the grave.

How the cold hurts. It bites like iron at my fingers. I must walk or the blood in me will freeze.

Down this street. Already it's dark. The shops are still open. Past a cleaner's, a pharmacy, another minicab office, a bank. But don't go far. This is a newsagent's – a general store. What if he comes? I mustn't miss him. There are grotesque costumes in the window, witches' hats, spiders, bats, webs made of rubber and masks – so many masks – and fake fanged teeth so white even Larry would be impressed. Larry won't win. I won't let him. He may have tricked us both with Marcus's statement – tricked me with so many things. But I'm awake now. He won't trick me again.

I glance back towards Curlston Heights. By the law of some bad fate he'll be sure to come, if I stray away from his threshold. Some fate – it seems – already begins to hang over me. One set of the fake fangs in the shop window suddenly flops open to form a ghostly mouth opened in a hideous laugh.

Hurriedly I move off, although I don't remove my eyes for one second from those grey adamantine doors.

In the next shop they are roasting birds. The smell of them punishes me. It makes my mouth water in a sudden flood of longing. I can see them all squeezed on a spit and turning and dripping golden oil and smelling of spices, of garlic and of hot barbecued wood smoke.

The smell of them unhinges me. I stare at them as they go round and round, all yellow and crispy, turning and roasting. My mouth is a-flood. It's a strange sensation, at once delightful and at the same time so urgent. I don't know what it means. My stomach starts to churn, as if it wants to grind holes into my being, as if acid is slowly dripping down inside me.

Suddenly, I realise with a shock, I want to go into the shop and have one of those birds. I want to sink my teeth into it. I want to rip tender flesh from barbecued bones. I stop, aghast. Such a craving! But I can't drag my eyes away from them as round they go, round and round.

**HALF CHICKEN: £3.50**

I have no money.

I'm faint with this feeling. Would they give me one? I'm too worried to ask. I remember the cabby's face, his demand for his spondulicks. No, I won't ask. Would they take my raiment? It's the last thing I have left from Heaven – spun of pure silk, flecked with iridium. I will offer it. I will offer my raiment for one half chicken.

I enter the shop.

A young man is there and – I think – seeing a thin-faced, shivering girl before him, frowns. I hold the raiment in my hand, but I haven't the courage to ask him for the chicken.

'Yeah?' he says.

I look at him. I can't speak.

'Yeah?' he says again.

'I was cold,' I stammer.

He nods. Inside the shop it's warm. The smell of roasting chicken fills every corner. Damp coldness clings to me. I shiver as heat chases the air around me. The smell is making my belly hurt. It feels as if demons have already started feasting on me. I look at the young man. He appears indifferent.

'You can't stay here all day,' he says.

I look at the raiment. I look at him. I look at the chickens. I'm too ashamed to ask. 'Sorry,' I whisper. And leave.

Outside the street is dark. I walk back towards Curlston Heights. My stomach twists. A car speeds past. Arches carrying high-speed trains tower above me, huge graphic letters spray-painted on them making no sense.

A car sped past!

I start to run. I run fast. I race back, past vans loading, lights flashing, traffic roaring, people streaming, kerbs greasy with old rain and fresh oil. But I don't stop to notice anything – because a car is drawing up outside Curlston Heights.

*And I recognise it!*

It seems to be driven straight out of another world. *So long ago. Someone's car, with music booming out of it. A proper gangsta sits in the driver's seat. The car slows. A window winds down.*

The car screeches to a halt and I know it with a melting of my bones, beyond a shadow of a doubt.

Marcus has come – at last.

# Zara 5

I run. I run, from the golden chicken shop. Run down by the nonsense-sprayed arches, dodging gutters, shoppers – run back towards the screeching car, bones melting, run and run, and I find that this new frail body can't move like an angel's. It's weak and tired before it begins.

'Marcus!' I cry. '*Marcus, Marcus.*'

Four men and a girl get out of the car. The girl is beautiful and the men are handsome. How gorgeous they are, dark glittering eyes and jeans fitting them in undreamt-of ways, leather jackets and hoods, gleaming gold and dazzling eyes, sultry looks and sombre stares, and there's Marcus.

My Marcus, more beautiful than all the rest.

I'm so glad. I run to him. I throw myself in his arms.

But his arms don't catch me.

I stumble.

I fall.

And land headlong on the concrete. His three friends, his blessed friends, laugh. I try to read kindness in their laughter. I smile, but it's not funny. What have they done to Marcus? Why is he so cold to me? Why didn't he catch me in his arms and call me his angel?

'Marcus,' I say, but something has caught hold of my

voice and broken it. I don't recognise this strange weak sound it's making.

'Marcus,' I try again, but he's stepping around me, stepping away from me.

I reach out to him.

'I've come for you,' I cry.

He stops. He peers at me as if he's trying to make me out.

'I Fell,' I say.

'You sure did, doll,' says one of his friends.

'Falling for Marcus is a well-known phenomenon,' says another.

'Enjoy the trip?' laughs a third.

'No,' I say quite truthfully, remembering the terrifying rushing, and the Devil. I look up at Marcus. 'I Fell from Heaven to find you,' I try to explain.

They start laughing.

Marcus holds up his hands as if to shush them. His face is perplexed. A thought is worrying him. For a fleeting moment his face lights up. He draws in his breath. He looks at me. But what he's looking for isn't there. There's a sudden smell, a blast of drains. I disappoint him. He shakes his head.

I know that smell, just like I knew that laugh. Larry is here. I can't see him, but I know he's here.

'I Fell, like I promised,' I say. I look at him. He must see.

He steps forward and takes my hand in his. My heart beats wildly at his touch. His touch, his dear, blessed touch. So firm, so real, so strange, so how everything should be.

I'm holding his hand – well, he's holding my hand – for he turns it now in his.

'Babes,' he says gently, 'you must have made some kind of mistake.'

'Mistake?' I squeak. 'No! Marcus, it's no mistake. I'm here for you.'

He smiles gently, sadly, even. 'No, babes,' he says. 'I don't know you. We've never met.'

'It's me,' I say, 'Serafina.'

The smile stays. 'I don't know any Serafina,' he says. Then he pauses. 'Although you do remind me of someone.' A flicker of recognition tries to break through; the trace of drains again. It dies. 'No,' he says, 'that didn't happen.'

'It *is* me,' I say.

He pulls me to my feet. 'I'm trying to help you out here.' He nods at the others. 'They'll rip you to shreds,' he whispers, 'just with their jokes.'

'*I'm Serafina*,' I whisper back. I try again. I remember how Kookie said it: '*Zara Finer?*'

One of his friends bustles forward. The girl; tall, long legs, short skirt, beautiful, scary.

'Is she giving you a problem?' she says, all possessive, all protective. She lays a hand on Marcus.

I blink.

The friends laugh.

I don't know what to say.

One of them pulls out his phone. He snaps a picture.

Another says, 'If you don't want her, Marcus, chuck her my way. Any skirt is skirt to me.'

Marcus turns and holds up his hand, stop-signs them away. There's a note of anger in his voice. 'Shut up,' he says. 'Leave the poor kid alone.'

'Sorr-ee,' says one of them. 'Didn't know she was so special!'

They hoot with laughter.

Marcus turns back to me. 'See?' he says. 'You need to go home.'

I grab hold of his arm. 'It *is* me, Marcus,' I say, 'you've got to believe me. I *am* Serafina.' But I realise with a sinking heart that I never told him my name, and suddenly I know the time has come to tell him everything, all the other things I never said as well. There may not be another chance. Larry may be here waiting to betray us again. Marcus may walk away. *Halloween is tomorrow.* I don't want to shock, but if a shock will awaken? I don't know what to do. But I do it anyway.

The street lies cold; the shop fronts glitter, a thin blowing of sleet slicks the pavements. I stand up straight. I unfurl imaginary wings. *'I am the Angel of Death,'* I say, even though I don't sound like one any more. *'The Seraph who held back Heaven and Hell for you. I took another in your place. I gave you extra time so that you could change your ways. The hour draweth near, Marcus. Take heed. You must repent by All Hallows' Eve or perish.'*

His friends are laughing so hard they're jumping about. The girl starts screaming in my face. Their cameras click. A passer-by puts his head down and hurries on.

I see a look of horror blossom on Marcus's face. I want to rush to him, to prove these things to him, to breathe

307

the dust of angels over him, to make a soft breeze blow in from the south, blow all the confusion from his eyes.

'What do you mean?' says Marcus. But his eyes are hard now, cold and angry.

I swallow. I don't know what to say.

'What's going on?' says the long-legged girl, grabbing at Marcus. She turns to me, her pretty face ugly with ignorance. 'Just eff off,' she says.

I chew my cheek. My legs are dissolving. I've said the wrong thing. I've said the right thing – in the wrong way. Why did I just spit it out like that?

Marcus grabs hold of my arm. He shakes off the girl's grip. He steers me away from his friends. His hand is quivering, his face twisting into something quite violent. 'I don't know who you are, who sent you,' he says, 'but I'm holding my temper down, and you need to leave. Now.' He pushes me away. I stand there. His eyes command me. GO.

I can feel the danger. I can see from the lines on his cheek, the twist of his mouth. My heart is pounding, my throat dry. 'Marcus,' I say, hanging on to his sleeve, 'I *am* Serafina, the angel, please remember. I Fell for you. I lost God's grace – my wings – my fire. I made a deal with . . . I look different now . . . I'm not an angel any more. You said *if it were always just us, you could be OK . . . If I were always here . . . I came . . . I promised. . . I didn't disappoint you . . .*'

Marcus shakes off my arm; a look of longing flickers across his face. Then he clenches his teeth. 'No,' he says. 'You're not.'

'But . . .' I start to say. *What can I say?*

Marcus balls his fists. 'I'm not going there again,' he says. I can see the effort it costs him; veins knotted and purple stand out on his neck.

With one powerful twist of his arm he casts me off. He strides back to his friends. He throws his arm over the shoulder of the closest one, rolls back his head as someone cracks a joke. He laughs. There they are all laughing and pointing at me.

And they think that's so funny.

# Zara 6

I don't know what to do. Tears well up in my eyes. I stand there in the driving sleet. I've never been in sleet before. I thought I'd like it. Rain and snow, all fresh from Heaven, cascading down on me, like bathing in some great outdoor shower. I don't. It hurts. Each splash of freezing water hits me in the face.

Soon it's not just sleet but an icy deluge drenching me, pooling at my feet. My little black gym flats are soaked. My make-up runs. My curtain of wild black hair falls from its spaniel ears. It hangs from my head, limp.

Where can I go? The pain in my stomach is back. *He doesn't know me.* I thought one look into my eyes would be enough. Larry has won. He's changed me beyond recognition. I'm not Serafina any more. He's tricked me. I should have said: 'And I wish to live on Earth *and look just like myself*' as well as all the rest. How can I matter to Marcus now? *He doesn't know me.*

He has ordered me to go.

Then I must leave.

I run.


My side stabs. My breath burns. I gulp in air. I must rest.

There's nothing worse than this. Nothing worse than rejection. No pain like Marcus's arm pushing me off.

A world without Marcus.

There's an empty lot ahead. A patch of darkness. I creep through the tin wall around it. I find a lump of concrete. I sit down, shivering. I think I'll die. This human body is very weak. It won't last long. My teeth are chattering. My fingers are white and numb. Soon the numbness will reach my heart. And it will stop.

So this is what it is to be human. To suffer hunger, cold and rejection.

But something inside me won't allow me to die. What, give up so soon? On my first night on Earth? Even Robyn managed eighteen years. If she could bear it that long, I can do one more night.

I will not sit here pitying myself.

I will not lament my lost Serafina.

I have a new self.

I'm Zara now.

With new powers.

I must find those powers.

And use them.

Tomorrow night, I tell myself. You can die tomorrow night, Zara – but not until then.

I set out back along the high street. Someone hurries past me, head down, raincoat pulled tight. He looks at me. He frightens me, and I turn aside. I catch sight of myself in the darkened glass of a shop front: a thin pale face peeps back, its eyes huge, edged about with smudged make-up; thin shoulders, skinny legs. It doesn't look like me. But no matter. I am her and she is me. I will try my best for you, Zara, I tell that pale white face. Together we'll find a way.

Behind my reflection the Halloween masks hang, leering at me from the darkness of the window, their white teeth stretched wide. I look at the teeth, and think of Larry and his treachery. *You will not feast on Marcus's soul,* I vow. *I will warn him of his peril. And I will carry on warning him as long as my voice lasts.*

Squaring my shoulders, I turn my back on the devils and the demons and I set out again for Curlston Heights.

Shivering, I retrace my steps. All around water drips. Underfoot pavements slip. My gym pumps are like envelopes of ice. And there are the adamantine doors, shut fast, their grey paint like an omen.

Dare I send up a prayer? Has news of my Fall raced through the streets of Heaven? Is my name whispered in horror? I send up my prayer anyway. *'Heavenly Father who sits on high, and knowest all things, please forgive your humble servant, Serafina, and send her your grace and blessings. Amen.'* And I make the sign of the cross over myself.

Then I tap 56 into the keypad.

No one answers. Marcus is there. His mother is there. But nobody answers. Timidly my hand hovers over the pad again.

Once more I make the sign of the cross. I press harder: 56.

I wait. The sleet drives against my back. I shiver. I'm no longer steady. A noise? Has someone come?

'What?' says a tinny voice. It's Marcus's mother.

'Please,' I say, 'for pity's sake.'

'Do you have any idea what time it is?' she says.

'No,' I say. I don't. In Heaven time is not important. Up until now time has only been a schedule to Collect souls by. But I hear from the tone in her voice it *is* important. And I know she's right. Time is a schedule and Marcus's soul is on it.

'It's five past four,' she snaps. 'It's the middle of the night.'

'I'm sorry,' I say. There's a tiny note of kindness in her voice that wasn't there yesterday. As if she understands what drives me to stand here in the early-morning cold and ring her doorbell. I want to appeal to it, fall on my knees to it, beg her to let me see Marcus.

'Listen,' she says, 'just go home.'

The tinny rattle of her voice fades. I hear another voice, a lovely, sweet high-flowing voice. It trills over the scruff and echo. I hear them talking, low, urgent whispers. '*Her again.*' '*You go back to bed. Try and sleep.*' '*Let me talk to her.*' The sound of sighing, a door closing. I wait.

'Hello?' says this new voice.

'Hello,' I say.

'Are you the girl who was waiting outside all yesterday?'

'Yes,' I say.

'You poor thing,' she says. 'You can't just camp outside our block, you know.'

'No,' I say. I know I can't. The sound of her sweet voice makes me realise how friendless I am. 'Please,' I say, 'it's so important.'

She knows from my voice how important it is.

313

'You better come up.' She sighs. 'We need to chat.'

The buzzer on the steel grille goes.

'What do I do?' I say, my voice hardly daring to believe.

'Just push on the door,' says the sweet one, 'and take the lift to Level Five. We're number 56.'

'Yes,' I whisper as the door opens. 'Thank you.'

# Zara 7

I press on the paintwork. I push open the grey adamantine doors and I'm in. I can't believe it. I can't even guess what it means. *I'm inside Curlston Heights.*

Quickly I stumble to the back of the foyer. There are the lift shafts. I remember how I adored lifts, how they clang around you, how they make your skin flutter. I step inside. The doors slide and clash. I'm encased inside steel. A prison. I'm scared. I'm scared to see Marcus again, scared he'll reject me, scared of what I've done. I punch in Level Five.

The lift rises. I tremble.

At the fifth floor it shakes to a halt. The doors clang open. I step out into the dark corridor. A low light flickers on. I look up at the door numbers.

'Here,' hisses a voice. Down the dim corridor I see a door has opened, a silhouette is outlined against it. I hasten towards it.

In the half light I slip into number 56 Curlston Heights. The figure, dark by the door, whispers, 'Be really quiet, everyone's asleep.'

I'm really quiet. I'm so quiet I float over the scratched plastic flooring. I tiptoe into a hall. Inside it's dark. I feel carpet thick beneath my feet, a small hand in mine. I'm led into the front room. *I'm inside.* There is the three-piece suite, the shelving unit, the sofa and chairs angled in outline around the rug, round the TV. Through those doors – down that corridor, Marcus is there.

The girl softly closes the door. I know who she is. I know her voice. I know her step. It's Jasmine – Marcus's youngest sister, not the tall, beautiful, haughty one but the elfin one who went with Marcus to St Jude's, who was so helpful at the funeral. I'm so lucky. I know how good she is. She switches on a side light. She takes my hand again. She leads me to the sofa and still holding on to me, she pats the seat next to her.

'Oh, look at you, you poor thing,' she says. 'You look half starved. Don't say a word. I'm going to fix you a lovely cup of tea and a hot toasted sandwich and you are going to dry out and warm yourself by the fire.'

She flicks on the electric fire and a sudden rush of fake orange coals light up. False shadowy flames dance out from the look-alike marble fireplace. But best of all a sudden rush of air, thick and warming.

'But please be very, very quiet,' she whispers. 'Mum is going through a rotten time. My brother got shot the week before last. He should have died; his best friend did. She's nearly beside herself with worry, and she needs to rest.'

'OK,' I whisper.

And she tiptoes out of the front room. I hear her moving down the hall. I hear some clicking and the soft purr of an electric kettle. I look around the room. There are the photos

316

of Marcus: Marcus as a baby, Marcus with his arms round his mum, Marcus in a football team, Marcus posing like the Original Badman, Marcus in dark glasses. Marcus looking manly.

Marcus.

I feel tears aching at the back of my throat, but they are very far away. I won't let them fall now; to burden this troubled family with my sorrows more than I have already. I just look at the photos and admire the curve of his arm and the strength in his jaw. I long for the touch of those strong hands. I think: *He is just a few doors away.* I think how lucky I am to know him, to feel this thing that springs up in my heart, to feel this ache. In all my thousands of years in Heaven never have I felt more alive, more real, more important, more unhappy.

Beside the photos is a calendar. October 31st has a thick black circle drawn around it as if the family already know that date is going to change their lives for ever.

*Oh Marcus, you must listen this time.*

Jasmine comes back. She's carrying a little tray and on it lies the toasted sandwich and the mug of tea and a paper napkin. The scent from the toast makes strange things happen in my stomach. I find my mouth watering, my throat swallowing in anticipation.

She smiles. 'Eat,' she says.

I eat. My eyes say, 'Thank you, thank you, thank you,' but my hands shake, the sandwich trembles, I juggle it to my lips.

Oh, it's so hot and crunchy and crusty and sweet and tangy and there's cheese and butter and relish and ham and each mouthful scalds my tongue, but it's tasty and I must take more. I can't stop. I burn my mouth.

'Slow down,' she says, 'I can make more toasties. You'll be ill if you eat it so fast.'

So I try to slow down, but this is the first time I've ever eaten a toastie. The first time I've ever eaten. And I love it.

'Now,' says the girl. 'I'm Jasmine.'

'Zara,' I say, still using the name Kookie gave me. I look at her. I look at the door. Marcus is very near.

'So Zara,' she says, 'where's home? Can I call your mum? Your friends? Will they come and get you?'

I look at her. I don't know what to say. How can I tell her about the Elysian Fields, the water meadows where a thousand songbirds chorus? I can't. But I can't lie to her, either, or make up anything, so I just look at her and say nothing.

'Difficult?' she says kindly.

I nod.

'Please don't mind me asking, but are you pregnant?'

I shake my head. It's a strange question. I'm not sure why she asks it, but I can see in her eyes that she means no harm.

'Oh good,' she says, sighing like that's a big relief.

She smiles encouragingly at me. 'But wherever home is, can you go back there?'

I shake my head. I can never go back to Heaven. The ache in my throat spreads. I blink rapidly, trying to swallow.

'I'm sorry,' she says, all kindness. 'I didn't mean to upset you.' She rises and comes towards me and puts her arm

318

around my shoulder. And suddenly I feel so drained. Her touch reminds me of other touches: Kookie, Marcus.

'I must speak to Marcus,' I say.

'Oh no,' she says, 'not now. He's been so ill. Don't get worried, he's had a miracle recovery – everyone says so – but he's weak. Let him sleep – please?' She looks at me.

I want to tell her sleep doesn't matter.

'No more questions for now. You need a wash, some fresh clothes and a good sleep. We'll talk tomorrow. OK, honey?' She pats my arm. 'You can sleep in my room, but you must be very, very quiet, OK?'

I nod. My heart has gone out to her. I love her. That she could be so kind to someone she doesn't know. She'll find her way to Heaven so quickly. She'll be fast tracked straight through to God. He'll be so pleased with her. Not like me. I shudder. In the quietness while Jasmine has gone to sort me out a bed I hear a clock ticking. There is no time for baths or sleep. I must make a plan. I'm in the flat. I must use this time.

But as hard as I try to think of the right words and how I will say them, my mind is shutting down. Warmth is flowing through me. My stomach feels so happy. The clock is ticking. Its ticks lull me. My eyelids start closing.

I slap at myself to stay awake. How strange, this human body. First it must eat, then it must be warm. Now it must sleep. I can't fight it. I *must* find Marcus.

Jasmine comes back and whispers, 'You'll be ill if you don't sleep.' She leads me to her room. The clock is ticking.

'Marcus,' I say.

'Tomorrow,' she says.

'I must see him now.'

'No,' she says firmly. 'You mustn't.'

I awake in Jasmine's room. The sun is shining in through her window. The pink curtains are still drawn, but the beauty of the sunlight and the sheer rosy pinkness of the cloth has flooded the room with a wonderful cheerfulness. I roll over. I'm alone. Jasmine's not here. *It's 31st October. Halloween! What time is it?* I've overslept. I sit up in bed. My bed is a long sofa with pretty silky sheets and a thick fluffy cover. I look around. On a chair placed near me lie a pile of clothes and a note:

*Dear Zara,*

*I hope you're feeling much better this morning and have slept well. Sorry about the sofa but we don't have a spare room for guests. I've left you some of my clothes to wear. I noticed you like the Gothy look, so I've picked out some black things. I hope you like them. I think we're about the same size. I've told Mum you're here. Please be very nice to her – she's very stressed. I know you'll want to talk to Marcus, but he's very grumpy if he gets woken up too early, so give him time. He's been very, very ill, he's mending like magic, but please don't upset him. There's food in the fridge and I've left you a fiver. DON'T OPEN THE DOOR TO STRANGERS. The door code is C3458X so you can come and go. I'll be back very late this evening, because I've been invited to a Halloween*

*party – on a blind date (!), but you can stay until we*
*work out a plan for you. I'll ask my friends if they*
*know of a room. You'll probably be able to get welfare.*
    *Love n kisses*
    *Jasmine xoxoxo*


  *My cell phone's 07978650345, call me in case of*
*anything.*

I read the note. I look at the neat little pile of clothes. I'm
overcome with some kind of emotion that makes my heart
catch. 'Oh, Jasmine,' I whisper.

I determine at once that I won't burden her with any
of the sad things I know. I won't burden Marcus's mother
either. They have too much to worry about.

I rise and wash. Quickly I put on the clothes that Jasmine
left: a tight lacy black top, a flared Victorian witchy skirt
and high-heeled, laced-up boots. I stand in front of Jasmine's
mirror. I look at my new human self.

I'm quite pretty. Not in the way I used to be, not in the
curvy way of the girls at the club. I comb out my hair. It's
truly jet black. I look at my fringe. I try pinning it to one
side. I settle for a dark wing over one eye. It frames my
face and makes it tinier than ever.

Jasmine has left her make-up bag out for me as well. I
think of Kookie as I look through it. God bless Kookie. In
honour of Kookie, who first baptised me with mascara and
black kohl pencil, I make my eyes up as dramatically as
possible. I put on the make-up she'd like me to wear. Red
lips, darker and huger eyes than ever, with teardrops drawn

on my cheeks, pale foundation and shimmery stardust high-lights. I'm not very good at it. I get make-up in my eye and it stings horribly.

When I'm finished I stand back and take a last quick glance at myself – small, pretty (make-up a bit weird). He doesn't love her, that scary pointed-little-chin girl in the mirror. There is no hope of that. *He won't love you*, I tell her. *His arms will never enfold you.* I don't cry. I didn't throw away Heaven to sit and watch myself weep in a mirror edged in fluffy pink. I just want her to get the message. She needs to stay strong and if she longs for his touch too much, she may weaken. *You love him.* I tell her. That's all that matters. And you'll save him because you do.

I catch my throat. I abandon hope. I don't let any thought of being loved back stay. It'll weigh me down with its sad longings. I wanted to become human. I wanted to be one with Marcus. But I left Heaven to save a soul. A soul which will surely burn in Hell if I fail.

# Zara 8

Mrs Montague is resting. Rayanne has left for work. Marcus is awake (please don't let him be grumpy). This is it. I steal to his room. He's taped on the door a picture of a skull made out of shining stars. Under the picture is a caption which reads: *Abandon hope all ye who enter here.* Only he would display such a message. I tap softly on his door. My heart is beating. My throat is dry. I hear a noise from within. I listen. I stand there as quiet as a mouse, quieter than a feather falling. I tap the door again. I hear the squeak of a mattress. The rush of covers thrown back.

'What?'

'Can I come in?' I whisper.

'Well come in, if you're going to,' says the voice I know so well.

Tentatively I turn the door handle. I push it gently in.

'And?' says Marcus.

So I step into the room.

Marcus is sitting up in bed. His dark hair is tousled, his voice gruff with sleep. But the room smells good, clean and warm and somehow scented. Marcus looks at me like he's never seen me before in his entire life.

'Who the hell are you?' he says.

He doesn't remember me. It must be the changed clothes, the new hairstyle, my clumsy attempts at make-up. Something inside me sinks, but it's not important. He doesn't know me. He doesn't need to, so all I say is: 'Please, don't invoke that fearsome place.'

He looks confused.

'Who are you?' he says, 'and what're you doing here?'

'I'm sorry,' I say. I don't know if I'm sorry or not. I've a mission to accomplish. I must do it.

Marcus waits. He looks at me and simply waits. I stare. Something thrills inside me. It feels all excited and shivery. But I must not be sidetracked. I fix my eyes on the floor. I must not look at his clean strong chest, the way his arm muscles flex. His wounds have healed well. There is only a patch of clean gauze over his heart.

I sigh. I don't even bother with 'I'm Serafina' any more; instead I say: 'For now you can call me Zara.'

'So,' he says, eyeing me, 'you think there's going to be a later – when I'll call you something else?'

I breathe in and tighten my resolve. 'There's something I have to talk to you about.'

He looks at me. Maybe there's something in my voice that reminds him of who I once was, for a certain curious, hopeful, puzzled look lights up his eyes. It's almost as if he recognises me – almost but not quite – as if my voice, or the light glancing across my face reminds him of something.

Quickly he grabs his T-shirt and pulls it on. He swings his legs out of bed. His bare legs are so taut and strong and smooth. I gasp as I see them. He stands up. I see he's wearing only shorts. I turn my eyes away. I do so out of politeness, and because looking at him makes me ache in a strange new way.

He sits on the edge of the bed and pulls on his jeans.

'OK,' he says, 'whatever your name is. Let's start with what you're doing in my bedroom.' He raises one eyebrow.

'I'm sorry,' I say.

'Well, if you'd walked in a couple of weeks ago, you might have been sorry – or maybe not.' He arches both eyebrows. 'But I'm a changed man now. I've had a heart attack.'

I look at him a bit blank. He points to where the gauze is taped on his chest. 'Heart,' he says. 'Attacked?'

I get it. It's one of his jokes. He's joking with me. I smile. Should I laugh?

'Marcus,' I say, taking a deep breath. 'This may seem like a strange request, but . . .'

Marcus looks at me. I nearly lose my nerve.

'Would you just listen to everything I have to say?' My heart is thumping so loudly I'm sure he must hear it.

'Are you one of Jasmine's friends?'

'Will you *promise* you'll just listen, *whatever you think?*'

'Hey, kid,' he says, 'I'll listen; don't look so nervous.'

I bite my lip. 'Do you remember Serafina?' His reaction is too fast and harsh for me to get another word out.

He's half off the bed. 'I see who you are,' he says suddenly. 'I didn't recognise you at first. You're that weirdo girl from yesterday.'

'I'm sorry,' I say again. I stammer. Nothing matters. Only listening matters now. I mustn't mess this up. His face looks

so serious. His lips so soft . . . so sweet . . . A mad idea
– should I kiss him – will he recognise me then? He must.
I would know his kiss anywhere. I want to kiss him. I let
it pass. Instead I say: 'I've news from the angel.'

Marcus looks at me. He screws up his face. 'News from
the angel?' he says.

I nod.

'Who the hell *are* you?'

He's seen the hesitation in my face. My throat goes dry.
I know I must speak. I take a very big breath and I say,
'On the night you were shot a number of things happened
that you may not have been aware of . . .'

He gives me a look, as if to say: And why would *you*
know them? But he doesn't. There's something that stops
him. 'I'm still listening,' he says.

'You were shot,' I say gently. 'Nobody could expect you
to know them.'

He's standing there poised, looking at me, trying to figure
something out.

'And you were dying,' I add.

He lowers his eyebrows. Maybe he's already considered
that.

'And . . .'

'What?' he says.

There's no easy way to tell him.

'I was sent –' I correct myself. 'Serafina was sent to Collect
your soul. Serafina was an Angel of Death.'

He shakes his head. He looks like he's going to react.
Like yesterday.

'You . . .' He opens his mouth.

'Please listen,' I implore.

He shuts up his mouth, and twists it into a disbelieving line.

'You were shot through the heart,' I say.

He looks at me.

'But you didn't die.'

He seems to be thinking about this, as if it has been puzzling him as well.

'I'm not dead,' he says, trying to turn it into a joke. 'Go on, pinch me. Here, have a squeeze.' He offers me his forearm.

'But you should be.'

He knows that's true.

'You're not dead, because the angel . . .' (I want to say: fell in love, couldn't bear to let you die, wanted to help you) '. . . the angel took out a contract on your death,' I say.

He leans back on his pillows.

'Well I've heard of a contract killer taking out a contract on a life, but never an angel contract killer who takes out a contract on a death!' he says flippantly.

'She signed a document,' I say, going pale, for it's not funny; it's not even the remotest bit funny.

But Marcus is suddenly smiling, as if taking out a contract on his death is the funniest thing ever.

'You must have wondered how you survived? Your recovery?'

'Not really,' he says, as if natural good health is his divine right.

'You must have wondered about the visions of the angel?'

He stops short. The blood drains from his face. 'How did you know about them?' he says.

'She told you there was a condition,' I say.

'How did you know I had visions?'

'She tried to tell you everything at the hospital.'

'*How do you know?*' he demands.

'She said she'd come to save your soul.'

He turns aside, seems to be struggling with something. Turns back, says, 'It was the side-effects of morphine, that's all.'

'She said she would heal your pain.'

Marcus shakes his head. 'No no no,' he says. 'Disorientation; irregular heartbeat; hallucinations; mood changes – exaggerated sense of well-being – shortness of breath; shallow breathing; sudden chest pain – all hallucinations.'

'She sent the Light of the Lord to heal you.'

'I'd pulled out the tubes.'

'She walked with you in the garden.'

'It's a normal reaction after life-threatening trauma.'

'She appeared again at the funeral.'

'She was bang out of order.'

'She told you to repent.'

'She should have told me about Joey.' Marcus frowns and turns away.

'She's been trying to tell you about the contract.'

'How the hell do you know all this?' His voice is suddenly sharp and loud.

I lay my finger over my lips. 'Shush,' I say, 'your mother . . . *please listen* . . . you said you would.' I take a deep breath. 'There was small print.'

'Small print!' He relaxes. As if the idea of angels and visions and small print don't go together. The spell is broken.

He breaks out in a fresh round of smiles. 'Of course there's always small print!'

So I wait. I wait until he can stop finding it so funny. For that is what he's doing; silently laughing out loud at a funny, pale, skinny girl who knows more than she should, who is trying to tell him something he doesn't want to hear. And maybe he'll never understand. For a minute I wonder about humans, but I'm human now; I'm no longer sure of anything.

'And . . .' he says, all mock serious, pulling a long face at me, 'what does the small print say? Will I be sent to the Devil after twenty years to fry for eternity? Come on, little Zara – who pretends to know everything – surely you know that too, don't you?'

I breathe a huge sigh of relief – so he does know. I nod. Thank God he knows. He must have been more awake than I thought.

'Only not after twenty years. Much sooner than that.'

The look on his face changes.

'Oh, really?' he says.

'Yes. And you don't *have* to go to Hell,' I say, 'not if you stick to the condition.'

'And what condition would that be?' says Marcus, all charming smiles, effortless grace.

'To repent, to mend your ways.'

He frowns.

'The condition is . . .'

'OK, OK,' he says. As if he is just testing me.

'Completely, in word and deed,' I emphasise.

'So, the small print?' says Marcus, leaning his gorgeous

face upon his hands. His eyebrows knit together in a new quizzical way. 'What *did* it *actually say*?'

'It said . . .' I continue, determined not to be put off. 'It said that an Extension on your mortal body could only be given if the books balanced.'

'And what exactly did *that* mean?' asks Marcus, narrowing up his eyes.

'That meant that another life was taken in your stead.'

'I see-ee,' says Marcus with a long-drawn-out nod.

My eyes fly wide. My jaw drops. I clamp it shut. This is it. I know what's coming.

'So let me get this right,' says Marcus. 'In order for my soul to remain in this gorgeous handsome body, somebody else had to take my place in Hell, is that it?'

'Yes,' I say.

'So, dear, pretty little Zara – who did that for me? Who took my turn on Death Row?'

I look up at him and gulp. Surely he must have guessed?

But his eyes (so very dark now) look back at me. Guileless.

I take a deep breath. This is it.

'Joey,' I say very simply. 'Joey took your place.'

'Joey?'

His face goes ashen. His jaw trembles.

It's not OK. He's not OK.

His eyes bulge. '*Joey took my place?*' He can't believe it. He's trying to believe it.

'Yes,' I whisper.

Marcus gets up, paces around the room. I watch, scared he will smash something. But it's worse. He's gone quiet like the hush after gunfire.

'I don't think *that*'s funny,' he says.

'Oh, it's not,' I say. I'm waiting for the screaming, waiting for the rejection. 'You need to understand –'

'What I understand,' says Marcus with ice in his voice, 'is that you've barged your way into my home . . .' He shakes his head, looks up at the ceiling as if it will dissolve. 'I don't believe this,' he says.

'But you must,' I say quietly.

'And you're telling me that I'll go to the Devil because of it?'

'Oh no,' I say again. 'Not go to the Devil at all if you repent.'

'So,' says Marcus, 'if I don't?'

'Then you'll die,' I say.

'We all die,' he says back.

'But you'll die soon,' I whisper.

He shakes his head.

'And your soul will be damned.'

'How long have I got, then?'

'The contract fixed the time – as midnight on Halloween,' I squeak.

'Halloween.' He says it so quietly, as if it might disturb a butterfly perched on some flower in Heaven. 'Tonight.'

'Yes,' I say.

Marcus pauses. Then he laughs as if the world has played its last joke on him. He laughs and laughs. He stands up and paces around the small bedroom again. He picks his guitar up, strums furiously, puts it down. He nudges a pile of discarded clothes with his foot. He picks up papers, CDs, books, games. He leans against the wall. He's very disturbed.

331

My heart quakes. I tremble. To have caused such pain, to have turned my smiling Marcus into such a whirlwind of confusion.

At length he turns on me. 'How do I know whether to believe you or not?' he says. I can see his doubt. I can see his confusion.

I've thought of this. I've thought of everything since yesterday. 'You can test me,' I say. 'Ask me to repeat anything that you said to the angel. If I don't know the answer then disbelieve me – but if I can tell you, then I beg you . . .'

'All right,' he says, 'I'll test you. But if you are lying, God help me, I'll make you suffer.'

# Zara 9

'Ask me,' I say.

Marcus squares his shoulders and turns around. Away he paces again, over the carpeted floor, away to the window, back to the bed.

'Tell me then,' he says. 'What were my first words to her?'

*Marcus, cushioned by my flame and my brilliance, opened his eyes, looked into mine and smiled, his eyes so full of trust. 'So, angels are watching over me, after all.'*

'Angels are watching over me,' I tell him.

'What were here to me?'

*'Only one,' I whispered back.*

'Only one,' I say.

A troubled look darkens his eyes. 'Where did we first sit together then?' he said.

*We reached the first huge spreading tree. One of its long limbs had grown so close to the ground it formed a horizontal seat . . .*

I tell him where we sat: on the cedar branch in the hospital garden.

Marcus sits down heavily on the bed. 'How can you know all that?' he says. He shakes his head. 'Who told you? Where? How?'

'Marcus,' I say quite steadily, for I'm no longer afraid, the worst is past. I've renounced immortality. I've suffered rejection. I've braved disclosure. I can tell him now. Now that I've confessed about Joey. So I do tell him, not to seek his affection nor convince him of my truth. Simply because it is the truth.

'I am that angel. I am she. I Fell from Heaven for your sake. I made my own contract with others. (I don't tell him of that terrible meeting in the Abyss.) I traded my fire and my wings and my beauty for this human shape.'

'Were you at the club? Did you overhear us?'

He doesn't believe me. But it is said. Finished. Done with.

'Are you a nurse? Did you work at the hospital?'

'I did these things for love, and it's for love's sake now I implore you to repent.'

'Do I talk in my sleep?'

'Let us seek out any holy person who can hear your confession and absolve you of sin.'

'How long have you been spying on me?'

'If you can't find anyone before whom you can repent, then fall on your knees and beg for mercy. At least it will save you from Hell.'

Marcus sits very still. He looks at me.

'Try to believe,' I whisper.

Marcus sighs. 'When I was ill and dying I thought I saw someone . . . I thought I had a guardian angel.' His face gentles a little as he seems to remember. 'Maybe it did happen . . . she made me value things I'd never valued before – you realise how good life is . . . how precious, how important.' His voice trails off.

I look at him. He does not believe in Serafina any more. Not fully. He's pushing her away – remembering her like a dream.

'It was the morphine . . .' he says, but I can tell he doesn't completely think that. 'I did believe for a while. I tried to do as she asked. I tried to go straight, dog my crew, turn Queen's evidence; I even went into a church. It didn't work out.'

Marcus jumps up. He seems disappointed, as if he has been struggling with himself and lost. 'So I don't believe you,' he says firmly. 'If there'd been an angel, she'd have made it happen.' But his face is shining, as if he has suddenly thought of something new. He grabs hold of me. 'But it *is* very strange – so I'll give you one chance. I'll make a deal with you! You show me my angel, I'll do whatever you say. I'll even repent.'

I feel the pressure of his hands on my arms. It sends spirals of electricity into my shoulders. I don't point out that if I *am* his angel – how can I show him myself? I just stand there.

He holds on, suddenly exhilarated. '*Show me my angel,*' he says. And he's holding on so tight, as if I can make a miracle happen. 'Come on then, I swear, I'll do it!'

*He's said he'll repent.*

He stands up. 'Hey, Angel!' he shouts. 'If you're there – show yourself!'

'Shush,' I say.

'*An-gel,*' he says again, as if he expects me to pop up in the centre of the room and appear before him in all my lost fire and glory. 'OK,' he says, 'she's not here. But you're going to show me her.' He shakes my arms. 'We'll get to the bottom of this and God help you if you're winding me up.'

'Yes,' I whisper. *He's agreed to repent.* 'Deal,' I say.

He sticks out his balled fist, touches my hand, knuckle to knuckle, touches his chest. A gangsta salute. 'Deal,' he says.

My brain is racing. I can't show him Serafina. Will he accept other proof? One step at a time. The testimony of another? But who? Who might be on Earth? Could I call on Raquel? Would she be on Collection Duty? Will she come? Would she apparition? I doubt it.

So who?

There's one person. My heart nearly stops in terror. *Not exactly an angel.* But proof. And I know where to find him. *He once was an angel.* I remember his exact words: *'If you make it to Earth and feel like partying . . .*

*I'll be in da club, with a glass full of . . .'*

I can show him the Devil.

# Zara 10

Marcus orders me to make us coffee, toast. He orders me to write a note and leave it on the fridge telling his mum he's fine, has just popped out, that'll he'll be OK, and he has a friend taking care of him and she doesn't need to wait in. Then he orders me to wipe off the make-up, that he's not going to be seen dead with a girl who looks like that. He orders me to leave with him.

He's very bossy. (If I was to stay with him for a longer time, and he was fully recovered, I think we'd have to do something about that.)

Then he says, 'Thank you,' with such a soft sweet smile. And my heart melts.

Outside Curlston Heights we stop. He stands in front of me. It's as if he's filled with a new happiness he wasn't expecting. He's bursting with life. He leaves me breathless. 'So, pretty little Zara, what now? You seem to know everything about my angel. So where do we go? Find her. Summon her, do whatever it takes. Come on, this is your chance.'

I can see his eyes racing, darting. I can feel his energy, his need.

'We go to the club,' I say.

337

'Good,' he says, as if that makes perfect sense. 'That's where it all started, so we'll start there too.'

A strange fever burns in his face. He grabs my arm again. Together we march down the street. As we go, he chants to himself: 'OK, OK, OK, Angel, I'll find you; I will.'

I can see the clench of his jaw, as he tries to hold something inside.

'We'll see if you're morphine.'

We stride down one street, through another. We don't talk. Marcus walks fast, as if he wishes every stone underfoot long gone. I try to keep up, but this new frail body I own is panting, struggling to trot alongside his mighty steps. I worry about his heart. I beg him to slow down. He laughs in a new reckless way.

At length we reach the club. It's open. It's a café bar during daylight hours. Larry will be here somewhere. I know it, like I know demons are everywhere, lurking out of sight. Waiting. Marcus rushes in, past the chairs and tables, past the bar and bouncers' desk, down the stairs, past the big mirror. I follow. Larry's not in the café. I don't stop. I don't look at myself. I don't twirl.

*How am I going to convince Marcus?*

We march through the empty club rooms, past black leather sofas, past upholstered walls. The place still reeks. In the centre of the empty dance floor he stops – there on the very spot where first I held him – where I watched him lay the wreath. '*Angel*,' he calls. His words hang on the air.

'*An-gel?*'

A hot stuffy draught belches through the room. A door

opens. A whiff of drains. The air catches the side of my face. A light flicks on. It refracts in the mirror in an orange glow.

'She's not here,' says a voice, a voice I know.

*He's here.*

In through the door strolls Larry.

That crisp white suit. How smoothly he apparitions. *I didn't even call him.* It must take millions of years to do it so effortlessly. If I didn't know he was the Devil, didn't know he had wings folded up under that clean tailored tuxedo, I'd think he was completely mortal. I must find a way to make him betray himself. All Marcus needs is to be convinced about angels. Then he'll repent. I know he will. If I could somehow show Marcus his wings.

I wonder if Larry will recognise me. I hope not. But it's a detail. Maybe I can trick him into doing something angelly – freeze time, conjure thunderbolts, something, anything, just show Marcus.

'So who do we have here then?' asks Larry. I don't smile. He doesn't flick an eyelid. Does he recognise me?

'Hello,' I say. He must know me.

Larry looks at me. 'Clara?' he says.

He never got my name right.

'Zara?' he says.

'Hello,' I say. How am I going to do this?

'So many names,' he says. 'So many girls.'

He knows exactly who I am.

Marcus looks at me, puzzled. He even flaps his hand at me, as if to say 'Why are we here? What's going on?'

I turn to him. 'This is *Larry*,' I say. 'He's the one I've brought you to see. He can tell you who I am. He can tell you all about your angel.' I wheel about and face Larry. 'Isn't that right?' I challenge. I don't know what makes me so bold. 'He's a Celestial Advisor, actually. *He knows everything.* He'll tell you.' My sarcasm is showing – even Marcus notices it.

Larry smiles in a very affable way. 'Cute, isn't she?' he says.

Marcus looks at me, shakes his head, then does something quite strange. He wraps an arm around me in a protective way. *He wraps an arm around me?* It's nice, but I can't make it out.

'Larry,' I demand, *'tell Marcus who I am!'*

'She's a *lovely* girl,' says Larry, turning to Marcus. Larry crosses his eyes, makes a screwy gesture with his hand, and adds: 'A little bit mental, but her heart's in the right place.'

'Larry, tell him you're the Devil.' I don't care if I sound mad or anything. It's Halloween. We've only got today.

*All Larry has to do is give himself away.*

Larry shrugs in a pleasant way, as if being called the Devil is a kind of compliment.

*'Larry!'* I insist. *'Tell him I signed the contract with you.' Tell him what it said!* If I could scream any louder I would.

He smiles. 'Got a copy of this contract, baby-girl?' he asks in an exaggerated way and ruffles my hair.

My throat dries up. My voice fails. He knows I don't have a copy.

Marcus sees I'm upset. He squeezes my shoulder. 'It's OK, Zara,' he says. 'Let's leave it, shall we?'

I look up at him. His face is tired. The strain shows in his eyes. 'Larry isn't a Celestial Advisor, or the Devil,' he says. 'He's the owner of The Mass nightclub. I've known him for ages.'

I look at Larry. Oh, I get it.

*Larry the nightclub owner.*

'So you're not the Devil?' I jeer. 'You couldn't even strike a match, get a little fire going or produce a demon or two. You're just a grimy old punter.'

I'm hoping to goad him into something – anything – just one careless flash of demonic power.

'Leave it, Zara,' says Marcus. 'For a minute there I almost believed you.' There's disappointment in his voice.

I look at Larry. There's something triumphant in his eyes. It seems to say, 'I know who you are. I made you what you are.' But it's just a flicker, then it's gone. He says nothing, except: 'Take that man's advice, Tara.' All the time his eyes stay on my face. He inclines his head very slightly, like I'm a trophy or an award he's been angling to win.

Before I have time to process all this, Marcus steps forward, 'Sorry, Boss,' he says, 'there's been a misunderstanding.'

Larry turns his face slightly towards me, catches my eye. He's enjoying my confusion. He smiles, all golden hair, blue eyes. 'No worries!' he says.

'*I'll prove it.*' I won't give up. Not after everything I've been through. I don't care. I step forward – determined to yank at Larry's jacket and reveal his wings.

Larry looks at me. His eyelids narrow. He warns me with a slight shake of his head. *But I don't care.* I have to show

341

Marcus. But before I can touch him, Larry starts to intone something. *'Bagabi laca bachabe . . .'* I reel back. *'Lamc cahi achababe . . .'*

I freeze. His eyes burn. I can't move. A band like steel tightens around my chest. *'Karrelyos . . .'* An unseen hand catches my throat, throttles me. *'Lamac lamec Bachalyas . . .'* I try to breathe. He's strangling me. *'Cabahagy sabalyos . . .'* Holding my tongue.

Larry smiles. His eyes grow opaque. *'Baryolas . . .?'*

I nod my head. I understand. He doesn't need to finish the incantation. Larry smiles again. The grip on my throat lessons. I can breathe. The pain around my chest eases.

*'Voilà!* Disco! There you go!' says Larry, smiling at me, Now let's go upstairs and have a coffee? Make a plan?' He playfully punches Marcus's chest. 'I can sort all this out.'

Marcus relaxes. He nods.

'Yes,' says Larry, 'I can sort everything out. You've come to the exactly the right person.'

# Zara 11

Larry leads the way up to the café. He selects a table beside a large picture window overlooking the main street. There are a few people there already. Two couples, a bunch of girls, a lonely man at a corner table. Larry orders espresso times three, 'Strong and sweet', and a large bottle of brandy: 'Three glasses and three stars'. I can't disagree. I can't walk away. My legs don't obey me. Every time I open my mouth in dissent my jaw freezes, my breath grows shallow. Larry smiles at me as I cough and splutter.

'That's it,' he coaxes, 'deep breaths, stay calm.' His eyes are dancing.

Mine are not.

Something in the way he moves reminds me of a cat slinking along a hedgerow. I wonder why I never noticed that before. That stink of drains that was always here at the club. Such a give-away. I wonder what the large bottle of brandy is for. Surely it's too early for drinking? Surely the Devil doesn't have nerves?

I do. Mine are raw.

Larry laughs; his lips pull back, well over his gums, his row of white teeth glistening. I find myself fascinated by his gums, their edges pink against the whiteness of his teeth.

343

Larry pours us each a generous measure of brandy. The liquid is clear, like honey, thick like manna dew. I've never drunk brandy before. I copy Marcus and warm it with my hands, cupping them round the bowl of the glass, gently swirling the drink within.

*How can I trick him?*

'So are we sitting comfortably?' says Larry like he's talking to small children. Even Marcus shoots me a conspiratorial wink. I don't shoot one back. I see Larry's game. He's inviting us to underestimate him. Sheer folly. I'm not fooled by his clean-cut white suit, his baby-blue eyes. Not any more.

*How clever he is.* I'd imagined horns and hooves and evil eyes. *And how beautiful.* Lucifer, Lucifer, Son of the Morning. Light bearer. Dawn Star. Why did I imagine the Devil would be ugly when I knew he was God's brightest and best?

'Let's drink,' laughs Larry. 'Brandy before business.' He lays a hand on Marcus's arm.

Marcus looks like he wants to shrug it off. But there's some power in Larry's hold that stops him. I know that hold. I know that power.

'This is not going to be easy,' says Larry.

'What's not going to be easy?' says Marcus.

'So we'll need a drink.'

*We're both powerless against him.*

'What are you on about?' says Marcus. 'It's just a silly misunderstanding.'

*What's his game?*

'Why don't you go and have a little wash up first,' says Larry.

Marcus looks at his jeans, his hoodie. 'I'm fine.'

'A splash of water works wonders,' adds Larry.

Marcus flinches a little. A spasm of pain crosses his face. He puts a hand suddenly to his chest.

'There – your wound's bleeding. Your dressing probably needs changing,' remarks Larry.

Puzzled, Marcus rises from the table, stumbles, clenches his teeth and makes for the restrooms.

Larry turns to me. 'So, Serafina, got your heart's desire yet?'

I'm not afraid of him. This surprises me, but I'm not. *How can I trick him?* I put the brandy to my lips. *What do I know about the Devil?* My first ever taste of brandy. How it burns, like fire against my lips. I can feel it, like an inferno in my throat. I taste the flame-hot, acid tang of alcohol. I let the heat race to my cheeks.

'Easy,' whispers Larry, 'you're not immortal any more.'

My chest smoulders. *What can I use against him?* I look at Larry. His face seems to morph. Is it the brandy? I feel dizzy, strange. Maybe I should eat. Do humans need to eat before they drink? I don't know. I look away to stop the strange swirling sensation.

*Salt.*

That's what the tales at the Cloisters said. Throw salt at him. *Salt in his eyes.*

'If you still wish to save him,' Larry hisses, 'you will do exactly as I say.' He smiles, all his white teeth glistening. 'Whenever I say. You understand?'

I understand. He doesn't scare me. But I understand everything. He wants me for himself. I've seen it in his eyes. He'll never have me.

*There's pepper and salt on the table. If I could just reach across and grab . . . when Marcus returns. If I could spray it over him . . .*

He might do something. Something that would make Marcus believe.

What a sad useless hope.

'And the first thing is – if you try to discredit me, or work against me from now on – I'll reach right into Marcus's heart and undo the all the amateur celestial healing you've put in place. You-get-me-babes?' He sighs and blows me a little kiss.

All hope dies.

'You're not an angel any more. You can't stop me now.'

I look at him. I nod. But in my heart I say, *I will not do what you want. I will work against you.*

Marcus returns. He looks weary. The bounce is all gone. He starts straight in: 'So?' he says. He places a hand over his heart and presses down. His wound is hurting. His face is drawn.

I stare at Larry. He did this. He's showing me his power. And at that moment I hate him. It scorches through me like a naked flame. It shocks me with its heat. *Evil malefactor.* How I wish the terrible Archangel Jehudiel were here. If I had his whip now; *how I would crack it down upon you: archfiend, enemy of Heaven.*

Marcus coughs. A spot of blood froths at his lip. How I long to shield him, wrap my arms around him, soak up his pain, enfold him in my wings. But Larry's right, I'm not an angel any more.

'Deal?' Larry mouths at me.

Marcus coughs again.

I nod.

Larry orders another round of coffees. 'Here, caffeine helps,' he says to Marcus.

Marcus sips the espresso. Instantly he looks better. *Oh, how you play with us, Lucifer, Son of the Morning.*

'So?' Marcus says, looking at Larry. 'What is it you've got to tell me?'

'Ah yes,' starts Larry. 'Lots of people come to the club now.' He rests his head slightly to one side and looks at Marcus out of the corner of his eye. 'Since the shooting.' He's all sparkling white teeth.

'Yeah?' says Marcus. 'So?'

'Seems like "word" is out,' says Larry. 'Blood is obviously good for business.'

'What word?' says Marcus.

'The Crow comes here too.' Larry smiles mischievously. *God forgive me for ever bringing Marcus here.*

Marcus's head comes up. The weary look disappears like smoke in the dark.

'The Crow?' he says.

'And his friends,' adds Larry, fiddling with the espresso, swirling the brandy.

'His crew?' says Marcus.

'And his girlfriends,' says Larry.

Marcus suddenly snaps his eyes wide open. 'What "word" is out?' he repeats, a dangerous new tone in his voice.

'Well,' says Larry, all white teeth, 'I should say, *girlfriend.*'

'What word?'

'His new girlfriend,' says Larry annoyingly, clinking the spoon against the cup.

Marcus is half out of his chair. 'I don't give a damn about his girlfriend,' he hisses.

'Ooo, I think you'd give a damn about this one,' giggles Larry.

'*What* is everyone saying?' says Marcus like he already knows. 'Come on, man, don't do that.'

'When a man's been shot and lost his best friend, naturally he's scared,' says Larry. 'It's understandable. Probably has a name like traumatic funk disorder.' He chuckles and pours himself a large slug of brandy. I look at him. His face swims in and out of focus. His teeth grow larger. He shoots a look at me. And he's not chuckling. A pain like scorching fire sears across my eyes. I look away.

'Are you saying man's bothered by the Crow?' laughs Marcus. 'Because let me put you right . . .'

And I want to applaud him. I want to kiss him, to hug him, because he's strong, he's not afraid of the Crow and he's not afraid of the Devil. Cautiously I peer at Larry's face, to see how he's taking this.

'Hey, hey, hey,' says Larry very pleasantly. 'Don't get me wrong, it's not *me* that's saying it. I understand, I'm a big man now. I know you've got to grow up and settle down.'

'Settle down?' Marcus looks at him. He scratches his head. 'That's crap,' he says.

I reach out to put my hand on Marcus's arm to warn him with a touch that he should be careful. But my arm freezes in midair. Larry throws me a cold smile.

348

And suddenly I see the danger. Larry is going to use Marcus's very fearlessness to trap him. I try to scream. *Don't follow his logic!* But my voice dies in my throat.

'Exactly,' butts in Larry, 'I'm only repeating the buzz from the club. That's what people are saying . . .'

'What exactly *are* they saying?' asks Marcus, a note of menace creeping into his voice.

'Well, don't shoot the messenger,' laughs Larry, 'but it's not nice . . .' He pauses, takes a deep breath, gulps down a large slug of brandy as if to fortify himself. He's playing with Marcus like a cat with a mouse. '*I* know it's not true . . . but they're saying you've lost your bottle.'

'What!' Marcus snorts with laughter.

'They're saying you're scared like a pussy.'

Marcus blinks at the sheer outrage of that.

'They're saying you're even glad Joey's dead, because if he wasn't, he'd make you do something about the Crow busting up your birthday party.'

Marcus stops laughing, goes grey. '*They're saying I'm glad Joey's dead?*' he whispers.

Larry nods. He picks up the brandy bottle. 'I told you it wasn't going to be easy.' He pours Marcus a generous amount. 'They're saying you fixed up Melly's job too.'

Marcus rocks unsteadily.

'They say you were shagging Melly all the time and you were afraid she'd blab it out to the brothers. That Little Joe isn't even Joey's kid.'

'*They're saying I arranged Melly's shooting?*' gasps Marcus.

'Now, come on, man, get outside that,' he says. 'It'll help calm you down.'

'They're saying I'm glad Joey's dead?'

'Don't let it get to you. Stay calm. It's not cowardice – he who fights and runs away lives to fight another day.'

'Runs away?'

'Better to live a coward than die a hero.'

'Live a coward?'

'Oh, do stop repeating everything,' smiles Larry, 'or I won't tell you the rest.'

I sigh. I want to say: *Don't listen to him.* But I can't. Every time I open my mouth some force presses down on my windpipe.

'Drink up first, or I won't say another word,' says Larry.

I look around for a cup to drop, a plate to smash, anything to break the charm. But I can't move. Larry is freezing me out.

Marcus drinks. Larry fills his glass. Each time a little more. He's planned this all along. I remember how Kamuel said: *'That's how the Devil works. He starts small but before you know it, he'll have Heaven under siege and angels falling like summer rain.'*

We are both just pawns in his game.

'Tell me everything,' says Marcus. His voice very quiet.

Larry sighs, as if he's really sorry to be the bearer of such vile news. 'They're saying that you've gone soft, that Joey's brothers want to avenge his death, but you haven't got the balls for it and . . .'

'And?' says Marcus, half standing, half ready to blow away the whole world.

'And any little gangbanger could take you out: you don't rank, all you can do is kill girls now.'

Marcus slugs down the brandy. Larry refills it.

'Word says if the Crow wants to he can take anything that's yours.'

Marcus laughs. Not a nice laugh.

Larry smiles. 'Like I said, the Crow comes here, this is *his* place now . . .'

Marcus smacks his glass down so hard it cracks.

'The Crow comes here with his girlfriend. . .'

*No!* I want to cry.

'A very pretty little thing she is too,' smiles Larry.

*Stop! Stop!*

Marcus drains his glass, grabs the brandy bottle, refills it himself.

'And there's no denying the facts,' says Larry sadly.

'What facts?' says Marcus. His voice is low and husky.

The ice around my chest has spread now to every cell of my body, ever capillary, every vein; it courses through my being like liquid nitrogen.

'The fact,' says Larry, very slowly, as if it's nothing to do with him, 'that every night your pretty little sister is down in the club making out with the Crow in front of the entire neighbourhood.'

# Zara 12

Marcus splutters, sinks into his chair, goes ashen. '*Jasmine?*' he whispers.

I stand up but my legs can't hold me. I look at Larry. He looks at me. He gently, very gently moves his hand and motions me to sit back down again. I do. I've no power to resist.

'And sadly,' says Larry, 'that's not hearsay. That's the truth.'

I look at him. I know it's a lie. Somehow he's engineered this. I remember Jasmine's note: '*I'll be back very late this evening, because I've been invited to a Halloween party – on a blind date!*' Somehow poor sweet Jasmine has become part of his war.

'And it gets worse,' says Larry, swirling the brandy thoughtfully round his glass. 'You see, every night the Crow puts his arm around pretty little Jasmine and says *"Here's to Joey Bigga,"* and Jasmine smiles and the Crow continues, *"Better off dead,"* and everyone else replies, *"Than with Marcus"*.'

Marcus stands up, pushes the table away. Glasses crash, the brandy bottle topples, honey liquid pours to the ground. I want to rise too. I want to hold on to Marcus, tell him, *You're being played! It's a trick!* I look at Larry. I'm held in my seat. '*No!*' I whisper.

Suddenly Marcus coughs, clutches at his chest. His lips grow pallid. *There's blood coming through his shirt!*

*'Yes!'* hisses Larry back.

*'Please,'* I manage. *'I'll do as you say.'*

*'Good,'* says Larry. He turns to me, full-frontal, eyeballs protruding. 'Make. Sure. You. Do. I'll. Be. Watching.'

A beat passes. Marcus straightens up. Colour returns to his lips. He pulls out his phone, unsteady. He taps in a link.

'Spider?' he says. His voice is harsh. 'You ready? The job?'

'Yo,' says Spider. His voice is faint but we can all hear him.

'The Crow.'

'Yess!' comes the reply.

'Right,' says Marcus, his voice still unsteady. 'Get the crew strapped, we'll hit the old club.'

'Yeah man,' says Spider.

'There's a celebration here tonight,' whispers Larry. 'A Halloween party.'

'Tonight. Friday. 31st October. Halloween. Fancy dress.'

So neat. So perfect. I look at Larry.

'Seen,' says Spider.

Marcus puts his phone down. He laughs, as if he's free now, free from some curse laid on him. He turns to Larry. 'Thanks, bruv,' he says. 'Must've been hard for you to tell me all that.'

'You know I'm your man,' says Larry. 'Was just waiting till you came.'

'I know,' says Marcus. 'Nuff respect, we won't damage your club tonight.'

'Don't worry,' says Larry. 'Like I said, blood's good for business.'

And Larry smiles at me and nods his head a fraction. The icy chains fall off my limbs. My tongue is free at last. And I look at him. I don't know what to say. Except to repeat back his own question asked of me so long since.

'Happy?' I say.

'Oh yes,' he says, turning conspiratorially to me and adding in a low voice, 'I'm happy, and I'll be happier still when both of you are safely delivered to the shores of Styx.'

# Zara 13

Marcus stumbles from the club. I follow. I take his arm. I hold him steady. *What shall I do? How can I explain?*

'Thanks,' he mutters, and leans on me.

'Marcus,' I say. 'Don't believe everything.' I want to tell him about Larry, but what if Larry is watching, listening? I daren't take the risk.

Marcus says nothing. He moves slowly. *Thou shalt not kill. I'll talk to him.*

'Marcus,' I start.

'Not now,' he says. 'Just let me lean on you.'

I shut up. He leans on me. I take his weight.

I send up a prayer: *Give me strength to stand firm, to oppose the Devil – and should I lose my soul and Marcus's to the fires of Hell, I pray for Your forgiveness.*

The streets are cold. The afternoon's nearly spent. A jagged range of buildings stands dark against the sky. The sun is setting somewhere behind the city. Its last rays streak the Heavens with red. Shop lights are on. They shine and sparkle in neon colours. The wind gusts, peeling corners off posters, rattling the grilles on shops.

'Thank you,' says Marcus and then, so softly, so I barely hear him: 'Oh Angel, where are you now?'

I want to explain. I can't stay silent. I won't give up. 'Things are not what they seem,' I say, 'and you should repent.'

'You know something, Zara?' says Marcus. 'I kind of like you. You are so certain about your angels and your repentance. You're completely cracked, but I like you.' He falls quiet. We walk slowly down the street. A bus rumbles past. It hits a pool of rainwater, showers us, continues, is gone. I can see he wants to say something else.

'You know,' he says at last, his arm still around my shoulder. 'I thought I saw an angel, I really did – you were right. I thought she held me in her arms and promised to be there for me. It's funny. I really believed it.'

'If you saw her, she was there,' I say. It's all I can say, because if I say, 'Yes, I was that angel' and all that, I might stop this thing he wants to say – this thing that's trembling on his lips.

'No,' he says, 'I was wrong. Must have been the bullets, must have been the wishing: she wasn't there.'

'But you saw her again? The hospital, the funeral?'

Marcus sighs and then he says: 'I remember the pain-killers, the buzz. I remember walking across a lawn with her, sitting on a tree. For fuck's sake, I was on a life-support machine. They found me on my hospital bed – you know, afterwards. I'd pulled out the drip – I was rambling –'

I hold my breath.

'I was so upset about Joey. I tried to believe in her. I tried to change.' He stops. His face is so sad. 'Then Melly died. I was confused . . . At the funeral I remember the stone angel, a flash of lightning. I was so angry with her.'

He's frowning. I bite my lip, remembering his anger.

'She should have been there for me. She should have told me about Joey, shielded me, helped me. She should have saved Melly. It's crazy how mad I was at her. She was supposed to love me – that's what I thought – and I needed her so badly.'

He stopped and took my hand in his.

'I was convinced that it was only her love that was keeping me alive and that if she stopped loving me I'd be as dead as Joey. I couldn't understand why she hadn't saved him too. If she really cared about me, she'd have known how much he meant.'

I don't know what to say. I hold on to him.

'If she could have stayed with me I knew everything would be OK – maybe I thought . . . I really believed – I must have been mistaken . . .' He puts his arm around my shoulder again. I guide him. 'Girls,' he says, 'just trouble.'

I look at him sadly.

'Not you though,' he says. 'You're insane, *and* you're trouble.' He laughs, then coughs. 'But I don't hate you.' He stops in the middle of the pavement. 'Where are all the others?' he says, and throws back his head and yells, 'Hey GIRL-FRIENDS, where the hell are you?'

His voice echoes down the street.

He sighs. 'Not there. They're never there when you need them.'

'Please?' I try to calm him. A window from a flat over a shop yanks open. A head sticks itself out; someone trying to see what's going on.

'There's only you left.' He stops to catch his breath. 'You know, Zara, when a guy's down and broken – all those girls run away.' He smiles again, a sad smile. 'Yo, Candy, where are you now, babes? Man saved your fucking life and all he got was a get-well card.'

'Just lean on me,' I say.

'She was the Crow's girlfriend, you know, she started all this.' He adds, 'She was hot. And trouble, that's why man didn't jump straight in. Man can get the girls, you-know, but I want the true one. I don't want all that: because man's the G and Man's got the dough and I'm some kind of badass trophy.'

'Let's go,' I say. I steer him back along the pavement. 'Can you make it home?' I ask. I've got Jasmine's money. I could get a cab.

'I really thought there was an angel.' He looks sadly at me. 'I really did. I wanted it to be true.'

'I could get a minicab?'

'She was the one . . .'

'There was an angel,' I say. 'And don't believe anything bad about Jasmine; she wouldn't do any of that.'

He stops again; he clutches at me. 'Do you think so?' he says earnestly. 'You're Jasmine's friend – aren't you?' In his face I see hope: a spark, a desperate wanting to believe. Perhaps after all there's still a chance?

'Yes,' I say, suddenly encouraged.

But then his phone rings. He snaps it open. The person at the other end is shouting. There's loud music even I can hear.

'Yeah, man, I've organised muscle. We gonna be so

358

packing, we gonna blow every mother to Hell,' someone
shouts down the phone.

Marcus laughs grimly, glances at me. 'Organise some
outfits. It's a Halloween party. We'll hide the burners under
the costumes, get in and dance with them first,' he orders.

I think there's laughter on the other end.

'Make mine the Grim Reaper. Pick me up before
midnight.' He slaps the phone shut. The moment is past.
The look of hope has died in his eyes. He grabs me and
says, 'There aren't any angels. Only badass gangstas.'

'There are,' I say.

'Girls!' he laughs.

'We're not all the same,' I say in a calculated tone.

'No?' he says.

'Some of us are very *Old Testament.*' I say it slowly and
clearly. I want him to know. I may not be able to stop him,
but he should know.

He stops. Spins me round. The look on his face! *'What
did you say?'*

'You heard me.'

He's confused. He pretends he doesn't understand. He
changes the subject. 'I like you, Zara,' he says. 'You're
nuts . . . I like you . . .'

I will not be put off. 'Don't do it,' I say. 'Turn your back
on sin. Pray for forgiveness. Leave God to dispense justice
– for the Lord says: "Vengeance is mine; I will repay."'

*'You sound just like her,'* he whispers. *'Maybe . . .'* He
changes what he's going to say. 'I wish you were her. If you
were her, I'd kiss her right now, like . . .'

Suddenly he moves in, driven by something explosive

inside him. He clutches me. He presses his mouth against mine. He strains me to him. The pain in me dissolves. I feel only his warmth, the violent pressure of his lips. I melt against him. His body melts against mine. He pushes his tongue against my lips, forces them open, slides deep into my mouth, probing, fierce. My knees melt like snow-flakes in the sun. He slides his arms around me, his hungry tongue searches out my soft and yielding places . . . his body grows hard against me . . . I am in Heaven . . .

I pull away.

'No,' I say. Every cell in my body is crying out: *'Yes.'*

But it's no good. He isn't kissing me. Not this Zara. Not yet. He's kissing his angel. I'm just a girl, any girl, to stand in for her.

This is not what I gave up Heaven for. This is something animal and raw, heady, powerful, but not love. Not for Zara. It won't do.

'No?' he says, looking at me, drawing back. *'But – it is you, isn't it?'* he says as if the words are being drawn out of him. As if in that one moment of contact the truth has dawned on him.

But it doesn't matter any more. He wouldn't repent for Serafina – he won't for Zara. And I'm *not* her. I'm Zara now. 'No,' I say, gently. 'And no more kissing.' But because he's wounded and to reject him would be cruel I add: 'Just no – not on the street – not while you're upset. You might wake up tomorrow and regret it.' I try to laugh. *There will be no tomorrow for either of us.* I grab hold of his hand. He sways a little. 'Because you're too important,' I say. But I don't say to whom or why, for already he's throwing his hands in the air.

'Let's go home,' I say.

'Oh Angel,' he murmurs. 'And I know it's you.'

I hear him. I say nothing. I've already spoken. He's chosen. Larry is waiting. The play will be played out.

'OK,' he says, 'OK, you're right.' His voice cracks a little. 'Why the Crow though, Zara? Why him? How could Jasmine do that?'

'It's a lie,' I say. I tell him about her note. Her blind date.

'I don't know,' he says, sadly.

'Trust yourself then,' I say. 'Trust her, you know her – do *you* think she'd do that?'

'Maybe,' he says. 'Take me home, Zara, I'll lean on you.'

Together we walk back down the street. Past the flower shop, past the chicken shop, past the graffiti, past the white vampire fangs, back to Curlston Heights, past the strange door entry, the number pad, up in the lift, into the flat. His mum's out. I take him to his room. I fetch him coffee. I bring him toast.

He sips; he bites; he says, 'Stay with me. Lie down with me while I rest – it's OK, I won't try anything.'

We lie on his bed. I put my arm round him. I let his head lie against my chest. I'm happy. He wraps an arm and a leg around me. He whispers, 'You're so skinny.' He winces if I move. I don't move.

I wish I had my angelic powers back. I could ease his pain, soothe away his sadness. I wish I could lie with him for ever.

Outside a blackbird calls. The afternoon wears away. I lie awake. The evening comes. Marcus rests. Our limbs entwine. My heart beats when his beats. Hours seem minutes. His body in my arms. I breathe when he breathes. I look at his face. Its dark curls, its sculpted brow. I think of the night ahead. My heart starts to pound. I think only of now: the blackbird, the evening, his beating heart.

I hear his phone buzzing. The world won't wait. Messages are arriving. Larry is working his mischief. By midnight it will all be done. Larry will have won. The shores of Styx are waiting. We will go there together.

Slowly I bend my head and press my lips to Marcus's curls. I wonder who will come for us. I pray it will be Raquel. I'd like to see her one last time.

Marcus stirs.

The hour has come.

# Zara 14

The entry buzzer goes. They slam the front door. Their voices fill the lounge. They laugh and sprawl on the sofa.

'Stay in my room,' orders Marcus.

I stay in his room. I sit on his bed. I listen.

'Got the stuff?' says Marcus.

I watch through the half-open door. Bags and bustle; guns and feathers spill on the floor.

Marcus picks up a costume. The Grim Reaper. He wraps the cloak around him, pulls the death's head mask over his face, straps a Mac 10 on to the angle of the scythe, binds it with black duct tape.

'Reckon we'll get in?' he laughs.

One of the brothers examines the scythe, adjusts the taping, straps another death's head mask over the whole thing.

'Yeah man,' he says. 'Bugs is on the door anyway.'

Marcus puffs, sits down.

'You cool?' asks Spider.

'Never better,' wheezes Marcus.

More bags spill on the floor. 'Anyone want to be the Angel of Death?' Spider shakes out a costume; black feathers flutter.

'Nah, too small.' The angel costume is cast aside.

'Nazi guards?' A mountain of greatcoats, boots, peaked caps with insignias.

'Yo, da SS.'

The gang pull on boots, drag their arms into greatcoats, tape hand guns inside caps, jam caps on their heads. Insignias gleam.

I watch. I listen.

A mobile rings. Marcus throws bags and costumes behind the sofa.

'What's the plan?' They look at Marcus.

'Get in, says Marcus. 'Get the guns in. Old Larry ain't gonna stop man dem – not the way he was chatting 'bout blood being good for business.'

Spider chuckles.

'Get inside – ready to roll.'

'I'll need a drink,' says one.

'See who's there. The Crow'll have his peeps out, you know – so you all sort out which ones you gonna take down.'

The brothers nod. Spider is smiling.

'Wait till the Crow is right on the spot Joey died and then I'll give you the sign.' Marcus raises the scythe and sweeps the air. 'That's the sign. Watch for the scythe. I'll get him there.'

'Yeah man!'

'You get to the bar; you take the door; you clear the stairs. You cover me, Spider, the Crow'll be right in my face. Man's gonna look him in the eye when he wastes him.'

'Then we go.'

'We take all of them,' says Spider.

'Every mother,' says Marcus.

'Hold up,' says Spider. 'We all want to do Crow, you-know, not just you, Marcus, the fam needs to see blood too.'

'OK,' says Marcus. 'I'll give the sign, then it's execution time.'

'Yeah.' They all agree.

A cell phone rings. The driver's ready. They slug back brandy. They leave. As they go Marcus returns to the bedroom. 'You stay out of this, Zara,' he says, 'stay home. You don't tell nobody nothing.'

I nod.

He hesitates, he bends. He kisses me on the cheek. His lips linger. Soft pressure. 'If it all goes ape, Zara,' he says. He bends again as if he wants to kiss me properly. His lips brush mine. A bolt of electricity flashes between us. A terrible longing dawns in his eyes. He stops. 'You were all right. Man could've got to like you, whoever you were, you-get-me, Angel?'

He leaves.


I sit there. Staring at the floor. But not for long. I'm not staying. I must see this night to its end. I stand. I take in a deep breath. It'll be cold. I drag a jacket from Marcus's wardrobe. I go to the front room. I look at the mess. I look at the bags. I pull the Angel of Death costume out from behind the sofa. I hold it up: a long black shift and wings that strap on over the top.

It'll fit. I slip on the shift. I put the jacket over the top of it. It's thick and kind of lumpy. It's leather and padded. I strap the angel wings over everything.

I twirl in the hall mirror. The black feathers stand rigid on my back. The long raiment is itchy nylon, the jacket is warm. I pull up the hood of the jacket. I put the five-pound note in my pocket. I have to go. I'm going.

But before I leave the flat, there's one last thing I must do. I find the note Jasmine left. I find the house phone. I've never used a phone before. It takes a few tries, but at last I understand. I call Jasmine.

'Hello,' she says.

'It's me,' I say, 'Zara.'

'Hi honey,' she says.

'Don't go to The Mass nightclub tonight,' I say.

'Oh,' she says, 'but it's a surprise . . . how did you know . . .'

'Please,' I say, 'I can't tell you more.'

'It's Marcus, isn't it?'

I nod. I can't speak. Tears catch my throat.

'That's why you were so upset? That's why you were waiting outside the flat?'

'Your blind date was the Crow,' I whisper. 'It's a set up . . .'

'*Oh my God,*' she cries. 'Does Marcus know? *Of course he knows* . . . Are they going to hit the club . . . *they are, aren't they?*'

I can't say anything except, 'I'm sorry.'

'I won't go,' she says. 'I'll call Marcus. I didn't know . . .'

'I'm sorry,' I say again.

'God bless you, Zara,' she says.

I put the phone down.

\* \* \*

Outside the road is empty. I need to hurry. I must get there in time. I start to run. They went in a car. They'll be there already. A car?

A minicab.

There's one by the Halloween shop. I have money now. I race to the corner. Past the clothes store. Past the cleaners. Past the pharmacy; here it is: the minicab office.

'The Mass nightclub,' I pant.

'We're pretty busy,' says the girl.

'How much?' I say.

'It's Halloween,' she says as if this affects the fare.

'I've only got five,' I say.

'Do ya mind being dropped off before the park? I've got a driver going northside just now.'

'No,' I say.

'Then I can do it for cheap – it's the one-way system, you see.'

'I'll take it,' I say.

I'm in the cab. And we're away. Streets flash past. Traffic lights flick from amber to red. The roar of the engine. The boxy thing starts talking. I look at it. Beside it on the driver's mirror something catches my eye. Something is hanging from it. Two furry dice and a glint of gold. A chain. And swinging from it a small golden crucifix. I recognise it immediately. It's mine. *It's my crucifix.*

I reach forward. The driver sees me. 'Pretty, isn't it?' He gives it a flick. 'Got it off another cabby for a tenner. Chain's broken, but I bet it's worth a lot more.'

He doesn't know its worth. I just look at it.

367

*It's a sign.*

*'Kamuel,'* I whisper, *'are you there?* You said you wouldn't desert me. *Don't desert me.'*

We slice round corners, spin down side streets and suddenly I feel a mad, crazy rush of hope.

I get down behind the park. I pay the driver. The streetlights are orange. I run along the empty street. My black feathered wings flap behind me. I pull the jacket tight. This is it.

I leap across the gutters.

I step through the city.

I'm coming.

For Marcus.

# Zara 15

HALLOWEEN reads the neon sign: COSTUMES ONLY. LADIES' NIGHT. I walk straight in, past the chairs and tables, past the people, past the bar and bouncers' desk. Someone yells, 'It's over-sixteens, but if you wanna drink you gotta show your I.D. and get a wristband.' He waves a handful of lime-green wrist tags. I don't want to drink. I jump down the stairs, dodging couples, past the big mirror, sidestepping revellers. I do not stop. I do not look at myself. I duck behind figures in costume: wizards, goblins and one huge green Frankenstein.

I'll find Marcus. One last try.

I march through the doors. I'm in the club: the black leather sofas, the upholstered walls, the reeking smell. Where is he? The music's too loud. It's too distracting. How will he hear me? What if I shout? There's no point – nobody can hear anything. Everybody's drinking. Nobody minds me. Their elbows poke, their shoulders jostle. And there're girls everywhere. Girls in witchy costumes, girls as cherubs, girls as skeletons – just too many girls, they cloud my purpose. Which one of them will catch a stray bullet? How can I save them? I catch myself. There's nothing like that, is there? If their names are on the Manifest nobody can save them.

There are guys too: guys as demons, guys as ghouls, and guys in zombie outfits. I can't save anyone. Not even myself.

And there's Marcus.

I see him as soon as I get there. The Grim Reaper, looking like he's in Hell already.

And there's the Crow. I know it's him. Nobody could mistake that bulk, that massive frame, that hook-nose, those jetty brows – and on his head is a black crow's crown, ravens' feathers, skeletal wings.

I stand by the dance floor. Just a moment. All the things that might have been and never were flood back to me. Someone turns the music up. For a brief second I remember what it was to be an angel. The music pounds. I start to sweat.

I watch Marcus. I watch him drag Candy into his arms. He's trying to wind up the Crow. Start the show. I watch as she moulds herself against his chest. Something inside hurts. I see the muscles in his arms straining against her. My throat goes dry. I try to swallow. I catch my breath.

Marcus smiles, but he's not smiling at me.

It's nearly midnight. What shall I do? At any minute his death will arrive. I must try and speak. I look around. Demons are dancing with angels.

Someone puts on a record. Marcus crushes Candy to him. Crow steps forward. He's unsure. Everybody else steps back. Someone whistles. *The Crow has figured out who the Grim Reaper is.*

. . . *Go, go, go, go, go, go* . . .

The Crow's eyes are wild.

Marcus reaches into his cloak.

*'God help me!'* I scream. *'Tell me how to stop it!'*

But it's not God who answers my prayer.

A figure detaches itself from the crowd. A tall, graceful figure. He slides smoothly forward and seems to push through the crowds effortlessly towards me. A rush of drains. The dancers fall back at his touch. He's dressed like the Devil. He is the Devil. I'd know Larry anywhere.

'Well, hello, Kara,' he says. 'Fancy meeting you here!'

I look at him. There's no point in saying anything.

'Do let me help you out,' he says.

Strange how I can hear him perfectly above the music. 'Help?' I say.

'There is a way,' he says.

'A way?' I repeat.

He laughs an enchanting, mischievous laugh. 'Yes,' he says, raising his eyebrows, 'a way out even for you, even at this late hour.' Larry smiles at me as if I'm being very slow. He cocks his head to one side. 'You still like him, don't you?' he says.

I look at Marcus. I look at Larry.

'And he hasn't repented, either, has he?' reminds Larry. The lights from the disco ball sparkle off his teeth.

'No,' I whisper.

'I see you've dressed for the part,' he says.

'The part?' I'm confused. I let it pass. *Don't get hooked in.*

'You can still be the Angel of Death, you know.' A smile plays cheekily around the corners of his white teeth. 'It'd be like old times.'

The music seems to have stopped altogether.

'And give him lots more time. That would be fun too, wouldn't it? It's really *very* simple,' smiles Larry.

I study him. The rubber horns on his head wobble. He flicks disappointedly at his limp tail. He pulls a 'this-outfit-really-isn't-me' face. Yes, Larry can always make things very simple.

'You can ask for an Extension,' he says.

All around us the club waits. It's held in a familiar time warp.

'An Extension,' he repeats in a charming drawl. 'Think about it. All you have to do is ask.'

'Ask you?' I say. He must be mocking me. Hasn't he won already?

'Go *on*,' he says. 'Give it a whirl; live dangerously. What've you got to lose?'

'More time is not enough any more,' I say slowly. Perhaps he is serious. 'I want his soul released from Hell.'

'Ooo, you little Devil!' cheers Larry. 'But you're learning. What fun this is going to be!' He rubs his hands together in glee. 'But – oh dear – oopsy-whoopsy – we have to keep the Rate of Exchange balanced!' he smiles.

'Take me,' I say.

'Excellent, I will,' says Larry. 'But – oh deary-weary – that doesn't seem fair. I've already got you in the long run. I could take Spider as well, perhaps?'

'No,' I say. No other deaths for Marcus.

'Oh,' says Larry, disappointedly. 'Just when it was getting exciting.'

'There must be something else you want,' I say, 'as well as me, to release his soul from Hell?' I'm sure of it.

372

Larry has his plan. Why else would he be here? He's just playing with me, trying to get me to suggest it. Soon he'll reveal all.

Larry looks instantly pleased. He does a little twirl and capers on the spot. 'I do want to take you, but I do want to make a profit too,' he says. 'Just squeeze out a little extra.' He dances his fingers over his cheek. 'Spider would have done, but if you're adamant on the point?'

I look at him. I wait.

'OK, I'll settle for both you and Marcus dead by midnight . . .' (Larry makes a squeezing motion over his heart – I don't forget what I saw this afternoon – he can take Marcus at any minute) '. . . Marcus can go wherever you like – I hear they are letting people back into Limbo again – but your soul is mine forever. And I call it generous of me.'

So Marcus must die too. I try not to bite my lip. If only I could have saved his soul *and* his life.

'OK,' I say miserably.

'But there is a slight hiccup,' says Larry.

There's always a hiccup when you're dealing with the Devil.

'You see, Subaru, there're rules even about getting into Hell.'

I don't know why, but I'm mildly surprised about that.

'Sadly you've got to have sinned in a deadly sort of way. And you, my dear, haven't done so yet. And I can't take you until you do. But don't panic – I've got an excellent plan!'

I start to panic.

'If you feel inside the breast pocket of that delightful jacket you're wearing, you'll find a handgun.'

I feel inside the pocket.

'Clever girl! Now all you have to do is point the muzzle and pull the trigger. Simple as a pimple.'

I don't need to ask who at.

'Think of it this way,' says Larry. 'You'll save him from committing murder. I'll strike him off *my* Manifest. (Heaven can do what the hell they like with their List.) You can shoot yourself as a punishment – fantastic, suicide too. We'll all come to a deal – I'll release him from Hell! And get you instead. *There you are! Your condition is met!* If Heaven wants him they can have him, but I really do recommend the new deal on Limbo – otherwise off he'll jog to Purgatorium. That's probably the best place for him anyway, don't you think?'

I've figured it out. *Larry wants me.* And he's making the rules up as he goes along. It's obvious, isn't it? If Marcus had repented he wouldn't be on anyone's Manifest. Would he? In fact since Joey took his place he's *not* on any Manifest at all. So Larry doesn't need *anyone* to balance the books. Oh he's clever, all right, but I've understood. *He wants me.* And he wants to be one hundred per cent certain he gets me.

He smiles. His white teeth sparkle. 'You get to have completed your Collection after all – a little late in the day – oh dear – but there you go! Ooo, *and* you'll have committed two of the most deadly of sins!'

*That's what he wants! Me to commit the most deadly of sins.*

But why?

'Then I can get you into Hell. A sinful little Seraph all of my own! What bliss! Together we'll pootle on down to Styx – you and me – just the two of us. Oh, how delightful – all done and dusted and delivered.'

I stare at him in amazement. So clever.

But I don't buy it.

I'm no longer a Seraph. There are loads of prettier girls everywhere. He hasn't set all this up just to get me.

He nods as if he can read my mind. 'Pretty straightforward, isn't it?' he says.

But it's not straightforward at all.

But I can't figure out why.

# Zara 16

I can't figure it out. There's not enough time. But I can take Marcus's place in Hell. And that's enough.

I'll do it.

Larry will take Marcus at midnight anyway. One twist will undo all the miracle-making I ever learnt at the Cloisters.

My hand curls around the gun. I draw it out from the pocket and slip it up the sleeve of the jacket. My heart is pounding. I look at Larry. I look at the dance floor. I don't even bother to ask for a copy of the contract. This is what Larry wants. I know, I can see the delight in his eyes.

Let him win. I've thrown away Heaven – what is my state of sanctifying grace anyway compared to that? Or my short little human life? Yes, it's better this way. Marcus may not go to Heaven but he will escape Hell. In Purgatorium he will find redemption. 'Kamuel,' I whisper, 'if you are there in Purgatorium saving the souls of the sinners, take care of him for me.'

Larry holds out his hand. I take it. We shake.

'Deal?' he says.

'Deal,' I reply.

I grip the gun. I move away. I can get close to Marcus.

He trusts me. He'll be surprised. He'll be angry. He told me to stay at the flat.

I'll tell him I love him. I'll implore him to repent. Ah, if only he would. We could both be saved yet. For my first contract with Larry still holds good till midnight. But he'll refuse. I know he will. So I'll tell him that when the Angel of Death comes for him he must say: *Sorry*. He must implore the angel to forgive him in God's name – just as if it were a confession. I'll tell him I've arranged it all. He will go to Purgatorium then. I completely dismiss the idea of Limbo, a horrible, forsaken train-station sort of place for those who cannot enter anywhere else.

I'll point the gun at him. I'll press it against his heart. From inside the sleeve of my jacket I'll pull the trigger. He won't know any pain. He won't know what happened. He'll understand when the angel catches him. I hope it's Raquel. I pray it should be her. She's beautiful and she's kind.

Then I'll shoot myself. It won't be hard. Without Marcus, life is nothing. My mind suddenly flashes to Robyn. I say a soft sweet 'sorry'; I tell her I understand now. I look at the crowd, at the girls, the men; I'm glad there'll be no stray bullets. I don't know what Joey's brothers will do. I pray they'll be confused and run away. Without Marcus they can't act. I've seen this already.

The music is back. Time starts up.

I push my way round the dancers. My feathers drag after me. I squeeze out on to the dance floor. Marcus has Candy in his arms. The Crow is there.

The music is pounding. Nobody notices me, this tiny

Angel of Death in her gangsta jacket and black feathers. I let the music guide me. I sway between the dancers. I'm almost there.

Suddenly Marcus raises his scythe.

*It's the sign.*

The Crow steps forward.

Candy screams. I slide in between. I raise my arm.

Marcus lifts his beautiful face up and looks at me.

'Zara?' he says, confused.

Candy screams again. She yells at the huge guy. '*Stop it, Crow. Can't I dance with anyone I goddamn want?*'

I prepare myself. This is it. I open my mouth and scream. '*I love you Marcus – please repent,*' I pause. The Crow steps in. I scream again, louder than any music. '*When the angel asks you, Marcus – when she says, "Turn. And. Look. Upon. Your. Death," when she asks you to repent . . .*'

Marcus turns and looks at me. He looks *straight at me*. His lips move. His eyes. *Oh, his eyes*. I can't hear him.

Candy throws herself at the Crow. Marcus hesitates. She's in his line of fire. I scream again, '*I'M SORRY. I LOVE YOU.*' I raise the gun.

'*You love me?*' he mouths back. Like being loved was all he ever wanted. His gun is drawn now. He's jerking Candy aside.

But all the music in the world can't drown out my words.

'*YES,*' I scream. I point the muzzle. '*I'M. NOT. THE. SAME. AS. ALL. THE. REST.*'

And then he smiles and his face lights up.

'*I. REALLY. LOVE. YOU.*'

It's like no one has ever told him how beloved he is.

Not like that. There's something suddenly radiant about him. I'm ready to pull the trigger . . .

*And I can't do it.*

I just can't shoot him. For some reason I can't bring myself to pinch out his life. I try. I jab at the gun, try to squeeze the trigger, but it's no use. I can't do it. All of this and my one last chance and I can't. It's not because I fear Hell, although I do. It's not because I distrust Larry – not about this. I don't.

*I just can't.*

The moment passes. My hand falls back. The Crow pushes forward. Marcus swings Candy aside. He faces the Crow. The dancers draw back. I see Jocy's brothers take position.

Someone screams and screams.

*'This is for Joey,'* says Marcus.

Dazed, I move in. *Thou shalt not kill.* I mustn't let him shoot the Crow. There may still be a way. Larry may be ready to make another deal. If he kills it'll be too late. Even Purgatorium won't have him. I step forward. The timing's all wrong. I see the look on Marcus's face. It's shining, like he's the Avenging Angel himself. *Radiance.* And then, like a miracle, I remember.

101 Curious Facts About Angels

77. Angels appear in their true glory at their own demise.

A sudden hope spirals through me. I remember Vincent. I remember the second the whip hit – how for one moment he'd appeared in his true glory – beautiful beyond compare. I think of Kamuel. Did he show me Vincent's end on purpose? Has he known all along?

And it's Candy who gives me the idea. *She is in his line of fire.*

'*I'll show you your angel,*' I scream at Marcus. '*You promised me if I showed you your angel . . .*' I'm screaming in his ear. '*You promised. I trust you.*'

He tries to push me away. *I'm here.* I won't be pushed away. I *will* show him. He raises his gun. I drop mine.

*I throw myself in front of him.*

*Marcus's gun goes off.*

Suddenly Larry is there. *Bagabi laca . . .* He's trying to freeze time. *Bachabe . . .* He's trying to stop me. *Lamc cahi achababe . . .* He won't win. *Karrelyos . . .* He's too late. *Lamac lamec . . .* He shouts in fury. *Bachalyas . . .*

Slowly, I pitch forward. Marcus shouts. Drops the gun. The dancers whirl. The room spins. His arms open.

He catches me.

He holds me. How breathtakingly beautiful he is. My eyes trace his sculpted features: the hard jaw, the soft full-ness of his lip. He smoothes back my hair. My wings are coated in blood. *How I love him.* My fire and brilliance light up the dance floor. I am a winged celestial creature more beautiful than a thousand stars.

How sorry he looks. He presses me to his chest. *I breathe when he breathes.* My blood coats his costume. I touch his hand. *My skin on his skin.*

He holds me as each throb of my heart beats and bleeds and ebbs.

All around us is pushing and shoving. The music is blasting. Joey's brothers have drawn their weapons. The Crow's crew are taking up position.

. . . *Hobgoblin nor foul fiend* . . .

Vampires and werewolves are screaming and screaming.

. . . *Shall daunt my spirit* . . .

Ghouls and goblins draw tight around us.

. . . *We know we at the end* . . .

They press in.

. . . *Shall life inherit* . . .

'Don't move her!' a girl screams. 'Don't move her!'

I look up. I wasn't too late. Thank God. I lift up my face. With a blaze of my eyes I freeze time . . .

For an instant all sound ceases. In the silence that follows, I say, 'Please repent, Marcus.'

There, I've asked him. He looks at me. His eyes are wide like bright jewels. Now I can go. I need to go. I feel a tugging inside. I've begged him to repent while he still can. I know he will. We had a deal. His eyes are shining.

I let time start up again.

The music coughs back louder than ever.

Someone screams.

Someone yells.

Everything goes very quiet, except the music. It winds on, stuck on a phrase.

*Go . . . go . . . go . . . go . . . go . . .*

# Zara 17

I'm still in the club. I see Kamuel. He's standing there right beside me; he's smiling at me. He looks so sad. He strokes my cheek. 'Little one,' he murmurs. 'Will you repent,' he says, 'and ask forgiveness for all the hurt you've caused others?'

'Oh yes,' I say. I try to look past him, to see Marcus.

'I promised you I would not desert you,' he says.

'Why are *you* here?' I ask. 'I thought you were going to Purgatorium?'

He strokes my brow so tenderly. 'Can't you guess?' he smiles.

I look around the club. It appears as if through some mist. Strangely quiet. Joey's bothers and the Crow's crew have been frozen in time. Everyone's been frozen in time. Except Marcus.

'It is his hour,' explains Kamuel. 'His choice now. Let all the angels watch and learn what true love can do.' He helps me gently to re-form my small human shape around me. Always those last few wisps. I glide into his arms. He shelters me with his wing. Then he whispers, 'I think they need to hear him in the Golden City too, don't you?'

Kamuel shows me where to look.

I see Marcus laying a shape on the floor. It's Zara. I see

him raise his eyes to Heaven. I hear him shout out. *'Forgive me?'* The sound is crystal clear. He cries, *'I'm sorry.'* His voice is so loud they must surely heed him and record his words in the Book of Days.

He looks down at the girl on the floor.

He bends down. He kisses her. *Oh, how he kisses her.*

Outside, far away, I hear a church bell start to toll midnight.

I hear Marcus whisper, *'I'm sorry. I love you. I've always loved you.'* He stands up. 'I'll show you, Zara, I'm sorry. I repent. I'll prove it.'

He drops his gun on the floor. He turns to Joey's brothers. 'It's over, guys,' he says.

One of the brothers unfreezes in time, steps forward. It's Spider. Perhaps it is his hour too, for his face is shining. The music sounds ethereal.

*Yea though I walk through the shadow . . .*

Spider's face is wet with tears.

Marcus stop-signs him away. 'Spider, it's over. It won't bring Joey back.'

But Spider's not listening. He's too pumped up. His eyes are bulging. There's no stopping him.

*of the valley of death . . .*

And Marcus sees it. He starts shouting at him to stop.

Spider raises his gun. He aims it at the Crow. 'Never,' he yells.

Marcus holds up his hand, both palms face-out. 'No,' he shouts.

'For Joey,' Spider screams.

Marcus steps in front of the Crow. '*NO!*'
The music winds on.
But Spider's gun is going off.
And Marcus falls.

*Earth to earth; ashes to ashes; Dust to Dust.*
*The Book of Common Prayer*

*We are floating outside time. It is not the future, nor the past. I am just a wisp, a soul still clinging to the memory of her mortal body. I look up at Kamuel and I want to know the truth.*

*'Kamuel?' I say. 'Did you know everything?'*

*'From the hour Satan declared war.'*

*'Right from the start?' I say.*

*'We knew he'd chosen you.'*

*So that was it. The last piece of the puzzle slots into place. Now I know why Larry wanted me.*

*'What did the Challenge say again?' I whisper.*

*Kamuel strokes my soul. It soothes. He quotes the words of Satan's Challenge:*

*'I will pick your brightest and your best, your loveliest and most innocent, from under your hand, and I will so corrupt and drive your chosen one that they will rather Fall and die and live in Hell with Me, than stay in Heaven with You.'*

*'He didn't win,' I say. 'I didn't betray Heaven.'*

*'No,' says Kamuel.*

*'But I did promise him my soul.'*

*'Yes,' says Kamuel.*

'And I sent Joey to Hell.'

'Yes,' says Kamuel.

'And I Fell.'

'Yes,' he says.

'So what will become of me?' I ask.

'All things are fair in love and war,' smiles Kamuel. 'We will make a case. We will appeal in the Halls of the Dead.'

'Thank you,' I breathe. Kamuel will take care of me. He will not desert me. Suddenly I wonder at that. 'Why did they send you?' I ask.

'Haven't you realised?' says Kamuel. 'From the minute you met Marcus, I've been there beside you.'

I think of the party, the water meadows, Vincent, the Abyss.

'I was assigned to be your Guardian Angel.'

I remember the lonely figure in the club the night Joey died, his presence again at Styx; the angel flying behind me when I talked to Raquel . . . the figure in the graveyard, the man on the street who hurried away when I met Marcus outside Curlston Heights, the man who scared me that dark night outside the Halloween display; so many times . . . Yes, he'd been there. How strange that I'd noticed and yet not noticed.

'Why didn't you tell me what would happen?' I say.

'Ah,' smiles Kamuel. 'You know we cannot interfere with Fate, we cannot direct choice – what would become of Free Will?'

I nod. I understand.

'But I tried to show you.'

'Yes, you did. You even tried to stop me,' I say.

He draws me near. 'I would have gone to Purgatorium to stop you.'

'What happens now?' I ask. 'What will become of Marcus?'
'Ah, yes!' he says. 'Marcus.' His face lights up.


We're back inside time. We're back in The Mass nightclub.
The bell has just finished tolling midnight. It is 31st October.
Halloween. Kamuel is there. I stay beside him. There is
Marcus lying on the floor. Poor Marcus. His arm is thrown
over Zara. He's cradling her thin frame. I can see the pulse
of his blood pumping out, coating his breast, coating her
feathers. His eyes are wide; he's whispering, *I'm so sorry.*
    The music is crashing out.
    People are screaming.
    It's nearly over.
    'I think we are just in time,' Kamuel says.
    I glide beside him.
    A white mist is starting to hover over Marcus.
    'Come and help me, Serafina,' says Kamuel. He is smiling,
radiant, in certain hope of the resurrection to eternal life.
'We have a soul to save.'


*fin*

**SARAH MUSSI** was born in Cheltenham, Gloucestershire. She grew up in the Cotswolds in a pretty small wooden cabin with her writer father, therapist mother, brother, sister, two cats, twenty chickens, three ponies and a donkey (plus some white mice which escaped and shall not be mentioned again). She loved to read and draw and climb trees and chat to the fairies who lived in the acre of woodland around the house.

She went to the local grammar school and managed to bunk a good few lessons by hiding in the library and reading novels that her dad didn't approve of, or truanting off to Cheltenham town centre and visiting book stores. Because both of her siblings went to university to study literature, Sarah decided to be different (plus her dad said she was too fanciful for academic rigour) and go to art school. After graduating from Winchester School of Art, Sarah went to the Royal College of Art and did an MA. She then set off across the Sahara with a handbag and a Sanderson scholarship and spent the next few years in Cameroon, West Africa.

Thinking to settle somewhere wild and wonderful like Nigeria and finding that artists were not in huge demand (there being so many talented ones living there already), Sarah retrained as an English teacher, studied literature anyway and started teaching. She taught English in Ghana for thirteen years and London after that.

Sarah still teaches English in London when she is not chatting to fairies, visiting Africa, hiding in libraries or writing books.

# Acknowledgements

I'd like to say a huge thank you to the Archangels:

Beverley Birch
Susie Day
Ruth Eastham
Sophie Hicks
Caroline Johnson
Emma Littlewood
Georgia Murray
Sarah Odedina

Without you Marcus would not have been saved.

Sarah Mussi
London